THE WOLF TONE

THE
WOLF
TONE

CHRISTY STILLWELL

ELIXIR PRESS | DENVER, COLORADO

THE WOLF TONE. Copyright © by Christy Stillwell. All rights reserved. Printed in the United States of America. For information, address Elixir Press, PO Box 27029, Denver, CO, 80227.

Author photo: Cindy Stillwell
Cover painting: "Landscape with power poles" by Edd Enders, eddendersart.com
Book design by Steven Seighman

Library of Congress Cataloging-in-Publication Data

Names: Stillwell, Christy author.
Title: The wolf tone / by Christy Stillwell.
Description: Denver, Colorado : Elixir Press, 2018.
Identifiers: LCCN 2018003156 | ISBN 1932418687 (alk. paper)
Classification: LCC PS3619.T557 W65 2018 | DDC 813/.6--dc23 LC record
available at https://lccn.loc.gov/2018003156

First edition: January 2019

10 9 8 7 6 5 4 3 2 1

For all those who work alone in the room.

And for my brother,
James Douglas Stillwell
1973-2018

The wolf tone is a wobbling or stuttering pitch caused by the vibration of a bowed instrument's string in competition with the vibration of its body. Described by musicians as "annoying," "hideous," or "monstrous," it is a fact of life for many cellists. Usually found on the instrument's lower strings, the howl can shift, affected by humidity, disuse, even room temperature. Well-adjusted cellos are more apt to reveal their wolf, since an instrument out of adjustment allows all pitches to wobble, hiding the howl.

A variety of wolf suppressors or eliminators are available. Experimentation is required. The challenge is to maximize the sound of the instrument but minimize the wolf. Some musicians refuse to suppress the wolf, believing it diminishes resonance and sympathetic overtones.

Be embraced, ye millions!
This is a kiss for the whole world!

—"Ode to Joy" lyrics from Beethoven's Symphony No. 9, fourth movement
(Adapted from the 1786 poem by Friedrich Schiller, "An die Freude")

THE WOLF TONE

One

Spring took its time. March in Deaton, Montana, was winter's final exhale. Robins had been spotted and the creeks were beginning to melt, but the surrounding mountain ranges still slumbered under blankets of white. The night of her accident, a new moon held the canyon in complete dark and Margot Fickett couldn't sleep.

Earlier her cello group played at the cider house, seventy minutes of Latin music that turned into one of those shows musicians live for: a sold-out crowd, a dozen players in their half circle gazing at one another, smiling as they bowed, plucked, and tapped their cellos. The audience was captivated; every soul in the room breathed in transcendent harmony. Once a musician felt this, knew that it was possible, she never wanted to do anything else. She'd rather play than eat.

Air whistled through the cracked window in the corner and a great horned owl called. Several weeks ago, a pair built a nest in the fir tree nearest the deck. During the day not much happened but at night there were calls and commotion, probably a transfer of food, the male bringing dinner.

Margot sat up, pulling on a sweatshirt. Next to her, Andy didn't budge. By the light from the hall she could see the dresser, its surface strewn with rings and bracelets, a performance program and her husband's pocket trash: his phone, coins, a crumpled list, half a roll of breath mints. She crossed the hall to gaze at her son, home from Minnesota on break. He was too long for the mattress—his legs hung off almost to the knee. Astonishing, the absence of boy. As recently as the holidays, that eager look was still in his eye. In its place now was an assuredness, a kind of knowing, as if he'd been let in on a secret.

He wasn't coming home this summer, he had told them. He would rent a room in Minneapolis and work for his professor, who was recording a film soundtrack. Benji was twenty-one and had toured or attended summer festivals since he was fourteen. Margot was used to his absence, had even encouraged it. Yet for the first time, she didn't know when she'd next see him. Movie music, according to Benji, was a new career path for string players like him. Also, music for computer games. You didn't really need a degree anymore, he said.

A bigger surprise was that the film music wasn't classical. He'd be playing fiddle with his rock band, something that came together six months ago. Margot was just hearing about it though she suspected Andy might have known earlier. Andy played bluegrass. Margot played classical. Benji's preference had been settled long ago. When questioned about his change in direction, Benji responded with a calm that was somehow patronizing, "It's still music, mom. Music is music."

Under the lamp's circle of light in the foyer, the telephone sat on the table in its tidy way next to the straight-back velvet chair. Over by the front door was a garbage bag full of the day's trash. Tomorrow, someone would take it to the shed. Seized by a wish to feel the outside, Margot decided to take it now. She picked it up, unbolted the door and stepped out to the porch. Her bare toes gripped the edge of the front step, benumbed. Her lungs froze in shock. The stars shimmered like something alive. If she reached out, the points of light would recoil like an underwater creature. There was no wind, no sound until the owl called again, fainter from this side of the house.

Railroad ties acted as bumper blocks along the edge of their drive, running along the crest of a steep hill. Wanting a glimpse of the yard, Margot stepped onto the tie, following it away from the house. The Suburban was pulled forward further than she realized; she had to sidestep around its front bumper, which turned out to be tricky. Barefoot, holding the bag aloft, Margot lost her balance. Her arms wheeled madly and she dropped the trash bag. There was a sense of cartwheeling, her legs pointing at the sky as she rolled like a Frisbee on its edge, missing by some miracle every stone that might have brained her. When she hit the pavers at the bottom she heard her collarbone snap like a pencil. The fall was over in seconds yet seemed to take forever, long enough for her to wonder: *How will they find me?*

Margot spent the days after the accident adjusting to the shock. Apparently it had all really happened. She broke a bone for which there was no cast. Nobody could even tell, unless she wore the sling, which wasn't required or even recommended due to the way it immobilized the elbow. When Benji was little, the thought of him falling down that hill haunted her. As it turned out, he rescued her. His bedroom window overlooked the slope. He heard her cry out.

The cello was off limits, ending her symphony season as well as spring shows with Strings, the cello group. Students were notified, lessons cancelled. Benji went back to school. Andy's bluegrass band, The Wilmas, started their tour. He put off joining them until after Margot had surgery. Seven screws and a plate raised her hopes for a full recovery.

Andy loaded Margot's favorite music on the iPod and rigged it to the stereo in the den. He stocked the house with groceries, brought her soup and crackers, rented movies with her until she finally insisted that he go. Seeing him bored was worse than being bored herself.

Andy toured often and Benji had been in school for years. Margot was used to solitude. Busy solitude and idle solitude turned out to be quite different. The sight of her large inert hands disturbed her. She spied on the owl. The bird was hard to find, camouflaged against the tree bark. Andy knew where to point the binoculars, but it took Margot several tries, scanning up and down the branches. When she finally landed on its huge yellow eyes, her hand jerked and she had to restart the process. The owl's face was terrible, startling in its hostility, the feather horns like angled eyebrows and the vicious, hooked beak. The creature appeared outraged by the invasion of privacy. Its stillness was impressive. An immunity to loneliness. Hours, days, sitting on those eggs. It was a good thing human beings grew their young internally, Margot thought; if a nest were required, we'd never make it.

The day after Andy's departure, she received a phone call, making this officially the strangest month of her life. Margot was in the den hooked up to an automatic icing machine, listening to Beethoven's Ninth. The Ninth was the orchestra's season finale piece, one she'd rehearsed exhaustively since January. She was out, of course—not a chance she'd play before three months. Bernstein's Berlin performance, from after the wall's collapse, was the recording their maestro liked best, though he felt it was too long.

Margot sat breathless after the first movement, that wild, leaping symphony in miniature. The section break was long, with no applause, only the sound of rustling clothing, crinkling paper, the ubiquitous cough. And a phone rang. Not in the recording but in Margot's house. The odds! It rang again and still the music didn't resume, as if everyone in that hall waited to hear who it might be. The answering machine picked up as the strings began their ecstatic tiptoeing.

Margot was sure it would be Satterfield, the maestro, but he was apparently still sulking. A female voice unknown to her, young, crisp, and insistent, said, "I'm looking for Mrs. Fickett."

The violins romped; the caller cleared her throat. "It's an urgent matter concerning your son," she said, then added, in case Margot had forgotten, "Benji."

The building, swelling call and response of woodwinds and strings rolled on.

"This isn't really phone call material," the young woman said. "I wondered, maybe, if you could come by Dolly's Second Hand Store on Randolph Ave. Where I work."

She hung up. The music rose to the surprising, boorish drum, then dropped back to its tiptoeing flutes. Sunlight spilled onto the carpet. The den was suddenly hot. *I imagined that*, Margot thought but the moment was ruined. She stopped the music with the remote and began the process of disconnecting from the icing machine, ripping open Velcro straps, detaching the hose. Standing on the warm tiles in the foyer, she stared at the pulsing red light on the answering machine. So it wasn't a dream. She decided she'd better get dressed.

Later this seemed rash, to immediately follow the directions of a stranger. Why not wait for a second call, even a third? The matter was urgent, said the voice, and it concerned her son. No woman had ever called for Benji before.

He was a violin prodigy; he didn't have dates. Following directions seemed like the right thing to do.

Though there was sun in the canyon, winter's inversion had socked the town in fog. Traffic was heavy and visibility was poor. She was driving Andy's huge Suburban as her Honda was too low to the ground. She hit traffic and a flare of panic rose in her chest: she'd made a bad decision. The accident did this, she was certain. Not that the accident *caused* the phone call. She felt separate from reality, almost immune to peril, which couldn't be good. A peculiarity was afoot, an ill wind. How absurd, to be summoned, to drive under the influence of painkillers. She ought to turn this rig around and begin the day again.

But Margot did not turn around. Switching the heater off to keep herself cold and alert, she followed the directions coming from her phone. Dolly's turned out to be one of several businesses in the Rock Creek Commons, a strip mall angled inside a moat of parking. Snaking around it was Rock Creek itself. Margot parked on the west side of the building where a thin stretch of woods stood between the creek and an auto parts store.

Dolly's was at the front, facing Randolph Avenue. An antler arch encased the entrance, hundreds of deer antlers wired together to create an arbor around ordinary glass doors. Inside the vestibule, the sounds of the busy street vanished as though she'd been swallowed. Through the next set of doors Margot found herself inside a warehouse, a mix of clothing store, furniture store, and haunted house. Old panel doors hung on the walls from industrial sized chains. Boudoirs and antique sideboards were set up among rack after rack of used clothing. The displays were not stalls, exactly, but more like sets, little slices of life. A miniaturist might be behind it all. The smell was of thrift store and furniture polish. Most surreal was the ceiling. The exposed ductwork peeked through a vast webbing of charcoal grey fabric that draped several feet and slowly swayed. It darkened the room and its movement made the ceiling feel close and alive, as if she were looking up from underwater.

The display nearest the front counter held a dining room set with an antique table and chairs. On the table a notebook lay open to a page full of numbers. Next to it lay a pencil, a calculator and a cup of coffee. She heard movement and turned. From inside a circular rack of dresses emerged a child, a barefoot boy in striped overalls, not more than three years old.

"Boo!" he shouted.

Margot jumped, sending a jolt of pain through her collarbone. She cried out and alarm widened the boy's great blue eyes. A woman emerged from a side room, short, with bleached hair cut severely at the jawline. She wore a low-cut dress and knee-high boots. Margot knew immediately that this was her caller. The look matched the voice, a girl trying to disguise her youth.

"A giant!" cried the little boy, pointing.

Margot turned and he withdrew, folding his body back inside the dress rack.

"I—I didn't dream you'd come right away!" said the young woman, giving her head a toss. She held out a hand. "I'm Eva Baker."

Margot stared at the girl's hand, then down at her own, peeking out of the sling.

"Oh!" Eva cried. "You're hurt! Aren't you in the orchestra? And your husband—Benji's dad—isn't he in a band? I remember the whole family was musical. I tell the Bird all the time, there's hope for you yet." She gestured towards the hidden boy. "Not from me. I think I'm tone deaf. My god, you're tall."

A great white noise began in the back of Margot's mind. "I'm sorry, do I—have we met?"

"Never," Eva said, raising her chin. Her neckline was low enough to reveal the edge of a chest tattoo, the tip of a wing.

"You said it concerned my son?" Margot asked.

Eva put her hands on her hips and blew out an exhale. "Wow. I don't know how to begin." She gave a hollow laugh and her left leg moved a little, a slight quiver at the knee. "It's probably not the best time. Well, let's face it, when *is* a good time to meet a grandchild you didn't know you had?"

The white noise became a howl. On the ceiling above, the banners moved with a faint creaking sound. They were not made of fabric but paper. Miles of it, stencil cut like Mexican *papel picado*, in intricate, unrecognizable shapes. Impossible to mass produce something like that; it had to have been hand cut, a detail that matched the carefully placed fringed lamps, lace pillows and rows of colored glass bottles. All of this came from the same mind.

"I know this is weird," Eva continued. "At least he's cute. Good company. Aren't you, Bird?"

The boy stuck his head out from under the dresses, grinning. He stepped out and stood in front of his mother, asking for something Margot couldn't make out. Eva reached into a pocket and handed it to him. He turned to show her. It was a pack of gum.

"What on earth are you talking about?" Margot asked. Her voice seemed to come from the distant end of a long tunnel. It vibrated through the fractured bone, a dull tapping. "What are you *saying*?"

"His name's Birdie. Birdie Ethan Baker, after my dad, Ethan," said Eva. "Who's actually kind of a prick. A wealth manager. He has a good person in him somewhere, he just lost sight of it. Kind of sad when you think about it. I try not to. Do you want a cup of coffee? It tastes like shit. Trucker's coffee. But it's warm and caffeinated."

Margot let out a breath, which sounded like a gasp. The boy was unwrapping one stick after another, stuffing them in his mouth. They had identical eyes, he and his mother. Exact color and shape.

"You're probably wondering why now. I mean, obviously, he's not an infant. But all of a sudden, boom." Her small fists opened like stars. "Here we are! But this isn't about getting Birdie grandparents. Or a dad. I mean, that ship has sailed."

Eva's chin lowered a fraction and she gave a little snort like she'd said something clever. She shifted her weight and her small hand came to rest on the counter.

"I need cash," she continued. "Five thousand dollars, actually. Benji technically owes me two years of child support."

Margot frowned. Had something happened last week when he was home for spring break? The little boy's cheek bulged. A mess of foil wrappers littered the floor by his feet. Following Margot's gaze, Eva cried, "Oh!"

She knelt and plunged a polished forefinger into his mouth, pulled out a pink wad then hurried behind the counter to flick it into the trash. The boy scowled at Margot and dove back inside the dresses.

"What you're saying," Margot stammered, "the idea—you and Benji, you—"

For all her nervous yammering, Eva displayed an astonishing patience. Her gaze grew heavy. She squared her shoulders. Among her eleven cello students, Margot was known to be demanding. She was quiet and watchful as they composed themselves, exactly as Eva was watching her now. This turning of the tables was uncanny. For the briefest moment, Margot believed the scene was a narcotic delusion; she'd been left alone in the canyon too long. Terribly hot, she wished she could shuck off the jacket wrapped over her shoulder. And how was it she couldn't remember the drive to town, all those curves through the canyon, the stop sign at the highway, passing under the interstate?

Later, tearing out of the parking lot, Margot couldn't recall exact words, only her own scalding voice. Fragments surfaced. *Now you listen to me,* she may have said, her tone identical to her beloved but frightening grandmother. There might have been finger pointing. Regrettable, all of it. Some kind of mix-up. Eva had the wrong boy. Margot may have suggested as much, for Eva mentioned The Wilmas, Andy's band. So what? That proved nothing. Type the name 'Fickett' in Google and anybody could come up with The Wilmas.

Her good hand trembled on the steering wheel. She watched it at each stoplight, dry and foreign. She would flush the narcotics, even if the pain kept her up all night. Definitely should not be driving. The thing to do was get off the road.

Two

The shop furnace shut down with a heaving sigh and the place grew quiet as a church. Even the music was gone. Mrs. Fickett had taken it all with her: oxygen, heat, sound.

There was the shock of having it over with. After years of silence, the secret was out. Eva stood at the counter turning one hand inside the other and felt a tremor of relief. She wasn't disappointed; she hadn't expected much. You couldn't make people do what you wanted them to do, just as you couldn't make someone like you. This philosophy probably accounted for the coolness people sensed in her, the element of her personality that led others to call her "icy." She'd been called a snob. Even, on occasion, a bitch. That awful word, as though the entire, varied universe of anyone could sit in that narrow little spoon.

Yet Margot Fickett did seem to be a bitch. She had a wide forehead and a prominent chin. That long, erect back with a Carhartt jacket draped over it like a cape. She wore no makeup and her hair hung untouched, but she was not ugly. Far from ugly. Dark eyes like blades. *You could be sued for libel!* The patronizing pauses. She was so certain it made Eva doubt herself. *Was* she lying? Was Benji dead? Had he turned out to be gay?

She pressed a fingertip to each temple and lowered her chin to her chest. *Just get the money.* Sully's words, this very morning. He was right. The Fick-etts were the fastest way to five thousand dollars, and investing in his business was the fastest way to triple her money. Enough to quit this job and open her own shop. She turned to the shoe rack next to the counter, a mess she'd had her eye on for weeks.

Birdie appeared, hands on his hips. "Why's it so quiet?"

This stopped Eva. Just past his third birthday, her boy could enunciate like an adult. He had a knack for finding and piercing the tension in a room.

"Good question," she said, smiling. "Paige must be in back changing the music."

She began dismantling the shoe display. Simple retail logic said to put kids' shoes on top. Smaller and cheaper. She formed a pile on the floor. Birdie joined her, tossing with gusto. After a moment he stopped and leaned forward to peer into her face.

"Are you happy?"

Eva took a moment before responding. Birdie, the human mood ring.

"Yes, Bird. I'm happy."

They went back to throwing shoes. Birdie went as fast as he could, racing her. It was satisfying, the naughty violence in it. They began to giggle. The music started and Eva cried out—a soul-sapping country ballad. She covered her ears, sinking to her knees. Birdie was scared until she reached out to cover his ears, too. They were both laughing when the clipped sound of heels approached.

"Who'd you get a visit from?" asked Paige, her boss.

Eva looked at Birdie and bit her lip. He slapped a hand over his mouth. Above them, Paige crossed her arms.

"Who was that tall woman?"

"Friend of my mom's," Eva said. "She had the wrong door."

"Oh? She didn't go back to the studio. She pulled out of the lot. She looked upset."

Eva shrugged. Birdie held up a stained, size-ten Chuck Taylor. Eva nodded at it.

"Something like that is never going to sell. It belongs in the trash."

Paige frowned. "You should take him now," she said, looking at the boy. "This can't keep happening. We can't have a toddler on the loose. You don't see Caitlyn hanging around all day."

Paige loved this defense: *her* child didn't come to work with her, so why should Eva's? Never mind that Caity was in school all day, and after school, her dad picked her up. Eva stared at the floor, trying to ignore the heave in her chest. The unfairness was lost on Paige. Her lack of intelligence was one of many reasons this place now sucked. "Dolly's." Even the name sucked. Before, it was The Unique Boutique, sellers of perfectly respectable vintage goods. Now it was full of Pottery Barn castoffs and outgrown clothing from Penny's, a dumping ground for the middle class.

Eva stood to go, taking Birdie's hand, vowing not to blow her plans by shooting off her mouth. She led him to the door without another word. Outside, walking along the building's west side, they were shielded from the wind. The sky hung low; the fog didn't want to lift. The roof dripped a steady line. Birdie pulled their joined hands under it, thrilled by the tiny blasts of frigid water. She had rushed it with Mrs. Fickett. She should have gone slower. Maybe been nicer? She never got her breath. She didn't actually *introduce* Birdie.

In the back corner of the Rock Creek Commons was Annie's Fitness, a hybrid gym and dance studio named for Eva's mother. Annie's offered classes in Zumba, modern dance, ballet, hula, belly dancing, and something new called EverCheer involving pompoms. The studio also offered full time day-care, where Birdie spent his days. Her mother had staffing issues, though, and "full time" often meant afternoons only.

Pushing open the door, they were hit with the smell of damp nylon and sweat. Familiar and unpleasant. Eva was thirteen the year her mother opened this place. She'd hated it then and still did. Birdie was getting too old to stay in one room all day. A source of unhappiness was that he, like Eva herself, spent so much of his life in a strip mall.

Class had just let out and several women lingered. Eva's mother was talking with clients, still wearing her headset; she jumped from the stage to the gym floor, a move full of strength. Her mother was at her best covered in a sheen, a fifty-something hottie who inspired others. Briefly, she met Eva's eye, offering a stingy smile, a minimal movement of the lips. She approached slowly, arms out, aiming at the boy. She crouched, put a hand on his back and smiled into his face. She picked him up, cooing and tutting as if his whole morning had been wrong until this moment of rescue. It pleased Eva that her mother adored him, but she didn't believe it would last. Once he was old enough to sass, she'd be done.

"It's been awhile," she said to Eva. "We'd love to see you soon for dinner. You should try to come by." With a significant look she added, "You and Birdie."

This meant, Eva knew, that her boyfriend wasn't invited. Sully was fifteen years older than Eva and that was only one of her mother's complaints. He ran the New Leaf, a medical marijuana dispensary and grow operation that had moved in behind Annie's Fitness. They shared a wall. The smell of weed came through the vent system. Eva's mother said it attracted riffraff, or would, when the dispensary opened.

The women filed out, stopping to greet Birdie, pat his back, tell her mother how superb her grandson was. She spoke to them like a proud hen. Eva knew she was still waiting for a response to the invitation. *Sounds nice.* Or, *I'll try to come*, any kind of acquiescence, no matter how meaningless. Her mother preferred a veneer of harmony over what they didn't like about each other. Politeness was important to her, as were appearances. She scoffed at the flabby and the thoughtlessly dressed. Invitations like this were actually commands. Two weeks ago, she said she wanted to meet Eva's "mystery man." Sully resisted, but Eva said if they were to have any staying power, this moment must be faced. They barely got past the threshold. When her mother recognized him, she made such a scene that the two left before any food made it to the table.

"Your hair's growing out," her mother said.

Involuntarily, Eva's hand went to her scalp.

"Are you going to let it be dark again?" She sounded hopeful. "Of course, you won't look like this guy with your natural color." Her mother nuzzled Birdie. "People will think you're his nanny."

The few remaining women heard this. They looked quickly from mother to daughter. Eva's eyes hardened as she leaned in to kiss her son goodbye. He was safe here—no physical harm would come to him—but she headed for the door with a roaring in her ears.

"I'll bring him down to you at five," her mother called after her. "Save you a trip."

"No!" Eva barked, turning.

Her mother cocked an eyebrow.

"I'll come get him," she said with a smile she knew looked anxious. "A little after five. I'm closing, so."

The excuse made no sense, but it would have to do. Her mother could not come to Dolly's. She must be kept away from Paige, who didn't know about Eva and Sully. Sully was Paige's ex-husband.

The complexity was tiresome; for six months Eva felt she'd been walking a tightrope. She was ready to be out with it, but Sully said it was too soon. Get a plan in place, he said, an exit strategy. Know where you're going and why. Mrs. Fickett was part of that plan.

Eva hit the gloomy air outside the studio and made a rash decision, turning not towards the store but towards the back of the building. In defiance of their pact, Eva was going to see him. The very thought of Sully lightened her step, put a curl at the corner of her mouth. Big, red-haired Sully. Eva, with a ginger! That hair was his defining feature. It grew like grass. Every few weeks he mowed it. Three short years ago, when she was still in school, a guy like Sully would have been invisible to her. He didn't try to be sexy, and if he did he'd fail. He was no hard-body, with his thick middle and broad shoulders. His signature outfit was Russell athletic shorts and old Nikes. Up top he wore a T-shirt or a sweatshirt, usually both. Her high school friends would call him a loser. An old man without prospects

Every one of those people had faded from her life since Birdie was born, including the girl she used to be. Sully might be old and out of shape, but he was a dad. He knew the layout of the children's museum and the dates and times of free pizza night. He knew the rec swim hours at the public pool and how many tickets won you a decent prize at Geyser Park. He was also an ex-soldier, missing half his left hand. His moody, pale eyes could be unreadable. He was prone to funks, and sometimes, an explosive temper. He was sexy.

There was no wind at the back of the building; the sound of traffic was blotted out and Eva could hear the chattering creek. In spite of the gloom, a warm anticipation burned in her chest. Her hands tingled and her senses were on high alert. Across the creek on the top step of a trailer, a yellow tabby cat sat grooming himself. A tattered screen fluttered in the window. As she passed the windows to her mother's studio, Eva straightened her back and walked with purpose, refusing to hide.

The New Leaf had windows back here, too. Peering in, she could see walls she'd painted herself, an earthy brown with white trim. Sully wasn't there, which meant he was in back, in the grow room. The chairs she'd ordered had come in, and someone had moved the three-foot ficus. Eva hadn't been here all week—Sully said they should be careful after the fiasco with her parents. But they needed her decorating skills, clearly.

Around the final corner the wind was waiting. Her eyes watered. She wiped them and stopped short. Dutch was leaning on his car, his back to her. Dutch was the boss, the California man fronting the money for Sully's business. His car was his alter ego, a sleek black Charger with vanity plates announcing his pretentious, one-word name. None of his people came from the Netherlands. She had asked.

He was the one requiring Eva to come up with the money. He didn't give a shit how much time she'd put into the business, nor did he care that Eva only wanted a loan, something to get her started in her own shop. He said she had to put in to take out. "Skin in the game, kids," he said to her and Sully when they approached him. "You gotta have skin in the game." Five thousand dollars. Who had five thousand dollars lying around? Sully would give it to her if he had it, but he didn't, and wouldn't until after harvest. Dutch wanted it *before* harvest or Eva didn't get a dime.

His car was next to the big stone planter, still full of snow. The skeletal hawthorn tree loomed above him. He was on the phone. Eva thought she could back away undetected but as soon as she moved, he turned.

"Eva," he said, pocketing his phone.

He never raised his voice, yet he was always audible, like a station on the radio that came in better than any other. He walked around the car's hood, his weird amber eyes scanning her body in a lazy, unhurried way. He wasn't particularly tall or muscular but he was sharp. Everything about him had an edge. His long fingers were in constant contact with his unnaturally red mouth.

"Four weeks till harvest," he said, standing well inside her personal space. Eva fought the urge to back up. "How's the investment coming?"

"You mean, do I have the money?" she asked. "It's coming. I'll get it."

He leaned back on his heels with a wry smile. She tried to step around him but he moved with her, blocking her way.

"Our pal's here," he said.

"Good," Eva said, thinking he meant Sully, hoping he'd appear by some stroke of luck.

Dutch turned to the side as if presenting her with a special view. He gestured with his head towards something in the parking lot. She saw nothing unusual; the north side of the building had only one other store, a bird supply place. There were a few cars.

"What?"

"Sully hasn't told you about our pal?"

Eva frowned, confused.

"The white Tahoe," he grinned, fishing in his coat pocket for cigarettes. "A spy," he added, raising his eyebrows for effect.

"What are you talking about?"

"Guy's here every day," Dutch said, lighting up. "Buys an awful lot of birdseed." Without turning from her, he said, "Look in the window of the store. See the reflection? A tiny bright spot?"

Eva saw it, a moving glint.

"That's his binoculars," Dutch said, exhaling a line of smoke, pleased with himself.

"Bullshit," said Eva. "You're making that up."

Dutch shrugged and took another drag.

"Jesus," said Eva, panicking. "A cop?"

"Federal agent, more likely."

The door swung open and Eva jumped. Sully stepped out, a wish fulfilled with his bright steady eyes. His coppertop stood on end from his hands running through it. Eva rushed over, threw her arms around him and kissed his surprised face.

"Eva!" he cried with an anxious look down the sidewalk. "Are you *trying* to get fired?"

"I was just showing her our pal," Dutch said. "The guy with all the birds."

"I thought you said the government didn't care?" Eva said to Sully. "There was a memo—it's legal?"

"The feds are watching everybody," Sully told her. "He's only trying to scare you."

"Doesn't matter who's watching," Dutch said, dropping his cigarette and pressing it under his boot. "We sell to card carriers. We're following the law."

Sully wrapped an arm around her shoulders and led her towards the corner of the building. He smelled of cannabis and detergent and something else, a fleshy, human scent all his own.

"You can't be down here during the day," he said in a lower voice. "You have Birdie to think about."

"I'm not afraid of Paige," Eva said.

"You should be."

They were at the corner now. He gripped her shoulders, coming in close to kiss her forehead. In a softer, encouraging voice he added, "Choose your moment."

"Five more weeks!" Dutch called to them.

Turning away, Eva scowled. She wished he'd go bald. Baldness would take all the steam out of a guy like Dutch.

Three

Margot drove home in a daze. Her hand on the wheel shook and her field of vision narrowed. She didn't take her eyes off the pavement for fear of disaster. She drove so slow a line of cars formed behind her. By the time the road widened at the underpass, enraged drivers gunned past.

The fog had reached the canyon. Details emerged from the gray, crowding her: three crows on the telephone line, jeering; a billowing plastic bag caught on a fence post; the bank of mailboxes at the fork in the road, the one in the middle open-mouthed. She sat a long time in the driveway, listening to the engine ping and hiss. The hand in her lap still trembled. Uninjured, she'd already be up the clifftop trail. Music and nature were her twin solaces. Anxious, excited, sad, or furious, the antidote was a bow and strings, or a walk beneath the lidless sky. With neither available, her mind skidded.

She pulled her bag into her lap and dug out her cell phone. She had no idea what Benji would be up to at two o'clock on a Friday. Margot still imagined him as a freshman in his dorm room, back to back with his roommate at those little desks. Perhaps he was at band practice, she thought.

"Nothing wrong," she said, shocked when he picked up. "This is a 'just because' call. Are you in the middle of something?"

"Sort of. How's the collarbone?"

"It's a pain."

"Ha ha," he said and Margot smiled, reassured by the way they fell into this old rhythm of bad jokes and easy banter. She could almost hang up now, tell him to carry on, get out of the vehicle and carry on herself, forget the last hour ever happened.

"Is your season done for?" Benji asked.

"I'm afraid so."

He was thoughtful, asking about what mattered most to her, so different from the average twenty-one-year old. Yet that was just what Eva accused him of being: average. This was a bind in which any ordinary fool might find himself.

"At least bones grow back," he said.

"How's it going with your rock band?"

"The Revelaires, mom. Taken from a song—yeah, it's going good. We've got gigs the next six weekends."

"How can you keep up with your classes, the school symphony?"

Benji sighed. "I just do. It works out."

Was he lying? Had he quit the symphony? She rubbed her forehead, noticed that her hand had quit shaking.

"What do you hear from your Dad?"

"They got a good review in Seattle, I saw on Facebook. And they're in Portland this weekend."

There was another lull. Surely it was obvious she wanted something. Used to be you could curl a phone cord in your fingers while you decided what to reveal.

"Benji," she said after a deep breath, "does the name Eva Baker mean anything to you?"

The question came out too studied. His pause was long enough to feel significant. Margot's stomach lurched.

"She was in my class," he said. "Why?"

"I met her the other day. She mentioned you."

"Where did you meet Eva Baker?"

Margot faltered. "A book group."

"When did you join a book group?"

All wrong. He knew she wasn't book group material. Margot loved to read but hated dissection and the inevitable off-topic meandering.

"A few months back. I'm trying new things."

"And Eva's in it."

"No," Margot said. "She was just visiting."

"What, you mean with her mother?"

"Yes." Eva had a mother. Did *Benji* know the mother? Did the woman read?

"Interesting," he said finally.

"What?"

"It's hard to picture."

Indeed. "Yes, well," she said. "I just wondered."

Bad on the phone, Margot tended to rush the obligatory parting phrases. Sometimes she skipped them altogether, going silent until she could hang up. Benji knew this and wrapped up the call for them.

She sat staring at the house, most of it swallowed by fog. The years of her life compressed. Benji was a baby and an adult in the same breath. She wasn't even going to have children! She'd cried when she discovered she was pregnant. Andy insisted a baby could be managed. They would hire a nanny; they could both still tour. They were living in D.C. at the time, Margot playing for the National Symphony Orchestra. Andy was miserable there, teaching part-time, wanting out of the city. They moved to Deaton, Montana, a place they'd first seen touring as students with the Peabody, when Andy still played classical violin.

Many called it career suicide, but as it was happening—quitting jobs, moving across the country, falling in love with Montana—it was all exciting. They believed they could defy the odds, live a life that satisfied them both *and* raise a baby. Andy's money helped; in graduate school, he invented a de-wolfer for string instruments, a suppressor that could be affixed to the instrument with putty. The kind of thing that was now everywhere, this device had made him a millionaire by the time he was twenty-five.

When Benji was born, Margot felt an almost crippling marvel. Hairless, appallingly fragile, she was overwhelmed with love and disgust. She wept as she nursed him, feeling both jailed and exultant. Within weeks his eyes took on depth and he began to notice light and movement. He would turn his head towards her voice. One night after a midnight feeding, she took him out to the deck and showed him the moon. When she played him his first note, he jumped, a full body startle, but he didn't cry. When he listened to recorded music, his eyes grew heavy and his limbs relaxed. Rachmaninoff and Tchaikovsky, her beloved Russians, put him in a trance.

The events of less than an hour ago—that bewitched emporium, Eva Baker in her low-cut top, those smug words—*This is happening Mrs. Fickett. I am happening*—were surely a dream. Benji! A kid whose idea of rebellion was to use his father's student-grade, greasy rosin instead of the darker stuff. In high school, he'd been rangy and quiet, considerate of others unless he was playing his violin. Then, the world vanished as completely as it did for his mother. He played with intense motion, the bow screaming back and forth as he leaned and swayed. The sight brought to mind a flock of furious birds. Nearby players scooted their chairs away.

Margot pulled the handle and pushed the door open with her foot. From out of the fog came a terrible screech, so unexpected and violent that Margot caught her breath. Her flesh rose, tingling with goosebumps. The sound ended in a blood curdling screech, the unmistakable hunting cry of the great horned owl. She got out of the truck and turned, scanning the sky, but the fog was so thick she couldn't see the benchtops east of the house. Halfway to the door, the scream came again, so close she crouched, thinking the bird was coming at her with its talons spread, eyes wild with rage.

Four

Sully stared after Eva, forcing himself to take slow, deliberate breaths. He outweighed Dutch by fifteen pounds. He'd seen two tours in Afghanistan, was divorced, and hated surprises. But he had to be careful.

When he was composed, he turned. Dutch was movie star good-looking and dressed the part. Women loved the guy. Dutch was watching him, his wolfish eyes reflecting the challenge Sully was trying so hard to hide.

"We could cut her in," Sully said. "She's worked hard and she'd repay the money within a year."

Dutch stepped forward, his jaw clenching. In the gray, dense air, his light brown eyes shone like gems. Be careful, Sully told himself, exhaling slowly. His luck was changing; the year looked good. The law was on his side. The justice department memo meant the government promised to live and let live. He'd found this space and not a week later Dutch waltzed into his life. The decision about Eva wasn't up to him. The guy with the money made the calls. As gently as he could, he tried again. "It's not really fair—"

"It's fair," Dutch snapped. "She's got nothing at stake here, Sully. You'd see that if you weren't thinking with your dick."

Sully's shoulders drew back in offense. Heat pumped through him. He crossed his arms over his chest to contain his bloated heart, anything to keep the moment from becoming a face-off.

"Here's a piece of wisdom," Dutch fumed. "You and I are from one world, Eva Baker's from another." He paused but his icy gaze never left Sully's. "She's slumming, my friend."

"You don't know what you're talking about."

Dutch rocked on his heels, unfazed. "Times are changing. Dope is legal. Great." He lifted both hands and turned them, a sarcastic gesture of excitement. "There might be crossover between this world and that, for the dope. But they'll never mix. It's like oil and water." He flattened his palm and made slow circles in the air. "You'll see the oil on top of the water, that rainbow shimmer. But they never merge, Sullivan. Never."

Looking away, Sully's gaze rested on the white Tahoe outside the birdfeed store. Dutch turned, too; he let out a scornful laugh as if his point were made.

Sully's phone rang. Relieved, he dug it out of his pocket and Dutch turned on his heels. It was Paige. Ignoring her would backfire. She'd stalk down here and scold him, then ignore his calls for a week. Once Dutch had roared out of the parking lot, Sully picked up.

Paige was already talking. " . . . sign her up for theater camp? Because they will fill up. And she needs new shoes and a dress for Easter with a coat to match. They have spring coats on sale at Penny's out at the mall. You could also check Dillon's."

He had not done any of these things, but he would. He'd do whatever she asked. She knew what he did for a living, that he had done it for years, long before it was legal. He could lose custody in a heartbeat. If he served time, she could sever his parental rights. Paige was no narc; she knew his grows were the source of her child support. Also, she had no interest in being a single parent. She loved her night life. Such was their understanding. She could call with this crap any time she felt the need.

Yes, he told her, he'd buy Caity a dress. Yes, he'd sign her up for theater camp. Yes, yes, yes. He was ready to hang up.

"Can you watch her tomorrow?" she asked. "I know it's my night but I want to go look at a living room set up in the canyon."

He was silent, staring at the snow piled in the planter, the little tree standing above it. Tomorrow night he had a date with Eva. He looked again at the Tahoe, astonished to see the driver's door open. A man got out. The guy had been here for weeks, yet Sully had never seen him. He probably had photographs. Was that in itself enough to sever your rights as a parent, if the FBI had your fucking picture?

"It's a velvet couch with matching love seat," Paige said. "If we haul, they'll throw in the dining room set. Including chairs. Somebody died. It's a *steal*, Sullivan."

"Can't," he said, walking towards the shop door. The agent wasn't tall, probably five-seven. Bearded. Cobalt blue ski jacket. He stood still, hands in pockets, looking Sully's way.

"Why not?"

His heart clanged.

"Hello!" Paige cried. "Sully, why not?"

"I gotta go," he said and hung up, pocketing the phone.

Briefly, the two men stood facing one another in the gray stillness, separated only by yards of sidewalk. As if by signal, they simultaneously turned to step through their respective doors.

Past midnight but well before dawn, Sully opened his eyes, fully awake. He stared up at the ceiling of his bedroom, which bowed slightly towards him, then rolled out of bed and pulled on his sweats. In the days before harvest, Sully rarely got more than five hours of sleep. Part of it was the constant contact; he groomed the plants daily and the bigger they got, the longer it took. Part of it was adrenaline, the excitement of studying buds through his jeweler's loop, scanning for signs of amber. His home crop was blooming now, the same three-light operation he'd run for years. At the New Leaf, he was weeks away from the biggest harvest of his life. Dutch doubted his yield estimates but Sully was confident. With sixty lamps, plus the seedlings they were nursing, no wonder he couldn't sleep.

Deaton, at night, without the students and tourists, revealed itself for what it was: an overgrown cow town. Sully drove exactly the speed limit, following the river, invisible under a band of fog. The houses on the north side appeared frail and vulnerable. He drove west, towards the newer subdivisions. These cookie cutter houses could be anywhere in America. Iowa. Nebraska, even his native Missouri. Street after street of three bedroom homes with yards. In the middle of a block like all the others sat Paige's, dark and quiet. He often monitored the street in front of her house, policing for foreign cars. If he spotted one, he'd confront her, demanding to meet the man spending the night with his daughter. It was only fair, but it infuriated her.

Next he drove by Eva's. He wasn't spying, only checking on those he loved. Her place was dark, the car in its spot. Eva was a thing of beauty. From the moment he first saw her in Paige's shop, it was an effort not to stare. His gaze could be too expectant, he knew. *Quit looking at me*, Paige used to tell him. But Eva's face wanted you to look at it, always full of expression, even at rest. A pouting, perfect mouth either pursed or turned up in curiosity. When he was in the same room with her, his mind was keyed to hers, reading her features, wondering about her thoughts. He'd studied her eating. Chewing hummus and crackers, never dropping a crumb. Not a drop of coffee on her shirt.

He tried joking with her once, when she was dressed all in black, black lipstick, black nail polish and heavy eyeliner. "What're you, Goth or something?" he asked, teasing. Without hesitation she fired back, "What're you, a douche bag?"

The hostility made him laugh, which shocked her. With her white hair tucked up under a black skullcap, her blue eyes jumped out of her face. He introduced himself and asked for a tour, which was the right move. He loved how small she was, how she charged through the store, kneeing furniture into place. The displays were pure genius. Some had walls of plywood with doors that opened like you'd see in a showroom. Paige got rid of the walls early on, saying it made theft too easy. What would they steal, Eva raged, costume jewelry? She hated sacrificing effect for practicality. She hated practicality. Going anywhere with her was like a walk through a fairytale. Her bedroom, with its canopy bed and fancy furniture, was straight out of a storybook. She was from Deaton, had never lived anywhere else, yet was unlike anyone he'd met here or anywhere, ever.

Sully came to Montana and saw right away that the good ol' boy attitude he was born to wasn't going to cut it. Back in Missouri, country boys liked moonshine, banjo, and dancing. The Montana cowboy liked bull riding and steer roping, was used to pain and lacked any attachment to leisure—a tougher biscuit by far. Without question the climate was part of it. Knowing nothing but winter, real warmth was unrecognizable to these people. Sully's mother came to visit one summer and they had to drive to the woolen outlet to get her a sweater. She used to ask when he was coming home, but once Caity was born, she quit asking. His fair-skinned, freckled daughter was the best of him. Hair straight as paper. Organizing his junk drawer. Tracing her name in window frost. Twirly skirts and the smallest boots. A pirouette.

He was deployed when she was born, and Sully admitted to no one that he wasn't sure the child was his. Then he saw her and the worry was over. A week in the world and she was topped by a swirl of unmistakable copper. He loved her instantly. After years of making an ass of himself over Paige, his feelings for his wife began to dwindle. He began what felt like an automatic transfer of affection from one account to the other.

If he was honest, it was more than his daughter that kept him in Montana. He'd come here young, just to see the world. A buddy was a farrier, wanted a new life, and let Sully tag along. As early as a year in, Sully knew he was home. Roughly half the people he met here were native to the place. The others were like him, restless souls. Not orphans, exactly, but they lacked the bond of family tied to place. This restlessness had nothing to do with childhood happiness or family ties. For Sully it was a temperament, some kind of wanderlust that cooled here in the ragged, unpredictable country all along the divide. The flat, long benchlands above the rivers, the ridiculous angles of the breaks, the deeply incised floodplains, the miles of empty highway provided an inner settling. Grassy plains undulating in the wind, canyons that dropped open without warning. The lack of symmetry to the place was consoling for a certain sort of person. Grandiosity was part of it: here, finally, was a backdrop that put you, a man, in the proper scale. You were small, and so was your angst. All your wandering would lead you in circles before this ceased to be true. In this sense, the connection he felt to Montana was religious. Impossible to explain, not to his mother, his relatives, or his old friends. Not even to his platoon mates. Certainly not to Paige.

Of all the people he had met, Eva might understand. She had never been anywhere else and still he sensed she would get it, whatever it was about Montana that spoke to people like him and claimed them. If he could articulate it, which he could not, she'd know what he meant.

———

He pulled into the Rock Creek Commons and drove to the north side of the building. There was a car in the lot, outside the New Leaf door, right next to the cement planter. The skin on the back of Sully's neck tingled. He was not afraid but wary. He pulled in near the bird supply store and shut off his engine. The car's dome light was lit; he counted three occupants. The one in back was small, probably a woman. They had clearly seen him.

He wondered what to do. They weren't cops. The car was a two-door sedan, heavy, with boxy fenders. Could be undercover, but he doubted it. A feeling told him otherwise, that prickle on his neck. He could back out and drive away, but everything he had was in that shop. A piece of him he could never get back had gone into making this place.

He got out, keys in hand, and approached the shop door. When he got close to the car, the driver's door opened. Smoke poured out, so much he thought it was fire. But it was odorless. Vapor. So they were from the coast. When the air cleared, he could see that all three held those ridiculous little e-cigarettes. The driver stepped out and cocked his seat forward. The woman climbed out of the back.

"Can I help you?" Sully asked.

"Maybe," said the driver. "This your shop?"

"It is."

"We're looking for somebody," the driver said. He was clean shaven, his voice young. The woman was young, too, small next to him, Eva's height.

"Who?"

"Name's Dutch," she said.

The wariness crept up his neck again, colder now. In the growing light he made out the girl's hair, the dark, tiny bangs across her forehead. Her features were sharp and small, a spiteful face. He needed to get rid of these people. Deny everything, whatever they asked. Since he was a poor liar, he resolved to say nothing.

"Not a big man," said the driver after a moment. He was as tall as Sully but not as old, and he carried the same dark energy as the girl.

"How many lamps you got?"

The words came from the car. Another cloud of vapor rolled out the open door. Sully leaned over to see the third man. Older, bearded, definitely the authority.

"Don't worry about it," Sully replied.

The passenger door opened and the bearded man got out. He was tall enough to make eye contact with Sully over the top of the car.

"Not worried," he said. "Just curious." He took another puff off his e-cigarette. Sully heard the hiss of his long inhale, then out came the vapor, encircling the man's head and creating a great funnel above him, into the lightening sky. He put a palm on the roof of the car. "Do you know Dutch? We were told he owned a shop here in town."

"Can't help you," Sully said.

"Can't, or won't?" said the man.

Sully began to move away from the trio, towards the shop door. In his mind, that is what they became, the dark trio that came looking for Dutch. They weren't the first sign, but surely the most obvious, that none of this was going to be as simple as Dutch said it would be.

They watched him unlock the door. Their gaze was heavy and unfriendly. Typical marijuana culture was open, social and welcoming. Decidedly not capitalist. Competing pot shops wished each other well. The law had been revised, but nothing touched these facts. Sully's guardedness marked him as guilty, just as they were marked by malevolence. He may have bought himself time; they would search the other dispensaries and growers in the storage units west of town. But they would be back.

Inside he didn't turn on the lights but stood listening, waiting for them to leave. For a long time, they didn't. He thought he saw movement out the reception room window. He crossed the room to peek out towards the creek and the trailer park. A light was on in one of the trailers but other than that, nothing. He sat in one of the reception chairs, holding his breath against this swell of dread.

Finally he heard car doors, the deep mutter of a big engine. They didn't turn on their headlights. He heard them come around by the creek, then pull around Annie's. He breathed into the silence for a second or two. A long, deep inhale the way he was taught in his re-entry program for the disabled. In his mind he hardly qualified as disabled, not compared to the others. But they insisted. Belly breathing. Expect high temper, they said. The civilian world will drive you crazy.

Five

By eight the next morning, Margot was showered, loaded up on Advil and once again behind the wheel. Her stomach roiled and she could feel the fracture every time she moved, but she was going to see Satterfield. She hadn't heard anything more from Eva and had no idea just what was supposed to happen next. Did one simply wait to hear?

The maestro was Margot's best friend, which was difficult to explain. He regularly told Margot she should tour more, and she should be in a quartet or a trio. She was wasting her talent with a group like Strings, which adapted popular music for cellos. Why, he wondered, would anyone want to do that? The matter would be different if Satterfield was a woman. Or a gay man. You saw that all the time, women admitting to friendships more intimate than their marriages. But he was a straight, bossy, philandering drama queen. Andy, who liked everybody, couldn't stand him. He thought Douglas was smug, and Douglas found Andy too careless with himself, his ideas and his music. Margot agreed. Andy was careless, and Satterfield was smug. But she spent more time with Satterfield; they played the same music; they understood each other.

Margot could have called Andy. As a rule, she didn't call when he was on the road. Performing was happiness to Andy. He loved to tour. The Wilmas put out a record as often as they could, and each year the band played the festivals in Telluride and Targhee, events Margot found intolerable. The smoky food stalls and partially clothed children, the drunk adults camped out like refugees made listening to the music impossible.

Late in the night, Margot had flushed her narcotics, then stood for a long time in their shared bathroom, ruminating. Andy's sink was covered in tiny hairs. His can of shaving cream faced its own reflection, a small foamy seed at the spout. He'd left behind his razor, his toothbrush, his squished tube of toothpaste. He was a poor packer, habitually forgot his essentials and had to buy more.

Long ago the two of them had learned that being apart could be good. They loved each other, and they loved playing music; no reason the two loves had to compete. The musician on the road ought to be left alone, without guilt. More often than not, that musician was Andy.

The drive to Satterfield's took twenty-five minutes. South of town, as she passed the country club, Margot saw a bald eagle in a stand of naked cotton-woods. The road was built up on the curve, high enough to be eye-level with the T-poles. The look the bird gave her, that sharp yellow under a white hood, felt like a recriminating glare.

The Satterfields lived in Doubletree, a showy subdivision full of massive homes on two-acre, treeless lots, with long driveways rolled out like pointed tongues. Gloria Satterfield opened the door wearing a silk, floor-skimming robe with matching slippers. At this hour, her ensemble might be a sleeping outfit except she was wearing earrings. She put a hand on her hip and they trembled. Did a mezzo soprano sleep in earrings?

"Margot," she said in a flat, unhappy voice. "What a surprise."

Of course, Gloria would be pissed, the chesty bulldog guarding her home. There was no way to explain that this wasn't what it appeared to be. Margot wasn't one of Satterfield's women. To say so at this moment would require acknowledging what everyone knew but no one mentioned: that Douglas had a lot of women. Among the players, Satterfield's promiscuity was forgiven, a byproduct of his intense personality. Gloria's chorale singers saw it different-ly. *Gloria is a saint!* you'd hear them say. *How she suffers!*

"I'm sorry it's so early. I need to speak to Douglas."

"You couldn't call?"

"It's important."

Satterfield appeared behind Gloria. He was dressed in shorts and a nylon shirt; he'd already been running, a good sign. Since they'd started rehearsals for the Ninth, his appearance had deteriorated. His impeccable dress—suit pants, tie, well-trimmed sideburns—had been replaced on more than one occasion with jeans and a button-down. His hair went uncombed and his sideburns looked faintly pubic. The violins swore he was wearing eyeliner. He liked to point out that the Ninth premiered when Beethoven was fifty-four—Satterfield's age.

"What on earth are you doing here?" he asked Margot. "And why are you still outside, for God's sake. Come in!"

He reached over his wife's head to pull the door open wide. Gloria crossed her arms and stepped back, glaring as Margot crossed the threshold. When they were in the sitting room, he turned to appraise her head to toe, his eyes resting on the bandage covering the right side of her neck. He was her height; they stood eye to eye. Margot held still while Satterfield reached out a hand and pulled aside the collar of her shirt. The incision was covered and taped, but he looked anyway.

"Is the wound really that long?"

"It is," she said.

He took a deep breath. She watched the hollows of his neck empty.

"We're a disaster without you," he said, raising his long eyebrows. "The singers are out of hand. There isn't room for us on stage. We've had to speak to the manager to change the curtain width so the balcony can see everybody."

"That's an exaggeration," cried Gloria. She started to say more but Satterfield cut her off.

"What were you thinking!" His arms flew overhead. "Running downhill in the dark? Christ! Were you drinking? You must have been!"

"I was not drinking—"

"Without a thought of us, of what was at *stake*!" he shouted, turning away. "You're irresponsible. You're selfish. Plus the goddamn violins and violas cannot manage to keep up." Satterfield was in full rant mode. All Margot could do was let him exhaust himself. "The timpanist has no muscle," he cried, "and the trombones are soggy."

"Stop!" cried Gloria. She turned to Margot, shouting, trying to drown him out. "He's making too much of everything! He's lost his mind! We still have weeks of rehearsal ahead."

"We're off the mark and you know it," Satterfield said.

Margot looked from one to the other, her head ringing. Slowly, she cradled her damaged arm with her good.

"Really, Margot," Satterfield said, "you couldn't have picked a worse time."

"Oh, you *ass*," she said.

He turned away from Margot sharply. Gloria harrumphed, crossed her arms, pleased.

"I was not drunk and I was not running," Margot continued. "It was a fucking accident."

They both gaped at her. Margot did not swear. "You'd know that if you'd bothered to visit," she added, "Or if you'd picked up the damn phone." She dropped into the closest chair, her hands shaking.

"Gloria, get her a glass of water," Satterfield said.

"I wanted to talk to you," Margot said when she'd gone. "Something bizarre has happened." Margot was stunned to find her mouth quivering. She was going to cry. "Shit."

"You should be in bed," he said, sitting on the coffee table in front of her.

He took her good hand. Fifteen years ago, his second year conducting, he made her principal cellist. When she protested, saying she didn't have the experience, he said he didn't care. He told her she played like her life depended on it, and that was all that mattered.

He'd made a pass at her once, not long after. They were on a summer chamber tour. It happened late one night outside a tavern in Moscow, Idaho. He leaned her against a car and kissed her. Next, her shirt was up and he had his mouth on her left nipple, right there in the parking lot. She supposed this was what women loved about him, the devouring. He tasted everything, left you weak-kneed but intact. He had languid, bedroom eyes, a big nose and a deep voice. He was six-four and he made the baton look like a toothpick.

Not her, Margot decided that night. She was a mother by then; she'd left Andy with the baby while she toured. That night in the parking lot, she slipped out of Satterfield's arms. They regarded each other in silence, then got in their cars and drove separately back to the motel. They never spoke of the incident. Margot remained the one who refused him, a status that turned out to have some power.

They were friends. She was closer to him than her own husband in some ways. But how was she to explain Eva? What a muddle all stories were. The matter of details, context, background. Balancing the general with the specific. A musical score was blessedly language-free. Same notes the world over. The Japanese, for instance, played the Ninth on New Year's Day. An anthem for a new beginning.

"I was seventeen when first I played the Ninth," she said, her voice cracking, as if just realizing this.

Gloria returned with a full glass of water, but Margot couldn't take it, her hand trembled too badly.

"Oh, you poor thing," Gloria muttered.

Satterfield took the glass and put it on the table. "Gloria, love, will you make a pot of tea?" he asked. She did as he asked and his gaze returned to Margot.

"You're scaring me. You don't do self-pity."

Margot smirked at him. He got up to pull the pocket doors closed, then sat again, right in front of her. Unlike many tall people, he had a careless way with his body, often sitting askew, knocking his knees or shoulders against his neighbor. Margot liked the contact, the smell of him, fresh and airy, like the wood of a new reed.

"Yesterday, a girl called me," Margot finally blurted. "Told me that Benji has a son."

Satterfield bushy eyebrows lit up and his mouth fell open. He was Benji's music teacher when he was seven years old. He helped the Ficketts find the best instructors in the region and guided them to the right camps and festivals. He opposed sending Benji to college at St. Thomas, though they had a fine performance program. He thought the boy belonged at a conservatory.

"Benji?" he asked, with a sound like a gasp. "A father?"

He shook his head and laughed in disbelief. When he saw her expression, he grew still. His eyes angled down at the outer corner, a detail that made him appear indolent, even sad.

"Impossible," he said. "The girl is lying."

"I thought that too, but why? Blackmail a musician? For *money*?"

He stood and began to pace. "She knows about Andy's gadget, obviously. Did she go to school with Benji? He must have talked about it."

Margot thought about this. It made sense. The Ficketts *were* unusual, a musical family with money. She felt the squeeze on her heart lift a fraction. Eva was after money, that was all. It really was just a stupid scam.

"Did you see the child?" Satterfield asked. "Did it look like Benji?"

"Douglas!" she cried. "It isn't Benji's child!"

He held up both palms in defense. "I was only curious," he said and crossed his arms, waiting.

Margot closed her eyes. "Yes, I saw him. No, he does not look like Benji."

Satterfield grunted again and resumed his pacing. "Why *now*?" he asked. "You said it was a little boy, not a baby. Why wait all this time?"

"Said she needs money. For an investment."

"*Investment?*"

"If she invests in her boyfriend's business, she'll get some of the profit."

"What business?"

"I don't *know*, Douglas!" she cried.

He turned his back, still thinking. Finally he clasped his hands and turned, saying, "Get a paternity test. Be sure."

Her breath quickened as if they were discussing national security. Margot had considered the need for proof, yet until he said it outright, a paternity test hadn't occurred to her. Of course it was precisely what was required, which made the situation feel more serious. Also, more intimate. *Couples* exacerbated one another's alarm, or mitigated it. Andy ought to be the one in this role. Yet if she called him now, Andy would wonder, why not last night? Why tell Satterfield before me?

Margot was sure that it was better to be certain before she brought Andy into the drama. Or Benji. If the situation didn't resolve on its own—meaning if Eva didn't go away—a paternity test should come first, before any phone calls.

In the hall there was a clatter as Satterfield's wife dropped the tea tray. She cried out and the maestro darted across the room.

"Wait!" Margot stopped him. "A paternity test—do you just walk in the clinic and ask?"

"I'll send you the name of a place. The report has to stand up in court, and for that you'll need Benji. Or Andy. It's easy. They swipe your cheek and you get results in the mail. Takes less then a week."

Margot's mouth dropped open. Satterfield did a double-take, surprised at her surprise.

"It's a Y-chromosome test!" he said. "You need the male!"

What alarmed Margot wasn't the particulars, but that Satterfield knew them. He saw his admission in her expression. He turned abruptly to the catastrophe in the hall, pulling open the doors. Gloria was on her knees, shrieking about the mess. Bits of shattered porcelain covered the floor and the far wall dripped with tea. He crouched to help. Margot stood. Careful to step around the mess, she opened the front door, listening to Satterfield tell his wife that it was all right, there was no harm done.

Six

Eva came into her bedroom after putting Birdie to bed and found Sully smoking by the window, naked. He had both windows open for ventilation, but the smoke was coming straight back at him like birdseed thrown in a fan.

He didn't turn when she entered, which meant he needed time to come into himself, be present. Eva undressed in the closet, pulling on a black silk robe and her rose petal heeled slippers. She crossed the room to her writing desk in the corner and touched her laptop. The Wilmas' Facebook page flashed up. There was Andy Fickett with his fiddle, a large, blond man. In every stage photo, his face was flushed with joy. Eva had seen the Wilmas play; the music revolved around his fiddling. If there was a lineup and Eva had to pick out the man most likely to be married to Mrs. Fickett, he'd be dead last. When she first showed this page to Sully, he said, "We got the wrong Fickett."

They thought Mrs. Fickett being alone would work to their advantage. Their idea was that since they weren't asking for much, she'd pay it just to be rid of the problem. When Eva told Sully that Mrs. Fickett was injured, he said, all the better. But he hadn't seen her, hadn't heard the way she spoke that day in the shop. She was not the lonely cellist Eva had in mind. Classical musicians were always pictured formally dressed, which made them seem fragile, especially the women with their tiny wrists and spaghetti straps. Mrs. Fickett was not fragile, even with a broken wing. She was more like the horse ladies at the barn near her parents' house, women who wore jodhpurs, had huge hands and were never afraid.

Eva switched to Benji's page, which was, of course, private. Neither of the older Ficketts had a personal page. She had scrolled these photos too many times. Facebook prowling always left her feeling smeared with inadequacy.

"Did you call her?" Sully asked without turning.

"I did," she said. "At least ten times."

"Good girl."

She closed the laptop and watched him pick up the metal trashcan to stub out his cigarette. His strategy was harassment. "Threaten to call Benji, or Andy, anything to make the woman want rid of you," he said.

"Just get your money. Don't give up."

To have a partner and a plan was nice, being in on something with him. And it was true that if he hadn't pushed, she probably would have kept her ideas in a notebook and waited. But there had been moments in these past three weeks when she missed the privacy of no one knowing about Benji Fickett. Keeping his identity to herself was a choice she made long ago, a way to run her own life and not ask anyone for anything. Telling Sully was like admitting that her life wasn't working.

Her life *was* working, up until last year when Bethany Meyers sold Unique Boutique to Paige. Bethany left, and so did Kariss, the two people Eva had worked with since she was sixteen. Everything changed eventually, she supposed. Dolly's was ziplining towards its death, and while it might be fun to watch Paige nosedive, there was the matter of the future. Sully was right. Time to make a move.

A long time ago, just after Birdie was born, Eva had called social services to ask a caseworker about her rights. She learned that student dads owed less in child support than those not in school. The rule was supposed to be an incentive for them to graduate and better themselves, but couldn't it also work as the opposite? Couldn't a guy just stay in school forever?

Finally, Eva lacked Sully's commitment to justice. She was unconsoled by the righting of wrongs. Dragging Benji's father into their lives wasn't worth the effort; a messy situation would become an all-out disaster. Of course her parents wanted her to. They hounded her about the father's identity. It still came up every time her financial situation was discussed. They bought the condo for her, and every holiday they thrust money at her, always with pride-killing commentary like, "We know you can use it." Or, another favorite, "Who would say no to three months of groceries?" Their handouts were humiliating, especially knowing that they could afford more. What they spent going to Maui every January could rent her a space and buy her opening inventory. That would have altered the plan. She could have skipped this middle step, which she thought of as begging Dutch, which in turn led to the confrontation with Mrs. Fickett.

Her parents would never agree and she didn't bother to ask. They had planned to pay her tuition and housing at the university. Going to school was a reasonable thing for an intelligent young woman to do. It was *not* reasonable for her to get pregnant and keep the baby. That they would not fund.

Sully came to stand in the middle of the room, looking at her. She moved to the edge of her bed, waiting. One hand resting on his pale thigh, he was unmoved by his own nudity, the smattering of hair across his chest and the darker fuzz around his crotch. People without their clothes were a different species. It was one thing to like a guy's forearms in his shirtsleeves, or the angle of the neck, the way his eyelashes curled. But naked, the slim, limp penis, the soft stomach and lean chest, a man was vulnerable, unsightly. So lovable.

So what if they fought more since she told him about Benji. Arguing was part of their thing. He provoked her, then retreated. If she went too far, he got angry and they fought. Rile and retreat. Maybe it was foreplay.

"You shouldn't come down to the shop when Dutch is there," he said. "I don't trust him."

"You're there," she said. "I never go when you're not there. And as a shareholder, I'm allowed to look it over."

"You're not a shareholder. We've been over this. Dutch is giving you this chance because I asked him to. It's a one-time thing, a way for you to get your money and get out."

Trying to control her aggravation, she said, as neutrally as you could say such a thing, "You're ashamed of me."

He didn't move. "It's not the right thing for you, long term. Surely you can see that."

"Yet it is right for you."

"It's what I do."

"That argument is lame."

He dropped his arms. She scooted back to the center of the bed, letting the robe fall open.

"You're the one who said that things were changing. You said it wasn't sleazy anymore. You said so to my parents! You said it was bullshit to call pot a gateway drug. That it's no stronger than Paxil!"

"It *isn't* sleazy. It's just, you could do anything, Eva."

He wasn't ashamed of her, she knew. If anything, he had her on a pedestal. He wanted to help her, make her happy, give her everything she wanted. Santa Claus Sully. Sweet, but absurd. He had college kids working in the seedling room, yet not once had Sully offered her a job.

"I need to be sure you understand it's a one-time thing." Gesturing to the room around them, he added, "*This* is what you do. You need your own shop."

Her room *was* a masterpiece, and she liked him saying so. The walls were a pale green with white brocade stencil she'd hand-painted. Her four-poster bed had a white canopy of soft gauze. The dresser was an estate sale find, with claw feet and bell clapper pulls.

He came to sit on the bed facing her. "Can I ask you something? I've wanted to know, but didn't know how to ask."

His voice had softened and Eva felt suddenly anxious. They did not speak of the past. She didn't ask for details about his life with Paige and he didn't ask about Birdie. Everything he knew, she had offered.

"You kept quiet so long, about the Bird's father—did you, was it —"

Eva sat up straighter, guessing what he couldn't quite say. "It wasn't rape. Not even close. My parents thought that too. They wanted that. They hated when I told them I initiated it."

"You did?

"Well, sort of—look, it was—it just happened. It was nothing exciting. Not even a broken rubber. We were at a party, we had sex, and I got pregnant."

He sat very still, listening without comment, his eyes open and patient. Here was Sully's strength, in Eva's mind. He was slightly out of shape and he dressed in Russell athletic wear, but he could hear the hard stuff.

"I could have had an abortion. I thought about it. Going to college seemed like a dumb reason to me. Or because I was embarrassed."

"I didn't mean —"

"I know. I'm just telling you."

He reached up to trace the edge of her neck with his forefinger. She shivered. Instantly, their argument changed shape. A different sort of tension filled the room. He leaned towards her.

"You didn't want a baby," he said. "You only wanted sex."

"That sounds bad."

"It's not bad," he said, pulling her towards him.

Seven

By Monday, the temperature had climbed well past forty. Spring slop was a torment to Sully. Fifteen years living out here and he never got used to the splatter and mud and black snow mounds, slipping on the pavement, tiptoeing through parking lots. In the morning he was short-tempered with Caity when she spilled her cereal milk. Dropping her off at school, he drove like an asshole, honking long and hard at a parent who turned in front of him.

He pulled into the parking lot and the first thing he saw was the white Tahoe; this, too, pissed him off. He was sick of being watched. When he told Dutch about the three strangers looking for him, Dutch asked for a description. They were standing outside by the planter, where all important discussions seemed to take place. Dutch was smoking, but he forgot the cigarette after Sully described the trio. He shrugged, said Sully did right, not revealing anything. The cigarette burned down almost to the filter. The ash fell in one piece and disintegrated.

The second he was inside, Sully knew something wasn't right. The air smelled damp. Without turning on the lights he crossed to the grow room door, opened it, and stopped dead. Water was dripping steadily from one of the pipes above the second row. Four planters were flooded; water had run over the table and now splattered the floor. The puddle reached from the back wall almost to the door.

Sully pulled out his phone, cursing. He told Marvin to go to the hardware store for mops, buckets and turkey basters. Marvin knew not to ask a single question. Next, standing in the middle of the puddle, furious, he called Gerald, the client who'd installed the irrigation.

"Get your ass down here!" he cried into his phone. Some favor this job turned out to be. Sully told him he'd better hope he could fix it. Walking into the office, he dialed his college-age crew, none of whom answered. Finally he dialed Eva's cell. "I need you!" he shouted. "This goddamn, cheap-ass PVC—I need people to mop!"

"I've got to get to work—"

"Can you just fucking get over here?"

"I'll be there in twenty," she said and hung up.

Sully used paper towels to soak water from the canvas planters until Marvin arrived with the supplies. Using a turkey baster, he carefully siphoned the water pooled around the plant stems, then shot it onto the floor. Marvin copied him, working on the next planter. Dutch's absence enraged Sully. Eva was taking too long. He sweated through his coat and sweatshirt before it occurred to him to shed a layer. When Eva showed up with Birdie, she was dressed in a retail outfit rather than sensible work clothes. None of this was her fault but it irritated him all the same.

"Grab a mop," he barked.

"Let me set Birdie up," she called, heading back to the reception room.

Sully looked over at Marv and saw him lift a stem with his finger; a sodden, ruined leaf came off in his hand.

"Motherfucker!" Sully exploded. "You can't touch them, you moron! Jesus Christ! You just lost us that much leaf weight."

Sully towered over Marv, close enough to see his eyes widen behind his thick glasses. It was inexcusable, to speak like this to somone he'd known so long. He sunk both hands into his hair, trying to gain control. In the next row over, high on the ladder, Gerald was frozen, wrench in hand. Eva stood in the grow room doorway.

"Not cool," Marvin said, shoving his baster in the soil. "Your temper is *not cool*."

It wasn't. Sully's body was rigid, his neck veins bulged. He turned his back and lunged into the wall; his fist connected in an explosion of drywall.

Marvin threw up his hands, exasperated. Gerald dropped his wrench. It hit the floor with a clatter that made everybody jump.

Eva was the first to recover. She stepped into the room, skirting the pool of water. Marvin grabbed his walking stick and limped straight through the puddle, muttering, "Oh man, oh man." He whipped the door open so hard it slammed against the wall and shut behind him. With caution, Gerald started down the ladder to retrieve his wrench.

Holding his fist away from his body Sully watched them, his people. He hated being a fucking terrorist. But here was Eva, in the same row with him, pulling on a pair of the surgical gloves they kept by the door. She picked up Marvin's baster and began sucking water from the soil.

"Like this?" she asked, meeting his eye, unafraid.

Sully's breath slowed. He crossed the space between them to stand next to her.

"You can't touch the leaves at all," he said, demonstrating with his own baster.

"Got it," she said, and began trying to save Marvin's plant. After a time, she said, "If you don't ice that hand, it'll be useless in two hours."

Without another word he walked down the row to the office. He pulled ice cubes out of the mini freezer, wrapped them in the rag from his back pocket and spread his hand flat on the desk, holding the cold on top of his knuckles. He wondered how this happened to him. He was never a dick in his youth. As a boy, he kept a jar of his own fingernails instead of insects. He had a collection of toy guns that he cherished, but it worried him. He thought it made him a bad person. A guy who loved weapons would turn out bad.

When he looked up he saw that Gerald was atop the ladder again, working to replace the failed fitting.

His first date with Eva, he took her to the bowling alley. It was early October and already cold. He turned on the truck's heater, could feel her watching him. He was older, had more experience and should not be the nervous one but he felt like he had royalty in his cab. Technically, she wasn't even old enough to be in the bar. He bought them vodka gimlets, delivered hers and said, "I could go to jail for that," which she did not think was funny.

He asked her to sit next to him in the booth, patting the bench. "You seem so far away."

"This is better," she said. "I can see you without getting a crick in my neck."

He grinned. "You're beautiful, you know that?"

She said, "I'm five foot five. 'Beautiful' is a stretch."

He said she was unlike anybody he'd known and she agreed this might be true. But, after another swallow of booze, she said, "You could say those things to any girl."

He laughed and leaned forward. "Yes, smarty pants, but to any other girl, I'd be lying."

She grinned. Apparently this was what she was looking for. Wit. A sign of life. He sat back, giddy. The top buttons on her shirt were undone and he could see the tattoo between her breasts. He imagined what the image there could be. Her skin was so pale she seemed dipped in milk.

She was looking at his maimed hand. He let her, explaining that when it happened he didn't feel it, didn't even know until he woke up in a ward hours later. Another guy had been killed by the blast.

"You were lucky," she said.

"Yes," he said. "Lucky me." He sipped his drink, watching her. "Is Birdie's daddy over there? In Iraq?"

She pulled her lips closed over her teeth, a shocked, spiteful look.

"I'm sorry," he stammered. "That's none of my business."

Still she didn't speak. Her small nostrils flared and her eyes bored into a spot near his right shoulder. He suffered, sure he'd ruined the night. Finally she sat back against the booth and said, "If I don't eat soon, I'm going to pass out."

They walked two blocks in the bitter cold to the pizza parlor, their feet thudding on the sidewalk. It started to snow and she didn't have much for a coat. Impulsively, he threw an arm around her small shoulders, pulling her to him for warmth. She didn't pull away, even slid a narrow arm around his waist. The restaurant was crowded and lively. Music and a low ceiling. A booth with a table made of bottle caps sealed in plastic. That hour in the pizzeria was one of the best of his life. Before they'd had sex, before they shared any real information. Before he knew his neighbor was her mother.

"I talk too much," he said when they had ordered. "I talk when I drink. I prefer pot." He looked at her. "How do you feel about pot?"

The waitress was setting down their drinks as Eva announced, "I have no feelings about pot."

This cracked them up. Sully even snorted, which made them laugh harder. They ducked their heads, covering their mouths and leaning towards each other. People were looking their way. Eva took his damaged hand in her own small hand; he had the feeling she was curious about it, what it would feel like.

"You really are beautiful," he said.

Back at his trailer, Sully hung his coat on a hook by the door. He flipped on the fluorescent light in the kitchen, opened the fridge. Eva didn't take off her coat right away. She told him later that she was impressed by the tidiness. Coat hooks. A boot tray. No pets.

He handed her a beer and sat down on the couch. After one sip he declared, "I don't know why I opened this. I don't want it." She laughed and handed him hers as well. He set both cans on the console next to the television. He sat down again, ran his half hand through his hair.

"Are you going to sit down?"

"I'm not sure."

He laughed, watching her hang her coat carefully over his. She came to stand in front of him, took another step, forcing him to uncross his legs. She straddled his left thigh and he stopped laughing. He took her hips in his hands and pulled her down, held her securely in place, then flexed his thigh.

"Oh," she said.

"Hockey," he said, flexing it again. "I play pick-up all winter."

She unbuckled his belt. He reached to turn off the light, but she grabbed his arm, then stood to pull down her skirt and leggings and stepped out of her boots. Sully had time to pull down his jeans before she swung her leg over and came down on top of him. He slid inside her, gasping, doubling over, grabbing at her hips, lifting her again and again. He pulled open her shirt and stared at the tattoo, a hawk with spread wings. She arched her back and unhooked her bra and he moaned, beginning to move again, but Eva stopped him, forearms on his collarbones. She met his eye and he understood. He stumbled a little, stepping out of his jeans, then hurried down the hall to the bathroom. He came back with a condom, sat on the couch to unroll it over himself while she watched. He got on his knees and faced her, pulling her off the couch into his lap. He came almost as soon as he entered her. She laughed; he was embarrassed but stopped her when she tried to move off him. He touched her and she gasped. Her climax was as immediate as his own, but far more beautiful. He was smiling at her when she opened her eyes.

"I wasn't going to do that," he said. "Have sex with you the first date."

She put her hands on his shoulders and said, "It's just as bad to vow not to as it is to vow that you will."

He smiled and said, "Aren't you the expert."

"Hardly."

He was quiet, looking at her. Moved her hair out of her eyes.

"We're bad," he said, thinking of their situation. Eva worked for his ex-wife. She was so young. "I'm a cradle robber."

She frowned. "Please don't say that. Not ever again."

He smiled. "We can't let Paige find out. She'll fire you."

"I can do sneaky," she said.

He shifted his body, moving her off of him onto the couch. He stood, thinking now or never. He pulled the condom off his shriveling penis.

"Come with me," he said, heading down the hall. "I've got something to show you."

He ducked in the bathroom and threw away the condom, washed his hands. Eva went in after him, and he was waiting when she came out. She looked down and laughed.

"What?"

"Shouldn't we put on pants?"

"What for?" he said, taking her hand, leading her down to what would be the master bedroom. Before opening the door, he turned to face her.

"What I'm about to show you, due to recent laws, could *not* send me to jail."

He opened the door, watching her survey his home crop, halfway to maturity, stems wrapped around the lattice of garden twine. The warm and heady odor of ripening marijuana.

She swallowed and said, "I need to get my pants on."

He followed her down the hall. She told him that she'd read about it, knew that people could be growers in their own homes. And she'd noticed the pot shops; you'd have to be blind not to notice. But it shocked her, he could tell.

He drove her home. It was snowing hard. The world was transformed. The whole ride he felt bad, and he hated feeling bad. In the parking lot outside her condo, he kept the engine running. Before she got out he turned to her and said, "The thing is, Eva, I can't do anything else. I've tried. I lasted a week at retail. Can't wait tables. Can't do trades, service furnaces, unclog toilets. I've got ADHD or something. Can't do the same thing every day."

He hoped she believed what he was saying. It was true—even mowing the yard drove him crazy. The inanity of growing a plant you never let bloom.

"I helped Paige apply for the loan to buy her store. I understand profit and loss. I'm a good grower. Two things I'm good at: business and growing."

"So farm," Eva said. "Nothing shady about growing tomatoes."

"Tomatoes. In Montana?"

"Wheat, then."

He sat back, studying her. She wanted to hear him defend his line of work. For fuck's sake, it was legal. It was *medicine*. He could have left it at that, kissed her good night. *Farming.* The image of his father alone in a combine cab all night cutting his fields was the loneliest thing he'd ever seen.

"I'd need land," he told her, raising an index finger. "And equipment." Another finger. "Irrigation pipe. Fertilizer. Combine crew in the fall." That was all five of the fingers on his good had. "But mostly, land." He turned. "I don't have any land, Eva."

"So it's pot in the master bedroom for you," she said.

She was smiling. He thought she was making fun of him but she said, "I'm good with that. God, give a girl a minute." She kissed him and was gone.

Her resolve scared him. One night together and they were doing this. She wanted him to come for dinner, and bring Caity. He might not have called, no matter how much he liked her. He could have avoided her in the store, talked himself out of what was surely a bad idea. But her number on his phone made him grin like a teenager. *What're you up to?*

Where was it headed? He didn't care. Could you love someone when you were twenty? He had, the wrong someone. How did age work, then? He suspected love was for your kids. He was a dad; his heart was occupied. No woman was going to pry in there. Eva was bushwhacked by her boy, too. So it was all right. Except maybe women were different. Maybe Eva was different, had more room in that chamber. She could somehow look at Birdie like that, then look over and annihilate Sully with whatever it was coming off her: faith, hope. That was love, brother.

Eight

Margot turned off the phone ringer to avoid Eva, who was calling three times a day. "I want your husband's cell number," she informed Margot in her last message. "I need to call him, because clearly, I'm not getting anywhere with you." She would come by their house; she said she knew where they lived. Margot refused to be bullied, yet for two nights she lay awake imagining Eva in her kitchen or standing over her bed with the little boy in her arms, his cheeks bulging with gum. She might have picked up the phone, demanded the paternity test, but she wanted the next move to be hers. She would initiate contact when she was ready. She didn't want to appear afraid.

She tried to predict Andy's reaction to Eva. He wouldn't ask for a paternity test, Margot supposed. He wouldn't care that the girl was lying. His approach to people, to all of life, was one of abundance: plenty of room, plenty of love. When Benji was young and decided to play classical violin, Andy didn't pout. Not once did he suggest that Benji's preference would wear off, as it had with him.

Like most only children, Benji grew up in an adult world. Margot and Andy felt no guilt over this because they did not think a life of music and practice was a bad one. They did not have to ask him to practice. His temperament led him to pursue excellence, to master a piece and be hungry for another. Both Margot and Andy were devoted to the idea of diligence, insisting always that nobody was a "natural." Embroidered on canvas, framed and hung on the wall was the phrase "Practice makes the Master." At the same time, they recognized their son's temperament as a gift and vowed to honor it. He had a violin at age three. Other kids played soccer or football; Benji got an electric piano with recording capabilities. They weren't trying to protect or deprive him; they did not rant against video games. This was simply how their life looked. Instruments lay half repaired on the kitchen counter. Tungsten string spread on the dining room table. Bow hair in the rugs. Tuning devices, pitch whistles, and sheet music were strewn on available surfaces.

Benji's switch in musical direction bothered Andy less than it bothered Margot. The bright morning before he left, Andy set up chairs on the deck and helped Margot get her first taste of fresh air since the surgery. She brought up Benji, saying she didn't see how he could stay in school if he hit the road with a band.

"Nobody said anything about him hitting the road," Andy said.

"But that's next, surely. He'll have wanderlust, just like you!"

Andy laughed but didn't gloat, gave no sign that this would be a triumph to him. "The more I think about it," he said, "the more sure I am that this isn't new."

"What do you mean?"

"I think he's wanted to try something different."

She sat up. "What are you talking about?"

"I just—I can't even say how I sensed it, exactly. Just the way he sounded a little rote in his playing last Christmas, even last summer."

"Rote? I never noticed. You didn't ask him?"

Andy shook his head. "I should have. I forget, now that he's not living here, how important it is to pry."

Margot smiled. Andy was good at prying. He pursued hunches, asked about Benji's inner world. He learned the most when the two of them were alone, far from home on a hike or a river float. Margot's intense watch over her son included his potential; she heard him play and saw all that lay before him. Andy focused on the boy he could see.

"At the time, I thought it was girl trouble," Andy said. "Now I think it might have been a change in taste. I think he wanted to branch out but he was afraid to tell us."

Andy spoke gently, without looking at her. Margot gazed out at the sloping yard covered in snow. "To tell me, you mean."

Andy picked up the binoculars and trained them on the fir tree, spying on the owl.

"Am I too hard on him?" Margot asked. "Did I push too much?"

Without lowering the binoculars, he reached over to squeeze her left hand. "We were careful not to push."

"I only want him to be the best he can be," she said. "I want that myself! I'm not at capacity. Neither is he. He's got more, Andy. I know he does."

"There is never only one way," he said.

She was going to say something sarcastic, call him 'Buddha' as she often did when he fell into his wise-man voice. But he lowered the binoculars to his lap and turned, his eyes bright with wonder.

"What if it's the trying that matters? The need to get as close to possible to your best—what if that is all there is? You never get there, and so what? It's the *effort*. We're all just making the effort."

She gave a dim smile and nodded. She hadn't forgotten this idea. What would it mean? Your best performance was an approximation, after all, of the original score, the composer's notes, the way it sounded in the maestro's mind. Rehearsals and practice were about chasing that nebulous ideal. Music was like parenting in this regard.

The foggy gloom of winter returned. On a cold afternoon, midweek, standing on the deck in her snow boots and down jacket, Margot gazed through the binoculars and made an astonishing discovery. She'd been staring at the mother owl, the intricate pattern of lines on her wings and head, the impossibly white chest, its feathers moving in the cold March wind. Movement at the base of the owl's body alerted her to two forms the size of adolescent kittens, heads downy white with huge eyes. They were so ugly they were adorable, peering at one another, heads turning in wonderment at the brand-new world. Margot's mouth widened in a grin; she could feel the cold on her exposed teeth.

She gave her first lesson since the accident. Markus Pippin, Pip, was a sixth grader with long arms who held the bow tight as a spear. He was small, with a tangle of soft golden hair. His quiet focus was a delight to watch. Like so many string players, Pip did everything with exquisite slowness. He arranged his sheet music on the stand, then arranged himself, pulling his instrument from its sticker-laden case, extending the endpin, adjusting his chair, then his bottom on the chair. He ran through the scales. Margot watched his wrist with dismay, thinking that if he stayed with music, carpal tunnel surgery was in his future. When he was ready, he looked over and appeared startled to see her there, smiling at him. He smiled back. Eyeing the white tape creeping out of her big button-down shirt, he asked without a hint of shyness, "Does it hurt much, Mrs. Fickett?"

"Not much anymore," she said. "It's more a dull ache. I've gotten used to it. See, I can raise my arm almost to the shoulder."

He watched with interest as she pulled the bow up. "How soon till you can play?"

"They said not to rush it. We'll see in another month, when I have better range of motion."

"It must be terrible not to play."

"Would it be hard for you, Pip?"

He considered a moment. "For a while, I guess," he said. "Then I'd get used to not playing. I'd do something else."

Margot smiled to put him at ease, but was thinking that if this was true, Pip probably ought to go ahead and do something else. Save his wrists. It was a funny thought for his teacher to have; teachers were supposed to encourage a lifelong commitment. She was feeling sorry for herself, wishing him a future different from her own. How wretched of her. He asked if he should begin and she said, "Please."

He dove straight into the first cello suite from Bach. His movements were labored, his wrists were not fluid, but she had somehow forgotten the beauty with which he played. Like her son, Pip put feeling into every note. Seconds ago she thought he ought to find something else to do and now she was thinking the kid was a genius. His small body swayed, eyes closed, radiating focused attention and respect for the music.

Margot lowered her instrument to the floor and stood, listening. He brought the prelude to a close, opened his eyes and began the allemande, not looking at her. Still holding her bow, Margot stepped to the center of the room, the music filling her head. He didn't notice her exit, the way she moved, entranced, through the door and down the hall, into the light-soaked living room, to the sliding glass door, which she pushed open using her left arm. Pip played on. Even outside on the sunny deck she could hear the cello's voice playing music so perfectly written for it. Tears streamed down her cheeks.

She stood on the deck with one hand on her hips, the other holding the bow like it was a stick she'd picked up. Above the house the red cliff face gazed down, its top exposed finally to the new year. The snow had receded like a hairline. For the first time in her life, Margot was lonely.

The music had stopped. Pip was behind her, small and blond in the open door.

"Mrs. Fickett?"

She turned. On either side of him and in the row of glass above, the valley was reflected, the sloping hillside beyond the deck, the fragile aspens, the distant ridge and of course the endless sky.

"Is everything okay?"

Margot did not bother to wipe her eyes as she took a step towards him.

"Let's call it a day, shall we Pip?"

Nine

Around noon on a slow Saturday, Paige came in with Caitlyn, who ran over to hug Eva, nearly giving her a heart attack. Caity was only seven and thus understood nothing about secrets. She'd been to Eva's often enough to know her DVD collection and the location of the drawer with the goldfish crackers. It was okay for them to be friends, but if she breathed a word about Eva's apartment, blowing bubbles on the patio, eating hot dogs in front of the television with Birdie, all was lost.

Paige scrolled through the sales record for the week and looked up at Eva. "Barely enough to cover your wages."

Eva was still earning what Bethany used to pay her, high for a retail clerk because Eva knew the business so well and Bethany had been training her to be a buyer. But Paige didn't need a buyer.

"Take the mats out and clean them," Paige ordered.

Eva stared. "It's snowing the size of Cornflakes."

"The mats are muddy," she replied, looking back at the computer.

Eva put on her coat and marched around the counter, grabbed the first mat and muscled it through the door to the vestibule where she dropped it, panting. It was too big; the door wouldn't close all the way. Eva came back for the broom. Paige was looking at her phone but Eva wasn't fooled. The woman was loving this.

Her last day in this place was going to be a celebration. She'd do the paternity test today if it would speed things along. Mrs. Fickett might refuse to pay. It happened all the time. You could fill a book with abandoned mothers. It was hard to imagine Mrs. Fickett ignoring her own grandson.

Eva swept the black plastic grooves with as much force as possible. The grit and dirt peppered the vestibule wall. Sweating, she had removed her cardigan to work in her tank top.

At the far end of the entry arch, her mother's white Lexus appeared, and honked. Eva's heart jumped. Here it came, the day she'd be fired. Caity was inside and now her mother. How long could this go on?

Eva opened the vestibule door and met her mother in the antler arbor. She was wearing white fleece with stretch pants and held out a bag.

"I bought Birdie some clothes," she said. "I couldn't help myself." She could hardly contain her excitement.

Eva looked inside. A collared shirt with ships. Pinstriped shorts. "Cute," she said, smiling. It *was* cute, but her mom's gifts were tricky. Sometimes they led to a request. Other times, they were apologies. Today her face fell slightly, as if she were hurt. Oh, what did her mother want?

"They were on sale."

"Great," Eva offered. "Thanks so much."

Her mother stood in the mouth of the arch, the snow raging behind her. She had left her car running, the door open. "Aren't you freezing?" she asked, turning to go. "You're half naked."

Eva opened her mouth to speak but her mom had turned away, swallowed by the storm.

When Dolly's closed that afternoon, the snow had stopped, but the sun didn't come out. The light was flat and dull as Eva drove Birdie across town to McLeod Park, the most mispronounced place in the city. Mah-Cloud, not Mack-Lloyd. The park was surrounded by proud old houses built for railroad executives at the turn of the century. The university president's house was in this neighborhood.

On one end of the park was a shopping district with the McLeod Park Bakery. A pastry and a walk around the park was a weekend ritual for Eva and

Birdie. They'd been coming since he was in a stroller. It wasn't their neighborhood but Eva loved it. The food tasted good; the coffee was rich and perfect. Wealthy people shopped here and that, too, was comforting. It was gentrified. The old buildings on the east side of the park had been turned into retail shops that sold beautiful things. The river was only two blocks away and luxury condos, hideous flat-topped structures, were being built around the old houses.

Eva had discovered a vacancy down the street from the bakery. A retailer had moved out and The Rhino could open here. Eva had been watching for six weeks, even before she told Sully her dream of opening the shop, before Sully suggested that the New Leaf loan her money, an idea that Dutch revised into making her pay. She had called about this space, knew the rent was high, but if things worked out the way Sully was saying they could, Eva could cover the deposit and rent as early as June. Because her shop would be a clothing exchange and furniture store, inventory would be cheap. She'd use her own furniture to get started; all she needed was a Shopify account, maybe a cash drawer, the rest could be done through her phone.

As they approached the empty space, a mean wind picked up. The awnings slapped and a short burst of rain dropped from the sky. They huddled in the entryway. A woman with a small terrier walked by. The dog sniffed Birdie, then barked, which gave him a fright. He looked at his mother, who laughed, so he laughed too. Eva watched them retreat. In her Uggs and ski parka, the woman was exactly the sort Eva wanted as a customer. Someone who might be buying used goods for the first time. A sculpture, maybe, or an oversized ceramic vase. She'd need coaching—Eva's shop would make her feel excitedly out of her element, the way Bethany's boutique had. Their customers were the sort who bought without overthinking it, who left with items hanging on their arms, shiny purses thrown over their shoulders, the only thought troubling them where they parked.

Eva was mystified by these women. The pocketbooks they carried, their shoes, even their wallets were mysterious. Black leather or shiny plastic, flat or bulging, the clasps snapped as the women extracted cash. Or there was that satisfying zip of perforation when someone wrote a check. Eva loved checks, the peek at a stranger's handwriting. Checks were from another time, when someone's signature meant something. When she was little she had found boxes of her parents' cancelled checks; she loved the way they smelled, stacks of them like playing cards. Fake money. Where did it all come from? Where did people make such vast amounts? Surely not from minimum wage work, which felt like breathing through a straw.

As they stood watching, snowflakes began to fly. Another woman passed, so focused on her purpose she didn't glance at them. Her face was made up; her coat, her shoes all looked expensive. Dear god, Eva thought suddenly. These women are exactly like my mother. How far could that motivation get you in life, trying to impress your mother?

Bethany had said she had talent. Every room Eva designed had a certain feel to it, homey but with flair. Lived in, but beautiful. Eva was drawn to metal work, wall hangings or sculpture. Her palette was more colorful than Bethany's. Customers loved her displays. People came from the canyons to seek Bethany's advice; their clientele were women who sought something more soulful than cowboy kitsch. Women who wanted show pieces, not stencil-back chairs in the shape of elk. One client had stood inside a living room Eva designed and announced that this was how she wanted her entire house to feel.

Bethany had taught her everything. Together they traveled to estate sales where Eva learned how to spot pieces of interest. Bethany didn't care about provenance so much as condition, weirdness, and function. A lady's chair was nice, but could you sit on it? The arrangement of objects created a mood, asked you in or shortened your stay. Fish tanks and the color blue were for waiting rooms, where no one wanted to be. Yellow and gold and rich brown were for rooms where you wanted to stay forever. Tin light fixtures, heavy fabrics, repeated patterns of brocade or fleur-de-lis, these consoled. Interiors were about mood, enchantment, something you had to feel with an inner eye. Not everybody had it, Bethany said. Paige did not.

And if Eva had talent, then she *still* had talent. Getting pregnant, being a single mother, did not erase that sort of thing. Bethany would agree; she said the inner eye was part of who you were, like your temperament or body type. The inner eye was also like a muscle: it could get flabby if you didn't work it, but it was always there, ready to be toned and useful.

If Bethany was disappointed in Eva's pregnancy, her decision to raise Birdie on her own, she never let on. She and Kariss, her co-worker, were the only people Eva was prepared to tell about the father. Bethany never asked.

Kariss and Eva were alone in the back room not long after Eva announced she was pregnant. Kariss, chewing her sandwich, asked, "So, who's the father?" Eva hesitated, and Kariss held up a hand. "Wise move, keeping it to yourself. You'd end up with another set of parents. Who needs that?"

Bethany gave her eight weeks off for maternity leave, then allowed her to bring Birdie to the shop when she needed to. Eva found an infant to be ridiculously different from the *idea* of an infant. You suppose you'll love it because all mothers love their babies. In fact they were difficult to love. They had mass; they were objects there in your arms, squalling, wriggling, suckling. Eva never blamed her roommate for moving out. Those first two weeks were unbearable. After ten days, the woman, a bank teller, was unable to take the mountains of clothing, soiled burping rags and shirts, sodden bras, shirts, tank tops, onesies, and rompers. Not dressing was much easier than stripping off your shirt every hour. Eva walked around like a topless zombie all day and half the night.

Her baby's cries, gurgling and mewling, were not quite human. But neither were they monstrous. They were incapable of any real harm, like Mrs. Vetter's birds at the feeders next door. Eva watched the birds fluttering in the space between their condos. Each frigid sunrise that February was marked by flocks of sparrows, siskins, and chickadees squabbling for a perch, a free-for-all of motion and noise. Eva kept time by their arrival, their chirping indicating that soon the sun would come up.

She lost track of the date. One afternoon she put the baby on the floor to check the clock on the microwave. Four-forty-five. Birdie was born in early February. Eva was wearing army fatigue pants, cut off at the calf. Her toenails needed cutting. Her belly was finally not in the way. It had become a soft, wide mass like bread dough. Her hair had grown almost to her shoulders. It hadn't been washed in a week. Two? And that squirmy form on the blanket—Birdie's little limbs flailed and his face was red—that creature came out of her, how long ago? She came back to look down at him, stunned. She couldn't remember how old he was. Two weeks? Impossible. She watched the baby working himself into a froth. It was terrible to find herself outside time and space. To see him on his own, so miserable down there, was also terrible. So *helpless*. One stomp and she could crush him like an insect.

Terrified, she ran for her phone on the kitchen counter, dialed Kariss at the boutique. It went to voicemail. Birdie was screaming now. Eva hung up and stood listening. Each time he paused to take a breath, she could hear traffic out on the street, students finishing up with classes for the day. The phone in her hand rang.

"Sorry, I was with a customer," Kariss said. "What's up?"

"What day is it?" Eva blurted.

"Monday. Eva, do you—"

"Date?"

"The twenty-seventh."

Birdie was nineteen days old. Her son was nineteen days old.

"Are you all right?" Kariss asked.

"I'm freaking a little, okay? I just…" she pulled the phone away from her ear, stared at its shape. The plastic case was cracked.

"Do you need me to come over?" she heard Kariss squeak from the palm of her hand. In the kitchen sink sat the remains of her microwaved enchilada dinner, hard as cement. Was that what she wanted? Was she hungry? Kariss could surely hear Birdie. His face was bright red; his body shuddered with effort.

"It's all good," Eva said. "I need some furniture."

"What happened to your furniture?"

"The bank teller took it. She moved out."

"*What*? When?"

Eva couldn't remember.

"I'm coming," Kariss said.

"You'll have nowhere to sit," Eva said, but the line was dead.

She dropped the phone on the floor and squatted to pick up the baby. She took him to the bedroom. He screamed every time she changed him, probably because she changed his clothes each time he had a dirty diaper. She had enough outfits to do this, and it made her feel responsible to have him completely clean. He was already screaming, so why not get it all over with?

His butt was bright, angry red, matching his face. She had gotten fast at maneuvering the little diapers, but not as fast as the nurses in the hospital. She zipped him into a white romper with a duck on it. He was still screaming as she carried him to the kitchen and poured water into an empty Gatorade bottle. She got thirsty when she nursed. She grabbed a bag of pretzels and the water, settled into the glider, her one chair, and filled his mouth with her nipple. His arms stopped flailing. His red face smoothed. The birds were gone now. It was dusk.

Kariss brought Bethany. Eva was confused by the looks on their faces. She'd sounded bad on the phone, she supposed. Her hair looked bad. Surely the best difference between blood relatives and the people who replaced them was the damage control. They were better at pulling you out of a mess than preventing you getting in one.

"You guys, I'm fine."

"This place looks like a fucking tenement!" cried Kariss.

"You don't have any lamps?" Bethany asked, flipping on the overhead light.

The baby winced and Eva cried, "Turn that off!"

She turned it off and they both came forward to stand over Eva, looking down at him. Kariss glanced into the kitchen and said, "Eva, it's like a bomb went off in here."

Eva let her head fall back against the cushion. "It did," she smiled. "A Birdie bomb!" She laughed. "A nineteen-day-old Birdie bomb." Looking up at their blinking shocked faces, she giggled again. "He's nineteen days old!"

Ten

Sully came home exhausted. He faced a long night of trimming his home crop. Eva had been right about the ice. His hand barely hurt anymore and his fingers were stiff but functional. He dropped his deli sandwich on the counter, kicked off his boots and slid out of his jacket. The days were stretching out—even without turning on the light, he could see across the room.

He stripped down to his boxers, socks and undershirt. Leaving his clothes in a pile, he crossed the kitchen to get a beer, took one long swallow and set it on the coffee table by the couch. He sat down to pack a bowl using Dutch's sample of Blue Dream. He lit it and inhaled, found it too grassy for his taste. Somebody'd jumped the gun on the trim. But it had a mellow, functional high that he knew their patients would appreciate. Two hits and he felt himself spread out, an opening in his chest and abdomen. He dropped his hands into his lap, palms open, closed his eyes, and straightened his body against the back of the couch. This was the transparency he liked to take into the trim. He believed that mental harmony affected the taste. That was why he never hired out the work.

He had six legal plants, all he had room for, though the state allowed six per patient. It was a vague law. Barely legal, he called his business. This crop marked his tenth with the same phenotype, Pink Dump Truck. His magic number was sixty-one days. He cut at thirty percent amber, using a jeweler's loupe to inspect the flower's THC glands. The cut stalks had been drying in trays for the last forty-eight hours. A fair amount of play was left in the stems. It was time.

The bud would cure in gallon glass jars, the kind his mother used to make sun tea. It would then be measured out in ounce baggies, the legal possession limit. Any profit after expenses went straight into the New Leaf. This wasn't the best idea; the two endeavors should be kept separate. Also, there should be paperwork on the business, clear titles and ownership documents. Legal or not, this was still dope, and it was a handshake industry.

He turned on his brightest lamp, grabbed his nippers and got to work, letting the buds fall into a long plastic tray. Sully worked bare-handed at home, loving the sweet buzz and the oily roll of the flowers. There was meditation in plant care, a way to stop the mind's hopscotching. Even the tinnitus he'd brought home from Afghanistan faded when he was grooming or trimming.

After an hour, he heard a sound. Sully hated interruptions, but he was paranoid and couldn't ignore it. The New Leaf had worsened this tendency. So *many* plants and so much money. That white Tahoe. The ugly trio looking for Dutch.

Sully turned off the light and stepped into the hall. Neighbors opened and shut doors. Tires crunched over the gravel lot and a dog barked in the distance. He walked to the front door, flipped off the porch light and stepped out. Nothing. The snow was gone. It had been a warm day, but nights were still cold. To Sully, even July nights in Montana were cold. Back inside, he stretched his arms and neck, opened another beer and headed back to work. Headphones made him anxious so he played music through his phone. He entered a trance-like rhythm in which his hands knew just where to make the cut. He could drop the bud perfectly into the tray and move on, like a chomping insect.

The first jar was full. He was almost through with the second when he heard another sound. A bump. He paused the music and swore the trailer shook as if someone had entered. The front door was locked, and no one but Eva had a key. He wasn't expecting Eva. He checked his watch. It was past ten.

He opened the door to the hall, calling hello. In answer came a knocking. Someone was at the door. Sully stopped in his room to pull on sweat pants. He pictured the short FBI agent standing on his porch. Or Dutch's trio. In the living room he crouched to peer under the front window blind. A lone figure stood on the stoop.

Sully slid out the baseball bat he kept behind the couch, held it behind his back and swung open the door. At the same time he flipped on the porch light, blinding the man, who lifted a hand against it. It was not the agent with the white Tahoe. He was tall and thick, wore a formal wool coat, unbuttoned. He lowered the hand from his face. Sully couldn't place him at first, stood staring until suddenly he knew. Eva's dad.

Sully leaned the bat against the wall and opened the screen door. "How'd you find me?"

"Can I come in?"

Sully stood back to let him pass, then closed the door. For a moment the two men mirrored each other, broad shouldered, arms crossed, Sully in his thin undershirt and Mr. Baker in his coat and pleated pants. His hair and eyebrows were the exact same color, a fact Sully had noticed the night he was at their house for the failed dinner. At the time this match didn't strike him as odd, just a fact. But tonight, it occurred to him that Mr. Baker must use dye. His wide hands hung at his sides; he wore two rings and a gold watch that looked expensive. Even his shoes looked expensive. I am surrounded by dandies, Sully thought.

"Is Mrs. Baker with you?" he asked finally. "She can come in."

"No, I came alone. Look, I'm not going to beat around the bush here, Mr. uh—"

"Stiles," he said. "Sullivan Stiles. You can call me Sully."

Mr. Baker stared at him as if the idea—calling Sully by his name—was repugnant.

"Do you want to sit down?" Sully gestured to the couch.

Mr. Baker looked at it, even bent over to inspect it before he sat on its edge. Sully grabbed a chair from the kitchen and sat on the other side of the coffee table. As an afterthought, he retrieved the bowl and lighter from the counter, then sat and packed it with more of Dutch's sample. He lit it, inhaled.

"Care to try some?" he asked, holding it out to Mr. Baker. "It's our first crop, almost ready."

Mr. Baker stammered, gave a gushing laugh and rubbed his knees. "Uh, no," he said. "No thank you."

Sully grinned. He hit the pipe again, then set it on the coffee table, exhaling, crossing one leg over the other, the picture of politeness in bare feet and sweats. Mr. Baker coughed, one of those delicate coughs non-smokers use around people, even outside, who are smoking cigarettes. He swallowed. Sully waited. He was going to stand up, Sully was sure. No way would he remain seated.

"I want you to stop seeing my daughter," he said, looking Sully straight in the eye.

Then, sure enough, he stood.

"You're too old for her. You are into things—" he held up a hand, "I don't want her involved in. I don't want to offend you, but I'm asking you. As a father."

His shins touched the coffee table as he looked down at Sully. He put his hands on his hips as if they stood in his parlor, on his estate. Sully the stable boy.

As insulting as it was, Sully understood the gesture. In fact, as soon as he recognized the man on his stoop, he felt an uptick of respect. Sully would have handled this situation differently, but if it were his daughter, he would sure as shit make the gesture. The gesture was key.

"With all due respect, Mr. Baker," Sully said. He stood slowly and wished he hadn't taken that second hit; the stuff was too tweaky. "Eva is an adult. You should be talking to her."

They were eye to eye. Mr. Baker nodded, hands still on his hips. "I intend to," he said in his king-of-the-manor voice. "But I wanted to speak to you first. I wanted to offer you, well, I don't know how to put this. I'll phrase it as a question. Something tells me, Mr.—uh—Sully, that you like questions."

He grinned and suddenly his affect changed from manor-Lord to wolf. With his dyed brown hair, his fat rings and his wrinkled hands, he was offering a sales pitch. Sully knew where this was headed. He wished it weren't so. He knew he didn't like the Bakers, never would, but he did not want to detest them. He suddenly suspected that Annie Baker was, in fact, out in the car. She didn't have the guts to face him, so sent in the marshal. Mrs. Baker came to visit him, once last fall, before he'd been out with Eva. He was clearing out debris from the new space, loading trash and boxes into his truck bed. She stood on the sidewalk wearing black tights and a white hoodie, hair pulled into a tight tail. He thought her appearance was a welcome-to-the-strip-mall visit. She asked what his shop would be, and he had the distinct feeling she already knew. He told her, gave his name, but she refused to shake his hand. "I'm afraid we can't be friends," she said. She intended to speak to the landlord, wanted him out.

He replied by pointing out that she did fitness and he did medicine; their businesses were related.

"They are not related," she replied.

He went back to loading trash, done being friendly. She walked away, her broad, proud back and perfect, tiny ass.

In his trailer, standing eighteen inches from him, Mr. Baker asked, "How much is it worth to you, Mr. Sully, to stop seeing my daughter?"

Sully ran his tongue over the back of his teeth. He sighed.

"Not *Mr. Sully*. You're not a preschooler. Just, *Sully*."

"A thousand dollars, Sully? Two?"

Sully dragged the back of his hand across his mouth. "Don't do that, you sick shit." He could still taste the weed, awful, like fermented soil. "Get out of my house."

The man's eyebrows shot almost to his hairline.

"I'm serious." Sully crossed to the door and opened it. "Get the hell out of my house."

The man looked assaulted. It was excellent to see him flustered, already striding towards the door. Sully wished this wasn't happening. This was not something he and Eva would laugh about later. He wouldn't even tell her; this whole episode was just too fucking sad.

"Your daughter's a great woman," he said to Mr. Baker's back. "And Birdie's a great kid."

He made no reply. Sully switched off the porch light and closed the door, watching through the narrow window as the man disappeared. He pulled off his sweats and kicked them onto the couch. Jesus, if Caity had been here. He ran both hands through his hair, clearing his head. That last bowl was a mistake. He made a growling sound that tapered into a roar. He heard Dutch's warning, *It's like oil and water.* As long as he could remember, Sully had fallen for people who were incapable of returning his ardor. In elementary school it started with Jimmy Bates, who never let him play, not even when Sully gave him his best remote control car. His mother was appalled.

Sully sat on the couch staring at his hands. The deformed left, the bruised right. Thick, hot shame erupted through his center. What had he gotten her into? He threw his hands forward and in one angry motion cleared the table of the lighter, his pipe, the bag of Dutch's grassy weed. His mostly-full, warm beer flew sideways, vomiting foam.

Eleven

Margot visited Satterfield on campus. Eva had left a message saying she found Andy on Facebook. She was going to private message him if Margot didn't call her back. No more dodging the affair. She needed reinforcement.

Traffic was heavy. She had to park north of the river and use the pedestrian bridge to get to campus. Midway across, vertigo struck. She stood perfectly still, eyes lifted so she couldn't see the water until it passed. The gray above wasn't uniform. Darker waves of fog loomed as backdrop to the mistier, lighter clouds closer to earth. Just over her head, a pale smear hung like a ghost.

The maestro's appearance was a shock. The eyeliner was evident and his hair, normally a point of pride, stood on end. The sideburns remained untrimmed and he wore a baggy pullover, loose pants and running shoes. He did a double take when he saw her come through the door. She nodded to him and sat in the back with the bass players, who were too busy to notice. They were working on the difficult third movement, which read like two pieces in one. Two different keys, two tempos. It was written last, and Satterfield said it was the most spiritual of the movements. The strings were on time but the woodwinds were behind. Over and over they played this heartbreaking conversation between strings and winds until finally Satterfield stopped them, frustrated. "People!" he cried, "Can it be beautiful? Is beauty too much to ask?"

The players visibly shriveled. It was hard to watch, mainly because he was right. The sound wasn't beautiful. The passing back and forth between sections wasn't smooth. How terrible to be locked out, yet still feel the humiliation running through the room. My god, she missed these people! Not only her section, but the entire group, an orchestra of real estate agents and schoolteachers. There was a shoe salesman among them, a radio announcer, and a caterer. Nobody besides the maestro made a living at music, except herself and concertmaster Sara Chen, a violinist who toured all summer. A handful of players commuted to Billings or Big Sky for additional gigs. Without exception, visiting talent commented on the distance; it took hours to get from one city to the next. Montana ate through your per diem.

Satterfield was wrong to shame them. She could feel the exhaustion in the room. Perhaps exhaustion was justifiable. Beethoven worked on this symphony for thirty years, after all. Twenty-three when he began it, fifty-three when he finished. His decision to merge two works was the answer. He knew he was onto something big, something that had never been done. The genius of the piece wasn't only in the voices, though the chorale was a radical addition. The symphony ran between fifty-nine and sixty-five minutes, depending on how you read the notes. Satterfield was going by the composer notes; he wanted a running time of just over sixty. When they started rehearsing the piece in January, he gave them long history lessons, setting up the context of post-revolution Europe and the Vienna Congress. Imagine sixteen years of death, he told them. Sixteen years of fighting. Then it ends and the aristocrats divvy up the world to look quite like it had before the war. Most people were too traumatized to care. Beethoven cared.

The story appealed. A deaf man writes a symphony to ignite the weariest, war-torn population, to offer them hope. Nearly two hundred years later, this music could still inspire. The players loved learning how horribly Beethoven's rehearsals had gone, how difficult it had been to organize the singers with the musicians. Satterfield promised that they would play his music more professionally, more precisely, more ecstatically than that first Vienna orchestra. The orchestra was thrilled by the idea of outplaying the original musicians, making music that would have pleased the composer, even if he couldn't hear it.

Nobody wanted to let Satterfield down. There was no grumbling, not even the mouthy violins. Everyone stared at the floor, the ceiling, their stands. They went through it once more and he dismissed them, not bothering to hide his disgust. Four hours of their Saturday they'd given him and all he said was *We're getting there.* Margot sensed a communal need to go somewhere and get drunk.

Her section crowded around her. Margot couldn't bear to tell the story of the fall again. Most of them understood this; nobody told her she was looking good, which would have been an atrocious lie. They said how nice it was to see her, how sorry they were, how they missed her. Margot had the horrible feeling that many would trade places with her, just to get out of these scoldings.

She joined Satterfield in his office. He was sitting in his desk chair, his baton thrown on the desk.

"You heard it. We're in trouble." He had bags under his eyes.

"You have five weeks."

"We need five months. I'm ruined," he muttered.

"Nonsense," Margot said. "Jesus, what's the matter with you? You've got to build them up, not ride them into the ground. You've been reading about him, haven't you?"

He looked up. "Who? Ludwig? I always read about the composers."

"Maybe not this time, Douglas. Might be time for a break."

He leaned back in his chair, gazing at her.

"They'll get there," Margot said. She missed this, she realized, the steady push towards what was always a glorious transformation: they went from a bunch of amateurs to a group of skilled artists, in tune with the music, each other and the maestro.

"Take them out for pizza," she said.

"*Pizza?*"

"Or drinks. Throw a keg party. Something to boost morale, not bury it. They are working so hard! Can't you feel the effort?"

He rubbed his face. "God I miss you. We all do." He scratched his scalp, tearing at his hair. "Did you hear Jerry? On oboe? What's the matter with him?"

"Numb lips, remember?"

Satterfield stared, confused.

"Hasn't kissed his wife since January?"

He grinned, remembering. Margot realized she should get him away from here, off campus. She had an idea. "Come with me," she said.

He watched her stand and pick up her bag. "An errand. You'll like it."

"Anything," he said, grabbing his coat.

They went in his car, a low-riding BMW. Folding herself inside took effort. She directed him towards Randolph Avenue. The gloom had lifted while they were inside; the fog was pulled back like a skirt around Mount Jumbo. The sight cheered them both as they drove through town. People were out on the sidewalks and the parks were busy.

They were going on a stakeout, Margot told him, telling him to pull into the Perkins parking lot across from Rock Creek Commons. They had to circle for several minutes before a space with a view opened. When they were parked they both pushed their seats back and Margot produced binoculars from her bag.

"Are you sure she's in there?" he asked

"I see her car."

"How do you know her car?"

"I'd bet money on the Subaru with the red door panel."

Fifteen minutes passed and not a single customer pulled in or out of the mall. The Perkins parking lot, however, was hopping. Cars splashed in and out of their places, diners yammered. Satterfield fidgeted.

"Spring makes me tired." He yawned and adjusted his knees around the steering wheel. "My god, all these people. There's always so much to do. One wishes it was possible to simply sleep through it."

When Margot didn't lower the binoculars, he went on. "This endless gloom. And the overly bright days get me down, too. Such false cheer. Runoff and filth. I'd rather skip it, just jump forward to yellow, parched July."

He dug an old newspaper out of the door pocket next to him. Still no activity. Margot watched customers at the auto parts store beyond the stand of trees. She saw a dog on a chain in the trailer park behind the building. After a time, cars began to arrive and park at the back. Women, mostly. In workout clothes. Margot's good arm ached from the weight of the binoculars. Briefly, a tree branch filled the lens. On its tip sat a perfect, whorled bud.

"You know, you could just go talk to her," Satterfield said finally.

She lowered the binoculars to look at him. "I don't want to *talk* to her. If

I wanted that I'd answer the phone."

"You can't avoid her forever."

"I realize that. I'm being discreet. Taking my time."

Satterfield looked at her wordlessly. "This is not discretion, Margot," he said. "This is spying. It's immature and cowardly." He smiled. "I support it wholeheartedly."

At five-fifteen, Eva emerged from the antler arch. She wore a babydoll dress and high boots. Bright lipstick. She carried a slouchy military style bag and walked determinedly around the corner towards the back of the building.

"Is that her?" came Satterfield's deep voice as he sat up.

Margot nodded. They both watched her enter a door at the back, then reappear a few minutes later carrying the boy. Satterfield reached for the binoculars but Margot elbowed his hand away. The boy was remarkable. Botticelli lips. Eyes alert and busy. Were all children so beautiful? He had a high forehead, wonder in his eyes, looking at everything. As they passed under the branch, he grabbed for it. Eva set him on the ground and they joined hands until they reached the patchwork Subaru.

"*Knew* it," muttered Margot. Satterfield put his seat up and started the engine.

They followed her to a mixed neighborhood with single homes and duplexes where none of the trees were more than a story high. Most driveways had a boat or a snowmobile out front. Eva turned into a condo complex. Satterfield pulled in, too. He drove past her parking space to the end of the cul-de-sac and turned around, pulling in a few spaces down. She went up the sidewalk and was swallowed by a foyer.

"Not bad," Satterfield said.

"What's not bad?"

"Well, it's not a trailer. She manages."

Margot said nothing.

"Are we done?" he asked, eyeing her. "Or will there be window peeping?"

She scowled and he laughed, sitting back. Glancing up, he said, "Oh dear god."

Margot turned with a start. Eva had come out, was walking straight for them. She stopped on the sidewalk in front of the car, both hands on her hips. She was barefoot. Her hair was pulled back. Before she said anything, she scratched the inside of her right wrist like a distracted teenager.

"You might as well come in," she said.

Margot stared straight ahead as if she hadn't heard. The driver's door opened. Satterfield got out, walking towards her with his hand outstretched.

"Douglas Satterfield," he said.

Eva stared, first at his hand, then up at his face. "Are you all oversized?"

"No," Margot said, still staring straight ahead. "You're short."

For a long moment, nothing happened. Satterfield lowered his hand and stood idly, his shirt collar peeking out his big sweater. The little boy appeared wearing nothing but underpants. The pale skin of his stomach and chest stood in sharp contrast to the juniper bushes, the brown siding, the lingering snow. He saw the visitors and hurried down the sidewalk towards them.

Following Margot's gaze, Eva turned. "Oh Birdie! Get some clothes on!" She covered her mouth with a hand, giggling. "He's so biblical," she explained. "Tears off his clothes."

She hurried towards him, telling him he would catch cold, but the scolding wasn't sincere. She was one of those mothers who pretended to be exasperated but was delighted with all her child's behavior, even the naughty.

Birdie looked over his shoulder as she picked him. "Giants!" he shouted at them.

"Yes! The giants have come!" said Eva, turning. "Well? Are you coming in?"

Satterfield followed, rejecting Margot's imploring look. She opened her door, turned her entire body and put both feet on the ground; using her good arm, she hoisted herself up by pulling on the car's door frame. She felt bovine and was glad neither of them waited for her.

She caught up in the short, dark hall just inside where Satterfield lurked.

"Shut the door," they heard Eva call.

As Margot's eyes adjusted, she saw batik tapestries on the walls, faintly Egyptian. Gauzy curtains shrouded sliding glass doors. The sofa was a claw-footed antique with brocade fabric. She spotted not one but two ceramic mermaid lamps. On the floor squatted an orange globular object, for sitting perhaps. Maybe a footrest. The usual detritus of small children cluttered all surfaces and the floor: an overturned bin of wooden blocks, a pile of naked Barbie dolls, and dozens of matchbox cars. Birdie approached holding a red car.

"That's Lightning McQueen," Eva called from the kitchen. "The Bird's favorite."

"Is he named for Charlie Parker?" Satterfield called to her.

"Who?"

Appalled, Margot whispered, "No he is not named for Charlie Parker."

"I've got to get our dinner going," Eva called. "We're hungry when we get home. You can sit at the counter." She gestured to the kitchen peninsula.

They looked at one another. Ignoring Birdie, Satterfield came further into the room. Margot followed. Eva was at the stove, buttering bread next to a fry pan for grilled cheese. She eyed them.

"Did you bring your lawyer to have a look?" she asked Margot.

Margot said nothing, watching Satterfield perch himself on a stool.

"I was beginning to think you'd dropped off the face of the earth," Eva said. She put the buttered bread into the skillet, creating a hiss.

The little boy had followed them, was tapping Margot's hip, holding up the red car. She took it. He stood quietly a moment, watching her, satisfied, then reached up for it. Margot handed it back to him. He climbed onto a stool, still staring at the visitors. Eva flipped the sandwich and the pan hissed again. She covered the sandwich and switched off the burner, then started building the second sandwich, slicing a huge brick of cheddar.

"You followed me home," she said without looking up. "That's creepy." She turned to face Margot. "Why? What do you want?"

Margot gave a short laugh. "You've been calling me, *blackmailing* me about my son and—"

"It's not blackmail!" Eva interrupted, turning back to the stove. "Blackmail is when I have information I'm going to leak if you don't pay." She used the spatula to point at Birdie. "A little late to keep him a secret."

Margot pulled her bad arm closer to her body, rankled.

"Since its legally my money," Eva continued, "It's not blackmail."

She pulled off the lid and scooped the sandwich onto the cutting board, sliced off the crusts with four quick moves and slid it onto a plate. She handed it to Birdie, warning him not to burn himself. He began to blow on it. Cheese oozed out the side.

"A paternity test," said Satterfield, leaning on the counter. "We're here to ask for a paternity test."

"A paternity test!" Eva cried. "You still don't believe me!" She looked at Margot and snorted. "If I was going to lie, if I *wanted* to blackmail somebody, wouldn't I choose, like, a senator's kid? Or the university president?"

Margot looked at Satterfield, speechless.

"How long did you two date?" Satterfield asked. Margot could tell he was hoping to catch her in a lie.

"Uh, I wouldn't say we *dated*," she laughed, turning on the burner again. She dropped the second sandwich in with another satisfying hiss.

"Well, it's irrelevant," Satterfield boomed, "until we get a paternity test." He cleared his throat with authority and stood. "If the test comes back positive, you'll be asked to sign a document, a notarized document that says this won't go on forever. There will be a settled upon amount, then, that's it. No calls when you want to send him to private school. No haggling over new clothes, or a car when he's sixteen."

Margot's jaw dropped. Was he making this up as he went along? What document? What was he *talking* about? Forgetting the sandwich, Eva turned to Satterfield, then Margot.

"You act like we're an illness."

"You *are* an illness!" Margot shouted. "You're blackmailing me and I want proof! How absurd that this might *hurt your feelings!*"

Satterfield glared at her and continued in his booming voice. "We will file for a restraining order. If you approach any member of the Fickett family, they have the right to take you to court. You could go to jail."

Margot's fracture was aching. She suddenly longed for her house, the view of the back yard, where the grass was showing now. The creek was thawing. She looked at Birdie, who was quietly eating his sandwich. She smelled burnt cheese. Where on earth were this girl's parents? How could anyone be so alone?

With deliberate, unrushed movements, Eva turned back to the stove and switched off the burner. Looking straight at Satterfield, she said, "That doesn't sound remotely legal. Whoever heard of a restraining order on a single mother wanting child support?"

He was silent. Margot knew he was thinking the same thing she was: Eva wasn't stupid.

"What kind of lawyer are you, anyway?" she asked. "Lawyers don't work on Saturdays. They don't *stalk* people." She looked at Margot. "Why aren't you saying anything?"

Weariness had settled over her. She said to Satterfield, "I think we should go."

Satterfield stood and headed towards the door.

"I'll do it," Eva said.

They turned.

"The paternity test. But I want you to do something for me, too. I have Monday off. Meet me here, in the morning. I want to show you something."

When Margot didn't say anything, Satterfield asked, "What?"

"Why I want the money."

Margot's throat was dry. She felt like she was coming down with spring flu, that sinking tightness in her throat. Satterfield was moving again, saying they'd be in touch about where to go for the test. Margot felt his long fingers gently encircling her upper arm, leading her to the front door.

Once they were driving away from the condo complex, Margot said, "You shouldn't have parked so close. That was horrible."

He didn't answer right away. His brow was knit. She was about to say more when he asked, "What did you say her name was? Her full name?"

"Eva Baker."

"And her father, you said—what does he do?"

Margot closed her eyes, tried to remember that first terrible conversation. "She said he was a wealth manager."

"Ethan—was that his name? Ethan Baker?"

"That's him," Margot said.

Satterfield covered his mouth with a weary hand. They were at a stop-light. He looked at her.

"What?"

"Donors," he said. "Gold level symphony supporters, Ethan and Annie Baker."

A gong pounded in her chest. Christ, the Bakers had been sponsors several years running, had bought a table at the spring fundraising gala. They were enthusiastic supporters of the adopt-a-musician program. This year, in fact, the musician chosen for their gold level cello section sponsorship was Margot herself.

Twelve

After the year's first luxurious thaw, it snowed. All day and all night it fell, burying the town in wet, heavy white. The radio reported that a group of intrepid students had trudged up Mount Sentinel to sled at midnight, waking local residents. The report called the snow a freak storm, which was clearly seasonal amnesia. Every year March and April were the heaviest snowfall months, and every year the people were shocked.

In the canyon, the placid, sharp eyes of Margot's owl were visible through the snow. The owlets were two weeks old, no longer small, and still the mother owl fit herself on top of them wings outstretched like a living tent. They did not yet have feathers; if they got wet, they would die of hypothermia. The risk was that high yet she appeared untroubled, her noble head barely moving, proving that the weather was nothing to get excited about. Margot thought of the fish in the streams, finning in torpor. The bears that slept on, nursing new cubs. She thought of Eva's apartment, how it had felt to stand amidst the overabundance of furniture. All that fabric: upholstery, curtains, lampshades, tapestries. How did she keep the little boy from knocking over those mermaid lamps or hurting himself?

Birdie. His bright eyes. Cheeks puffing out as he blew on his sandwich. He had lined up his Hot Wheels, bumper to bumper, behind the sofa. At least thirty of them, organized by color. The magnets on the refrigerator were also grouped by color. The place smelled of cooking, dust and candle wax. What happened if she paid Eva the money? Was it over? She'd never see either of them again? Satterfield maintained that their blunder was not in going over there, it was getting caught. He said that if Margot paid the money, she would never be free. The boy would need a winter coat. Eva would want to take him to Disneyland, and here they'd come. The fact that her parents had money didn't matter because she clearly didn't have access to it.

Margot wasn't so sure. For all the makeup and flashy clothes, Eva did not feel devious. She did not seem like a schemer. Ten days ago, inside that awful shop, a schemer was exactly what Margot thought she was seeing. But there were the stupid things Eva had said on the answering machine: that she would call Andy, or post it all on Facebook. She was stalling; if she meant to do any of that, she'd have done it. Watching her grill that sandwich, the efficiency with which she sliced off the crusts and warned the boy not to burn himself proved she was a mother, not a schemer. A woman could be both, of course. But Eva lacked the ambition Margot saw in many of her students' mothers. She was too guileless, which was a strange thing to say about a girl demanding money. Satterfield would disagree, but he wasn't a parent. He hadn't noticed Birdie at all, other than one good look when they first stepped inside. He didn't notice the boy's awe, how he stared at Satterfield's hands and face. His reaction to the man's deep voice wasn't one of fear but curiosity. He wasn't afraid of men, or strangers or much of anything. That kind of courage didn't happen on accident. To have such a secure little boy, Eva had to be doing something right.

In spite of the snow, Margot walked on the rim above the house, resuming the old ritual. She came in to find a phone message from Andy. He was checking up on her, unusual when he was on tour, he admitted. Even recorded on the machine his baritone voice hit her straight in the chest. *I know you can't play your cello. And you miss me.*

He cleared his throat in an exaggerated way to signify that he was kidding. He often accused her of not missing him at all. Standing in the foyer, Margot smiled. He was having fun, he said. The best tour yet. Before he hung up he exaggerated again, "Fun, fun fun!"

The concept of fun was a longstanding Fickett debate. In fact, Benji was at St. Thomas, a liberal arts college in Minnesota, instead of a conservatory like Peabody because Andy had hated Peabody. He hated the lack of fun in classical music, he said. The players themselves twitched and convulsed with controlled passion but the audience was meant to sit still. No toe tapping. No clapping, for god's sake. Finally Andy decided he didn't like the audience either, laced-up, prim and cerebral. Quartets were meant for a despicable aristocracy. He didn't last the year, but stayed in Baltimore, joining the legions of other musicians who played the clubs and traveled to New York for more gigs.

In the troubled days before he left the conservatory, Andy asked Margot why she played cello. "Is it because you love it? Is it fun?" It was not love, she admitted. What she *loved* was reading while soaking in a hot bath, or walking the dark streets before the sun came up. She loved *listening* to music, but playing it was something deeper, in some ways less personal. Later, when Margot had students of her own, Andy admitted that "fun" was not the purpose of playing, certainly not something you could tell students. Satisfying, perhaps. They both liked the athlete analogy: athletes trained every day, skipped dessert and rarely partied. The performer must hone his skill just as diligently, keeping his goals in mind. Practice was essential, and practice was far from fun. Satterfield claimed that the musician's discerning ear and nuanced hands must be trained as thoroughly as a surgeon's. But musicians most resembled writers, he said. "We deal in the intense."

Even love itself could hardly be called "fun." Margot had her first love affair when she was seventeen, at a summer music festival in Colorado, the only time she'd been lost to herself. Surely fun meant enjoying yourself while still *being yourself.* Years ago, when Benji was fourteen, they all played cards on the deck of a cabin at Lake Mary Ronan. Margot got up to make popcorn and, returning to the table, said aloud: *This is fun.* On the same trip, she caught a fish. Trolling for kokanee salmon, her pole arched and the guide began shouting directions, *Pull the tip straight up! Straight up!* Margot wrestled the rod against her hip, squealing so loud her voice carried back to the lodge. The fish was not a salmon but a fifteen-inch trout. She was talked about, the screaming lady who caught her first rainbow. *That* was fun.

Last year, cocktails with the cello section after the Christmas concert was fun. At the end of the night they stepped into the giddy silence of a snow-covered world. The flakes were still falling; a third cellist's car was stuck at the curb. All the cellists to the rescue. The zipping sound of his tires spinning, the drunken laughter as they positioned themselves around the car in their heels and coattails to push. Hysteria when Chester Poole face-planted in a snow bank, the unified triumph when the car finally pulled free and fish-tailed down the street.

She was glad Andy was having fun. He was being sarcastic, but he was right: she couldn't play and she missed him. On impulse, she sat in the chair in the foyer and picked up the phone.

"Margot!" he cried. "You know how to dial!"

His deep voice, rich as butter. A strangled laugh came out of her throat. "Yes," she squeaked. "Fun, fun fun!" she quoted him.

Unexpectedly, tears filled her eyes. She could say, "Come home," and he'd do it. She knew nothing for certain, had no real facts. If the situation were reversed, he would protect her. She'd be furious, later, that he didn't tell her, yet it was also true that knowing would ruin her tour. If she told Andy, he'd want Eva's phone number. Who knew what he'd say?

Next week, Andy would see Benji. The Wilmas' drummer lived in Minneapolis, and the band was flying there for several gigs. Of course Andy would tell Benji. School would be a lost dream. This drama would be the excuse he was looking for.

"So?" Andy asked when Margot didn't say more. "What's new?"

She could hear the sound of voices in the background, the drone of an engine. He was on the tour bus. "I can lift my arm to shoulder height," she stammered. "I just wanted you to know."

He spoke to someone else, then told her he was glad to hear it.

"All is well," Margot told him. "Don't worry."

She used the number Satterfield gave her to find out what was required for the test. Since they didn't have the alleged father, they'd be using a home kit to collect an "unusual sample," in this case, Benji's toothbrush. Because there would be no way to prove the origin of the sample, the data would not stand up in court. Margot decided this was a good place to start. If lawsuits became necessary, they'd deal with it later. She booked the appointment for Birdie's cheek swab the first Monday in April. Early, as soon as the clinic opened. Margot had the address. She used caller i.d. to find Eva's number.

Eva answered on the second ring.

"Mrs. Fickett?"

"How'd you know?"

"I have you on speed dial," Eva said with irony.

Margot smirked into her empty house.

"My place doesn't always look like it did when you were here," the girl said. "It's usually spick and span."

"I see."

"We relax on the weekends."

Margot gazed out the window in the den. Snow again, coming from all directions, like a light show. "About the paternity test," she began. She gave Eva the information, said they could meet at the clinic. Eva agreed, saying that Monday was her day off.

After a pause, the girl said, "You agreed to come with me. You said that if I did the test, you'd let me show you why I want the money."

Margot swallowed. "I did say that. Yes, I did."

"Can you do it on Monday, right after?"

Margot paused. What good would it do to know why Eva wanted the money, if the results were negative? Was Eva trying to get Margot to feel sorry for her? Satterfield would say don't do it.

"If you want to wait until after the results come, we can," Eva said, reading her hesitation. "If you're busy."

Margot wasn't busy, was the thing. She had a student coming later in the day. Pip would be back on Thursday. She planned to attend another symphony rehearsal. The days were long, in fact.

"All right," she said at last. "I will drive to your place. Next Monday. We'll do it all on the same day."

"Right on," said Eva. "You won't regret it. You'll see that I—"

Margot hung up.

Thirteen

Deaton was divided by water, not a babbling brook but the muscular Black Fork River, populated by boulders and eddies and overspill drains that in the summer backed up with foamy flotsam. In winter its banks grew wide, icy shelves making the river appear narrower and tamer. But in the spring, the Black Fork came to violent life. Snowmelt raged down from the higher elevations, storming the newly exposed banks. Mornings, the river's foggy exhale crept through neighborhoods, and in the afternoon there was the sound of ice cracking, breaking off in chunks bigger than a human head. The river pulsed like blood through an artery, thick or thin but never still.

A system of parks and footpaths followed the riverbank and the bridges connected the two sides of town. The Cedar Mountain Clinic sat on an industrial street that dead-ended at the water, in an unmarked cinderblock structure with few windows. Both building and parking lot were surrounded by an iron fence accessed through an automatic gate that stood open during business hours. A small group of pro-life picketers formed a ring around the entrance to the parking lot. Though the day was bright, one of April's finest, the people were grim-faced. Their hand-lettered signs struck Eva as limp and sadly inconsequential.

Parked in Mrs. Fickett's Suburban, she sat gazing at them without speaking. She had been here when she was pregnant with Birdie, but there were no picketers that day. Now he sat in his car seat, happily munching a granola bar

while the women contemplated abortions and clinics and other unmention-
able things associated with their gender.

"Let's don't cross a picket line for this—" began Mrs. Fickett, but Eva
opened her door.

"You can't be scared off by these losers!"

"Who?" Birdie asked her. "What losers?"

"Haters," said Eva, unbuckling him.

She marched around the front of the vehicle, wanting Mrs. Fickett see her
fearless, forward motion, the way she made eye contact as they approached.
She led them across the line; holding Birdie up, she called, "Don't shit your-
selves! We're not here for an abortion, obviously."

They reached the door and Eva pressed the buzzer. Mrs. Fickett was
ducking her chin to hide her smile. Eva felt her face flush with pleasure.
"What?" she asked.

"Nothing."

"Embarrassed?"

Mrs. Fickett met her eye. Briefly, so quickly neither could believe it happened, they smiled at each other.

They were buzzed in, held briefly in a vestibule until a woman appeared
behind bulletproof glass. Through a speaker she asked their business. Another buzzer sounded and they were admitted into what might have been any
pediatric clinic, with beat-up toys, primary colored walls, worn out seating,
and month-old magazines. While Margot spoke to reception, Eva pulled out
a pack of wipes and crouched to clean Birdie's hands. "Don't put anything in
your mouth," she whispered and turned him loose.

There were forms. They sat side by side with clipboards, asking each
other for addresses and phone numbers. Eva remembered coming here,
scared and bewildered. She'd left with pamphlets on adoption and pre-
natal care. Not long after that visit, she had told her best friend, Heather Copenhagen. They were going to be roommates at the university.
Throughout their senior year, they had discussed the horror of going to
college a virgin. Neither of them was an abstainer, those sad kids who
wore T-shirts that read, *I'm Waiting!* Who cared? No, it was far better to
get it over with before you hit campus, they thought, though neither of
them had a boyfriend.

Late in the summer, Eva arranged to meet Heather at the food co-op. They sat at an outdoor table on a sunny day, and Eva listened to Heather chirp about curtains she'd found for their dorm room. Curtains, Eva remembered thinking. *How cute.*

Eva made her announcement and Heather gave a breathy laugh. "You're *pregnant?*" she said. "And you're telling me you're going to *have it?*" Her small mouth made an unpleasant rectangle, half scowl, half shock. "Are you crazy?" she shrieked. "Jesus, Eva! Get an abortion and get on with your life!"

Eva sat blinking at her friend. Everyone was thinking this. Certainly her parents were. At least Heather had the nerve to say it. But Eva did not forget, would never forget, that laugh, the way her friend's college-bound, bug-eyed excitement vanished like a popped balloon. Eva had expected questions: *Who? When?* Even, *Why wasn't I informed?* Best friend material. The giggling, whispering demand to know did come, but it wasn't first. Instead, Heather panicked.

Panic could not be called a strange reaction. Eva herself panicked. Her parents were away when she bought a pregnancy test and saw the pink line. Her thought was, *Holy Shit.* She threw herself on her bed, crying so hard that her body shook the headboard. The fact itself felt oddly unrelated to the act of sex. She did not rethink her graduation night, that moment by the river. She didn't feel regret or worry so much as primal shock. The concrete way she had always thought of herself vanished in one afternoon. She immediately missed who she'd always been. She wailed, longing for the days when she and her brother got home from school and hurried out behind the house to the river to wash away the heat and boredom of the classroom.

She bawled and slept, woke in the night and felt a horrible overwhelm. Somebody else had begun. What in god's name was to be done? She cried again, only this time as her body shook and she gasped for air, she wondered if she could cut off the thing's oxygen. She was suffocating, so it was suffocating in her womb. Womb. What a word. I have a womb and in my womb is a mass of cells growing a spine.

She got up, filled her parent's big tub, stepped in and went under. Her hair, still long and brown then, swirled above her face. She stared through it, up to the ceiling, which was dimly lit by the outside yard lamp near the garage. If I drown, we both die.

The silence was broken by the splash of water against porcelain, the gasp of her deep inhale, water dripping off her shoulders and hair. She breathed in and out, gripping the tub's sidewall, bile in her throat.

The cosmic nature of the experience intensified when she heard the heartbeat. A hushed room in another clinic. Eva and the nurse holding their breath, the Doppler wand moving through thick gel on her lower belly, white noise like static between radio stations. Suddenly the nurse looked up, grinning. They both heard the resplendent Martian rhythm. All that business in science class about the universe expanding and nanotechnology was right here in her uterus. The dark void, this swimming pulse, a racing, insistent, flutter. Contact! Birdie had begun.

Eva and Mrs. Fickett finished with the forms and turned them in, then sat with one seat between them, waiting. Eva glanced at Mrs. Fickett's blank face. She sat erect in her chair, the arm in a sling. Didn't move a muscle while Eva fidgeted endlessly. The chairs were uncomfortable, the upholstery cheap and pilled. Her left foot pumped. She wrapped it around her right ankle to keep it still but this pulled her tendons and her elbows flared from her sides. She propped them on the armrests, but that, too, felt unnatural. She adjusted her bangs, uncrossed her ankles and all the while Mrs. Fickett didn't move. It was her work as a musician, Eva thought. You couldn't fidget. Other jobs that required little movement: Truck driving. Toll booth operator. Bank teller.

"You'd have to be invisible to get a bomb inside this place," Eva said.

"Comforting."

"How are you managing with a broken arm?"

"I'm all right."

"Where's your husband?" Eva asked, though she knew, from The Wilmas' Facebook page.

"On tour with his band."

"Shouldn't he have stayed? I mean, how do you cook? Get dressed?"

Mrs. Fickett had astonishing dark eyes under her scraggly bangs. Eva looked away and back, drawn to them.

"I told him to go," she said. "Playing music is everything to him. And anyway he can't cook. I was awfully sick of tea and soup."

Astonished, Eva smiled slowly, realizing that Mrs. Fickett had made a joke.

Birdie came over, delivering a handful of plastic, hollow shapes. "Hold those," he said with his bright gaze. Eva accepted the load in her lap but hesitated to touch them, drawing her hands up. Mrs. Fickett stared at him in the way older mothers look at little kids, with longing. When he left, Eva used her shirt to gather and dump them into the vacant seat.

"Do you ever worry he won't come back?"

"Andy?" Mrs. Fickett laughed, surprised. "I have never worried about that, no."

"How does Lambchops fit in?" Eva asked. Mrs. Fickett was confused. Eva said, "The tall guy with sideburns?"

"Satterfield," she said. "He's the symphony maestro."

At first Eva thought this was a joke. *Maestro?*

"The conductor," Mrs. Fickett explained, amused.

"I knew he wasn't a lawyer," said Eva. "Does Andy know about him?"

Still amused, Mrs. Fickett's large left hand moved to her knee, brushing away lint or hair that Eva couldn't see.

"Nothing to 'know.' We've been friends a long time."

Eva tried to imagine being married to one man and friends with another, a man like that, someone you'd notice on the street. He looked like an old-fashioned aristocrat. Put a wig on him and he could be in Parliament. Eva didn't believe that men and women could be friends, if they were both straight.

"How long have you been married?" Eva asked.

Mrs. Fickett thought. "A long time. Almost twenty-five years."

"Did you tell him about me?"

To Eva this didn't seem a weird or impertinent question, but Mrs. Fickett looked alarmed. She shook her head and for a second her dark eyes lost their guard. Eva saw a flash of regret. What did she regret? Keeping Eva and Birdie a secret? Did she worry that Eva would be hurt because she hadn't made the marital news? When Mrs. Fickett was in Eva's house, she claimed not to care about Eva's feelings, but now she revealed a softness. She *did* worry about other people's feelings. She would probably give up the money, in the end. Eva's throat felt thick and she stared at the floor.

"What about your parents?" Mrs. Fickett asked. "What do they know?"

"They know nothing," Eva said. "But they think they know everything.

You should probably thank me, actually. If I had given them your name back at the beginning, it would have been a nightmare."

Mrs. Fickett's uninjured arm dropped to her lap. She looked snide. Eva wished she hadn't said that.

"Why didn't you tell them? Why all the secrecy?"

"It wasn't any of their business!"

Mrs. Fickett dropped her chin, pinching the bridge of her nose in exasperation. "I don't believe Benji is the boy's—Birdie's—father, but *somebody* is," she said in a clipped, scolding voice. "Shouldn't you tell him?"

Eva's regret deepened. For a while there, things were getting friendly.

"Can you imagine finding out something like that? He should have been told years ago!"

"It could be worse," Eva retorted. "Birdie could be twenty, knocking on your door."

Across the room a young woman looked up from her magazine.

Lowering her voice, Mrs. Fickett asked, "Do you hear how self-serving you sound? Like a child. You *are* a child."

"A child with a plan!" Eva said, crossing her arms. "I had given up. I wasn't going to leave any more messages, no matter what Sully said—"

"Who's Sully?"

"My boyfriend. Then you showed up at my house with your goon."

Again Mrs. Fickett tucked her chin, a gesture of restraint. "I might as well ask," she said at last. "Five thousand dollars isn't very much. Why not ask for fifty? A hundred?"

Eva's jaw dropped. She turned in her chair, crying, "I'm *polite!* I only want what I'm owed!"

"That can't be right! Over three years a guy only has to pay *five thousand dollars*? For his own child?"

"It depends if he's a student," Eva said. "There's an education incentive. In the summer, when he can work full time, the rate goes up."

Mrs. Fickett pushed her bangs out of her face. "That's pitiful."

"Agreed," said Eva with a nod.

A tight silence ensued.

For so long, Eva meant to be a person of integrity, to show people she could do it on her own, that she was not a cliché. The Ficketts became dead to her. Deaton was a big enough city; months passed and she saw or heard nothing of them. Only a year ago, right before Bethany left, Eva was at a music festival in Riverfront Park and saw The Wilmas perform. Mr. Fickett dominated the stage. When he played his fiddle the crowd went wild, clapping and dancing. Benji himself appeared, joining his dad on stage.

With Birdie perched on her hip, Eva stood among her dancing friends, gazing up at them. Benji looked the same as he had in high school, the same floppy hair he couldn't quite pull off with his polo shirt and white gym shoes. She scanned the edge of the crowd and found tall, stately Mrs. Fickett, not dancing but at least smiling, looking proud.

All the famous Ficketts. Eva left before the set was over. Seeing their blissful ignorance made her ashamed of the tattoos she got when she was pregnant. She had cut off her hair and bleached it, got a nose ring, the typical, juvenile acts of defiance. Her big stand against the status quo was that she had kept her baby. How noble. She was still dead in the water, while Benji got to pursue his dreams. Talk about status quo! She wasn't a *wife*, for god's sake, trapped at home keeping house. She could still *do* things.

That night she got out her notebooks, the sketches of the store she wanted to open. She would model it after the boutique, but not as upscale. Eva's place would be a clothing exchange, an idea popular with the college crowd, who liked to recycle everything. She would stock furniture, of course. The best she could find. She'd be discerning: she'd take antiques, and settees, day beds, unique lamps and solid wood chairs. Nothing from a chain store, ever. You could bring in your stuff and trade for cash or store credit. Her boutique would be cheap, but not Salvation Army cheap. The Rhino. She'd even designed the logo, her favorite animal pair since grade school: the African rhino with a oxpecker on its rump.

Eva and Mrs. Fickett were called, led back by a nurse. They walked down a narrow hall to a small exam room, which got even smaller when she closed the door. The process took under fifteen minutes and most of that was the nurse messing with the plastic vials and the shipping envelopes.

In the parking lot, the picketers had gone. Eva was going to take Mrs. Fickett to see the New Leaf, an idea that now struck her as bad. What were the chances that Mrs. Fickett would be for it, would say, *Great idea! Of course I'll give you the money!* She was more likely to charge into Annie's Fitness and introduce herself to Eva's mother. Climbing into the Suburban, Eva almost felt sorry for the woman. She was going to flip out when she discovered that this was no lie. My god, Eva was tired of people flipping out.

Fourteen

The easy way Eva ordered Margot through Deaton matched the way she had charged through the picket line, mouthing off. At one point, Eva dug through her bag, searching for something; Margot glanced over and got a look inside: a paperback book was jammed in there. She saw a plastic lighter, a diaper, a tampon, lipstick, old receipts. Eva pulled out a granola bar, ripped it open and handed it to Birdie, stuffing the wrapper into the console cup holder.

They passed a strip mall and Eva pointed out a hair salon on the west end.

"That's a walk-in place you should try," she said. "They're good. A friend of mine from high school."

Glancing over, Margot asked, "What are you saying?"

Eva's back straightened with embarrassment. "Not that you look bad!" she gushed. "You don't care how you look, in a cool, Chrissie Hynde kind of way."

Offended, Margot quipped, "Better Chrissie Hynde than Debbie Harry."

Eva gave her a blank look and asked, "Who's Debbie Harry?"

She shut her mouth and listened as Eva described her financial situation. The exchange concept baffled Margot. How were you supposed to make any money? Her shop seemed like the kind of idea you'd go hoarse trying to talk your kid out of. Eva's confidence, her blindness to limitations, was also confusing; she wasn't frightened enough to be a twenty-year-old single mother. Perhaps modern women didn't feel fright or limits. Nor did they have abortions, apparently. So what if you made bad financial decisions? What mattered was faith in yourself, this blind belief that you could do it all. Still, money had to be made. Time had to be put in. Somebody was going to pay, sooner or later. Right now, that somebody appeared to be Margot.

Eva claimed her boyfriend stood to make three hundred thousand dollars, and that she could triple Margot's investment. The business wasn't actually her boyfriend's; he was running it for another man, the one who was requiring her to buy in, rather than just loaning her the money. She was confident in her idea of a clothing exchange, knew she could make back her initial investment within a year.

The confusion intensified when Margot recognized where they were headed. She had no wish to return to the haunted emporium where Eva worked. Then again, more than thirty years ago Margot had vowed never to see the inside of another abortion clinic. Revisiting places she didn't want to go was the theme of the day.

"Are you taking me to work?" she asked, turning into the parking lot.

"Not exactly," said Eva, directing her to pull around back. They parked by the little tree outside an unmarked door.

"What is this place?" Margot asked, unbuckling. "I don't see what this has to do—"

"Just come on," Eva said, unbuckling Birdie from his car seat.

For the second time that day, they rang a buzzer and waited.

"Feels like a speakeasy," muttered Margot. Eva's tentative smile revealed she didn't know the term.

A gaunt man opened the door. The smell, even from the threshold was unmistakable. Margot was following a woman carrying a child into a pot shop. She was introduced to Marvin, who wore thick glasses. He stood with them in the waiting room. After a pause, as if it took him that long to notice, he smiled at the boy in Eva's arms, crying, "There he is!"

"Can you get Sully?" Eva asked him.

Marvin hesitated. "Dutch is back there."

"Just say I've brought Mrs. Fickett."

Satterfield would advise against this, certainly. *Leave at once*, she heard him commanding. What did it mean, *I've brought Mrs. Fickett?* What did these people know of her? Why did Marvin limp? Three brown upholstered chairs sat along the wall. The shoulder-high countertop held an open laptop. Everything looked brand new.

Marvin returned through the door behind the counter. With him was a thick-chested, red-haired man wearing a denim work apron. He crossed to Eva, kissed her on the cheek, then wiped his hand on his apron.

"Sullivan Stiles," he said, holding his hand out to Margot.

She looked down at her sling, which she wore to alert others that she couldn't go around shaking hands. He lowered his hand and smiled.

"Welcome to the New Leaf."

"The what?"

"It's a medical marijuana business," said Eva. "Grow operation and dispensary."

"Pot," Margot said. The word was so full of disbelief it sounded like a question. Looking at Birdie, she asked, "Should he be here? Breathing this?"

For a time, no one said anything.

"'S'no different from sniffing a geranium," Marvin offered. "Which by the way is poisonous to eat, harmless to inhale."

Margot turned away, suddenly beset by pain. She stepped over towards the chairs to take her arm out of the sling. The elbow hurt when she extended her arm. She heard Eva say to Sully, "She's got a broken collarbone. You should let her try something. For the pain."

"Would you like a cup of cannabis tea?" Sully asked Margot.

Margot shook her head, but Marvin headed behind the counter towards a tray on wheels. She heard the sputter of an electric kettle coming to life, the rattle of a spoon against a ceramic mug. Sully and Eva were whispering to one another. Margot stared out the window at the creek and the trailer park beyond. Did he actually mean pot tea? Was there such a thing? A pot shop was Eva's big plan. This adventure just kept getting better and better.

Birdie came over with a Lego brick in his hand, grinning up at her. His cheeks were streaked with dirt from the planter in the corner. Margot took in the boy's skin, like fine silk. His bright-eyes and neatly spaced, perfect teeth. Such beauty. She thought of the owlets in her backyard up in the canyon, shielded by their mother's body.

"Sit," Marvin said. "Take a load off."

He was coming towards her with a mug. Good Christ, she thought, catching sight of his shiny-tipped cane. She took the mug, saying, "I'm fine, really."

"The tea will help," said Sully.

Behind the counter a door opened and another man entered the room. He was thin, not as tall as Sully, with dark hair and light brown eyes, almost gold. His effect on the others was remarkable: all activity in the room came to a halt. Even the little boy stood still.

"A party," said the man, gazing at them. His eyes rested on Margot and he stepped towards her, asking, "Who's this?"

Margot found she couldn't speak. She took umbrage at beauty in men. The faint stubble surrounding his mouth did not obscure the curve of his upper lip or the wry smile that played at the left corner of his mouth. His bone structure, his fair skin, the fine nose and his narrow build were all feminine, yet the sharpness to his looks, the width of his shoulders, the way he eyed her with interest was decidedly male.

He put his hands on his hips, letting his gaze wander up and down her body. Unsure what to do, suddenly self conscious about her unwashed hair, the weight of the injured arm hanging at her side, Margot sipped the tea. The taste was neither pleasant nor repulsive. Mostly the liquid was hot, which jolted her senses, distracting her from the pounding in her chest. She glanced at the others, trying to figure out what was infecting the room. Power, certainly. Perhaps fear.

"I'm guessing you are not a new customer," he said at last.

His voice was soft. His jacket was pulled back, revealing a wide leather belt around his narrow waist. The buckle formed the twisted face of a dragon; the leather sash was its tongue.

"This is Mrs. Fickett," Eva said. "My guest."

He swiveled his torso to look at Eva. "Nervy," he said. "Bringing guests."

The skin around Eva's eyes tightened. "Meet Dutch," she told Margot. "Our financial backer."

He swung back around, smiling, but did not offer his hand.

"I'm to pay *him*?" Margot asked, looking at Eva. "*He* is going to triple your money? Perfect. Just excellent."

Dutch's smile broadened. "Whoa! Why would you pay me?"

"She'd pay me," clarified Eva. "I'd pay you."

"Oh, this is getting interesting," he said, stepping closer to Margot.

The lump in her throat doubled in size. Margot had no use for flirtation, recoiled at silliness between people. She found banter insufferable, shrank from giggles and word play. At the moment, however, not grinning took real effort. She scowled and sipped the tea.

"Can I show you around?" Dutch asked her.

The question was polite, oddly sincere in contrast to the mocking look on his face. At least they have a leader, Margot thought.

"Please," she said, following him to the door.

Margot felt all eyes on her. She saw Eva's anxious expression as Dutch's fingertips grazed her upper arm, guiding her into the back.

The smell in the grow room was high-pitched, potent, and destabilizing. Margot could taste the plants, a bitter herbal weight in her throat. A sea of green. There was the high ceiling, the fans and exhaust running. The top of the plants were woven through a double lattice system that spread over the planters like a second and third ceiling. Dutch watched her take it in, then said with a dazzling smile, "Welcome to the jungle."

Leading her up one aisle and down the next, he talked about clones and varietals and THC content and other details Margot did not hear. She was remembering news stories; this was happening in Deaton. Andy was in favor of legalization. He'd always been a weed smoker. And The Wilmas' bass player had a medical cannabis card—when he heard about her fall, he'd offered to send cookies. But the business of marijuana was another language to Margot. Raising the tax base, protestors, limits to storefront locations, doctors who prescribed marijuana for conditions like chronic back pain—she had ignored the controversy, the way she did most local news. Now that she was strolling the aisles, staring at the crop, passing college students stooped over the planters, Eva's evasiveness made sense. Margot ought to have guessed this. She'd read that over half the legal card carriers in the state were under the age of twenty-five. What could possibly be ailing them?

They reached the back office, where Dutch flipped on the small fan on top of the fridge. Margot was grateful for the moving air. He motioned to the chair, which she declined to take, leaning on the desk instead. She had been sipping the tea as they walked. The mug was half empty. Dutch filled a cup from the water cooler and handed it to her. She set down the mug and took the water, aware of him watching her swallow.

"When did you break your collarbone?"

"How could you possibly know I broke my collarbone? I'm not even wearing my sling."

"Your body told me." He gave a quick imitation of her posture, back straight, right arm immobile.

"Maybe I'm just uptight."

He shook his head. "Nobody's that uptight."

He moved around her, pouring his body into the desk chair. "I broke mine when I was eighteen. I know the pose."

He wheeled the chair closer until she was standing inside his open knees. "You have no idea how beautiful you are."

Margot froze, the empty cup still in her hand. Heat crept up her legs.

"Those eyes. Like chocolate. I think I'm drowning."

She was sure her face was red, could not look him in the eye. Not since Nigel Webster, the violinist to whom she'd lost her virginity, had Margot felt this affected by a man she didn't know. And this man wasn't even a musician. His words were ridiculous; the whole scene was embarrassing. Yet she did not move away from him.

"What's your name," Dutch asked. "Your first name?"

She laughed, at a loss. When she said it, he repeated it like it was precious. He stood up, his face very close to hers.

"What do you do, Margot?" he asked.

"I play cello." Saying this composed her. She handed him the empty cup.

"Cello," he said. "I'd like to see that."

"You won't. Not any time soon."

"The injury," he said, eyeing the side of her neck. "Too bad."

Without stepping back, he crossed his arms over his chest, spread his feet wide.

"What's she got on you, Margot?" he almost whispered. "Why would you give her five grand?"

Here was a man who needed to know all angles of a situation. Clearly he expected her to look away, or fidget, or confess. Instead, she asked a question.

"Sully's her boyfriend?"

His smiled widened. "He's a genius, that man."

"A genius?"

"This is all his design, everything you see here."

Margot thought about this. She was aware of her own mass, leaning on the desk.

"A pot genius," she said.

He grinned, then shrugged. "Eva's a big girl. You shouldn't worry."

"From where I stand, you two look like a couple of perverts."

Dutch's face opened in surprise. He laughed.

"Taking advantage of a single mother, a kid," Margot continued. "Leave her alone. Let her find another way to make her money. You're toying with her. And I suppose Sully wants what all grown men with young girlfriends want."

"A workout!" Dutch cried with a mocking, hyena-like laugh.

The vulgar sound brought Margot to her senses. She stood, forcing Dutch to take a step back. He put his hands on his hips, again exposing the open dragon's mouth at his waist. Unable to move for the door, Margot said, "You overheard that, about my collarbone."

He smiled. Margot could feel her heart in her chest, the blood rushing in her ears.

"Have dinner with me," he said.

Her mouth dropped open in surprise.

"Tomorrow."

She began to grin with such dumb force her face hurt.

"Give me your phone number."

"No!"

"Come on," he said with a crooked smile. "When's the last time you had fun, Margot? I'd like to see you having fun."

He could have no idea the load that word carried.

At the sound of approaching footsteps, Dutch reached around her to pull open a desk drawer, pulled out a scrap paper, scribbled something and thrust it into her hand. "My number," he said. "Put it in your phone."

She could smell the soap on his skin, in his hair. Up close his eyes were the lightest brown, with green flecks. The groove above his lip was deep.

The cupid's bow, she suddenly remembered, the name for that divot in the upper lip.

The door opened and Eva appeared. Realizing she had interrupted, she took a half step back. Dutch, too, stepped back. Margot slipped Dutch's phone number into her pocket and asked, her face aflame, "Shall we go?"

Fifteen

Eva was closing the register on a Tuesday, trying not to panic because Sully was in the shop. Normally he didn't linger when he dropped off Caity, but Paige had set up a new sectional in front of the television in the back corner. Caity wanted to show him something on her video, and was searching for it with the remote. Paige was in the office behind the counter going through new donations. Eva could feel every nerve, as if she'd drank too much coffee.

The tinkling of the bell indicated a new customer. Annoyed—it was after five—Eva looked up from her receipts and jumped. There stood her mother. She had brought Birdie in his stroller; he was struggling against the straps. She hurried around the counter, trying to keep her mother from seeing Sully.

"Well, thanks mom," she said. "I said I'd come down, but okay."

"I saved you fifty steps," said her mother, leaning a hip on the counter, in no hurry. Birdie squirmed out of the shoulder straps and whined until Eva's mother undid the belt. He ran to the back of the store to see what was on the television. Doom was upon Eva, for now Paige came out of the office, happy to be distracted from inventory. The two women greeted each other. Paige asked her how business was at the studio. Eva's mother launched into a dissertation on the surge of attendance right before swimsuit season. Eva stood frozen, arms at her sides, her lungs constricted.

"Well, thanks for bringing him!" she squeaked, reaching out for the bag of supplies on her mother's shoulder. "See you later!"

From the back came a shout of excitement. Eva saw her mother's glance shift up and over the cash register to the back corner. Recognition flooded her expression. She called to Sully, "It's getting mighty fragrant down at my studio! Like the back of a van on the west coast." Flashing Paige a knowing eye roll, she added, "I'm probably stoned right now."

Sully ignored her, but Paige gave a sympathetic smacking sound with her lips. "That's too bad," she said. "It'll probably get worse when harvest begins."

"I wouldn't know anything about harvest," said Annie, still trying to get Sully's attention. She looked at Eva. "What should I expect? Just how bad is it going to get?"

"I don't know," Eva said, flattening her expression, her voice like wood. She couldn't move her arms and her eyes were glued to the floor.

"You don't *know?*" her mother asked. "I thought your pot farmer boyfriend there was educating you."

She put a spin on the word, *boyfriend*, making it unlike anything a mother would say. She spat it, with mocking bitterness. Paige took a second to register what had been said. A jolt seemed to go through her body. Her head snapped in Eva's direction.

"*Boyfriend?*" she repeated. She turned towards Sully and said with more volume, "Boyfriend!"

Eva saw Sully slowly stand, unable to ignore the situation any longer. Eva's mother still didn't understand what she'd walked into. She called out, "Okay, Mr. Sullivan Stiles, how bad is the smell going to get?"

Eva stole a glance at Paige. She was glaring at Sully as he approached, leaving the kids in front of the video.

"Hello Mrs. Baker—Annie," Sully said. The look he gave Eva said he was sorry. This wasn't what they'd planned.

"Well my customers are starting to complain—"

"You are *such* an asshole!" Paige screeched, bringing conversation to a halt.

Both kids peered towards the counter. Eva's mother turned to Paige, eyebrows up.

"What'd you do, swear Caity to secrecy?" Paige demanded. "How long has this been going on?"

Briefly, Eva closed her eyes, telling herself this might have been worse. Try as she might, she could think of no scenario in which that would be true.

"She's a *child*, you idiot!" Paige shrieked at Sully, her arms flying over her head. "What are you *thinking*!"

Birdie climbed off the couch and trotted towards them. Caity didn't move. Paige suddenly turned to Eva and cried, "Are you aware that everything he touches turns to shit?"

"Stop it, Paige," said Sully.

Paige threw up her hands again, saying, "Doesn't matter. Not my problem!" Then she slammed her palm on the counter so hard that Eva's mother jumped. "You're *fired*," she shouted, pointing a finger in Eva's face. "Take your little boy and everything you own and *get out*."

"What on earth!"

"Mother," Eva said to her, "Please go."

"Get that kid out of here!" shrieked Paige.

"*That kid* is my grandson!"

Paige turned to her. "I don't think you've been informed," she said icily. "Sullivan is my *ex-husband*. He's *Caity's father*."

Eva swooped Birdie into her arms. She grabbed the stroller and pulled it around the counter to the office to collect Birdie's toys, books, and Tupperwares, piling it all in the seat.

"Make sure you get it all," Paige called, coming to stand in the office doorway.

Eva was coming out; they were quite close to one another. Jabbing a finger in Eva's face, Paige said, "Whatever you leave, I'm throwing out."

Enraged, Eva slapped the finger away. "You'll never make it without me," she hissed. "You're all wrong for the market. This place is filthy. I know more about your bills than you do. You're going to *sink like a stone*."

Her voice had risen. The hair on her forearms stood up as if she'd been electrocuted. She stepped around Paige, dragging the stroller to the back room. She picked up a box and began emptying her personal shelf, saying to Birdie in her calmest voice, "Time to move out!" Spare shirts, a sweater, extra shoes, a hairbrush. Books, magazines, an old hat and a coffee mug. It filled quickly and she found another. She was all over this place. Six years of her life.

Sully appeared. "We'll figure this out, babe."

He did not look at all confident. Funny, she thought. The man fought in Afghanistan and three hysterical women made him quiver.

"Take this," she told him, handing him the full box. She carried the other under her free arm, still holding Birdie on her hip.

Her mother was approaching. "Eva—" she began, then turned to Sully. "Your ex-wife!" she sneered. "Brilliant. Really?"

"Go fuck yourself," Sully said, shouldering past her.

Annie gasped, turning to Eva, but Eva didn't stop either. She balanced the second box on top of the stroller load and pushed it towards the front of the store. Caity was crying. Sully stopped to comfort her but Eva kept going, heading for the door.

Paige stood behind the counter, arms crossed. Passing her, Eva said, "You are a terrible mother."

"*Get out!*"

Eva pushed the door open with her hip and struggled through the vestibule, under the antler arbor and into the bright afternoon. The arm holding Birdie was shaking under his weight. He squirmed against her tight grip. Unable to bear the idea of loading her car in front of the store, Eva aimed for the New Leaf.

"Here," Sully called, catching up with her as they passed her mother's studio. "Let me push it."

He put his box on top, steadying the tower with one hand. Eva switched Birdie to her other arm. The whole crew of women standing by the door watched Eva and Sully pass with the overloaded stroller; they stopped speaking to one another when her mother appeared.

"Oh, Eva!" she cried. "You should have told me! I didn't mean for—but Jesus Eva, her ex—"

"You never liked me working there!" Eva shouted, failing to hold back furious tears. "You ruin *everything*! You don't even have the manners to make us fucking dinner!"

She turned the corner of the building. The women were still watching, hands over their mouths. Eva's mother, their fearless leader, tried to say more, but Eva screeched, "Don't say another word to me! *Ever!*"

She wiped her eyes and kept walking. Sully was beside her. Around the final corner, the day was warm and silent. He let go of the stroller to unlock the door, then held it for her. Eva kissed Birdie and put him down. He ran to the planter where he kept his Legos.

"Are you all right babe?" Sully asked when they were both inside.

Eva nodded, wiping her eyes. She sat down.

"I'll get you water," he said, moving behind the counter.

"I just need a minute. I don't want to get in the car yet," she said. She was strangely calm, no longer shaking though her arms felt dead. Her voice didn't tremble. There was even relief to have it over with. "I just need fifteen minutes."

"Stay as long as you like," he said, bringing her a cup of water.

"That was not how I wanted that to go."

Sully crouched in front of her, smiling. He put a hand on her knee. "Get the money, Eva," he said. "Get the money to Dutch. He's going to come through." He stood, hands on his hips, confident. "This weed, Eva! It's superhero pot!"

She looked at him.

"Dutch has done this before, in Seattle. He knows the laws. He's got like an unofficial law degree."

As if on cue, the grow room door opened and Dutch came through, headphones around his neck.

"Hello kids," he said, seeing them. He stopped, noticed Birdie playing in the planter. "Why the long faces?"

Neither of them spoke.

"Could she trim?" Sully asked, turning to Dutch. "Didn't you say you were bringing on more crew for harvest? You could hire her."

"Gentlemanly, but no," Dutch said, hands in his pockets. "I am hiring an *experienced* crew."

"It's okay," Eva said. "It's—I just got fired."

Dutch whistled. "Paigey found out?"

Eva turned to Sully and said, "Don't worry. Please. I'll be fine."

"You heard the lady!" said Dutch.

"You're a dick," Sully said to Dutch, which made him laugh. Not smiling, Sully said to Eva. "I can give you a ride if you want."

"No, go back to work," she said. "I'm going home in a minute."

Exhaustion was settling in. Her mind raced. Her cell phone bill was already late. She had half a tank of gas and her rent was due. Sully bent over to kiss her. "I'll call you later," he said.

Dutch followed Sully, but when he got to the grow room, he stopped and came back to sit next to Eva. His presence was like a smell, impossible to ignore. Did he make everybody feel this way, she wondered. She'd seen clerks in gas stations fall over themselves to wait on him. Male and female waiters at the bowling alley were forever trying to impress him.

"Gonna have to ask mom and dad for help?" he asked.

She saw that it pleased him to ask this. "What do you know about my mom and dad?"

"Oh, I've met mom," he said, nodding towards the back wall. "Charming." He leaned forward, elbows on his knees. "Counting on Mrs. Fickett?"

Eva didn't speak.

He gave her his best smile, showing teeth. "I've got an idea for you."

She eyed him, feeling wet under the arms. Their eyes locked. He leaned back in his chair and spread his legs. The fabric of his pants was thin, revealing the outline of his penis. She tried not to look, but he reached into his pocket, pulling the fabric tight. He was getting hard. She could not look away from his lap, the transformation going on there.

He slid out a hundred-dollar bill and set it on his knee.

"Show me what you've got."

She could feel the horror creeping into her expression. He reached in again, pulled out four more hundreds and set them on his knee. His crotch was tented now.

"Five hundred. Lift your shirt."

"You're kidding," Eva whispered.

"Do I look like I'm kidding?" He leaned against the chair back, adjusting himself, leaving the money on his knee. "Gas for a week. Groceries."

"Fuck you," she said. Then, as though some other voice pronounced the words, she asked, "Here? Right now?"

"Show me."

His hypnotizing eyes shone steady. The longer she waited the more his smile faded. Soon it was gone. She felt the pulse in her neck, the breath moving in and out of her chest. She looked at the money on his knee, then sat up straight and lifted her sweater.

"Blue," he said, meaning her bra. "That too."

Eva put her fingertips under the wire and lifted it over her breasts. The cool air actually felt good. There was something horribly wrong about doing this with your son in the room. She went to pull it all down, aware she'd made a terrible mistake, but Dutch's right hand shot out to catch her wrist. He squeezed her tightly, wouldn't let her lean over.

"Touch your nipples. Scissor them."

"No," Eva said, trying to twist away from him. His grip tightened.

"Do it," he said, squeezing harder. They were struggling; Birdie would notice and come over. She stopped struggling and still he squeezed her wrist, hard enough to hurt. With her other hand she quickly took her left nipple between her first two fingers and pretended to cut. It hardened and her face burned with shame.

In one motion Dutch let her go and knocked the bills off his knee. He was out of his chair, across the room and through the door before she got her sweater back in place.

Sixteen

Spring was on. Clouds chugged overhead, flat-bottomed and wispy-topped, as if caught in motion. No wind. The snow would be back, but here was that first taste of delicate, skittish April. In the canyon, the owlets were out of the nest. Not far, only to the end of the branch. Pale white fuzz clung to their heads but they had wing feathers now and their bodies were as long as Margot's forearm. The mother sat on a nearby branch. She wouldn't leave them until they could fly and hunt for themselves.

Only days after she met him, Dutch left a message on the landline. Margot hadn't given him her number, which meant he found her the old-fashioned way. His voice was deeper than she remembered it; she could tell from his exhale that he was smoking a cigarette. Lowering herself into the chair next to the phone table, she replayed the message several times, especially liking the part when he said he couldn't get her out of his head.

The encounter with Dutch awakened a bedeviling vanity in Margot. He stayed on her mind. Without the cello to focus her energies, she was subject to April's caprice. She got her hair cut and colored, an indulgence normally reserved for three set times per year. Her appointment was still months away; she had to call a salon she'd never been to, a move that felt radical. She let them apply makeup and she bought a new dress, no easy feat with one underpowered arm.

Preoccupied by her looks, she was out on the deck working with the Theraband and caught sight of her reflection, fascinated by her shorter hair and bare shoulders. She noticed herself in the chrome handle of the fridge. Brushing her teeth at night, she gazed in the mirror, watching herself blink.

As was often the case in spring and fall—unstable seasons—the past was suddenly available. A door opened and all time flowed, a warm beckoning light. Into it she stepped, an experience beyond simple remembering. She re-inhabited her young body, could hear the loud, insect-laden Midwestern night filling her teenage bedroom. She felt the pulsing aliveness of the world outside their ugly rectangular house. The smell of the grass and trees, the fleshy scent of unfurling green. She dreamt of Nigel Webster, the London violinist she met that summer in Colorado. The shock of life outside the nest, the beauty of people her own age, all musicians. She spotted Nigel the first day, struck by his assured beauty. He was tall, with sandy blond hair and pale eyes. The way he dressed, his casual slouch, his brilliant playing—he was perfect. When he caught her eye and smiled, her legs wobbled. New to such immensity of feeling, she was sure their meeting could not be random; it was fate. Other times she felt she'd created him, imagining the perfect match for herself. The universe, in its grand benevolence, provided.

Nigel said that real beauty was found in how it was used. Margot must appreciate her height, which for her had always been a source of unwanted attention. "You should enter a room with your shoulders back and your chin up!" he claimed. He was an expert in appearances and impressions, in the surface of things. He demonstrated how she should sit on stage, where to rest her hands when she wasn't bowing, even how she should position her face, her lips, and her eyes. An audience wanted to see a female cellist's décolletage, he said; that pale, untouched skin must always be protected. Never let it burn or freckle. When she played she ought to wear soft fabrics like velvet or silk, anything to invite touch.

By the time she was at Peabody Prep and met Andy, Margot subscribed to an opposite ideology: how a cellist *played* mattered more than how she looked. In fact, playing music was one of the few times a person could forget her physical self. An audience responded to transparency, not studied dramatics. Yet the value Nigel placed on her looks was difficult to abandon. In spite of all that went wrong with them, Margot never forgot his lessons.

Big, confident Andy was a great relief. He lacked pretention. He responded to her with his whole body, touching her all the time, stroking her face, her hair, her upper arms. *So soft*, he'd mutter. When they were younger they'd made passionate love. These days their sex life was like a large, placid lake. Occasionally a storm moved through, stirring up the darker waters, but for the most part, it was a friendly, weatherless place.

On a fine spring day late in the week, Margot drove to campus. For the first time in a month, she felt like walking, didn't mind her distant parking spot. Students sprawled in the grass, their pale skin shocking in the sunshine. The ground would still be damp but nobody cared. Any absence of snow, rain or fog was beach weather in Montana.

She caught Satterfield on his way to the recital hall. They met on the steps of the music department and stood a moment, scrutinizing one another. He was less disheveled. No more stubble. Wingtips on his feet. He appeared almost his old self, though without the tie. Today he wore a bohemian shirt with wrist ruffles peeking out from his jacket sleeve.

"You cut your hair," he said to her.

"Yes."

"It's quite noticeable," he said. "Very good."

"Thank you," she said with a wry look. He knew she disliked flattery but even to her this complement felt limp. "I see you've cleaned up."

"Spring inspires us, I guess."

They walked together and as usual when they were side by side, the two drew stares. One tall person might blend but two could not. Students watched them crossing the campus oval. Satterfield's looks were unusual and Margot in her long skirt and good wool coat looked glamorous. She felt Satterfield's pleasure with the attention. She didn't mind it herself. She took his arm, filling him in on the appointment with Eva and the New Leaf. Margot had dropped Eva and Birdie at McLeod Park that day. She'd learned all about her illicit love affair with her boss's ex-husband.

"A strip mall soap opera," Satterfield called the story.

"The girl's a walking time bomb," Margot said. "Her mother works right next door. And then there's Dutch."

Satterfield watched her carefully as she described the investor behind the New Leaf. Eva reported that no one knew much about him, including where he got his money. They only knew he came from the west coast and that he'd opened other medical marijuana businesses.

They reached the recital hall and stopped under an apple tree, days from bursting into bloom. "He's a little man," Margot reported. "Fair skin, the kind of guy who might front a pop band. A British band. He lacks the high dollar smile of American singers."

"You mean he has poor teeth?" Satterfield asked.

Margot laughed. "His teeth are fine. Just not perfect, which gives him a vulnerability."

Satterfield clasped his hands and leaned back with a knowing smile.

"He's the reason you've done your hair," Satterfield said at last. "I flattered myself at first, but I see how it is."

Margot felt her face redden. "You're being idiotic," she said, cursing her pale skin, her horrible transparency.

"Please," he retorted. "I've known you fifteen years. You do your hair once a season, when you buy your new outfit."

The heat in her face increased. She put up a hand to shield her eyes from the sun, a lame attempt to hide. "Why would I spiff up for a hoodlum?"

"I've no idea," he said, amused. He started to head up the steps, then stopped. "Do you need a ride this weekend?"

She looked at him, confused.

"To the gala? Oh, Margot, you haven't forgotten!"

"Well, I'm not going!" she cried. "I'm enfeebled! I'm not even playing until fall."

Satterfield eyed her. He required all musicians to attend the symphony's fundraising event, especially those sponsored in the Adopt-a-Musician program. Just playing music was no longer an option, he told them; one had to carry part of the fiscal responsibility. Satterfield held workshops to teach the players how to inspire giving without groveling. "Graciousness 101," he called this, another name for charm training.

"Well what about the Bakers?" she asked when she saw he wasn't budging. "Eva's parents!"

"Exactly. They will expect to see you. They're your patrons, after all."

"Douglas, you understand the awkwardness."

He shrugged. "You're not certain of anything yet."

"I am certain that their daughter wants five thousand dollars to invest in a pot shop. Shall I mention that?"

His eyes narrowed. "I'd advise against it."

He turned to go, but Margot took a step towards him, suddenly anxious. She wanted to catch him off guard, to discover his honest opinion.

"Douglas," she said in a hushed voice, "do you think it's possible, what Eva is saying about Benji?"

"Of course it's possible."

"My god, what if he has parented somebody?"

Satterfield came down a step, put a large hand on her arm. "Margot, I have no children. I'm the last person to consult about such things. Maybe it's time to call the fiddle player."

He left her shocked on the sidewalk. The men didn't like each other, never had. Just before he went through the door, he looked back. His expression held regret, bordering on pity and Margot understood that Douglas not only thought it was possible, he was quite certain that Benji was a father.

Seventeen

For the first time since she was old enough to work, Eva was out of a job. Her first morning without anywhere to be, she started in on deep cleaning the condo. Wearing cobalt blue industrial gloves, she cleared the counter of appliances, sprayed 409 and dug in. She took an SOS pad to the oven door, moving in circles, sweating, until the glass was free of brown food flecks and blackened grease. She moved on to the bathroom, attacking the toilet, tub and sink with Comet, then mopping the floor of both kitchen and bathroom with neon Mr. Clean.

Her mind hovered on her finances. She spent some of Dutch's money on gas for the car and Mexican carryout. She could not think of the incident between them without revulsion. Happily, she was good at steering her mind elsewhere. She had ten days until bills were due; it wasn't uncommon for her to be short at this stage in the pay period. Of course there wouldn't be any vow to do better next month. No splurging on toys for Birdie.

On all fours, scouring the tub, a bolt of inspiration hit. She would sell the condo. She wished she'd thought of this a month ago. She might never have bothered with Dutch or the New Leaf. The condo was in her name. Real estate was a sure thing in Deaton. The news said that new home construction was slow, like the retail economy. But existing houses still sold, it just took longer. Eva would sell the condo, rent the space on McLeod Park, and live in back. She'd clean up her furniture and sell it for starting inventory. The Rhino would become a reality.

She dug out the rental agent's phone number, told him she could hand deliver a check later in the day in exchange for the keys, if he would promise to hold it a week. Eva couldn't be sure the condo would sell that fast, but once she had the keys she could stall for more time. The agent agreed to her scheme only because he would be out of town for ten days; if she'd pay a deposit of five hundred, he'd hold her check. The horrible moment with Dutch would pay off.

Once she had Birdie up and dressed, they spent the afternoon making plans. She paid the deposit and delivered the bad check, got the key. They drove to the space to take measurements. At the hardware store she bought a For Sale sign. She researched the cost of a dorm-sized refrigerator and a countertop stove. They spent the afternoon packing up clothes, exhilarated to be busy. She and Birdie would share a futon. She'd sell the canopy bed, and his bed, and most everything else.

At almost eleven that night, her doorbell rang. She was in her robe and little else. Expecting Sully, excited to tell him, she swung the door wide and found her father. For a stunned moment neither of them moved. He'd been fishing, was still wearing his vest and canvas hat. Eva wondered if he was drunk. His eyelids looked heavy and his skin had a hint of pink to it from the sun. His beard was coming in; it only took a day for her dad to look like he'd been on vacation for a week. She pulled her robe closed, aware of its thin fabric.

There was a time when she loved to fish with him. Then she got old enough to be bored by the waiting, and conscious of the silly outfit. Waders with built-in booties. On shorter excursions she'd go with him in her cut-offs and bikini top, hauling a stack of books and magazines. Occasionally he'd get her to row. But most often her dad went alone. He was notorious for not checking in. Once he floated miles beyond where he parked and had to spend an extra night out. Her mother called Search and Rescue, assuming he was drowned.

"Can I come in?" he asked.

She opened the door and led the way into the kitchen. He sat on a counter stool and she offered him a drink.

"Bourbon is what I'd really like," he said with a smile.

She nodded, registering his surprise as she pulled out a bottle of Maker's Mark and two glasses. Her movements felt exaggerated as she poured and set his in front of him. Looking around the room he asked, "Did you paint?"

"Last Thanksgiving."

He nodded. "It looks good in here."

She smiled. "Dad, what's up?"

He met her eye. "I didn't expect to find you alone."

"What, you were going to raid us?"

"I wanted to say something to him."

"Sully, Dad. His name is Sully." Eva sipped her bourbon, trying not to reveal that she had no taste for it. "Were you going to ask his intentions?"

"I guess so," he said. "It may seem silly to you but, Eva, he's quite a bit older."

"You realize that's absurd."

"Absurd?"

"Dad, in case you forgot, I'm living the life that everybody's so scared of." She opened her arms. "You won't serve me booze and you're worried about my older boyfriend. *Hel*-lo! I got pregnant at eighteen. I *had* the baby!"

"All bets are off, huh?" He gave a weary smile. "I don't see it that way. I'm not giving up on you."

She blinked at him. "Giving up on me?"

"Maybe this is a gift, you getting fired."

She straightened. "Mom told you."

"You could still go to school, Eva. Get a degree. You could still have a future."

She blinked at him, cut to the quick. "I have a future."

"We could find a nanny to look after Birdie," he said, his volume growing. "I'm willing to pay for that. And your tuition. I don't care who Birdie's father is, the goddamn deadbeat. Say you'll think about it."

His expression was pleading. He appeared to sway a little, though he had not touched the booze. He, neither of her parents could believe she wanted a child. They refused to accept that she didn't want to go to fucking college.

"Where were you today?" she asked, uncrossing her arms, putting her hands on the counter.

"The Blackfoot, way up by Nevada Creek."

The subject change broke his fixation. Just saying the river's name allowed his shoulders to relax. He picked up the bourbon and shot it back.

"Any luck?"

He shook his head. "Not even a nibble," he said, letting the glass slap the counter.

"Does mom know where you are? Have you called her?"

He shook his head. This would infuriate her, Eva knew. She supposed it was on purpose, a throwback to when he was younger, when nobody wondered where he was or when he'd be back. She'd seen her father out on the water and knew that it altered him.

"I'm going home," he sighed. "She'll know soon enough."

He gave her a last pleading look. She didn't say anything and prayed he wouldn't either. She wanted to have a good feeling about him, the way he was before all the pity and disappointment. He stumbled a little when he got to the hall by the front door. She turned on the light and they both saw her For Sale By Owner sign leaning against the wall.

"Jesus, Eva, what is this?"

"Dad, go home. We'll talk about it tomorrow."

"But where are you going to fucking live?"

He never cursed. It didn't suit him. She reached around him to open the door, ushering him out, then closed it behind his fuming figure on her stoop.

Eighteen

Margot and Pip sat in the practice room under the stairs, deeply engrossed in the Bach suites when the door swung open and Eva burst in, carrying Birdie. Margot jumped out of her chair and Pip yelped, dropping his bow. Margot slapped a hand over her heart trying not to hyperventilate. In all the years she'd taught, no one had ever barged in during a lesson. The Ficketts respected practice time above all else; interruption was unheard of.

"Holy crap!" Pip laughed, leaning over to retrieve his bow.

"I had no idea you were here!" Eva cried. "I—we rang the bell and we knocked! The door was open."

For a moment no one moved.

"Really, I'm sorry," said Eva. Looking at Margot, she added, "I got fired."

Margot lowered her hand and smoothed her shirtfront. "Do you mean, just now? As in, that's why you're not at the store?"

Eva eyed Pip, who was listening intently. "Two days ago."

"Well, I'm sorry," said Margot. "You knew that was coming."

The girl blinked twice and said, "You cut your hair."

Margot's face felt hot. She said defensively, "I wasn't home, so you thought you'd take a look around?"

But she obviously hadn't thought that far ahead. She looked dazed. Birdie was twisting in her arms, trying to get down. She clamped him harder. He did something astonishing: he reached for Margot. Unable to take his weight in her injured arm, she grabbed his anxious hand.

"I'm sorry," Eva stammered. "I don't know. I guess I was going to wait."

"We're just finishing," Margot said, sitting down again. "You can wait. Help yourself to anything."

Pip's ride was a half hour late. Margot made bacon. She toasted frozen waffles and put out cereal bowls with milk and Cheerios for dinner. Pip was delighted when Birdie put his fingers inside the waffle squares, then sucked the butter off each fingertip, grinning.

"That's the best way to eat them!" Pip cried.

Eva drank several glasses of water but didn't eat. A fit of shyness seemed to have gripped her. Pip wanted to know how long she'd known Mrs. Fickett, if she played cello. Eva grew less comfortable the more Pip settled into his interviewing mode. He asked her age, what job she'd been fired from, where she'd graduated high school.

"Are you always this nosy?" Eva finally snapped.

Pip, the mini professor, adjusted his tie and said, "I'm afraid so."

Margot hid a smile; he was himself in all situations, a miniature old man.

"Eva is a new friend of mine, Pip," she explained.

"I was wondering," he said, standing up. "The little guy seems a bit small for bowing!"

"Shall we all go out on the deck to watch the sunset?" Margot asked, also standing.

Pip led the way. Already the sun had dropped part way behind the ridge, which made it seem bigger; they had to shield their eyes. The air was chilly and the night would be cold but in these final rays of light, dark felt impossible. They stood shoulder to shoulder and Birdie pointed as the great eye slid out of sight. In the afterglow, the sloping yard appeared a rich, deep green; the willows at the bottom of the hill looked silver.

"How gorgeous," said Pip.

"Yes," agreed Margot.

Eva let Birdie down and for a time they all watched him explore. The snow had melted; the deck was dry and Birdie crouched to slide his hands between the slats. Pip led him to the edge and helped him down. As they wandered down the hill, Margot faced Eva. Tension radiated from her like mist.

"It sucks to be fired. More than I thought it would."

"You'll be all right, Eva," Margot said gently. "I really believe that."

Eva gave an exasperated sigh, then asked abruptly, "Did you get your test results yet?"

"No—wouldn't you get yours, too?"

"I never check my mailbox," Eva said.

Of course not, Margot thought. Nobody under the age of thirty had any use for actual mail. "Well I've checked," she said. "It hasn't come."

As Pip and Birdie chased one another in the fading light, Eva told Margot about putting the condo on Craigslist and the space she'd rented in McLeod Park, where she intended to live. She spoke quickly, almost manically, not the self-assured girl Margot had seen at the clinic. In short, Eva acted scared. She wondered if something had happened or if this was just the adrenaline of making decisions. For the first time she was struck by how young Eva was, younger than Benji in many ways, in spite of his privileges.

Margot remembered that the other day when they left the New Leaf, Eva had her drop them at McLeod Park, saying she didn't want to be stuck at home. She had a car, Margot pointed out; she wouldn't be stuck, but Eva said she was almost out of gas. Seeing Margot's shock, she laughed, "We take the bus! He's three years old, Mrs. Fickett. We've learned how to get around."

Of course they had. And yet this move seemed poorly thought out.

"Where'd you get five hundred dollars for a deposit?" she asked.

Eva's face quivered slightly. "I had some rat-holed."

"Rat-holed? Last week you didn't have money for gas. And do you have to sell your house? Could you maybe ask your parents, just to help you get started?"

"My parents?" Eva asked. "Uh, they don't really get me, Mrs.—Margot."

Her tone was so earnest and her expression so tragic, Margot thought she was joking. Pregnant at seventeen, and a much older, pot-selling boyfriend—no, she supposed Eva's parents didn't "get" her.

"Can you afford McLeod Park? Isn't that neighborhood for tourists and doctors' wives?"

Eva's face darkened. "You sound just like my mother!" she cried, petulant. She began to pace. The deck creaked under her weight. "There are a million reasons *not* to do something," she said. "*No* stays the same, day after day. *Yes* is the risk. It's the risk that matters. What happens to people! Jesus! It's like you turn thirty and there goes the fun!"

That word again, thought Margot. Eva sighed and crossed her arms against the cooler evening air. The smell of the creek reached them, as if it had waited to exhale until the cover of dusk. She could barely see the boys.

"I'm sorry. I shouldn't have yelled," said Eva.

"You told me the other day that you weren't worried about your boss. You said you could get another job. It would be easy."

"I don't need my words thrown back in my face, Mrs. Fickett."

Margot grew still. The rebuke made her see her assumption: that Eva was here for support in some kind of crisis. She had been mildly flattered. Now it seemed that Eva wanted something quite specific. Margot wasn't sure what. She supposed that if she was Eva, she'd be doing a lot of yelling. She remembered being twenty, the fanatical need to get life started. Nigel and the messy aftermath, the plodding business of finishing high school, begging her cello teacher to help her find a school, applying to Peabody Prep, none of those events went fast enough. The hurry of youth, especially for those desperate to put events in the rearview mirror.

"The year I applied to my first music festival," Margot told her in a low, deliberate voice, "no one thought I'd get in. I was seventeen. My parents, my classmates, none of my relatives. Worse, nobody understood *why* I'd want to go so far away. They were insulted by my need to leave. I wanted more than what they had."

Eva came towards her, listening.

"My applying had nothing to do with them," she explained. "It was for me. I wanted to see if I could get in. I had to audition by video. It wasn't so easy then, with no smart phones. You needed a video camera, a tripod, good light and sound, and quality tapes. I asked the city symphony conductor to help me."

"Did you get in?"

"I did. My grandmother paid my airfare."

"Were you glad you went?"

"Yes I was. It changed my life."

Eva moved towards the edge of the deck, satisfied with the story. Of course, there was more to it. Margot did not regret that festival, but what happened there was unexpected, certainly. On this cool spring night, speaking to a lost twenty-year-old, the secret she had made of her abortion seemed wrong. Not telling anyone made it pulse like a magnet, drawing every other accomplishment into it. Eva had made the same mistake. She couldn't keep her son a secret, but she'd done everything in her power to keep the father unknown, as if Birdie was something she decided to do, without consulting anyone else or asking for help.

The paternity test results were the reason Eva had come out here. She wanted her money. They said it would take a week; it had only been three days. She could have called. The girl wouldn't have driven all this way if she wasn't confident what the results would be. Margot felt a sudden chill. Her injured arm hung heavy. She felt she'd been on her feet for hours.

To the east, headlights appeared, aimed at the house. Pip's ride. Margot called him and Birdie, who made their way back up the hill. The whole party entered the house, climbed the stairs, and passed through the front door to the driveway. While Margot spoke to Pip's father, Eva buckled Birdie in the car seat, then got in, started her engine. She lingered. Margot came closer, arms crossed against the chill. She could not speak, didn't want to know what it was Eva was waiting for. She saw her hands gripping the steering wheel. Such small fingers!

"It looks good," she said.

Margot was confused; she couldn't see Eva's eyes. The car was in gear, moving backwards.

"Your hair," Eva called.

Margot's hand went up to touch it. She stood a long time watching the car bounce down the lane.

The Symphony Spring Gala was held in the Baxter, a grand hotel built during the railroad boom. Sturdy and graceful, the ballroom had marble pillars wider than old fir trees. The chandeliers dripped with crystals, casting low, glamorous light on the women in their gowns. In the corner, a jazz quartet played. Satterfield and Gloria stood in the lobby greeting all comers. Gloria was dressed in her usual drapey lavender, complete with chiffon shawl. "Oh Margot, you poor dear," she gushed dramatically. "How do you stand it? To be on your own, and in pain, on top of it."

"No pain anymore, Gloria," Margot said lifting her arm to shoulder height. "I'm a month out of surgery. Getting stronger every day!"

As she walked away to find her table, Satterfield followed, whispering in her ear, "Be nice. No matter what happens."

She stood in line at the bar, took her mojito to circle the room, casing the tables for her seat assignment. The Bakers had not yet arrived. Only Angela Gold was at the table, a first violin. She appeared to have four sponsors, which Margot commented upon. Angela pointed out they all had the same surname, so two were probably children. She was right. They appeared within the half hour, a couple of women sharing food from a small plate and their teenage children. Angela Gold asked if either of the children played violin. They did not, though one of the mothers had played viola in middle school orchestra. The girl played clarinet and marched with the band; the boy was a pianist. The family sponsored a string player to broaden their horizons.

Still the Bakers didn't come. Satterfield turned on the microphone to announce that people should take their seats for the first course, they still had thirty minutes to bid on items.

A boisterous group of people moved closer and got louder; the couple at the center of the hubbub announced with glee that this was their table, they were Annie and Ethan Baker. Margot stood up and, reaching out both hands, started to explain about her injury but it was too late. Mr. Baker took hold of her right palm and gave it a vigorous pump. Margot gasped, letting her hand go limp and still he didn't let go. When he finally did she had to physically turn away, a hand slapped over her collarbone.

"Oh!" cried Angela Gold. "She's injured!"

There were apologies. Margot nodded and grimaced as introductions continued. The Bakers took a long time to sit down. Mr. Baker kept speaking, even after Margot sat, and the women with their polite children, and finally the violinist. Mrs. Baker touched his elbow. He met her gaze, lowered his volume and sat. His grin remained wide and his color high as he finished saying how happy they were to finally meet Margot Fickett, whose name and picture they'd seen for so many months. He did not mention seeing her actually play, which meant the Bakers were the sort who sponsored the orchestra but did not listen to it. It wasn't that unusual, though most people who wanted a tax write-off didn't come to the gala. If they did, they usually confessed, blaming hearing impairment or scheduling conflicts. Satterfield taught his players that if they gave, you thanked them, no exceptions.

Mr. Baker did not confess, nor did he cover his tracks with tactful silence. He doomed himself with a loud toast for the table. "Annie and I are so happy to be supporters of this terrific band!"

"Band!" cried the teenaged boy.

Angela Gold smothered a smile. His sister chortled. The woman with shorter hair glared at the teens in admonishment.

"We really are pleased to meet you, Mrs. Fickett," said Annie Baker. The shawl she was wearing fell down to the crook of her elbow, revealing a sculpted shoulder.

"Please, call me Margot. I so appreciate the sponsorship," Margot said politely. "You surely know how much the symphony depends on people like you, long time patrons of the arts."

Annie Baker looked pleased that Margot knew they weren't first-timers. Ethan Baker picked up his drink, eyeing his wife over the rim of his glass. The plates were being served on the far side of the room. Soon the silent auction would close, winners would be announced and the whole evening would be over. If Margot was going to say anything, it had to be now. Her mind went blank. How did you interview people without being obvious? *I actually know your daughter. Funny thing.* She leaned forward and asked what the Bakers did for work.

"I'm a personal trainer," said Annie Baker. "You know Annie's Studio, in the Rock Creek Commons? That's me, I'm Annie!"

Margot said she knew it, then worried Annie would try to recruit her. She started to ask about the New Leaf, but how would that look, a cello player asking about a pot dispensary? She could say she'd read about it, but why that one and not another? The interest itself would be a mark against her. Legal or not, the stigma remained. Even in Deaton, people weren't always as liberal as they thought themselves to be.

"Do you have children?" she asked, sipping her mojito.

Annie Baker spoke of a son at Stanford medical school, a brother Eva had failed to mention. Mr. Baker beamed. There was a pause. She watched them exchange glances.

"And you?" asked Mrs. Baker.

Astonishing! They weren't even going to mention Eva.

"I have a son," Margot said. "Benji. He's studying music at St. Thomas in Minnesota. He graduated from West High." She mentioned his class year and the Bakers both sat up straighter.

"He must know our daughter," said Mr. Baker. "Eva was in that class!"

Margot smiled, feeling smart. Now they were getting somewhere. "Benji played music. Mostly he knew other musicians. Was your daughter a musician?"

Annie Baker's expression grew strained. She shook her head. Mr. Baker looked at his drink but did not pick it up. Margot's heart started to pound. She thought, Benji could rob a bank and I'd still claim him. I'd still *talk* about him.

"What does your daughter do?" she pressed.

"She works in town," said Annie, picking up her water glass. "Sadly, we couldn't get her to go to college. Circumstances became such that—"

"We still have hope!" interrupted Mr. Baker. "She's a very bright girl. With a lot to offer." He smiled weakly at his wife.

The teenagers, sensing parental treachery, listened and watched.

"They do have minds of their own," said Margot with a glance at the young people. "We don't always get a say."

She picked up her drink, waiting. Annie leaned over; Margot thought maybe she was picking up her purse, would pull out a photo, but she was only adjusting her shoe strap. Mr. Baker touched his tie. The Bakers weren't going to mention their grandson.

Was she being too hard on them? Her own repugnance came to mind, how appalling she found the idea of being a grandparent. She imagined telling Eva about this. *They didn't even speak of him!* Eva would nod excitedly. *I told you they were pricks!* But under the excitement there would be sorrow, that particular kind reserved for parents who didn't understand their offspring. Margot felt sorry for her own mother and father, who were happy for her but did not understand her ambition. Only her grandmother understood. After her abortion, sorrow came to that relationship, too, for she would have never accepted such a decision, and therefore was never told. Her grandmother had always maintained that self-pity was the artist's enemy, because it robbed you of the energy to try. The secret remained between them until her death, a fact that Margot hated.

The servers were approaching with the plates of beef and potatoes. The

Bakers stood up to go to the bar. Angela's couple also went for drinks. The teenagers were looking at their phones. Margot looked across the room to find Satterfield. He wasn't at this table but in the far corner, sitting with a young woman who looked familiar. Briefly he put his arm around the back of her chair to say something that made them both laugh.

"That's Collette Smith," said Angela Gold, following Margot's gaze. "It's been going on all spring."

"A violinist?"

"Flute."

Margot felt a fluttering in her throat as if she might cry. She thought of that day they walked on campus, how he'd cleaned up. She felt a flush of envy. Margot glanced around for Gloria, spotted her at a table full of people, pretending not to watch Douglas and the flutist. He was in for a rough ride home. As if he'd heard Margot's thoughts, Douglas suddenly turned, looked directly at her. She studied her lap, her plate. When she looked back, Satterfield was still watching her. He adjusted his tie and headed for the stage to announce the auction winners.

Nineteen

The following Monday, Margot's cello student Josiah brought in her mail, leaving it on the phone table in the foyer, where it sat all through the lesson. When he had gone, Margot tossed it on the bed while she changed into hiking clothes. Then she sat, sifting through the shopping circulars and catalogs and bills until she came to a formally typed letter. Ripping it open, she scanned the letter three times without really reading, looking for the one word that would settle this for good: *Negative*. Instead, she found her full name and date of birth, Benjamin's full name and date of birth. The unusual specimen had proven successful; the lab was able to get good DNA from the toothbrush bristles. Here was Birdie's full name and date of birth, and the word that did indeed settle the matter: *Positive*. A 99.9 % match in the genetic line.

Benji was a father.

Margot's hands trembled. She lowered herself into the chair by the window, cranking it open. Air whistled through the crack and the letter was swept off her lap. She watched the paper shoot sideways on its crease, landing under the bed.

She drifted into Benji's room and sat facing the bookshelves. A pressure squeezed her chest, a caving in. She was about to cry. Foolish to weep over a lost child, as if you'd ever stop them from growing. Yet once they matured and left the enchanted forest, the whole family was evicted. When Benji was little, Margot thought of him as limitless, dreamed of his future. Once innocence was over, his flaws took precedence. His disinterest in school. This preoccupation with his band. Now, fatherhood.

On the shelves in front of her sat several picture books and an X-wing fighter made of Legos. These were the only fossils of his childhood. Everything else was music related: biographies of composers, sheet music, an old tuner, the complete score of the William Tell Overture, which he'd learned to play in high school. Music, the mighty distracter. If he'd had more time to read or become obsessed with Legos, would he *not* be a father? Was it music that clouded his judgment? Had it clouded hers? If an individual was not well-rounded, if he tended towards obsession and pursued an art, was his judgment in other areas—sex and love, for instance—necessarily impaired?

Ridiculous. Where was it written that a sexual awakening must be delicate? Did anyone experience the loss of innocence as a sweet, gauzy deflowering? She recalled the burden of virginity. The shocking physicality of sex. Those first tries with Nigel felt like a failed experiment. Once they got the hang of it, how naughty it felt! Up all night in the dorm room, then seeing each other the next day in rehearsal, remembering all that they'd done to one other, a private, delicious shame. The pregnancy was a different chapter, a whole separate book. Benji's fate now looked similar. The somber hall of adulthood stretched before him.

Margot hiked. The day was warm. She wore only a sweatshirt and by the time she reached the cliff top she tied it around her waist, letting the sun hit her arms, which would mean a burn. She didn't care. The motion of putting one foot in front of another, the warmth on her back and arms soothed her nerves, allowed her to breathe. She followed the route she took most every day in the summer, all the way to the property line. That wasn't far enough. She wasn't ready to stop, so she lay on her back and scooted under the fence. Her injured arm hindered her—a barb caught her shirt sleeve and tore it. The north slope was still covered in snow. Halfway down she slipped and slid twenty feet but managed to remain standing. She came to a halt, her feet soaked, pants wet to the knee. Imagining the disaster if she'd fallen, she admitted the extended hike was a bad idea and turned around.

On the rim above the house she stood for long time with the binoculars, looking for the owlets. She found the nest and felt a tightening in her chest. Empty. No sign of the mother owl. This development worried her beyond all proportion. Of course they were not dead—what could hunt a great horned owl? They had fledged was all, as they were supposed to do. Still, she hurried down the stone steps to the deck determined to call Andy. He must be informed. The owls were his project. He'd found them last February and checked the nest every day since. He would want to know.

Inside, she dug her cell phone out of the basket on the kitchen counter. He answered with an anxious, "What's wrong?"

"Nothing," she said.

The word was a grievous understatement. Bordered on a lie. It *was* a lie. The phone shook in her hand.

"You must be doing push-ups by now," he said, "Pumping iron."

"I'm fine. Better. I can lift my bow to shoulder height."

His joke felt inappropriate, as did the ensuing stories about shutting down clubs in Eugene, Oregon. Dancing students overturning tables. Finally he asked how Margot was filling her days. He phrased it like that. Not *How are you?* or *Why did you call when you never call?* He was careful, trying to help her get to what she wanted to say. It didn't help. She felt unhinged. She didn't know how she'd been filling her days. She'd lost contact with reality, like an astronaut floating untethered on the outer rim.

"The owls are gone," she blurted. "I searched all the branches. There's no sign of them."

"Flew the nest?"

"I guess. I don't hear them at night."

"Moved up higher, I bet," he said. After a pause he asked, "Am I on speaker phone? You sound so far away. Margot?"

She didn't say anything.

"Margot? Margot!"

Still she didn't answer, letting him think they'd been disconnected.

Margot took days to decide what to actually do. She kept trying to sell herself on the idea that being a grandmother was no big deal. So what if you had a grandson? This wasn't a death sentence. Accidents happened, she knew too well. You wanted your kid to be happy, at least, that's what everybody said. But it wasn't quite true. What you really wanted was for them to be happy doing *something you approved of.* Who could approve of this? An unemployed, impetuous girl with family issues. A little boy, a darling, perfect boy—a *child!*

She listened to her beloved Russians: Prokofiev, Rachmaninoff, Tchaikovsky. The mental handwringing would not abate. It followed her into lessons, into her headphones, even into sleep.

At the end of the week, Margot shampooed her hair and blew it dry. She put on her new dress, black, with a wide neck, and a cardigan to hide the scar. She drove to town, headed for the bank. The thought of the tellers deterred her. They all knew her, would surely comment on such a hefty withdrawal. She couldn't bear the idea of what they might say, something inane like, *Going on a trip?* Instead, she made several withdrawals at different banks, stuffing the cash in a plastic grocery bag. She meant to find Eva. Together they would deliver the money to Dutch, ensuring that the girl got her share of the profit, as promised.

Eva wasn't home. A sad looking 'For Sale By Owner' sign had been stabbed in the front lawn. She supposed they were at McLeod Park. The New Leaf was closer. She decided to check there first. In the east, deep blue night was already on its way. Birds roosted. Traffic thinned in that pause before a Friday night.

She drove to the back of the building and felt a jump in her chest. Eva's car wasn't here, but Dutch's Charger was. She pulled in next to it. Almost immediately, the door to the shop opened and Sully stepped out, lighting a cigarette. Margot sat still behind the wheel, understanding that there was no backing out now.

He walked over to her window, saying through the glass, "Mrs. Fickett?"

She rolled down the window and said, "I brought Eva's money."

He looked past her to the bag in the passenger seat. He rubbed his face, astonished. "Do you want me to take it? I could give it to Dutch."

Margot knew he wouldn't steal from Eva. He loved her, she'd seen that at once. He had an apologetic face, not sorry for himself but for the world. Something about him felt quiet, not insecure or shy, but reluctantly wise.

How such a man could be a soldier was a mystery.

"I need to see him," she said. Another lie. Weeks later, Margot would trace her actions back to this moment and decide here was her biggest mistake.

Sully hesitated, assessing. The light from the setting sun made his face boyishly pink, revealing his freckles. His shoulders slumped as he said, "I'll send him out."

Margot rolled up the window, grabbed the bag and got out. She waited by the Charger, feeling a cartwheel in her chest. The door swung open.

"My lucky day!" Dutch cried, clapping, smiling wide. "I woke up this morning and I *knew* I'd see you! I just *knew* it!"

Margot smirked, enduring his wolfish stare as he took in her dress.

"What's in the bag?" he asked. "Are we having a sleepover?"

"Eva's money," she said, handing it over. "Your money."

He stood still a second, eyes wide, then took the bag, peering inside. "Five thousand dollars?"

"She's in," Margot said. "She gets a portion of your profit. Or crop. Whatever your terms were."

He took another step closer and his smile suddenly widened; the amber in his eyes shone in the evening light. "One condition," he said. "Come out with me tonight. Right now."

"That was not part of the—"

"Terms changed." He held up the bag of money. "We hit the town. Have some fun. And then Eva gets to profit share."

Dutch was already digging in his pants pocket for his keys. He unlocked the Charger and hurried over to open the passenger door, throwing the bag of money in the backseat.

"Party time!" he called.

A cottony muffle of anxiety welled up in her mind. She was aware of the snaky thrill of his gaze as he waited, then finally said, "Margot?" holding out his hand as if a chariot awaited her.

This is a terrible idea, she thought, lowering herself inside. He closed the door. The windows felt high and narrow, as if this were a gangster car from the twenties. He grinned as he climbed in and started the engine, which made the seats vibrate. He reached in front of her to open the glove compartment, took out a pipe and a canister.

"Medicine," he said, arching an eyebrow.

She looked away as he packed the pipe. She had not smoked dope in twenty years. She could refuse cleverly: *Advil is strong enough for me!* Refusal would be like going to Disneyland and not riding the rides. Dutch lit the pipe and his lips, the sloppy flame, the sucking sound of his inhale, embarrassed her. His exhale coiled between them as he passed her the pipe. She took it, worried he'd try to instruct but he didn't. He gazed out the window, offering privacy. She took the smallest sip of air, trying not to cough. The smoke felt light and smooth. Her lungs seized but she didn't cough. She took another small inhale, implicated now.

Dutch took another two hits and set the pipe in the console, put the car in gear and backed out. Margot stopped herself from asking should he be driving, which would be like saying she needed to be back by ten. He revved the engine, let the tires squeal as he pulled into traffic, headed south.

Twenty

Margot's awareness moved in and out. They seemed to cover several blocks, even miles, in hardly any time. Beyond town, along the Bitterroot River, the houses were more spread out. Dusk had fallen. Their headlights were on, as were lights in the houses. Dutch reached out and pressed several buttons on the stereo until he found a song he liked, something pulsing and rhythmic that perfectly matched the road, the twilight, the sense of descent.

Lolo came and went. The road narrowed, becoming curvy as they entered the foothills. He put on another song, seemed full of music, could produce any song to match the mood. He was a man in control of his surroundings. She felt what he wanted her to feel, and right now that was out of sorts, slight fear masked by aloof amusement. Also, a deep sensation of beauty. Not a noticing, but a feeling. The dissociation was not unfamiliar. It was like crossing campus at dusk, seeing the rise of starlings. Or noticing the slant of afternoon light across a wild field, hearing the hiss of grass in the wind—these liminal places where time sunk and spun away.

"How you feeling?" Dutch asked, shouting over the music.

Margot cracked the window. "Stoned," she said.

He laughed. "Nice, isn't it? Mellow. And your injury?"

The wind whipped his hair as smoke was sucked from his mouth. She had forgotten the fracture. For the first time in over a month she'd failed to think of herself as injured. He began to laugh. Margot, too, began to laugh and couldn't stop, even when her stomach ached from it.

They pulled into the gravel parking lot of an old saloon, shaped like a large cabin with a peaked roof and a covered porch. On the hill behind the place cabins were scattered, an unincorporated enclave around a bar in the woods. They had gained elevation. Margot could see her breath as they approached the door. The porch steps were made of railroad ties. Already frost was forming in the cracks. A hand-lettered sign nailed to the railing read *Bruno's*.

"Ready?" Dutch grinned, taking her good arm in his hand.

She smiled, feeling the portent. The door opened on a hinge. He let it slap behind them. Heads turned their way. A ripple went through the room. Margot felt it like a soundwave. People sat up straighter, snatching glances. The light was warm, the music not too loud. These people could have been turn-of-the-century gold miners. The wall behind the bar was a mirror framed with ornately turned wood. Above that, lining the room, were the heads of stuffed ungulates: moose, elk, antelope, and deer.

The bartender, presumably Bruno himself, shook Dutch's hand as he and Margot sat on the short side of the bar. Dutch ordered two martinis. He glanced in the mirror, nodding at people. His phone rang and he took the call, turning away from her. Margot looked in the mirror, didn't recognize herself, a woman almost fifty. Her flushed face. Her dark, shorter hair.

She studied the population around her. Grizzled, bearded men sat next to ranchers in Carhartt jackets. Several tables were pushed together for a group of college kids in T-shirts and trucker's caps. The few women were dressed in outdoor boots, wore no makeup and looked like lumberjacks. Margot touched the edge of her yellow cardigan, wished she had a coat.

Dutch watched her, smiling. Their drinks had appeared and he raised his glass, saying,

"I love tall women. You know why? You can wear anything you want."

This was so unexpected that Margot laughed, a shocked, loud bark.

"I'm serious," he said. "The cowboyed-up Montana girl look suits you just as well as this prim sweater. I could see you in a velvet gown, on stage, playing your cello."

She never wore velvet, but didn't say this. He stood, held out his hand. Some invisible signal had been given. They were changing seats. He walked close to her. People watched as they crossed the room. Unlike walking with Satterfield, which made Margot feel regal, safe and powerful, walking with Dutch made her anxious. She felt a sense of inadequacy about the picture they made: she was taller, more sophisticated, and yet she somehow knew that in this crowd, she was the one who didn't measure up.

They passed under the closer archway that opened to a huge back room and stepped into the intimate hold of a booth along the back wall, across from one another. There was a stage nearby—most of the room was a dance floor.

A man approached, a Deaton college kid, judging from his gray sweater and young face. They greeted one another as Dutch took something out of his coat pocket and set it on the booth bench. Neither of them looked at it but the young man leaned over and put his hand over it. An exchange. After him it was an older cowboy. Now that they were seated, it was like he was open for business. He had to make a trip out to his car. A stream of friends, each collecting an unacknowledged parcel. Margot sipped her drink. Food arrived, though she didn't remember ordering. She cut into her steak and fries, hungry.

When Dutch returned from the parking lot the second time, Margot asked, "Is what you're doing legal?"

He laughed, unwrapping his silverware. "Almost."

"What is it?" she asked. "Tell me it isn't something that will rot these people's teeth and turn them into wretches."

"Pot, Margot. Tincture, mostly. A little grass."

Grinning, shameless, he placed a forkful of steak into his mouth, chewing with gusto.

"Have you always done this?"

He swallowed, picked up his fresh martini. "Done what?"

"Dealt drugs."

He ducked his head, pretending to choke.

"Cocaine is a drug. Meth and crack are drugs," he laughed. "I sell pot."

He sipped his drink, set it down and smiled at her. "Yes, I've done it a long time. Successfully. You should come to my place in southern California. I have a pool. Cabana bar. I'd love to see you there, in a swimsuit, big sunglasses, sipping from a straw. Live like royalty. My trophy wife."

Nothing about him suggested he was kidding. He was hunched forward, excited, like he was actually seeing this scenario, Margot in designer gowns.

A *trophy*? She was embarrassed but her eyelids felt heavy with pleasure, picturing it. *What color bathing suit*? she wondered.

The corner door by the stage opened, letting in the cold air. The band entered, hauling equipment. Night had closed in. Like animals emerging from the woods, people filled the bar. Dutch and Margot worked their way through their second drinks and she stopped trying to hide how much she was enjoying herself. Royalty, he had said. Traffic to their booth slowed as the band warmed up. They leaned towards one another to be heard. Dutch suddenly took her hand.

"Show it to me," he said. "Your wound."

Her smile faded a little.

"I'm serious. I want to see it."

"You're sick."

He locked eyes with her. People didn't tease Dutch, she saw.

"Take off your sweater."

Heat crept up her neck as she slowly obeyed. She freed her right arm first, sliding the sleeve down her weakened arm, its first public appearance. She pulled the sweater around her back and down her left arm so she was sitting there in her scoop neck dress, letting him look. The scar was red and raised where it crawled from her neck to her shoulder, taped with only four fresh steri-strips.

"Jesus," he said. "It's long."

"You haven't asked how it happened."

"I know how it happened," he said. "Skiing. You were in Big Sky, over spring break. With your husband."

She didn't contradict this, even made an effort to look impressed. She picked up her sweater but Dutch said, "Don't. Leave it off."

She put it down and picked up her martini.

"How does it feel?" he asked, "After you smoked?"

"It's tight. I can tell it's broken."

"But it doesn't hurt," he said, smiling.

It was true. No pain. Her entire body felt distant from her mind, not an unpleasant feeling. Dutch picked up his drink.

"Are you going to tell me what Eva's got on you?"

She looked at him, felt the lazy weight of her eyelids. "Why don't you like her?"

"She's a poser," he said without hesitation. "Spoiled rich girl who wants to make her life a little less boring."

"Isn't that how you just described me?" Margot asked with a laugh. "Skiing in Big Sky?"

He gave a sly grin. "Am I right?"

"No, smartass, you are not."

"You're not married?"

"I am," she said. She leaned towards him, a grin curling the side of her mouth. "But I don't ski."

Amusement spread over his face, beginning in his eyes, reaching his mouth last. She heard his laughter, felt it ringing in her head, mixing with her own.

"Did some girl do that to you?" she asked him. "Use you to spice up her life?"

"Please, no dime-store head shit," he cried, holding up his hands in defense.

"You think you'll teach her," Margot pressed.

He grew still, lowered his hands.

"You probably *like* making women do what they don't want to do."

"I give women what's good for them," Dutch said, swallowing the rest of his drink.

Margot sat back. Dutch reached into his coat pocket and pulled out his cigarettes. There were no ashtrays. No one else was smoking, but he lit up anyway. A waiter approached. Dutch gave him a cold, level stare and said to Margot, "I don't care if she's stringing Sully along, wants to piss off her parents. I don't care if Sully sells kiddie porn so long as his focus stays where it should be. On my crop."

Standing at their table, the waiter stammered. "There's no smoking. I'll have to ask you to put that out." Dutch dropped his cigarette into his water where it gave a lethal hiss. He handed it to the waiter.

Margot excused herself, hoping to sober up, maybe figure out a way to wrap this up. She had to pass into the other room, which was now crammed with people. Sober, it would have crushed her, but pushing through the crowd she picked up on the merriment around her, felt buoyant, in charge. Passing the last table before the hall to the restroom, she stopped. There was

Satterfield, leaning over his plate to speak to his date, the flutist Collette Smith. He didn't see her but Collette did. She froze and Satterfield turned.

"Douglas?"

"Margot!" he cried, wild-eyed with shock. He stood up to kiss her cheek, looking behind her. "What on earth—how did you end up here of all places?"

She laughed. Couldn't stop laughing. To have caught him here was suddenly hilarious. Bruno's, discreet and lawless. She'd found his hideout.

"That looks awful," Collette shouted, eyeing the wound. Her tight, flutist lips.

"I thought I'd air it out." Margot, too, shouted to be heard. "Wreck people's appetites."

Satterfield asked again where she was sitting.

"With a friend," Margot said, gesturing loosely. "I won't keep you."

"What friend?"

Both Margot and Colette looked at him. She backed away, waving. On her return, she made a point not to pass them, pushing through the crowd towards the front door, intending to enter the back room through the other arch. The crowd jostled her down the bar to where they had begun the night.

Dutch had returned to the same stool. Draped on his shoulder was a young blond woman in a low-cut dress, not at all the lumberjack sort. She was the kind of woman that showed up later, when the night heated up. From the stage in the back room came the sound of a twanging bass. Margot was close enough to speak to them but turned abruptly. She wished for her sweater to cover up. She started to push her way back into the crowd, but a hand wrapped around her wrist. It didn't yank or pull, just held on.

"Margot," Dutch said, and she turned.

His eyes were softer now, almost reassuring. He lifted her hand to his mouth, pressing his lips along her knuckles. The younger woman faded into the crowd as Dutch slid off his stool, leading Margot back to their table like a pet.

He slid onto the bench beside her in their booth and pulled something out of his coat pocket, set it on the table. A cookie, a Mexican wedding cookie.

"What's that?" she shouted.

He leaned over and said in her ear, "Dessert."

She looked at it. He picked it up, broke it in two and popped half in his mouth. She took the other half and ate it, a sweet, crumbly confection with a grassy aftertaste. They chewed, looking at each other. He grinned, put his arm around her neck and pulled her face close to his. The kiss was long and lingering. His tongue moved around her mouth with curiosity.

She opened her eyes, just as the explosive, deafening guitars began. An electric keyboard and a heavy drum pounded through the amplifier not five feet from them. Margot covered her ears, on the verge of panic until the other instruments stopped for a fiddle. A woman about her own age, hair up, arm flying. No one sang. It wasn't pop or rock or country but a blend of all three. The fiddle player had skill. The others let her lead, making a mournful yet danceable tune. What a mystery music was! Without words, no definitive meaning, yet the mood was easy to read: longing and joy, the strangest blend, so unapologetically sad it made you happy. Margot began to smile as the tempo increased and people began to tap their toes. Then the whole floor was bouncing in time with it, people joined at the elbows, spinning each other.

Dutch had gone. She scanned the room but couldn't see him. His absence was as intense as his presence, as if he never was. Had she come on her own, landed here, just to see these people play?

The night moved at odd intervals—slow at times, and then with great speed. The buoyancy did not wane. The singer was the guitar player, a tenor with a full head of hair and good enunciation but she couldn't make out the words. The guitar ran over his voice. It didn't matter, the fiddle had the melody. Who cared what it meant? The room sparkled. The people were loveable—cowboys, college kids, and hippies together.

Someone asked her to dance, and the injured cello player, feeling no pain, said yes. She shouted in her partner's ear that she could not move her right arm. By the third song, she stopped announcing this, swinging it high, circling her partner or sashaying around him. Another song began and she turned to find Satterfield behind her, his face red and merry. They laughed when their hands touched, both sweaty and drunk. Margot saw Collette pouting by the wall and this made her laugh harder.

After midnight, the band took a break. Recorded music was piped through the speakers. People danced on. Margot came out of the bathroom, pushing through the crowded front room when she saw Dutch seated at a small round table. A bearded man stood talking to him while a woman and man sat opposite. The woman was dark-haired and small. The seated man had his back to Margot, angled slightly with both hands under the table, like a child waiting for dinner. Margot stopped. Something was off about the picture. Dutch's face lacked all trace of amusement. He didn't look angry, either. The closer she got the more his expression alarmed her. It looked like fear.

The seated man's hands moved in his lap and Margot caught the glint of metal. Her spine stiffened. The sweat on her bare shoulders suddenly cooled, as if someone had opened a window. She turned around, pushing her way back into the other room, to their booth where she stood a second, thinking. She picked up her sweater and bag, turned and scanned the room for Satterfield. She made her way to where he'd been sitting, but they were gone. Mild panic rumbled in her gut. If he'd been here, he would have insisted she come home with them. She would have left Dutch, she realized. If the situation were reversed, Dutch would do the same. Her certainty of this, looking back, should have been a warning. Neither of them trusted the other, and this ought to have meant more, prevented all that was to come. She might even have got her money from his car. There was a pay phone by the bathroom. She could have waited the hour it would have taken for a ride. Or just called the police.

But that wasn't the way it happened. She did something stupid. Even dangerous. She put on her sweater and shoved her way through the crowd to the bar, keeping an eye on the table. Even the wait staff was giving them a wide berth. Margot put her bag over her shoulder, ran both hands through her hair and bounded over to the foursome like a drunk co-ed, squealing, "Dutch! *Dance* with me, Dutch!"

The voice that came out her mouth was high-pitched and overdone. People were staring. The bearded man grabbed her forearm—her left, thank god; she was able to twist out of his grip. Pulling Dutch by the lapels of his jacket, she practically lifted him out of his chair. The woman made a sound resembling a growl. The bearded one made another attempt to grab her. Margot shrieked. Heads turned. She laughed and hopped around Dutch, a giraffe on speed. His hand gripped her waist, pushing her. He was hopping too, laughing, his mouth wide open in over-blown pantomime of hilarity as she led him to the back room where the horrid recorded music blared.

In the archway, she glanced over her shoulder. The bearded man and the woman were following them. The man with the gun stayed seated, his face awash with rage. They rounded the corner and Dutch grabbed her good arm by the wrist, running, shoving people out of their way. People glared. Some cursed or shoved them back. Margot was screaming at him, crushed and pulled, not feeling a thing. He charged on through the crowd towards the stage door, which he pushed open. They tumbled out into the shocking silence of snow.

They were in a small space along the side wall of the kitchen. Stacks of outdoor chairs sat collecting snow, like white totems. Dutch sprinted, pulling her, both their feet slipping in the slush. They ran to the back of the building where a dumpster sat with its mouth open. A prep cook smoking by the kitchen door jumped when they came around the corner and shot past. Dutch's Charger was on the far side of the lot. He was shouting at her to fasten her seatbelt before she had the door closed. He seemed to have the car in gear before he started the engine, was already in reverse before he'd turned the key.

Dutch gunned the engine, spraying slush and gravel over the parked cars. As they flew past the front porch the two men and the woman were jumping off it. Margot saw the gun—*it really was a gun*—when the younger man lifted it to aim.

"Get down!" yelled Dutch as the thing went off, louder than possible. People screamed, leaping off the porch like falling dominos. Margot let her torso fall forward, head between her knees and stayed there as he fishtailed onto the highway, her seatbelt digging into her fracture. She felt sick.

There was a back way to Lolo, he was saying, but if he took it they would see his tracks in the snow. He cursed, pounding the steering wheel. Margot sat up. He took one look at her and stomped on the brakes, reaching over to open her door. Vomit hit the pavement with a splat. She felt the snow and slush hit her in the face, a relief. Pulling the door with both hands, she shrieked, "Go!"

Dutch floored the gas, and again they fishtailed on the wet highway. Margot put her head back on the seat rest. Dutch was howling with laughter, cackling like an animal.

"Thank you for not puking in my car!" he cried. "Thank you for getting me out of there!"

He pounded the steering wheel again, cursing and laughing. Her head was still plastered against the seat back. She wondered if it was even snowing in Deaton, or if this was just a local storm.

"Margot! Where'd you learn to move like that? *Fuckin*-A!" he cried, slapping the dashboard.

She held onto the seatbelt to keep it from sawing her collarbone. The snow came straight at them. They were going fast. And how funny. Shot at. She had a vague sense that she was laughing. "My hero!" he cried. Ahead were the lights of Lolo. She was right about the snow. The next time she looked, they were speeding along the river and it had stopped.

Twenty-one

A commercial harvest took days and required gloves. Even with no skin contact, after twenty-four hours Sully felt he was clawing his way out of a heavy sleep. He didn't like not touching every flower himself, knowing each leaf was properly cut, trichomes saved for kief or to make hash, butter or juice.

Dutch's new hires were two Hispanic brothers, Tristan and Carlos. Paid in weight, they weren't big talkers. Only yesterday Sully had arrived to find them leaning against the tree planter, no visible means of transportation. They each had an intricate beard, and both had full forearm tattoos. They stood up when Sully got out of his truck. He braced for trouble until the taller one stepped on his cigarette and held out a hand. He said in accented English, "We work for Dutch."

When Sully unlocked the shop, the men walked straight into the grow room and grabbed gloves. They had their own trimmers. Without asking for permission or direction, they chose a row and got to work cutting the larger leaves and gently placing them in trays to cure.

So it went, row by row. Marvin joined them and the college crew came at noon. Sully didn't like the strangers, their private language and their dark, watchful eyes, but the company wasn't bad. The crew worked straight through the night, sharing the exhaustion and jumpiness. Well into their first twenty-four hours together, Sully realized that this communal, giddy camaraderie was similar to being part of a platoon, a happy feeling. Late that night one of the brothers—he couldn't get their names straight—held up a three-millimeter bud, crying, "Holy shit!" All heads lifted. Faces lit. Laughter and thumbs up. Marvin whistled and snapped a photo.

In the morning, Sully came outside to smoke a cigarette and found a dusting of snow covering his truck. Judging from the light, it must be seven or eight in the morning. He saw Mrs. Fickett's Suburban still in the lot, also floured with white, meaning she'd been out all night with Dutch. She'd brought Eva's money and that should feel good, seeing Eva get justice, but the idea of Mrs. Fickett and Dutch made his guts churn.

Sully smoked, noting the absence of the white Tahoe. The agent was probably still in bed. Saturdays started slow in a college town, a fact he liked. The pace here suited him, even if the weather made you want to go home. He recalled a similar alien feeling to life overseas, where the days got so hot Sully wept. Crossing a courtyard alone, firearm slung over his back in one-hundred-fifteen degree heat was enough to make him sob to himself.

He wandered closer to Mrs. Fickett's Suburban, idly peering inside. He was stunned to see her body sprawled in back. "Jesus," he muttered, tossing his cigarette. He pulled open the door and put a hand on her shoulder, calling, "Mrs. Fickett?"

She opened her eyes and gasped. Sully jumped back. Mrs. Fickett tried to sit up, cried out in pain and rolled off the bench onto the floorboards. Her confused look, her ruffled hair, the impossibility of the situation struck him as funny.

"Holy shit!" he laughed. "*Somebody* had a rough night."

She glared. Sully swallowed his amusement. Mrs. Fickett turned her long body in an effort to get back onto the seat. The neck of her dress gaped. He saw half her breast.

"Here," Sully said, reaching in to put a hand under each of her arms. He lifted. Her legs scrambled like a colt's. Sitting up, she winced with pain, her injured arm held to her chest.

After a moment she raised her head, gave it a proud little shake to knock the hair out of her eyes. Sully knew nothing about classical music. He heard it in three-second intervals when the radio scanned past the station. But his idea of the people who played such music was not this.

"Are you okay?" he asked unable to help smiling.

In a gravelly voice, Mrs. Fickett told him, "I gave Dutch the money."

Sully had a near perfect poker face, he knew. Margot Fickett had a similar skill. Her face was blank, not a flicker in her eye or around her mouth.

"What did he say?"

Margot rubbed her eyes. "If I went out with him, Eva was in. She's a partner, or whatever you are calling it." She swallowed and met his eye. "Did you tell her I had the money?"

He shook his head. "I haven't seen her. I've been here all night."

"Is Dutch in there?"

"Haven't seen him."

She pursed her lips. Sully waited. He had no idea what she was thinking and hoped his expression was equally unreadable. He didn't like Dutch having that money, he realized. He'd invited Eva into this place, and now that the demands were met, he didn't like it. Last week she'd called him to help her move furniture. Eva had lost her mind a little since getting fired. Not once had she mentioned the New Leaf or Mrs. Fickett, as if investing with Dutch was yesterday's idea. Instead, she'd decided to sell her condo. She'd rented a space where she planned to open her shop. She wanted to start moving furniture over there, especially the mattress so they'd have someplace to sleep.

"Do you need anything?" he asked Mrs. Fickett.

"Water would be nice."

He held out a hand for her. She leaned on him as she swung her legs out the back door, pulled her body forward, wincing, and eased out. She stumbled a little and he caught her, felt her strong body under her clothes as they stood a second with her arm over his shoulder. She reeked of booze and cigarette smoke and faintly, vomit. When she had her balance, he let go, leading the way to the door. They walked inside, behind the counter and through the grow room. One by one the men looked up from their work. He took her into the back office and poured her a cup of water from the cooler. She knocked it back and held out the cup, which he refilled. She did that four times, wiped her mouth on the sleeve of her sweater and crumpled the cup.

From next door, came the thump of dance music and an amplified voice, barking cues. Mrs. Fickett and Sully locked eyes.

"Is that Mrs. Baker?"

He nodded. "You know her?"

"We've met," she said. "Thanks for the water." She started to leave, then turned to him. "This is harvest?"

"That's right."

"What happens next?"

"We'll let them cure. We've sold about half this crop in pre-orders."

"How much is that?"

He grinned. Like a landowner and his acreage, Sully didn't like to speak in specifics. "A lot," he said.

"Why did you need Eva's money, if the profit is going to be so high?"

"We don't need Eva's money. Dutch refused to loan her cash. He wanted her to pay, to make it fair."

They stood a second, gazing at the huge plants. The branches snaked along the lattice like a small grape arbor. Sully watched her take it in, admitting to a certain pride. He led her down the aisle to the waiting room. When he had shut the door, Mrs. Fickett spoke.

"Last night—there were people, a woman and two men. We were chased. They had a gun. People were screaming, running away."

Her left hand was shaking, he saw. "It was like a dream," she continued. "Or a game. I'm not making any sense."

"Tall guy with a beard?"

Her eyes widened. "Do you know him?"

Sully shook his head. "Where were you?"

"A saloon, out in the middle of nowhere."

"Bruno's," he said, and she nodded.

"Dutch was, all night long—what does he sell? Is it only pot?"

Sully's throat caught. He could see from her expression that she had no idea what she'd just told him. His mind crumpled into a fist. Of course the shady prick would be selling illegally, on the side.

"Did you see it, the product?" he asked.

She shook her head. Dread spread through him. He followed her outside. They stood in the brilliant morning sun next to her car. The shadow of the hawthorn's bare limbs stretched across her face. Arms crossed, elbows in her hands, she closed her eyes.

"Are you high, Mrs. Fickett?"

To his surprise, she opened her eyes and smiled. He had not once thought her beautiful, hadn't thought about her looks at all. Her smile was quite a sight. She had a wide, disarming mouth. Was not yet old. Once again she gave her hair the gentlest shake.

"I think I am. We ate a cookie."

"Those can be strong."

"We split it."

Suddenly embarrassed, Mrs. Fickett turned to her vehicle. He watched her get in, fumble around looking for her keys, then start the engine. He had a bad feeling, watching her drive away.

He didn't like Eva's McLeod Park idea either. She couldn't afford it, for one. That day they loaded her furniture, she had chattered on and on about the half dozen calls she'd received since she posted her place on Craigslist. She had three showings the next day, one that very evening.

"I know I'll get an offer," she said. "I bet I have one by the time he deposits my check."

"It'll still bounce." He heard his own pessimism, couldn't deny his irritation with how easy this shit came to her.

"Okay, Mr. Cheerful," she said, getting in the truck.

"Ignore me," he said, sliding behind the wheel. "I'm tired and crabby."

They rode across town in silence. In the rearview he watched a piece of baling twine whipping in the wind like an angry tail. Even then the bad feeling had begun, and that was before harvest, technically. The plants were in the dark phase of flowering, nutrients cut off, which was why Sully could be spared.

He followed Eva's directions to McLeod Park, not somewhere he'd ever been. When they got there, he saw why. It was full of hoity shops and restaurants, imported cars, people strolling in pale clothes, pretending the weather felt like spring. He parked and followed Eva to the vacant space; she already had a key, said a lease was imminent.

"Don't you love it?" she enthused and he nodded, smiling, just as she had done when he showed her his shop, months ago.

But he didn't love it. The place was not somewhere he would ever be at home. As they unloaded, people walked by the front window, stopping to stare, curious. In neighborhoods like this there were always curious people.

"Do you really like it, Sul?" Eva asked when they were through.

If he looked at her, she'd see he was lying. He said, "I do!" and faced the back. "It's perfect for you. A little high-end, compared to where you were."

"That's good, though," she said. "I can design houses, room by room. And I can wardrobe college girls!"

An interesting combination, he thought. In his experience, people who hired home designers wanted nothing to do with used furniture. Or college girls. But what *was* his experience? He knew nothing about this sort of thing.

"So, you'll live back there," he said, indicating the storage room. "And work out here."

"'Till I get going, yes," Eva said, brightening.

He smiled at her. "I've got to get back."

"Sure?" she stepped towards him. "Come in back and we can christen the mattress."

"Can't," he said, kissing her forehead. "We're almost there, babe. So close." He couldn't believe he was walking away from sex with her. He should be shot.

From McLeod Park, Sully drove to Paige's house. He hadn't seen her since she fired Eva. He was supposed to have Caity this weekend. He needed to rearrange their schedule for the harvest, but when he tried doing it on the phone, she hung up on him. The confrontation had to happen, might as well face it.

For three straight minutes after she opened the door he stood listening to her shrieking abuse. Every foul name she could think of. "Asshat" was new to him. He stood gazing at her, shoulders slumped, taking it, until she slammed the door on him. Caity's scared face appeared in the front window. He heard Paige shout at her, which pissed him off.

He walked around the house to the side gate. Her little yapping dog nipped his ankles. He kicked it, flattening it briefly. He crossed the patio and came in the sliding door to the kitchen. Paige was there, stunned. She picked up a coffee mug and hurled it. He caught it and kept coming until he had her cornered by the pantry. She was shrieking and Caity was behind him, crying, "Don't hurt her! Don't hurt her!"

He whipped around, dropped to his knees, immediately contrite. He put his hands on the sides of her small, earnest face. Her two front teeth were bigger than the others. He kissed her forehead, and told her he'd never hurt her or her mother. He rubbed his face and his hair, letting himself sit in front of her. Paige came out of the pantry and scooted behind him without a word. He explained to Caity that he'd be gone a few days—he'd be working and she would have to stay here.

"I'm not going anywhere," he told her, wiping away her tears. "Daddy is never going anywhere. I'll be back in a week to get you after school."

She nodded and he hugged her. The feel of her thin arms around his neck was more comforting than anything in his memory. He kissed her cheek and stood, picking up the mug he'd set on the floor. Paige leaned on the counter, watching.

"You've dated plenty of men," he said, putting the mug in the sink. "I don't know half of them."

"*Men*," she said, glaring. "Not children."

She didn't want him happy, Sully knew. Even if his girlfriend was the right age and didn't work for her, Paige would still be furious. He wasn't supposed to date. She could, but not him. This was understood for all six years since the divorce. He was supposed to remain devoted and quietly in love with her.

"What am I supposed to do with her after school?" Paige asked, switching off the water. "I have to work. I have no one to cover those hours."

"Aftercare," he said. "The Eagles."

"Eagles!" shouted Caity behind them, raising her fists. Sully grinned at her. Afterschool Eagles meant popcorn and kickball on dry days, Pop-Tarts and movies when it was wet.

"Afterschool Eagles is for—" Paige stopped herself and faced him finally. "It's basically no supervision. They let the kids run wild. That horrible woman, Mrs. Carpenter—"

"Paige," he said. "It's one week."

"It's awful." She raised her chin in defiance.

He turned away, unwilling to console her for a problem she created when she fired her only employee.

"It's what we've got," he said.

Back inside the shop, Sully sat on the stool a minute before rejoining the crew. He explored his bad feeling, admitting that the New Leaf was bigger than he wanted. Too many plants, too many lights, too many men. Sully had thought he wanted a big business, but it turned out he liked his home grow, his fifteen thousand dollars a year. His crammed, stinky trailer.

What was Dutch up to with Mrs. Fickett? What was Mrs. Fickett doing with Dutch? The little rooster side-selling meant he was effectively stealing from the business. On a hunch, Sully jumped up and went to the corner, crouching in front of the heating vent, which opened on a hidden hinge. This was a detail Dutch had come up with, a false front to a safe. Sully spun the combination, fingers moving quickly. What he saw inside took his breath away. Piles of bills, hundreds, mostly. Some fifties, some twenties. He removed one stack, set it on the floor and counted it. Fifty thousand dollars. There were at least four more like it. His throat was thick. He ran a hand through his hair, over his forehead and face, lowered himself to his knees. He put the pile back in the safe and drew his hand away taking a chunk of bills before he closed it again.

Sitting on the floor with his back against the safe, he stared at the bills in his lap, several thousand dollars. Through the windows across the room, he saw the clouds race across the morning sky. He could hear the thumping beat next door. He jumped to his feet and stuffed the money in his pocket, heading back to the grow room.

Twenty-two

The thaw was on for real. Mount Blackmore's white face began to look pocked with black earth. The foothills surrounding town emerged. And the wind blew. Not the warm chinooks of January, but a scouring April wind, spring's final weapon against winter. It blew the exposed detritus down empty streets and alleys, up against yard fences and into gutters. In other seasons, it might drop off at noon, but this one kept up for days, howling over rooftops and through city parks.

North of town in the canyons, the wind found narrow channels to knock up and down, throttling trees and shaking power lines with satisfying violence. Margot's head hurt and nothing about her physical self felt right. The appalling memories of being chased, being *shot* at, were made manifest by the weather, appropriately savage and dire. Could anyone find this fun, ingesting dope and having one's mind bend like a paperclip? Debauchery so intense it makes you throw up? She recalled buying the woman fiddler a drink during a set break. They were the same age, and she, like Margot and Andy, had a classical background. There was a vague memory of telling this woman the whole story, beginning with the accident, then Eva and Birdie, even the paternity test results. Margot was no storyteller. My god, the words, the sheer number of them, more than she'd spoken at once in her memory.

The adventure caused a setback in healing. She could no longer lift her bow to shoulder height without pain. All that dancing, swinging, and do-sidoing had put her back to square one. Forced to dig out the lightest Thera-band, Margot cancelled her lessons. She dragged a chair out to the deck, sat in the wind wrapped in a blanket. Satterfield left messages; she ignored them. She would have to speak to him or he'd show up at her door, but for now she took a vow of silence, one of Benji's inventions when they all lived together. The vow was used when someone was working on a difficult piece or needed rehearsal space or just had intense need for alone time. The vow gave you a ten-hour exemption from talking. If you needed to make a phone call, you walked up on the cliff with a cell phone. You fed yourself. You watched a movie in your room. You asked no questions, made no comments. Andy struggled with it, but to Benji and Margot such silence was lifesaving.

She had finally told Dutch about Benji being Birdie's father. Margot had no memory of the context for this confession, could not imagine what possessed her to reveal something so personal. She did, however, recall his response: *I thought God was the father.* Which was funny.

"Apparently not," she wisecracked.

This disgusted her now, the way she had adopted Dutch's disregard for others. *Apparently not.* He had shrugged and said, "Just tell him to come home and man up. Eva's a tasty treat. Hell, I thought she was bribing you with something serious."

This comment ought to have sobered her, walked her out of the dream. The ubiquitous baby bias, an abiding belief that nothing but good comes from them. This adoration was a cultural given, the idea behind those hateful car window stick figures, the family represented from biggest to smallest. And the caution signs, *Baby on Board!* slapped on minivans as though procreation were a badge of honor. To not want to breed, or to choose against it, was blasphemy. Even, apparently, to drug dealers. But last night she'd laughed it off, positioned high and away from her own life.

"Oh you don't understand about Benji," she'd told Dutch. "He has a future!"

"That's exactly what I mean," Dutch snapped, his amusement transformed to flat disdain. "He's still got a future. He didn't burn down anyone's house. He's not going to jail."

She hated Dutch's patronizing, but the reproach made sense. Benji would survive this. People could make music and raise children. Margot and Andy had done it. The gloom she felt now was more difficult to explain. She nursed a sense of betrayal, the early, deep kind, like being ten years old and catching your best friend at the movies with someone else. Margot had pitied Eva! And felt virtuous for it! It turned out Eva was only trying to build a future for her, *Margot's*, grandson.

She was haunted by idea that Benji's future was ruined. Children put a ceiling on one's life. You couldn't keep soaring once you were a parent. The pressure was crushing. A musician's life of auditions, solos, competition—all that was cotton candy in comparison. Children were relentless in the way they were *always around*, from that delicious weight of them in your arms, to their young, hopeful gaze, watching, mimicking, following.

On Monday, Margot drove to town and parked in a loading zone across from the music department, determined to see Satterfield. She stayed in the vehicle until he came down the steps with Collette, the flutist. His hair was blown back from his forehead and his suit coat caught in the wind, as did Collette's long skirt. Satterfield wore his black wingtips, giving him a presidential look. As if he sensed her, his gaze lifted. She wore sunglasses but he recognized her, gave Collette's arm a squeeze, and strode across the street to speak to her. Margot felt herself shrinking, hoping she didn't look as bad as she felt.

"I see," he said. "Hiding behind your Jackie-Os."

"I think I ruined my arm."

"I wouldn't be surprised," he said, losing the smile. "You're an idiot."

Before he could get any further with his scolding, she blurted, "The test results came in."

He crossed his arms and looked at the ground. Margot turned her gaze straight ahead, facing the windshield.

"Call the fiddler," he said at last.

She put her forehead on the steering wheel.

"Really Margot, you must. You must!"

When she still didn't speak, he gave the side of the vehicle a knock, then went back to Collette. Margot watched them walking side by side, the wind whipping their clothing. With the old buildings behind them and the bright, cold sky above, they looked like a postcard.

Margot reentered traffic and drove towards the strip mall. She meant to confront Mrs. Baker, like a grown up would. Talk to another grown up. It was what they would have done if all this had taken place years ago, when it should have. But halfway there, she lost her nerve. Eva's apartment was between campus and the Commons. She decided to go there.

She pulled into the first parking spot she found, ignoring the assigned numbers. Though there was no sign of Eva's car, Margot got out to ring the bell anyway, passing the For Sale sign on her way to the stoop. The windows next to the door were mottled glass, revealing nothing.

Next she drove to McLeod Park. The cottonwoods knocked against one another. Branches were down and twigs flew, hitting her windshield, pelting her as she crossed the park to the shops. The sidewalks were fairly empty and awnings slapped in the wind. Margot had dropped them here the day of the paternity test. She found the space again, saw Eva inside and knocked on the glass.

"Welcome!" Eva cried, opening the door.

The place smelled of floor polish and paint. Music was playing. Eva had a paintbrush in her hand, was working on a wall mural, in gray.

Margot pulled off her sunglasses. "So this is it?"

Eva nodded with enthusiasm. "In back we have a mattress and a stove top cooker. There's a bathroom with a stall shower."

"What's the rent on something like this?

"A lot," Eva said. "I'll cover the deposit with the sale from the condo."

"If you sell it."

Margot had her back turned. She was glad Eva couldn't see her face. In the history of one bad idea leading to another, this sequence had to be one of the worst. The girl's silence meant she sensed Margot's unfriendly skepticism.

"What about the New Leaf?" Margot asked, turning.

"Fuck Dutch," said Eva, her face turning grim.

"Wait, you *changed your mind?*" Margot took a step forward. "You can't do that to me!"

"Do what?" Eva asked.

"I gave Dutch the money! I drove all over town collecting cash. I gave it to him last weekend!"

Eva looked worried. "We can get it back," she said. "I'll tell Sully—"

"I don't want it back!" shrieked Margot. "Get your share of the profit!"

"No!" Eva cried. She shook her head and said, "Yes! That's what I meant! I will!"

The hand holding the paintbrush fell to her side. Her free hand showed the faintest tremble. Only now did Margot notice Eva's appearance; she'd never seen the girl in sweats, with no makeup. She was barefoot; without heels, she came to Margot's shoulder.

Birdie came out of the back room and lit up when he saw Margot. She had not considered what it would be like to see him knowing that Benji was his father. She didn't want to look at him, but here he was, reaching out to her. The bluest eyes! Oh, why was he always handing her something in these heartbreaking ways! It was a plastic orange fish.

"Nemo," he said.

She took it, staring at his dainty teeth. She reached out to stroke his cheek with the back of her finger, his skin so soft it felt like nothing. Did he have Benji's head shape? Really she saw nothing of her son. Benji was pale and dark-eyed with unruly hair; Birdie was blue-eyed with hair straight as straw. The boy looked like Andy, she realized. Margot crouched in front of him, hiding her emotion from Eva. She lost her balance and nearly fell, had to drop the toy fish to catch herself with her good arm. Her laugh sounded more like a sob and concern flashed over his face.

"Careful!" he said, picking up his fish.

"What's your mom painting?" Margot asked him.

"A rhinoceros," he said without hesitation. "For The Rhino." With his small hand he pointed. He swung the fish back and forth in front of him, returning to his game, a shushing sound coming from his thick lips.

"So you believe me now," Eva said when Margot stood.

She opened her mouth to respond, found she could not. "Can we go next door, to that bakery?" she asked at last. "The smell in here is making me queasy."

They stood in the wind while Eva fumbled with the deadbolt. Nobody wore a coat, so they dashed down one door. The bakery smelled like bread and Margot immediately felt better. They ordered and sat down with coffee. Birdie and Eva each had a chocolate croissant.

"I don't know what to say to you," Margot said once they were settled.

"You don't need to—"

Margot stopped her by shaking her head so quickly that it hurt; she closed her eyes and inhaled, feeling Eva's eyes on her. She lifted her coffee mug. Birdie swung his legs, holding his croissant with two hands. Eva reached out to help him with his water glass. How cozy, Margot thought. Here we are having pastry, me and my grandson. And who? Not her daughter-in-law. Who were she and Eva to each other?

Still chewing, the little boy climbed off his chair and walked over to explore the bin of toys in the corner. People watched as he passed, smiling.

"Does Benji know?" Margot blurted when he had gone.

Eva took a second to understand, then said, "No."

Margot gripped the side of her neck. Even if it was the answer she wanted, she felt the unmoored sensation between herself and her son, a severed live wire that was cutting her in half.

"Why not?" Margot asked. "Why didn't you tell him?"

Eva avoided Margot's gaze, her expression anxious but undefeated, about to justify the inexcusable. She was that kind of girl.

"I couldn't. The circumstances—" she turned to look out the window. "I initiated it. It was my idea, the sex. And he called a few times, wanted to see me again. Who wouldn't, after a night like that."

Margot tried to unhear this.

"I avoided him. I didn't want a boyfriend. Didn't want—no offense, Mrs. Fickett, but a lot of days Benji came to school with his shirt inside out. I liked him, don't get me wrong. We were lab partners in AP science. Had fun burning hair over the Bunsen burner, making ice cream with liquid nitrogen. But even as a senior he could have trouble finding his locker."

Margot believed her. That sounded like Benji.

"He'd've wanted to discuss it, I knew," Eva continued. "Shit. I didn't want to *talk*."

She swallowed, still unable to look at Margot, and yet there was a heaving relief coming out of her, confessing this. Margot hadn't meant to get the whole story, only meant to ask why in god's name she wouldn't tell a boy he was a father. Yet she *did* want to know. She waited greedily for Eva to continue.

"After I found out," Eva said, "nothing changed. I mean, everything changed, but I still didn't want to talk to him. I guess I was embarrassed. I felt bad. And I didn't want to—I knew he was this big deal musician, headed to private school. Everyone knew he was going places, Mrs. Fickett."

"You were being nice?"

"No, not—well. I'm not some saint."

Margot sighed. "We should have been involved from the beginning. We should have been part of the decisions."

"You would have told me to get an abortion."

"Yes," Margot said. "Benji is too young. *You* are too young."

Eva face reddened. "I'm not so sure about that. I think we're doing pretty well."

Margot took a breath. "You are, Eva," she said. "You're doing very well. But it's a—"

"Don't tell me it's a fucking shame," she snapped. "Don't say I should be in college, living it up. Partying with idiots, having sex and staying out all night. *Fuck* that. I like this better. I like him better!"

Conversation stopped at the neighboring tables; people glanced over. The two women both sat back, gazing over the room, getting their breath.

"What do we do now?" Eva asked after a time.

"I don't know."

"What's your lawyer say? Lambchops." She fluttered her fingers and added, "The maestro."

"He says I should call my husband."

"You haven't?"

Margot sat still. Eva looked horrified. "He's your husband!"

"Eva, It's complicated."

"How is it complicated? You call, you say, guess what? You're a grandpa!"

"I need time to think about this. To digest it. Andy and I are very different." Eva grew still, considering.

"I know you went to Bruno's with Dutch. Sully told me."

Margot felt her face tighten. Her jaw clamped like an animal trap.

"Mrs. Fickett, I don't know what happened, but Dutch is..." Her eyes shifted and she wiped at the paint on her fingers with a paper napkin.

"Dutch is what?"

"Awful. And anyway, you're *married*!"

Margot shifted in her chair. "Nothing happened."

"But you want it to."

Again Margot felt her jaw clench. A nerve in her temple throbbed.

"Dutch has nothing to do with my not telling Andy and Benji." She leaned forward. "I went with Dutch for *you*. I gave him the money because I thought that was what you wanted. Now you're telling me you want something else. You have got to stop jerking people around, Eva. Be honest. Direct."

"Ha! You're one to talk about being honest."

Margot shut her mouth. Eva was right. She could hardly lecture about honesty. Yet the last thing she wanted was to call everybody home. Part of her hesitation was an aversion to drama. She feared her own rage. She was furious with Benji, that he could mess up like this after all they'd given him, all *she'd* given. Margot and Andy had shared parenting duties only to a degree. It was Margot who had the connections, who found the festivals and oversaw applications and auditions. Benji used to come home after a week of lessons in Seattle and play for her, and she could see all that he'd learned in his face, his hands, his technique. Then he could put his instrument away, eat dinner and watch videos on his laptop. This entitlement was precisely what Margot wanted for him. He never questioned his right to the best teachers or the opportunity to be great. How proud she'd been to offer that!

She could see the heroics in her thinking, the martyr trying to get out. But the anger wasn't something she could talk herself out of.

"We've never had to deal with anything like this before," Margot said at last. "Andy will want to meet Birdie. And you. He'll want—I don't know what he'll want. I can't believe you're scolding me about speaking up when you didn't say a word for years. *You're* one to talk."

The two women regarded one another.

"Touché," said Eva, the corner of her mouth curling.

Unsmiling, Margot said, "My god, Eva, don't you see that telling them will change everything?"

"I know!" Eva cried. "That's how I felt! I didn't want to be that kind of earthquake for anybody!"

"But Eva surely you can see, he *is* an earthquake!" Margot gestured towards the boy in the back room.

"A good earthquake," Eva said in mild defense.

Margot didn't know how to respond. Was there such a thing? Could upheaval and destruction be positive? Buildings crumbling. Futures ruined. From now on the world would be about repairs and rebuilding. A whole new city.

"He's adorable. Of course he is. He's exquisite. That is hardly the point."

Eva's expression softened. What Margot had not been able to see until now was how badly Eva needed to hear just such useless optimism. A crumb of approval. Margot did not believe everything would turn out all right and she didn't forgive Eva, or Benji. But Birdie, how could he be blamed?

"What about your parents? What do they say?"

Eva slumped in her chair. "They think that whoever he is, he should help support us."

"Of course he should."

Margot glanced at Eva's small, paint-covered hands. She'd probably been good with him as a baby. Awkward at first, but efficient, one of those mothers who could hold his head and move him through the world with ease.

Outside, the few people on the sidewalk walked leaning forward, using the tops of their heads to cut the wind. Bursts of sunlight soaked the street, only to be swallowed again by the racing clouds.

"Did you know," Eva said, "that songbirds can't go out on days like this? My neighbor told me. They're too small to fly in the wind."

"I didn't know that," Margot said.

"If they venture out," Eva continued, turning to face her, "they'll roll along the ground like crumpled paper." Her face looked sad, as if she'd just delivered bad news.

Margot said nothing.

"It's harvest at the New Leaf," Eva said. "Dutch has hired two scary men from out of town for the trim. The whole team is going bowling this weekend."

Margot felt pierced. She knew this. Had Dutch mentioned it? She was supposed to go with him. She recalled him asking, laughing, hunched over a piece of paper, scribbling his address. They were in the back seat of the Suburban—Christ! What were they doing in the back seat?

"You could come," Eva said, as she dunked the last bite of her croissant in her coffee.

"I could," Margot said.

Eva stopped chewing. "What's that mean?"

"It means, I could."

Eva swallowed. "That's the last thing I expected you to say. Bowling with the pot growers?"

Margot fidgeted, crossing her legs. "How did you leave things with your mother?" she asked, changing the subject. Eva put an elbow on the table.

"I don't want to see her again," she said. "I'm sick of being wrong. Everything about me, wrong, wrong, wrong. How I speak, how I dress, how I parent. My job, my boyfriend. A weight has lifted."

Birdie came to the table, thirsty. Eva helped him with the glass of water. Margot was sure there was more to the story—their side, for instance. But at least Eva was thinking about it, not just calling them assholes. She said the relationship was non-existent, yet they seemed to affect her life as deeply as if she still ate at their table.

"That's quite a statement," Margot said.

Eva smiled wanly. "Quite."

"Parents are human, you know," Margot said. "They can't live up to what you want. You will be that way, too."

"Don't sympathize with them," Eva said.

"Of course not. I wasn't—"

"Just don't, okay?"

Margot closed her mouth. She didn't nod or smile. Yet in picking up her bag, joining Eva in the gathering of their things, she felt she had chosen. She was on Eva's side.

Their parting was a shouted good-bye in the wind on the street. Margot made her way across McLeod Park, leaning so heavily forward she worried she'd stumble. Once inside the Suburban, she dug out her cell phone, found Dutch's number. A vague memory of him holding her phone, entering the numbers. She dialed.

"What happened?" she asked before he said hello. "I don't remember how I ended up—tell me about when we got to Deaton."

She heard his inhale, his breathy laughter. "Margot."

Out the windshield, she watched a plastic grocery bag fly across the park, turning over on itself like a lost parachute. Again the sun flashed through the clouds and was quickly extinguished.

"You really don't remember how I tried to get you to come home with me? Drove you to my apartment?"

"I was in your apartment?"

"No," Dutch laughed. "You wouldn't get out of the car. You said if you went inside you'd regret it. You insisted I take you to the shop, to your car. You promised you wouldn't drive."

"I didn't."

"I know. I helped you get in the back. I put your keys under the floor mat, left you passed out."

"In my backseat."

He laughed again, sounded distracted. Where was he, she wondered. Certainly not behind a desk or at a computer, nowhere she could imagine. Was someone speaking to him? Was he in line at a drive-through? With a woman?

"Are you coming this weekend? You promised you would."

Here was the invitation. Bowling. She would go. To get the money back, or make certain that Eva got her share of the harvest. Margot wasn't going to fly to Minneapolis to meet Andy and Benji for The Wilmas' show. Nor was she going to tell them to cancel it and fly home. She was going to league bowl. Disaster was certain. The world was crumbling. But the symphony had begun: they were past the andante, well into the third movement's delicate minuet.

Twenty-three

Eight months after their first date at the bowling alley, Eva and Sully were going back. He was picking her up at the condo. The New Leaf had a league team, with shirts. Eva's right to a share of the business was first introduced here, on New Year's Eve. She asked Dutch for a shirt. Innocent enough. But the question was weighted: was she a member of the team? She thought back now to the weeks she had thrown herself into so much of the labor—at great personal risk—just to prove that yes, she was a member of the team. It seemed like a lot of work just for a fucking bowling shirt.

Birdie was next door at Mrs. Vetter's, an older woman Eva used on occasion. The place felt strange without him. Everything felt strange. Her plan was working. Earlier today she'd signed a buy-sell agreement on the condo. The buyers were a couple, young enough to shop for a house on Craigslist but old enough to want a lawyer and a title company to handle the sale. They would close in two weeks. It was good news, a triumph, yet all was strange. Eva felt a bizarre out-of-body sensation. She was both herself and watching herself from a slight distance. Half her furniture was gone; she was living in two places. The condo wasn't really hers, but the new space didn't feel like home. Last night, their first sleeping in the store, went poorly. The back room turned out to be drafty. Even with the thermostat set on high, they were cold. The old building was full creaks and sighs. There were mice, probably drawn by the bakery next door. Birdie heard them in the walls. Thinking he'd like to imagine them in their world, busy and awake, Eva made the mistake of telling him the truth. He was up all night, worried they'd trample over his legs or sleep in his hair. At dawn, they drove back to the condo, exhausted. Eva took a bath and came out to find Birdie asleep in his bed, naked, clutching his teddy.

Something was up with Sully. Since the day she got fired, he felt distant. He was busy with the harvest, but his distance felt like more than distraction. She felt doubt coming off him the day she took him to McLeod Park. Seeing the new space and neighborhood from his perspective was unsettling. He didn't say anything specific, but after he left she felt burdened. The Rhino looked impractical, like more work than she'd ever manage. The gloom he left behind was not dissimilar to that left by her father's nighttime visit.

The New Leaf felt different. She had visited midweek, after scanning for Dutch's car. The smell was so potent it stung the eyes, and in spite of the trimmers and their music, there was a felt silence to the place, as if the absence of growth could be heard. The scene was one of assault. Desecrated plant stems were draped over the trellises. Paper bags full of detached leaves lined the shelves along with glass jars full of curing bud. Chopped and packaged, the plants lost their glamour. Sully and the crew referred to it as medicine, but to Eva it now looked like dope. It smelled like dope. Pounds of it.

Marvin and Gerald worked alongside the two new men, trimming the buds with quick, efficient movements. Sully had told her about Carlos and Tristan, but in person they were scarier. Carlos had a forearm tattoo that Sully said linked him to a Tijuana cartel. Tristan had the three R's tattooed on his upper arm: Respect, Reputation and Revenge. The presence of these two changed everything. Just as the room was no longer a tidy indoor farm, the team was no longer a bunch of guys growing weed. Legal or not, they were doing something risky, even dangerous. For the first time, Eva wasn't sure she should let Birdie be around all this. It didn't help that Sully had become watchful, following Birdie around, worried he'd get into something. Probably the lack of sleep made him paranoid. He could barely stand still to speak to her. Eva wanted to throw her arms around him, breathe in the clean smell of his breath, his clothes, his skin, but some new, unwelcome caution prevented her.

The bowling alley seethed. All twenty lanes were taken and people packed the concourse. The energy felt swashbuckling, as if they'd all been at sea for months and someone had finally spotted land. The shoe rental man, a notorious grump, grinned as he sprayed the shoes. The New Leaf team, half-stoned from days of contact, stood gathered in their assigned lane settee when Eva and Sully arrived. Marvin leaned on his cane, speaking so slowly Eva couldn't make out his words. Gerald laughed with the three college kids. Compared to the tall, fine frames of Carlos and Tristan, the rest of the men looked like a pale subspecies. Even Sully looked small as he shook their hands. Eva could barely speak to them, they were so huge and dark and *well made*. She pressed against Sully, holding not just his hand but his entire arm. When he arrived, she'd tried to get him to come inside, to be late, but for the second time in a week, he put her off, saying Dutch had some kind of surprise for them, had ordered them not to be late.

Dutch appeared, hopping down the two steps from the lounge carrying a tray of whiskey shots. Eva had never seen him so animated. Grinning, moving fast, about to get rich, he passed around the drinks, coming to her last. They met eyes over the tray and he said, "Welcome to the team."

All the men were watching. Sully was smiling. Eva picked up her shot glass and Dutch set down the tray, picked up a brown bag and passed out shirts, pale blue with the oval name tag. Who did he find to buy such things? She could not imagine Dutch mail ordering. Marvin and Gerald buttoned theirs up. Sully left his open. Even the brothers got one, though the armholes were too small for their biceps. In front of Eva, Dutch pulled one more out of the bag. He held it open while she put her arms through. Sully began a cheer. Marvin and Gerald joined him.

Silly as it was, the shirt and the cheering pleased her. Her face hurt from smiling. She gave a half turn, showing it off. The California men grinned. Sully leaned in to kiss her. When he stepped back, Eva nearly jumped out of her skin. There, standing next to Dutch wearing a sexy black dress was Mrs. Fickett.

"I think some of you know my date," Dutch said.

"Mrs. Fickett!" Eva couldn't help crying.

Margot gave a little patronizing laugh. Dutch was showing teeth, beaming with pride. Oh, he was enjoying her shock! Eva saw that Sully, too, was bug-eyed with surprise. Eva felt sick. Dutch held up his whisky glass and called out, "To new partnerships!"

Everyone lifted their glass. When Dutch leaned over to touch his glass to Eva's, a knowing look came into his eyes, almost a warning. What did it mean? That if he could get to Margot, he could get to Eva, too? To do what?

"We'll take Carlos and Marvin," he announced, pointing at them. He took one of the college kids, too. "Sully," he cried, turning. "You and Eva take the rest. Go get your shoes!"

Dutch made his way across the room to fetch his personal ball. The others went to the counter for shoes. Left alone, Eva and Margot looked at each other.

"Congratulations," said Margot. "Partner."

"What are you *doing* here?"

"I said I might come!"

"I didn't think you were serious! Jesus, Mrs. Fickett, what—"

"Look at my arm!" she interrupted. "See how I can bend it!" She watched herself bend and straighten her right arm as if it belonged to somebody else.

"Oh my god," Eva said, stepping closer. "Are you *stoned*?"

Mrs. Fickett blinked her dark eyes. "We ate cookies."

Eva's jaw dropped. "A *whole* one?"

The tall woman sank to the horseshoe-shaped couch behind them. Eva sat beside her.

"Mrs.—Margot—are you *with* Dutch?" Eva hissed. "On a date?"

Her gaze was slow and heavy, lacking the shrewdness Eva had found so unnerving. In contrast, the vacancy was downright creepy.

Dutch returned, put his ball in the return, and busied himself at the scoring stand. Eva knew he had hearing like an owl. She turned her back to him, leaned in to whisper to Margot, "I don't think you know what you're into."

Margot gave her a mild look. "Where's Birdie?"

"With Mrs. Vetter, my neighbor."

"How often do you—" she began, but someone laughed nearby and she lost her train of thought. She smiled, looking over as if she were in on the joke, completely distracted now. Eva squeezed her good arm but Margot turned the other direction, interested again by her broken side. She bent and straightened it, muttering, "Incredible." This would have been funny if it wasn't tall, proper Mrs. Fickett. Birdie's *grandmother*.

"Dutch is bad news, Margot." Eva whispered. "Those two guys he brought from California—did you see their tattoos? Sully told me that's from a *cartel*."

Margot met her eye.

"You've got to *go home*. You can take a cab."

"What about you? You're just a kid." Her eyes drooped and she smiled vacantly. The woman was a cartoon version of herself.

"Oh my god," Eva said.

Sully joined them, sitting on Eva's other side. "What is she doing here?"

"*I* didn't bring her! I have no—"

"Oh shit," said Margot, straightening, looking past Eva and Sully. At first Eva thought she was sick. Then Sully turned and jumped to his feet.

Three people were crossing the concourse, shoving through the crowd coming directly towards them. Their swagger, the violent, self-important way they pushed people drew attention. The woman was heavily made up and wore a dress that stopped just short of obscene. Her hair was so black it might have been a wig. The taller man had a beard and pale, hard eyes. A biker's chain swung from a belt loop to the wallet in his back pocket. Most disturbing was the smaller man's grin. Whatever was about to happen, he was looking forward to it.

Eva saw Margot and Sully meet eyes. "What?" she demanded. "Who are they?"

Sully gripped her upper arm, pulling her to her feet. "You should go," he told her. "Right now. Both of you."

He let go, moving quickly around the couch to meet the strangers outside the settee.

"Who are they?" Eva asked Margot. "What's going on?"

Margot sat, mute, hands still, eyes big as plates. The trio leaked past Sully. When the New Leaf team returned, they found the strangers gathered around the ball return. The woman draped herself over the grinning man's shoulder like a cape. Marvin, Gerald, the college kids, even Carlos and Tristan were as clueless as Eva. Everybody looked to Dutch for a reaction. He turned from the score screen and froze for a split second, his eyes stunned. Eva knew that whatever happened, it wouldn't end well.

"Hey, hey!" Dutch cried, stepping down from the scoring stand, arms spread in welcome.

He was a terrible actor. Margot covered her mouth with a hand. Eva swallowed with difficulty, her mouth had gone dry.

"The more the merrier!" Dutch clapped. "Sit down! Let's talk this over."

"Talk *what* over?" Eva whispered to Margot.

Nobody moved.

The ball return gagged. Up came Dutch's red eighteen-pound ball. The bearded man looked at it, then at Dutch. Jutting his chin, he picked it up and walked onto the floor in his street shoes. Swift as a cat he approached the foul line and released it. The ball traveled straight down the center, picking up speed. The noise in the room seemed to peak. Bowlers laughed, pins crashed and pint glasses scraped tabletops. Time stopped on lane eighteen.

Everything that came after happened quickly. Later, Eva felt there had been no chronology to it, the room simply exploded. The roll was a strike. The shoe man shrieked from his desk, "No street shoes on my lane deck!" Dutch walked up to the bearded man as if to congratulate him but instead picked up his foot and stomped on the man's left toe. The man doubled over and Dutch hit him on the back of the neck. The guy dropped like a board.

Sully came forward, but the woman in the dress blocked his way, shouting, "Hold on, Carrottop!" He pushed around her, shoving her in a way that meant he'd lost his cool. The woman turned and crouched, about to jump on his back. Eva sprung on her, tackling her to the ground with a wad of hair in her fist. Eva was making noise, a long extended howl, and the two of them rolled over the floor. The younger man grabbed Eva, trying to pull her off. Sully punched him in the side of the face. The man fell and popped up again like a toy. He came at Sully with both fists, hitting him on top of the head like a post pounder. The woman elbowed Eva off her back and swung her purse, which connected with the side of Eva's face. The room tilted as she fell to her knees. What the *fuck* was in that purse?

Marvin's cane was swinging. The brothers' tattooed arms moved like pistons. A fleeting image of Mrs. Fickett standing on the bench, her long legs swinging over the back of the booth, escaping the settee. College kids from the next lane poured into the fray like water through a crack.

Eva tried to get up, stumbled, caught herself on the booth, and was hit again. The shoe counter man was shouting, *Break it up! Break it up!* Mutiny was upon them. Eva stayed down, listening to the shouting and screaming and the sick, heavy sound of thudding flesh. After a time—impossible to tell how long—police officers invaded, clubs in the air. By the time they were loading people into squad cars, the place was wrecked. The music was shut off and the lights felt over-bright.

Twenty-four

In the parking lot, Sully was led past the squad car where Eva sat crying. He appealed to her with his eyes, offering reassurance, but she didn't see him. He felt the cold and realized his shirt was gone. He wore only his tank top. Placed in the back seat of another car, Sully heard the radio in the front, men's voices. The noise, the lights, breaking glass and shouting combined with exhaustion and days of THC contact, triggered a flashback: he was back in the desert, that hellhole of oppressive heat, the smell of cooked meat and smoke and blood.

He let his head rest against the seat, focusing on the car's dome light and the feel of his lungs expanding and contracting. His knuckles were bleeding. A memory flickered. He latched onto it, an isolated moment, an image of the Devil's Slide. Way back, before Caitlyn, before Paige. He was nine years old in the hot, wide back seat of the family Plymouth. Summer, somewhere near Gardiner, Montana. His mother's finger pointing at a wide, curved track up the side of a mountain in the middle of nowhere. The mountain looked like the curled spine of a creature hiding its face. People wondered what had happened to the dinosaurs. Here they were, frozen in these spiny ridgelines. This one wasn't covered by grass or snow—every vertebrae was exposed and twisted as though it had been hit by some kind of electric pulse. Did no one but Sully see it?

Wooden chairs in a brightly lit hallway. What they didn't put in Hollywood movies or cop shows was the endless waiting. Hands cuffed in their laps like naughty children. Sully stared at the split knuckles on both hands. Eva held an ice pack to her left cheek, silent, waiting for him to speak. Marv wasn't here, nor Gerald. The kids got away of course, but how did Marvin escape? Across the room the Hispanic brothers looked untouched, though they'd fought like machines. They stared straight ahead with dead eyes.

Sully lifted both hands to dig at his eye sockets. Hard data, one of his counselors called this. A pinch, a squeeze. You could even bite the inside of your own cheek, anything to land you inside your own body. He was going to reach over and take Eva's hand. Any minute, he would take her hand. An officer came out and spoke Spanish to the brothers. They both stood and followed the man down the hall. Sully turned to Eva.

"No matter what, keep your mouth shut."

She shrank a little.

"You don't know a thing. You've never seen those two Mexicans before tonight. Got it?"

"Jesus, what is all this? It was a *fist fight*!"

"I'm serious. These are the feds."

Now he could do it, lift his hands across the armrest and lower them into her lap. She dropped the ice pack and gripped them both in her own. More hard data.

"Who were they?" she asked. "Those three?"

Before he could answer, a man appeared. Even without a hat Sully knew him: the agent from the birdfeed store. He stood before them, hands on his hips.

"I'm Evans with the Federal Bureau of Investigation," he said. "Sullivan, I need you to come with me."

"You've got no right to hold us here," Eva said. "What are we charged with?"

Sully freed his hand, glaring at her. Ignoring him, she said, "My son is with a sitter. I have to go."

Evans cleared his throat. "Shall I call your mother, have her come get you?"

This slowed her down. "What do you know about my mother?"

"Oh, we go way back," said the agent with a smile. "I met her a month, six weeks ago."

Sully stared, imploring her to shut up. Finally Eva bent down to retrieve the ice pack and returned it to her cheek. He thought she'd be all right but she looked at Evans and asked, "What is taking so fucking long?"

Sully closed his eyes. He heard the agent answer, "How soon you get to go home is up to him."

He gestured for Sully to stand, which he did. He looked at Eva once before they started down the hall. Her tears were starting again.

In the interrogation room another agent was waiting, wearing a tie and a DEA jacket. He was dark-eyed and wore tight pants. Full head of hair. Evans felt familiar, but this guy was an asshole, Sully could tell. Evans uncuffed him, told him to sit. The asshole stood with his feet spread wide. "You picked the wrong partner, buddy boy." He slapped a photo on the table in front of Sully. It was a grainy close up of Dutch, younger, less polished, with longer hair.

"James Whitney Joyner. He's been on our watch list for over a year," said the asshole. "Skipped town out of Bremerton, Washington. Owes people money. A known trafficker."

When he was sixteen, Dutch helped rob a bank. Something went wrong and a teller was killed. The ringleader of that escapade was serving a life sentence in federal prison. Dutch spent two years in juvie till he turned eighteen, then was sent to California state prison for seven years. He'd been in trouble off and on ever since. They offered Sully walking papers if he'd give them everything he had on Dutch.

Sully wasn't stupid. He knew they could do what they wanted. They could take Caity. They could jail him for his home crop. He told them he met Dutch last September, when Marvin brought him to the trailer. How prophetic that felt, only days after he'd found the vacant space in Rock Creek Commons. He stuck to the facts, both hands on the table. They'd interview Marvin because of this, but it couldn't be helped.

Caity had answered the knock at the door that day. Sully was watching from the kitchen. He could tell by her face that she didn't know the visitor. He crossed the living room and opened the door wide, standing behind her. Marvin was there in his pleather coat and wraparound sunglasses. Next to him was a clear-eyed man with no sunglasses, in possession of all his hair. He was an inch shorter than Sully but the clothes, his confident half smile, gave the effect of stature. Sully didn't take his eyes off the stranger as he said, "You got your weed last Tuesday, Marv."

"I know that, Sully," said Marvin, leaning on his old wooden cane. A car wreck had left Marvin crippled years ago. The injury had qualified him for one of the first medical marijuana cards in the state. "This is Dutch. Dutch, meet Sullivan Stiles."

Dutch held out a hand, still wearing that secretive half smile.

"Dutch what?" Caity asked.

He looked down. Sully told her to go watch television, but she ignored him.

"Most people have two names," she said. "I happen to have three. Caitlyn Caruthers Stiles. My mom calls me Caitlyn Caruthers."

"And your dad?" Dutch asked her.

"He calls me Caity."

"See?" he said. "One name. Just like me."

That was how the New Leaf began. Dutch said he was looking to invest, the time was right. He liked to get in on the ground floor in situations like this, meaning: Montana, where the law was ambiguous. Marvin had told him Sully was the best grower in town. Dutch wanted to see for himself. Sully showed him his plants, he told the feds, certain they already knew about his home grow. Full disclosure might indicate an allegiance to the law.

Dutch told Sully he had better clones out of California, some west coast buzz called Blue Dream. He said all they needed was space, he'd pay for everything else. "You put in the muscle. I've got the money."

"So we'd be partners?" Sully asked him.

A jaw tendon pulsed. "I'm an investor," he said. "I'd expect returns. That's all."

Even at the time, Sully thought the plan ought to be more clear. There should be a lawyer, papers signed. But it happened so fast, with such serendipity. He told Dutch about Rock Creek Commons and Dutch said, "Rent it." Handed him a roll of money. Said he'd be in touch.

"How much money?" asked Agent Evans. Next to him the asshole was taking notes.

"Eight thousand dollars," reported Sully. Enough for the deposit on the space and the first month's rent and all the equipment: planters, lights, trellis, filters and fans.

"He showed up later with fifteen grand, for renovations. We built a seedling room, a drying room. We knocked out walls, built an office." He thought of the safe they put in, disguised behind the heating vent. The cash he'd found there. In a split second, as he looked at Evans, he decided not to mention this.

"He told me to buy some clothes," he said instead.

"Clothes?"

"He didn't like my look. Wanted me to buy a suit. He said I was a businessman, not a dealer."

Gazing at Sully's undershirt and athletic pants, the asshole remarked, "You didn't comply."

Sully smirked. Marvin had stood next to Dutch, nodding like an excited parrot. Marv bought a suit, new shoes, the brass tipped walking stick. This was only the beginning, Marv kept saying. Their future had begun.

Twenty-five

A ringing phone woke Margot. The walls of the room were bare, dingy white. The bed beneath her had no sheets and the room had no furniture other than a side table and a beat-up highboy, drawers open and empty. The ceiling angled sharply over the bed. She was in an attic. Wainscoting circled the room, gray with age. The open closet door was made of thin paneling, revealing a narrow chamber under the eaves, entirely empty. She wasn't wearing any clothes.

The ringing finally stopped. She sat up, wincing in pain. Her clavicle beat like a timpani. No sign of her clothes, shoes or bag. No clock. No curtains on the window.

"Hello?" she called out. Something about the way her voice hung on the air told her she was alone.

She swung her legs over the side of the bed. Her head throbbed. She blinked several times until she could focus. Holding her forearm protectively to her torso, she stood. Pain crushed her. She stumbled towards the highboy, leaned on it to get her breath. The phone started ringing again. She recognized it as her own, somewhere outside the room. She teetered towards the door, braced herself and reached out. The knob turned but the door was bolted from the outside. She was locked in.

Margot shook the doorknob and kicked the door, then cried out from the jolt through her bones, a pain so acute she felt sick to her stomach. Gasping, she turned around to lean against the door. Images of the night flashed before her. Dutch had her go up the narrow stairs to his apartment in front of him, snaking a hand between her thighs. Outside the door he came up behind her, pressing her between his body and the door. His voice in her ear, whispering things as he fumbled with the key. "Go," he breathed.

There was a full apartment, she recalled, with a kitchen and a bathroom. But it was in this room that he pulled off her dress, his gold eyes locked on hers as he lifted the hem, slowly pulling it over her head. There had been a lamp—she remembered the bullhorn of light it threw on the floor. He unhooked her bra and dropped it on the floor. She groaned when he touched her breasts, cupping one then the other, letting the weight of them rest in his palms. He went after them with his mouth, lapping her nipples, biting them as he reached around behind her and palmed her buttocks, separating them, bringing them together again, murmuring what sounded like *my my my*.

He bent her over the edge of the bed, slapping her smartly eight times, then nine, ten. Shocked, stinging with humiliation, she registered a naughty thrill, exactly as she had that summer she was seventeen. This night felt connected to those few weeks in Colorado. Unspeakable pleasure. Her lungs constricted. She was panting, looking over her shoulder to watch him. Dutch met her eye and stopped, stood abruptly and left the room.

She waited. She did not get dressed, though there was time. She stayed where she was, on her knees, listening to him move around. She lost track of time, lay on the mattress, dozed. When he returned, he was naked. He was sinewy, with thighs bigger than she expected. His penis was long and thick for such a lean man. He held a glass of water. Margot reached for it but he lifted it out of her grasp, tipped it forward, pouring it down her front. The water ran over her chest, around her nipples and down her stomach onto the bed. He moved it to his own torso, letting it run over his chest, down his stomach and over his penis, now pointing straight at her face. He dropped the glass. It hit the floor with a thud but didn't break. He guided her head, filling her mouth. She relaxed her jaw and let him move her head. Like the spanking, it went on too long. She was choking when he finally let her go and again turned her over the edge of the bed. He took her broken arm and bent it back, so far she cried out. There were tears; she specifically remembered weeping. Had it cracked?

Then they were on the bed, on all fours. He was thrusting into her from behind, her head repeatedly smacking the wall, which explained her headache. Not once did she tell him to stop. She *didn't want him to stop.* She recalled him whispering, "You like that." Yes, she told him, she did.

Leaning against the door, Margot looked down at her body. In the dim light she could see bruises running up and down her arms and all over her breasts. Wounds on her nipples. She felt a cut at the corner of her mouth. Her playing arm was ruined, she feared. She took a step towards the bed and vomited. It fell out of her quickly and violently, splattering the floor and hitting her lower legs.

She held still a moment, hand over her mouth. Longing for a drink of water, she crossed to the window, noticed that the house next door was an office. Saturday, she remembered. No one was coming to work. She tried to lift the window but it was painted shut. She crossed to the empty closet and squatted in its farthest corner, covering her face with her hands as warm urine flooded her bare toes.

Her four weeks at the Aspen Summer Music Festival was the first period of her life during which not one person asked her what was wrong, why she wasn't smiling or what made her so serious. Nigel was from London, in his first year at the Royal Academy with sights on the LSO. He had thick, dark hair that he wore long because who wouldn't, she thought, if you had hair like that. He played with great flourish, scowling and sweating, the muscles in his arms tensing. He was one of the few men she'd met taller than she was. They were in quartet together. Within a week, they were lovers. Margot experienced sex as a magnificent alternative to sound, a physical consumption. She held nothing back with Nigel. Her adoration was obvious. She waited for him every day at the lamppost just outside the school's campus. They would stroll hand in hand to town. If there was time before rehearsal, they'd sneak back to his dorm room. Even before they got up the first flight of stairs Nigel would put her hand on his crotch, stiff with pressure. "You like that, don't you?" he'd whisper. "That you do that to me?"

She did. The power was part of the pleasure. Sometimes he'd stop what he was doing and say, "Feels good, doesn't it?" He would wait until, half crying, half laughing, she'd beg him to start again.

They became a nuisance to others. In quartet, the viola and other violin were openly disgusted with their fawning stares. At breaks the others would put down their instruments and hurry away, eager for fresh air.

"Watch out," warned Danielle Carter, Margot's roommate. Danielle was a piano prodigy nobody liked because she practiced more than anyone and had a superior air. The orchestra was playing a Mozart piano concerto to showcase her talent. "Wild affairs tend to end badly," she said. Margot ignored her, wondering how the hell this small girl from Spokane would know.

In the third week, just midway through the festival, Margot came out to their lamppost and Nigel wasn't there. She waited twenty minutes. When he didn't appear, she walked back to the building and searched the basement rehearsal rooms. She checked the auditorium twice, the second recital hall, and finally the great outdoor stage. She roamed campus, near panic. Only something terrible would make him break their routine. At dinner as soon as Margot sat down, Danielle asked, "Trouble in paradise?"

Margot explained. Danielle's small face grew hard. "He's met someone else," she said, turning back to the score she was studying. "You've been dumped."

Seeing Margot's shock, she added with venom, "Close your mouth."

Margot gathered her things and walked out, leaving her tray on the table. She went back to her room until evening rehearsal. Nigel appeared, ten minutes late. Margot could not catch his eye and when it was over, three hours later, he had vanished again.

That night Margot's stomach knotted in on itself with hunger and angst. She lay doubled over, waiting for daylight. When Nigel appeared at the dining hall for breakfast, Margot was waiting. She stood behind him in line, out of her mind with worry and panic and hurt.

"What happened to you? Where have you been?" she demanded, speaking too loudly.

"Oh, hello," he said, patting her shoulder as if they were meeting months, years later. His expression was utterly empty. Neither malignant nor hostile, simply devoid of feeling. "How are you?"

For a long moment she doubted her sanity. Had she dreamed the entire two weeks? Had he truly *forgotten*? Maybe she had misread what was between them. Her all-consuming desire for him clouded her perception. He filled her mind all day, canceling out bodily needs such as food and water, even music—*music*! She thought it was love. Tears sprung to her eyes. He looked alarmed, the first real response she'd seen from him.

"Stop it," Margot said, raising a hand and waving it in front of his face, checking his reflexes. "What is *wrong* with you?"

"Hey, whoa!" Nigel said, holding his tray in front of his chest like a shield.

"Why didn't you meet me?" she asked. "What's happened to you?"

"I don't know what you mean," he said. He turned to the tray guide and dragged his along the metal bars. He reached beneath the sneeze guard and helped himself to a plate of biscuits and bacon, a gesture that disgusted her.

"Yes you do know what I mean," she hissed, wiping furious tears from her cheeks.

Nigel glanced at the others in line behind them. He shrugged.

"I got carried away with some percussionists from London. We decided to go round to the pub."

Nigel wasn't looking at her but at the buffet. He reached out for a bowl of diced fruit. Her fingers tingled with the first flash of hatred. Seeing her crumpled face, he said, "What? It was just a bit o' fun."

He was talking about the pub, but maybe this was what their affair had been to him: a *bit o' fun*. Horror rooted her in place as he moved away, carrying his tray.

"What about last night?" she asked, coming after him, her voice like a squeaking balloon. "What happened to you after rehearsal?"

"I was still drunk!" he laughed, now taking a bowl of yogurt onto his tray. He set it all down with care in order to fill a mug of coffee. Two boys moved around Margot to get to the yogurt.

Nigel carefully lifted the mug onto his tray, picked it up and said, "Look, I've got to eat this or I won't make it through the morning."

Her arms hung at her sides. Her hair was uncombed, her clothes picked up from the floor of her room. She stepped towards him. Nigel froze, alerted by something in her expression. The light coming in the high windows threw the room into a dazzling relief. Sound ceased and movement halted. Margot took another step and lifted both hands, palms up, against the underside of his tray, forcing it into his chest. Hot coffee splashed over his neck. Yogurt splattered down his front. Strips of bacon flew over his shoulders. The bowl, the plate and the mug hit the tile floor and cracked in two, restoring sound and motion to the room. The tray clattered endlessly, flipping back and forth on top of the broken porcelain. Nigel's cry hung in the air, his arms out, stupefied. Margot spun away from him. All eyes were on her as she marched through the cafeteria and pushed through the turnstile into the morning.

She wasn't the first to be dumped. Accepting this fact—that people got together, had sex, broke up—took years. Her performance that August at the end of the festival earned her the maestro's highest recommendation, her ticket to Peabody Prep. She left Colorado with supreme confidence that what had happened to her that summer, that kind of untempered surrender, would *never* happen again.

She was pregnant. She suspected this before she left Aspen and confirmed it when she got home. She drove herself to the clinic and marveled that an abortion turned out to be shockingly similar to a routine exam. Took ten minutes, twenty, tops. The doctor was a man. A woman nurse held her hand. It was very early in the pregnancy, no machine was required, only a series of pipettes opening her cervix, a hint of a cramp. That was it. She drove herself home, ate dinner and later slept on towels that she laundered herself.

Twenty-six

Across town, on the same Saturday morning, Eva opened her eyes to find Birdie awake, gazing at her. He pulled his arm out from under the covers to pat her cheek. Smiling at him, she fumbled for her phone on the table next to her bed. Seven a.m.

A police officer had escorted her to the condo at one-thirty. The porch light wasn't on. He stood on the stoop shining his phone light until she found her keys. Mrs. Vetter was on the couch, the last remaining piece of furniture. Eva helped her get home, came back, locked the door and leaned against it, crying with relief. She swallowed her sobs, hoping not to wake him. She sprinted to his room, gathered him up, and moved him to her bed, where she watched him sleep for what felt like hours.

"Good morning, sunshine!" Eva said, hugging him. "It's always a good morning with you in it!" She sat up and dialed Sully but the call went straight to voicemail.

"We have a job this morning, Bird," she said. "We have to find Sully."

"And Caity!" he said, jumping out of bed.

"Yes, let's find them both," she said, pulling on pants.

She had him dressed in a half hour. She packed water and protein bars and loaded him into the car. She drove downtown, heading to the bowling alley. The morning was crisp and clear. The streets had that abused feel she noticed every Saturday. Trash, broken glass, the odd coat or shoe left by a reveler. This view of Deaton was normally a favorite part of working week-ends, the city in recovery. Today, however, the mood felt portentous and eerie. Probably she should have stayed put, waited to hear something.

There was a point last night when she believed that she was going to jail. One of the tattooed brothers was led by an officer to a chair across from where Eva sat, still in cuffs.

"What happened?" Eva asked when they were alone. "What'd they say?"

He looked at her a second and his eyes switched off. Incredible. He was like a Tibetan monk, gaze fixed on a point above her head.

"Where's your brother? Tú hermano?" she tried, but got nothing. He ignored her as though he were asleep.

After an hour, Evans returned, sat next to her and dropped a manila envelope in her lap.

"Open it."

It was a photo of Dutch. She took Sully's advice, denied knowing him.

"Look again," Evans said. "I think you do."

Still she denied it, played dumb. Evans didn't press, though he reminded her he'd seen her in the shop and spoken to her mother. He said she should call him if she remembered anything. He let her go. Sully must have coop-erated. What about Caity? The business? Their plans? Jesus, all that money. And Dutch. What would he do if he found out Sully had cooperated with the cops? Who the hell were those people, that trio of hate that waltzed into the bowling alley like animals? And what about Margot? Eva glanced once more at the tattooed brother and followed the officer to his car.

This morning she would get answers. She took deep breaths as she drove, a hand on her chest. *Calm down, Eva.* All that mattered was right here in the car. She glanced in the rearview mirror and saw that Birdie had fallen asleep, listing sideways in his seat.

Sully's truck was still in the bowling alley parking lot. Her stomach dropped. He could be in jail. She turned around and headed out Randolph, towards the New Leaf. She ran the heater, trying to stop herself from shak-ing. She passed Up in Smoke, Harvey Mankiller's dispensary. A small crowd stood on the sidewalk; a police cruiser was parked in front. Eva's heart skid-ded. She slowed down, saw men in FBI vests and Drug Enforcement Agency guys. Eva saw Harvey himself smoking a cigarette next to the curb. A man emerged from the front door wearing a respirator mask and white coveralls, carrying a full plastic bag. A pit opened in her gut. She tasted bile. She drove on several more lights and her worst fears were confirmed. Flashing lights in front of the Commons, cruisers blocking the entrance. She turned into the Perkins across the street, dodging early morning diners to park facing the street. She could barely see the back of the building, but caught sight of more men in respirators moving in and out. Several black Suburbans, the unmistakable FBI vests.

Hands shaking, Eva put the car in reverse. She drove north to Lucky Lane, clinging to the possibility that Sully had called Marvin for a ride home. Maybe he was sleeping. Maybe he didn't know. In the back seat, Birdie's head fell to the side. The sun came over mountains, bathing the town in the warm, tentative light of April.

Dutch's Charger was parked next to the trailer. Her heart thudded. Could Dutch have brought Sully home? Eva got out, shut the door softly and left the car running so Birdie wouldn't wake. The front door was ajar, which was unusual. With that much product inside he always locked it, even when he was home.

"Sully!" she called, pushing the door open.

The place was dark other than the light from behind her. She saw a figure moving and reached out to the light switch. Dutch stood holding a pillowcase, his skin ghostly white under the fluorescent overhead. The trailer reeked of weed. Confused, Eva thought he had Mrs. Fickett's money in the pillowcase, that he'd come here to give it to her.

"Where's Sully?"

"Gone, cutie," Dutch said, smiling. He came forward to shut the door behind her.

"Is that my money?" A part of her knew this couldn't be right—he didn't have money in that pillowcase.

He grinned. "Money's gone, too. You're on your own."

She was rooted in place. He was between her and the exit. It was weed in the pillowcase. Slowly he came towards her, backing her up against the kitchen peninsula. He came so close his chest nearly touched hers. He snatched her wrist. She slapped at him, but he dropped the bag and grabbed both wrists in one hand. His other hand gripped her waist. An edgy hunger came into his gaze. He pulled her closer and with his mouth very close to her ear, whispered, "Show me."

He began to lift her sweater, snaking his hand under it and her bra to pinch her left nipple. She held still, believing it was imperative that she not move, make no struggle. She kept her eyes on his teeth, his mouth, the tongue moving inside his lips. *Make your mind work!* she screamed at herself.

"Down you go," he commanded, still whispering. The hand on her waist was pushing. He stopped, began to fumble with his belt. Eva looked at the pillowcase on the floor. In the distance a dog barked. He pushed on her shoulder, trying to get her to her knees. With a surge of adrenaline, Eva tried to lift her arms, but he yanked down so hard she fell to her knees, feebly crying out, "No!"

He moved fast, wrapping her wrists with the belt, grabbing her by the hair and pulling her across the room. Her feet scrambled underneath her. She was screaming, trying to stand, like an animal being dragged to its death. He yanked on the end of the belt and she fell to her knees again. He hauled her around the corner into Sully's bedroom, opened the closet and deposited her like a satchel. She screamed and thrashed but he kicked her legs until her body was all the way inside. He slid the door closed and left.

She heard his retreating footsteps. The front door slammed, leaving a stunned silence. She held her breath, heard a car door close and began to writhe with panic. Screaming aloud, she twisted and kicked. Her foot came straight through the cheap paneled door. Still kicking, she sawed her wrists back and forth until her hands were free. The escape took under thirty seconds, including her dash down the hall and out the front door, but she was too late. Dutch's car was still there, but Eva's was gone.

Twenty-seven

Margot discovered that if she pressed herself against the window, she could see the front sidewalk. She stood that way a long time, until her nipples and stomach were numb with cold. She heard footsteps, caught a glimpse of someone passing out front. She slapped the window stiles with the heel of her hand, shouting. The pedestrian didn't hear her, but Margot had an idea. She knocked the glass, watching it shake in the glazing. The she lifted the side table, took a step back and hurled it at the window. Her one-armed throw was feeble. The table bounced back, barely missing her right foot. If she could use both arms, hold it in front of her chest like a weapon, she could force it through. She didn't consider how she'd get past the broken glass or scale the outer wall. She turned to the highboy, thinking it was heavy enough to do the trick.

She got into the corner next to it and wedged her good arm behind, inching it forward until she could get her shoulder in the space. With her knees bent, her left breast smeared against the side panel, right arm hanging uselessly, she pushed with all her might, face screwed down in effort. An animal groan leapt from her as the thing took a tiny skid forward. She stopped, rested, then hurried to the other side. Unable to use her right arm, she repeated the process only this time with her back to the dresser.

Back and forth she went. She was sweating. The better part of an hour had passed before the highboy was within a foot of the window. The room was now flooded in sunshine. Hair stuck to her forehead. She had to sit on the bed to get her breath. Her left arm quivered with muscle spasms. A desperate sob escaped her. She lay a palm flat on her belly and watched it rise and fall until she was all right, then stood, pressed her shoulder to the dresser's back, inhaled and gave a shout.

The highboy tipped forward at a slight angle, then a corner made contact with the glass, shattering it. She bent her knees, thrusting her left shoulder into the dresser while lifting its leg and shouting. The dresser tumbled through the opening, taking a chunk of the window stile with it. Margot's momentum kept her coming forward a few steps. Her bare feet pressed into the broken glass. She stopped herself by slapping her hand against the window casing. The highboy appeared suspended in space, held motionless for a split second before it exploded on contact. Splinters of wood flew across the grass, the sidewalk, even as far as the side of the house. She saw a flash of movement below at the corner of the building. There was a shout. Margot gasped. Eva was down there.

The women stared at one another, aghast. It was impossible. Neither could take in what she was seeing.

"Help me!" Margot called at last.

A bright white rectangle marked the highboy's place against the wall opposite the bed. The interval between Eva's disappearance below and the sound of her entering the apartment was eternal. The room continued to brighten, the light so intense it felt shrill. Years it took her to come up the narrow staircase, through the door, and to stand outside the bolted bedroom. An eon to turn the deadbolt. There she stood, her face distorted with horror. Margot sobbed once, naked in the full sun.

The outside air accentuated the stink of sweat, sex and urine. Eva gagged. Margot came forward a step and crumpled in pain, not realizing she'd been standing in broken glass. There were bloody footprints on the floor.

"Go run the bath," ordered Margot.

Eva obeyed. Margot sat on the bed, swung her legs up and rolled across to the other side. Walking on her heels, she crossed the threshold. On the couch in the front room her clothes sat folded in a neat pile with her bag. He took the time to do that.

Still on her heels, she crossed the kitchen, pausing to open the refrigerator. Inside was one item: a Mexican wedding cookie. Next to it, a Post-it that read, *XO*. She snatched the note, crumpled it, threw it into the sink, then continued to the bathroom. Eva stood in the corner while Margot made her way to the edge of the tub. She lifted her right foot and held it under the spout. The water ran pink on the porcelain.

"If you hadn't come—" Margot began. She met Eva's eye, saw the girl's lip trembling and said no more.

There were no towels so she folded a length of toilet paper and lay it on the floor, carefully setting set her foot on it. She repeated the process with her other foot. An animal sound came from Eva. Margot looked over to see the girl leaning on the sink, about to collapse with panic and ruin. Margot turned off the water.

"Where's Birdie?"

"Dutch," Eva sputtered but couldn't manage more.

"Eva, why did you come here without Birdie?" Margot's voice had risen. She was sitting up straight, hand on her knee.

"He, Birdie was in my car—Dutch took my car, Dutch *has him*." She clamped both hands over her mouth as if she could take it back.

A dozen questions raced through Margot's mind but Eva's wild eyes silenced her. She stood, walked past Eva to the front room. The toilet paper stuck to her feet and disintegrated, leaving a trail of white clumps on the floor. Margot went to the pile of clothes and unfolded the dress.

"What are you doing?" Eva cried, following.

"We'll go to the police," Margot said.

"No!" Eva shrieked. "I was at the police station all night! They'll take him away! I lied! I said I didn't know Dutch!"

With her good hand, Margot grabbed Eva's wrist. The girl screamed as if she'd been burned. Margot held on. Eva clamped her other hand over her mouth. Leaning in close, Margot said in a steady voice, "We are going to get him back."

The girl's eyelids fluttered. She removed the hand covering her mouth. Margot squeezed harder and said it again. "We are going to get him back."

When Eva's eyes stilled, Margot gently let go. She slid the right sleeve of her dress up her injured arm and said, "I need you to hold the other sleeve."

Eva complied. Margot slid her left arm in and Eva pulled the garment over her head. Margot straightened and pulled it down around her body. They looked at each other. Margot turned to pull on her underwear. The socks required Eva's help; Margot sat on the couch and let her unroll them carefully over the cuts. Finally she stepped into her boots, picked up her bag and led the way out.

The sky was a ridiculous blue. No wind. Sunny and crisp. Robins chirped. The world felt foreign and new, a revelation. They were in Margot's Suburban. Eva tuned the radio to news of the raids with huge, frightened eyes. All the Deaton pot shops were closed, product seized. Neither of them said a word.

At the police station, Eva refused to leave Margot's side. They entered the interrogation room together. Eva sat with one hand clutched inside the other. She answered all Evans' questions, explaining how she and Margot knew each other, admitting that she knew Dutch. He was from California, provided the clones, bought the equipment. At first, Dutch only made visits to Deaton, but by Christmas, he had the apartment. Eva had only been there once. She had no idea how she'd found it again, driving Dutch's Charger, barely able to see straight.

Evans asked for a description of her car and they put out an APB. They had enough to arrest Dutch. Even if he didn't know Birdie was in the car, the charge would be aggravated kidnapping.

After a silent moment, Eva asked, "Where's Sully?"

"He was released. You missed him by twenty minutes."

Evans turned to Margot. Decades ago, in green rooms before performances, Margot had learned how to keep anxiety in check: inhale slowly and look it in the eye. She admitted to sex—yes, it got violent and yes, it was consensual. Margot felt Eva recoiling with disgust. The agent's expression remained neutral. He explained that an officer in front of Dutch's apartment had seen them arrive last night. He'd seen Dutch leave several hours later, but couldn't follow because his tires were slashed. He called for backup but all available men were involved with the raid.

"He eluded us," Evans said, his mouth forming a grim line of obvious fury. He sat back in his chair and said, "There were other women. You appear to have been his finale, intricately planned."

Margot didn't respond. She didn't believe Dutch had the night planned. She recalled arriving at his apartment early in the night, before the bowling alley. She had climbed the stairs with a pounding heart, breathless with anticipation. What a fool she'd been, so confident that something extraordinary was at work.

The unlit front room had been invaded by the April twilight. Dutch lay on the couch under the windows wearing headphones, eyes closed. She crossed the room to stand over him, studying his narrow hips, his mouth, his strong, clean hands. She was too old to be swept away by beauty, yet her mouth went dry. Her hands trembled with the desire to touch him. His crackling energy drew her to him. In spite of what happened last weekend at Bruno's, Margot had thought of him constantly, dramatizing this reunion again and again, each time with a different flourish.

As if he'd heard this confession, he opened his eyes. Margot jumped. He pulled out the ear buds and sat up. She allowed herself to be kissed, his hands cradling her face. He led her to the refrigerator, pulled the door open and made her close her eyes. *Open your mouth*, he said. Enthralled, she obeyed. He placed a whole cookie onto her tongue and watched as she bit down. Together they chewed, grinning.

Perhaps that much was planned, getting her high. But the rest of it? His actions did not unfold according to any sort of scheme. Her presence excited him. She sensed him performing for her, leading her through his life like a tour guide, though he tried his best to hide his enthusiasm. Nobody had tipped Dutch off about the raid, Margot thought. He slashed the officer's tires as a prank. He probably did it when he left the bedroom to undress. He was gone a while, could have slipped downstairs, through the front hedge, used a knife he undoubtedly carried with him. Locking Margot in and skipping town was likely improvisation, his exit an obscene gesture at those guilty of living unaware of him. Dutch was like the worst kind of visiting soloist, the egoist who treated the other musicians like background noise.

She told Evans about the odious three, the bearded man and the couple with the gun.

Evans listened, hands on the table, eyes steady. He didn't write anything down. She told him about Bruno's, about the exchange of money she'd witnessed and the car chase. He seemed unimpressed, as if it were old news.

"Where are your husband and son?" he asked suddenly.

Her eyes jumped to his. Why bring them up, after what felt like a full confession? They were together, in Minnesota, she said. This was the weekend of the shows in the Twin Cities. This could not be relevant. Evans only wanted to shame her.

"I don't see how that matters," she said. "They are not involved."

Agent Evans raised his eyebrows and ran a hand over his mouth. He cleared his throat.

"If the boy is your grandson, I'd say they are involved."

In response to his patronizing tone, Margot raised her chin. "Benji goes to St. Thomas, in Minnesota," she said. "My husband is on tour with his band, The Wilmas."

Evans leaned back. Let him stare, she thought. Judge all you want. We make music. Who cares what kind?

After a moment he stood and thanked her. They were free to go.

"*Go?*" Eva sputtered. "I'm not going anywhere! You've got to find him."

"We're doing our best," he said. They had officers heading to Bruno's, had alerted highway patrol and the city police. "We'll get him," he said and whipped open the door, exiting without a backwards glance.

Twenty-eight

Last year a girl Eva had gone to school with lost her child in a house fire. Scrambling to get out, she woke the boy, thought he was following her, but when she turned, he wasn't there. He was six and he couldn't withstand the smoke. Days later, the woman ran into a classmate, a woodworker, who offered his condolences. The mother thanked him and with very little pause said, *I need a new kitchen table. You should put me on your schedule.*

This story circulated with hushed horror, proof of heartlessness. She dropped out of school to have a child, then lost him in a fire and she wanted a kitchen table? Crazy. But in the hours after Birdie was taken, Eva recalled the rumor and understood. The woman was insane with grief. The overtaxed mind will turn to the mundane, something it can comprehend. Eva examined every detail of the police breakroom, imagining the paper plates and powdered creamer inside the cheap cabinets. The refrigerator would contain old meat and limp lettuce. She studied the officers down the hall, holsters wrapped around their middles like girdles. She thought about the furniture she had listed on Craigslist: Birdie's bed, dresser and night stand for seven hundred fifty. Would there be offers by now? Had she deleted the condo listing?

Eva remembered a nurse at Birdie's birth, the woman who stayed all afternoon, breathing with her. She took no breaks, didn't look at her phone or eat any food. He-hee-*heave*. For hours Eva's body contracted, her lungs moved like bellows and her eyes fixed on the nurse's calm, steady gaze. Eva never learned her name, never saw her again.

A sharp memory of kindergarten. The distant whine of an airplane. The smell of freshly cut grass on a clear day. Holding hands in pairs at a crosswalk. The crisp sound of a tennis ball being hit on the courts across the street.

By noon there was still no word of Birdie, and no sign of Sully. If only Eva had stayed home, waited for him to call. If she had made eggs, even a cup of coffee before she went flying out of the house. If their timing had been a minute later, Dutch would have been gone.

On television the cops were always finding people and FBI agents knew everything. They were young and good-looking, not middle-aged men with saggy middles and splotchy skin. Little puddle jumps of horror kept flashing through Eva's mind. Birdie's current reality. When he woke he would rub his eyes and see the driver wasn't her. Once he understood that she wasn't in the car, he'd be still, thinking. Wondering. His confusion would build until he'd ask where she was, maybe start reciting his address, which Eva had made him memorize. Dutch looking at him in the rearview mirror. Dutch ignoring him. Dutch touching him in any way.

Margot moved stiffly around the back of the couch to sit next to her, startling Eva.

"Have you heard from Evans? What did he say?"

But of course Margot had not spoken to Evans. She hadn't left the room. She gazed at Eva.

"They aren't doing enough!" Eva cried. "Why aren't they telling us anything?"

"I'm sorry, Eva," Margot said. "I wish I could say that Dutch wouldn't— that I saw something good in him."

She stopped talking. What she was suggesting was unbearable. Eva held up a hand. "Please don't say more," she said. "What were you thinking? You're *married*!"

As soon as the words were out of her mouth, Eva thought they were the stupidest ever said to one woman by another. Margot had bags under her eyes and her skin had a gray tint. Her neckline revealed bruising, and of course

Eva had seen under the dress. She watched Margot rub her temple wearily. She was suffering, yet Eva couldn't help her disgust. She felt sick, thinking about what went on between the two of them.

"We'll get him back," Margot said.

Eva couldn't bear to look at her. She felt her eyes fill with tears. The break-room door opened and Eva's mouth opened in shock. Evans was escorting her parents inside. Her mother's hair was pulled back. She was wearing her spandex. There weren't going to be any classes today with the FBI mess. Her dad looked like he was off to work, in his khakis and button-down, wearing a suit jacket on the weekend.

"Oh my god," Eva muttered. Her mouth quivered with effort but she couldn't stop herself from sobbing. Her dad in those fucking khakis.

"What are you doing here?" she heard him ask. He was speaking to Margot, which confused Eva. Margot was on her feet, towering over her parents. Her dad's face was red and her mother, too, looked astonished. Margot looked uncomfortable, glancing down at Eva.

"You know each other?" she cried, dumbfounded.

She had imagined this moment a thousand times, but never like this. The fan in the corner refrigerator shut off. The air in the room reverberated with debilitated silence.

With a faint sigh, Margot announced, "My son is Birdie's father."

"*You?*" Eva's mother cried, back straightening. "From the symphony?"

"*What?*" cried her father.

Margot lowered her bad arm and gave a tired smile. "I am Birdie's other grandmother."

Eva's mother dropped to the couch beside her. She grasped her knees and stared at the floor a second, then turned to Eva, as if waiting for corroboration. Eva's dad remained frozen in place, staring up at Margot.

"How could you not mention this the other night?" he asked.

"That was hardly the time or place."

Hearing this, her mother moved like a spring had snapped inside her, jumping to her feet.

"You should have arranged to speak to us later then! You pretended not to know Eva, or anything about us!"

"What are you talking about?" Eva interrupted. "What 'other night?'"

"You played dumb!" her mother continued, stepping closer to Margot. "You were afraid! You thought you'd lose our funding!"

"That's ridiculous," Margot said. "I'm adjusting to the news myself. And it's Eva's place to tell you, not mine."

Eva stood up. "Wait a minute! You *know* each other?"

"We're sponsors of the Deaton Symphony," her father said to her. "We've been part of the adopt-a-player program. This season we adopted Margot Fickett."

The skin around her mother's mouth quivered with rage. "We met last week, at the symphony fundraiser."

"And you didn't tell me?" Eva said to Margot.

"I didn't see how it mattered," Margot said with placid, exhausted eyes.

Eva understood the inadequacy of this response, one she'd used so many times, both to her parents and Mrs. Fickett. How degrading. *Manipulated* was not too strong a word. That it wasn't an outright lie hardly mattered. For someone else to decide what you should or should not be aware of was demoralizing.

Stepping around the women, Eva's father came towards her. "Is it true that he's been kidnapped?"

Eva felt his question like a lance run through her middle. "Yes, Dad," she sobbed. "He was in the car. I left him sleeping in the car." She bent over her knees, rocking with shame.

A hand touched her shoulder. She heard her mother say, "Baby, I'm so sorry."

Eva looked into her mother's teary face. She felt wrung out and shredded, at the end of her strength, but could still register shock at the honest emotion she saw there.

"Birdie's father is a violin prodigy," she blurted with stiff defiance. "I never told him. I never told anyone. I didn't think it mattered. It *didn't* matter. I did all right. I did better than all right!" She glared at them all, daring anyone to disagree. "He's not a rapist or a druggie. He's not riffraff. He's a genius. So you can stop being such pricks."

At this her father dropped into a chair, his shoulders heaving with sobs. The sight was abhorrent. An officer entered, caught sight of the weeping man and did an about-face.

"Dad," Eva said.

He held up a hand to indicate she should give him a minute. Eva's mother crossed to the water cooler and brought two paper cups of water, one for Eva and one for her dad. Margot limped to the far sofa and sat down, trying to give them privacy.

"He's hungry," said Eva's mother. "You're hungry," she repeated, looking at her husband. "You never had breakfast."

Her dad wiped his nose and face with a white handkerchief, nodding. He downed the water and stood, announcing that he would go get food. Eva said she wasn't hungry. Nobody asked Margot.

"He needs something to do," her mother said when he was gone. "Men can't sit still."

Eva gave a bewildered laugh. To her it looked like her mother ordered him away, as if she couldn't stand his presence. Did they not see the insanity of their relationship? Nobody was hungry! Her mother was saying that Eva should come home, get some rest. Evans would call if there was news. Eva needed rest—she should come home.

"I'm not leaving, Mom."

They sat side by side on one couch, staring at the opposite wall. On the other couch, Mrs. Fickett stretched out on her back, grabbing a box of tissues to bolster her injured shoulder. The scene felt absurd, far too intimate—all of them mothers. Eva ran through the equation: Benji is to Margot as Birdie is to Eva; Eva is to her mother as Benji is to his mother as Birdie is to me. I had sex with Benji. And Margot had sex with Dutch.

Repulsed, she leaned back on the couch. A brown amorphous shape stained the ceiling tiles. The fluorescent lights hummed. Eva liked how Margot was with her parents. Not ingratiating or intimidated. She made no excuses for herself, or Benji. She didn't *apologize*.

She wondered if her parents remembered Benji Fickett. He was at their house the night of the graduation party. Kids, including Eva, called him Yo-Yo Ma. He'd grown his hair long senior year, a look he couldn't quite pull off. Eva's parents hosted the party but didn't provide the alcohol and they didn't want to know who had. Her mother had been against the whole idea, telling her father he'd end up with puke in his vegetable garden.

Eva was chopping wood for the bonfire, using a sledgehammer to break up palettes her father had collected. She had the job covered, but Benji joined her, picking up a second sledgehammer. After a time, he removed his shirt. She was shocked that underneath all that baggy clothing he was no waif—he had shoulders and a back. Could you get that from playing a violin?

They worked for several minutes in silence. Without stopping, she shouted to him, "So, how much do you practice?"

"Six hours a day," Benji called. "More on weekends."

Now Eva did stop. "Holy crap," she said. "I've never done anything for six hours a day. Except work. For which I get paid."

"It's like my job," he said, unsure if she was making fun of him.

"Oh, sleep," she added. "I sleep six hours, easy."

He laughed. It was a delightful laugh, familiar somehow, something you wanted to hear again.

The air was cool and clean-smelling that June night. Later, walking with a group to the swimming hole, Eva positioned herself near him and slowed down. She let Heather Copenhagen get ahead, watched her red shorts disappear down the trail and grabbed Benji's hand. She wanted to show him her childhood fort, she said, leading him deep inside a willow tree. What happened between them was Eva, all Eva. She'd had two shots of whiskey, but as they stood facing each other in the hideout, her head never felt clearer.

"Nobody knows where we are," Eva whispered.

"Nobody," he whispered back.

Even in the dark she could see the white flash of his teeth. Then she pulled her sweatshirt and tank top over her head, stepped out of her shorts and underpants and stood in the clearing naked except for her shoes. She could hear him doing the same. They both laughed when he stumbled and ended up on the ground. She went to help him up but he pulled her down to him. She was aware of the chill and the intense smell of mint, the first plant of summer along any body of water. It lined the trail and covered the riverbanks. They were probably lying in it. Forever after it was the smell of arousal and trysts. He groaned with pleasure. The air turned still as their bodies got serious, an intensity overcoming them both. They fumbled a little, but didn't laugh. Eva bent her legs to help him, was shocked by her hips rising, moving against him. There wasn't any pain, not the way other girls made it sound.

It was mostly just this yawning emptiness being filled up, filled to the very brim and over the edge, an all-encompassing skin bath, so shockingly close.

When it was over, sound came rushing at her, the swollen river, the rustle of leaves, the muffled screams of the others, not two hundred feet away. Sex would not occur again for nearly two years. She was at a dance club with Kariss while Bethany watched the baby. Eva ended up with a college boy in the alley. An urgent need to be entered, and afterwards, this same clarity of sound. A diesel engine a block over. The sound of heels on a sidewalk. The thumping music through the club walls. That night by the river was less efficient, sloppier and clumsier, but still, the knowing what to do, how to do it, was remarkable.

"Jesus," said Benji Fickett, sitting back. He grabbed his pants.

"I can't believe we did this," Eva said, pulling her shirt over her head.

He laughed and said, "Can we do it again, as soon as possible?"

This cracked her up. They were stumbling around the clearing trying to pull on their clothes. She could see nothing of him except his long, dark outline, his hair a shaggy halo. Walking back to the yard, they held hands until they entered the light from the fire. Her classmates appeared drunk and happy, huddled in towels and blankets. The astonishing accident in these relationships was apparent. Their shared experiences, over now, added up to nothing more than a weightless gas, the sort that would simply up and float away. Eva and Benji let go of each other's hands. They would never be a couple, Eva was certain. There was a good chance they'd never see each other again.

Her father returned to the police station with three shrink-wrapped sandwiches, a box of donuts and two Perriers. He set them on the table in front of Eva and her mother like treasure. Margot did not stir.

"My god, Ethan," said her mother. "That's it?"

But she did something astonishing. She opened the box of donuts, lifted out a chocolate sprinkle and bit into it. As Eva and her dad watched, she ate the whole thing, daring them to say anything. Eva grabbed a glazed donut, comforted by the sugary dough moving in her mouth. She watched her father eat a blueberry cake donut. Her mother reached for an apple fritter.

Twenty-nine

Leaving the police station, Sully caught a bus downtown, a local, which meant that every two blocks people poured on and off. It took twenty-five minutes to get close to the bowling alley. His gut churned. He hadn't eaten or slept in over thirteen hours. He walked the final four blocks to his pickup, then drove himself out to Rock Creek Commons. Cop cruisers blocked the entrance and FBI rigs ringed the parking lot. He drove past, did a U-turn and doubled back to the auto parts store, where he parked. On foot, he jumped the creek and approached the building, passing Annie's studio. It was closed, as was Paige's store. The morning was clear and cold. The tails of his bowling shirt—returned to him at the police station—billowed behind him as he came around the corner.

Crime scene tape formed a square around the shop door, encircling the hawthorn tree and its stone planter. News crews hovered fifty yards back, by the birdfeed store. Outside the police tape, wearing sweatpants and slippers with no socks, stood Marvin, smoking. Sully had never been so glad to see him. Marv picked up his walking stick and hobbled over, holding out his hand. They hooked thumbs and clasped hands.

"You got away," Sully said, and Marv launched into his escape story. He'd stayed close to the wall, he said, limping around the perimeter to the back door. Sully knew but didn't say that Marvin escaped because the feds weren't after him; they wanted Dutch. Evans had told Sully that the FBI was acquainted with the evil three. The woman had no record but both men did, in California and Nevada. Sully told Marvin what he knew about the raids across Montana.

"This is some crazy shit," said Marvin. "The cannabis apocalypse."

A mound of dirt was piled next to the door where at least two dozen planters had been dumped. Stalks were wrapped in blue plastic tarps. Agents moved in and out of the shop wearing blue gloves and respirator masks, some carrying cameras, others with notebooks. The curing jars, now empty, were lined against the exterior wall. The cured bud would have been bagged, probably on its way to an evidence room in Helena.

"What's the case against us?" Marvin cried, loud enough for the agents to hear. "We were in compliance. Every one of those jars filled orders for card-carrying customers!"

Sully put his hands in his pockets, not in the mood for one of Marv's libertarian rants. He started shouting about Sully, asking hadn't Sully served his country, with multiple tours in Afghanistan? Didn't everybody in this shop love his country? They were following the law!

"This is some Fascist, martial-law dictator shit," Marv cried, dropping his cigarette and smothering it with the sole of his slipper.

The lack of reaction meant that Marv had probably been spouting like this for a while. The door to the shop stood open. Seeing no immediate obstacle, Sully ducked under the tape and marched inside like he belonged, closing the door behind him. No one was in the reception area. Their laptops had been piled in the corner along with the printer, the paper files they kept in the office, two external hard drives and every scrap note, Post-it and pencil. Appalled, Sully gazed at the pile. On a hunch, he moved to the heat vent in the far corner behind the counter. They hadn't found it. He squatted, turned the wing nuts and swung open the false front, revealing the safe. His fingers flew through the combination and the door opened. Empty.

He fell onto his rear, hung his elbows on his knees, seeing white. Rage ripped through his intestines and spread across his chest. He slapped the vent cover so hard it bounced against the wall and fell off its hinge, hanging like a broken tooth.

Marvin's cane and hairy ankles appeared.

"How much was in there?" he asked, eyes magnified by his thick glasses.

"A hundred, two hundred grand. The guy hated banks."

Marv whistled. Sully gave a halfhearted snort, dug his fists into his eye sockets. It wasn't Sully's money, exactly, but Jesus the *man hours* he had in this place. He pulled a hand through his hair slow and hard enough to stretch the skin of his scalp.

"I knew this was too good to be true," Marvin said.

"Have you seen Gerald? Anybody?"

Marv shook his head.

"You brought Dutch to my house that day, last fall," Sully said.

"I regret that. Boy do I."

"Where'd you meet him? Where'd he come from?"

"Bruno's. I was at the bar and he came up to me, wondered if I'd know how to connect him."

"You'd never seen him before?"

Marv shook his head. Sully looked at the floor. It was about six months too late for this line of questioning.

"How did he know?" Sully asked, jumping to his feet. "How did he *know* they were coming? It just doesn't figure. "He leaves the bowling alley and *poof!* Vanishes into thin air."

"Fucker's lucky," said Marv.

Sully stared. Could it be that simple? The infectious cloud that followed Dutch, the mesmerizing charm and good looks was nothing more than infuriatingly dumb luck?

Two agents came out of the grow room. Seeing Sully and Marvin, their hands went to their holsters. Sully raised his hands, repeating, "We're going, we're going." He thought about telling them about the missing money. But the safe was now exposed. Let them figure it out.

He swung open the outer door, marched through, ducked under the tape and kept going, ignoring Marvin's calls. It had become an obscenely bright day. Fucking schizophrenic weather. Tulips along the boulevards. Birds. They're gone all winter and suddenly they're back, cracking open the silence of the longer season with their irritating cheer. A fat, chirpy robin on the street sign. Clouds of sparrows darting through the park.

He pulled into Lucky Lane, parked in the gravel outside his trailer. He saw the front door was ajar and knew his worst suspicion was true. He spent ten seconds beating his steering wheel, then stepped out, took the steps two at a time. Gritting his teeth, he made his way to the back room. The planters were still intact, his seedlings were alive. His curing jars were just as he left them, except they were all empty.

Rage leapt out of him. He was in the hall, didn't remember exiting his grow room. He drew back a leg and put a foot through the paneling, had to struggle to extract it and ended up on the floor. He jumped to his feet and stormed down the hall, put his fist through the door to his bedroom. The ruined closet door gave him pause, but his body couldn't stop. Sloping into the bathroom, he gripped the sides of the medicine chest, stared at his own reflection and ripped the cabinet out of the wall. The mirrored front swung open, toothpaste, toothbrush, shaving cream and razor tumbled into the sink. He threw the thing into the tub. Its weight ripped the shower curtain from its plastic rings. The plastic fabric deflated on top of the cabinet in maddening slow motion.

He paced his front room, feeling the rage drain from him. The shades were drawn, which was good—the darker the better. He saw the clock. It was fucking Saturday, his day to get Caity. He'd have to explain this mess. Daddy lost his temper. Her pale brows, knit with disappointment.

He listened to his messages standing outside next to his pickup. Eva's news squeezed the breath out of him. He spun around to lean on the truck. Three messages, the first unintelligible, the second panicked, early this morning: "Where are you?" The wretched third: Dutch took her car *with Birdie in it.*

He lowered the phone. It made no sense. Dutch left with the cash, the weed, and the little boy. What the fuck did he want with Birdie? Sully felt a volcanic surge in the center of his body, had the forethought to get himself back inside. In his front room he bent over, pounding his thighs with his fists, screeching like a wounded animal, unable to fill his lungs. He had to stop screaming in order to inhale, then out came one horrible, deep sob. Evans had warned him to forget Eva, "for her sake." He suggested Sully try the straight and narrow from now on, put him on probation for a year. Sully imagined he'd give it a week before he found Eva, a scene he saw taking place in her new shop. He'd report what Evans had said. They would laugh about the "straight and narrow." *What exactly is the straight and narrow?* he could hear Eva ask. *A hallway? Alleys are straight and narrow.* My vagina *is straight and narrow.*

He stumbled out to the porch and stood with his hands on the railing, gulping air. The whole of Lucky Lane felt still, as if the place itself was trying to recover. Curtains shifted, sparrows looked down from the naked trees. A muddy trough had formed around the base of his trailer from the dripping roof. He stared at it, listening to the distant sound of a cartoon show coming from next door. Above him, the blue sky.

He drove to Eva's. No sign of life, nor her car. He got out and pounded on the door anyway. Her homemade For Sale sign filled him with a sorrow he didn't understand and he kicked it flat as he marched back to his truck. She might be at her new space and though it was out of his way, would make him late to pick up Caity, he drove across town, parked, and peered in the windows, even walked around back to pound on the bay door. He could simply call her—but no, he told himself. He could *not*. What would he say? What was there to say? He should call her. If he loved her he would call her. He imagined her at her parents' house, in that massive front room full of windows, and could not do it.

He was heading north on the Russell Avenue bridge. Without a signal, he pulled over, threw the truck in park and got out. Cars honked, veering around him. He marched around the hood of his truck to the rail and hurled his cell phone over the side, watching it vanish with a little splash into the gurgling, frigid current.

In front of Paige's house, Sully blew out a long slow breath and headed for the front door. Paige opened it wearing what looked like pajamas though it was almost noon. She turned her back without a word, leaving the door wide open. "Daddy's here," he heard her say in monotone as she disappeared into the kitchen.

Caity leapt up from the couch, wearing a tutu and tank top. Her smile, her bouncing self, woke something in him. He knelt to wrap his arms around her narrow shoulders and felt an inner sigh. Her hair smelled dirty. Paige couldn't make her wash or pick up or do much of anything.

"Get your stuff," he said quietly. Looking around, he noticed her school backpack thrown by the door, untouched since yesterday. The television was on. She watched too much TV.

"Can you get your toothbrush?" he asked. "Some clothes for school on Monday?"

She bounced up and down on the balls of her feet then sped down the hall to her room.

Paige was in the kitchen. Dirty dishes were piled in both sides of the double sink, even along the counter. This morning's breakfast and maybe last night's dinner remains still sat on the table. Plastic placemats soiled with dried milk. It stunned him, that she lived like this. He took off his coat, let it drop to the floor and pulled up his sleeves, started removing dishes from one side of the sink.

"Oh no you don't," she hissed from her seat at the table. With her hair down, without makeup, she looked older, more like her mother. His hands kept doing what they were doing.

"I said, stop it!" she cried, standing. "You don't get to come in here and be a big hero. You're no hero, Sullivan." She was coming towards him. "You realize that in the span of a week you've wrecked my life? Sleeping with my employee. Shutting down my shop. They won't let anyone in the parking lot, thanks to your little scheme."

"I had nothing to do with that," Sully said softly. "It was Dutch they wanted. The business was legal."

"Doesn't look legal from the street, to all the people driving by, gawking."

"They can't keep you out."

"Oh, no! They told me I could go back to work! But federal agents buzzing around the place like wasps isn't that good for business."

He stopped moving the dishes. Staring at the drain in the bottom of the sink he thought, She's lazy. She doesn't want to go back to work or clean up this house or be a parent. He recalled the last time he was in this kitchen, how he'd cornered her. What did it matter? He was done spending energy on her.

"It'll blow over, Paige."

"It'll blow over!" she shrieked. "Blow up is more like it! Jesus, you've wrecked my life and that's *all* you can say?"

He took a deep breath as he unrolled his sleeves. He picked up his coat and told her, "My payment will be late. I have some clients who owe me, but it might be a while till I get back on my feet."

She crossed her arms, ready to dig in again. Before she could, he said, "Dutch robbed me," he said, blinking at her. "Took everything, even my crop."

Paige shook her head with disgust, arms still crossed over her body. "You thought you were going to be so slick," she said. "Big business man." She puffed out her cheeks and blew at him. She wanted a fight but Sully was done, limp as rodent in the jaws of a predator.

"He skipped town, took Eva's little boy."

The slight jump to her eyes, the way her arms dropped to her sides when he said it meant she was not a monster after all.

"What did you—are you saying he *kidnapped* Birdie?"

He looked into her face and pursed his lips.

"For fuck's sake, Sully, why did you—they're still gone? Since when?"

"Early this morning."

He was braced, ready to hear how she knew it all along about Dutch, and what an idiot he'd been to go into business with him. Instead, Paige put a hand to her mouth.

Caity appeared with her toothbrush in one hand and a pillow stuffed with clothes. They both looked at her, the two people who made her. The one good thing they'd done. Caitlyn Caruthers Stiles.

"Leave her," said Paige. "Take the week. Get yourself together."

Sully looked up, surprised. Caity was shouting protests, clinging to his leg, but he knew it was for the best. He hugged her, rubbed her back and promised they'd have Dairy Queen for dinner when she came again. Paige looked anxious and sorry as she walked him to the door, holding Caity's hand. Backing out of her driveway, Sully hoped to god the vision of them on the porch would be the low point of this mess.

Thirty

Late in the afternoon on Saturday, Deaton traffic was heavy, which happened when the weather was fine. Droves headed out of town, towards Flathead Lake or into the mountains for spring skiing. Crossing the river was a slog. Margot and Eva hit every red light. On the tracks by the fairgrounds they met a freighter and sat with the windows down as it hammered by. With every mile after the underpass, Margot felt a familiar lift in mood. Traffic, people, and sound thinned as they snaked through the canyon. Open fields roared over the hillsides under the blue sky, the freshly turned soil dark as night. They passed the fencerows of the horse farm, then the wilder creekside miles, the banks greening up, willows budding. Margot smelled the swelling water and knew that, broken and shamed as she felt, she was not destroyed.

She wanted to share the optimism with Eva, but sensed the instinct was wrong. What could the canyon offer Eva? The girl surely blamed herself. How could she not? A single different decision that morning would have kept Birdie from harm. She glanced over at her shriveled form in the passenger seat. At the police station, Eva had jumped to her feet when Margot announced she was going home. *I'm coming with you,* she cried. Her parents were both stunned, even hurt, sitting there with a box of half-eaten donuts.

"Are you hungry?" Margot asked her now.

In answer, Eva scoffed without moving.

"I have bourbon at home. That might help."

They passed the final ranchettes before the Ficketts' driveway. Until the grader could get out here, the hill would be a slog. "Hold on," she said. The back of the Suburban sashayed like a duck's tail as they sunk in the swampy road, but they made it to the top.

They took off their coats in the foyer and she led Eva downstairs, poured her the drink at the counter. Eva sat on a stool, not touching it. Behind her, through the huge windows, Margot could see the valley bathed in the wheat-colored light of late day. The roof was no longer dripping and the deck was dry. She opened a window, letting in the breath of spring.

"My mother will find us," Eva said. "That's why she asked for your physical address. She'll use her phone to find your house."

Us. Eva used that pronoun, Margot noted. What was that, exactly? *Us* was being invented, right now, as they spoke. "That's okay, isn't it?"

Eva shrugged, listless. "Apparently, you already know my parents?"

Margot picked up a rag and gave the counter an idle swipe.

"Only as sponsors. It's not like we were friends," she said, which sounded embarrassingly adolescent, the deny-everything defense: *I'm not friends with them! God!*

Eva gave another airy shrug. "Sure."

The immaturity of the mood felt appropriate; Margot's hangover made her feel like a whoring coed. In an attempt to re-inhabit her adult self, she came around the counter to sit on the stool next to Eva. Clearing her throat, striving for her teacherly voice, she said, "Last night, Dutch and I—" Here she hit a wall. What about them?

"You're lucky he didn't hurt you. I mean, really hurt you."

"I know," Margot said. "I just wanted to say that it was bad judgment on my part."

Eva snorted. "You don't have to explain. I'm not going to tell anyone."

"No, that's not—I want to explain. I'm happily married. I love my family. I was temporarily insane."

Eva regarded her. "I don't think you were insane."

Margot straightened, brought up by the challenge in her tone.

"You didn't call your husband. You told me earlier in the week you needed more time."

"Not for *that*, Eva! Sex with Dutch was not what I had in mind."

"Wasn't it?" Eva smirked. "You knew you'd go to the bowling alley, yet to me you acted undecided."

An icy stillness spread through Margot.

"You can *say* you didn't know what you were doing, but you had your reasons."

Eva picked up the little glass of bourbon and slid off the stool. She walked past the stairs into the living room. In the slanting light, her face looked twice its age. How fitting, Margot thought, when she has just shamed me like a parent.

She slid off the stool and headed up the stairs, calling to Eva, "I'm going to take a shower."

Eva's head snapped up. She met Margot's gaze through the wire balustrade and said, "The best shower of your life."

Margot undressed and studied the horror of her reflection. In the fluorescent light, her skin looked gray. Her scar was purple at the center and a sick yellow-green towards the edges. Scabs had formed on her nipples. Her breasts had finger bruises, as did her hips. Using a hand mirror, she saw that her back ribs were also bruised. The cuts on the bottoms of her feet were raw but not bleeding.

The Advil and the dope had worn off, and shame's high tide was upon her. She'd had sex with a bad man, only the third man ever. His smoldering sexuality, the way he kept daring her to prove she wasn't the slumming phony he accused Eva of being, had worked. All their encounters were a long seduction, she saw. His feelings did not go beyond a lust for dominance. He wanted to win. The cookie he left in the fridge said as much. A taunt. Margot deserved Eva's jabs, she knew. If she had disappointed Eva, imagine Andy's reaction.

He'd have trouble believing it. Margot had no interest in dope, largely ignored the legalization battle. She scoffed at the stoned girls who trotted into his shows like ponies, with their long braids and gauzy skirts. She didn't worry about him straying. If he wanted such specimens, good luck.

In the sobering light of her bathroom, Margot saw her puffed-up apathy as trust in disguise. She *trusted* Andy. Always had. This thought settled into her chest with a terrible weight. She lowered herself to the edge of the tub, recalling other comments she'd made about his audience. She called them "a bunch of sloppy stoners." Her cockiness was so obviously rooted in trust. Derision was a way to dare him. Andy would smile, sometimes laugh in assent. Now she wondered if he saw through her, if he knew that showing off was a way of not minding his long absences, all the clubs and festivals he played.

Eva was right. Margot was not insane. At any point during the past week she might have avoided all this.

Infidelity. Treachery. Ugly words, the overblown vocabulary of the unfaithful. She jumped over to the toilet just in time to vomit. She had nothing in her stomach, which felt like it was folding in on itself. Her bowels seized. She had to turn quickly and sit, losing what remained of the last twenty-four hours in a quick, hot gush. She stepped into the shower, foul and demoralized, weeping like miserable child.

By the time she got out of the shower, the doorbell was ringing. Margot dressed quickly and opened the front door to find Annie Baker standing on the porch holding a pizza and a bottle of wine.

"I hope you don't mind. I can't stand being away from her."

Margot let her in, led her downstairs. They both stopped short when Eva came out of the downstairs bathroom, hair wet, dressed in one of Benji's old T-shirts and her underpants.

"Mom!"

The sight of her half-dressed daughter flustered Mrs. Baker. She coughed and looked away, but Margot was happy to see Eva making herself at home.

"Any news?" Mrs. Baker asked.

Eva shook her head. Her mother turned towards the kitchen, set the pizza box on the counter and started opening drawers. Margot stepped over, dug up a corkscrew and handed it to her. "Mrs. Baker—"

"Please," the woman smirked. "We're family. Call me Annie."

This remark landed with a thud. Eva turned away, crossing to the living room. Margot handed Annie a glass.

"Most kidnappings that end well do so in the first twenty-four hours," Annie said in a lowered voice, pouring the wine. "Agent Evans said so after you left. We're on hour eleven."

Unsure how to respond to this, Margot led Annie to the living room. Eva was lying down, had a blanket pulled up to her chin with her eyes closed. Annie sat in the chair and Margot sat opposite Eva on the other couch.

"It's so funny the way life turns out," Annie said, reclining the chair.

Oh boy, thought Margot.

"We never dreamed we'd be grandparents so early."

"I'm finding it hard to adjust to, myself."

"Have you told your son?" she asked. "Does he know?"

"I haven't, no."

"Can I ask why not?"

Margot inhaled, wondering what it would be like for Eva, growing up with this kind of aggression. "You can ask, you just did," she said. "My answer won't satisfy you."

"Try me."

"He's in school. He's a musician, like me. Classical violin—well, he's transitioning to other forms—anyway, I want him to stay in school. I want him to finish. The last thing I want is to wreck his future."

With an anemic smile, Annie said, "Tell me about it."

Margot's usual reluctance to explain herself wasn't going to fly, she saw. She glanced at Eva. The girl's eyes were closed but Margot doubted she was asleep. Annie Baker wanted a defense, and didn't care if Eva overheard it.

"I needed to be certain," Margot said. "We only got the results last week. You probably don't know but eight weeks ago I fell in the middle of the night. I'm a cello player. I don't downhill ski, don't ice skate, don't ride horses. I protect my assets like an athlete, and I broke my collarbone taking out the trash. I know it sounds ridiculous, but the world fell apart."

Annie Baker lowered her glass. "Don't get melodramatic. This didn't happen only to you."

As rude as it was, Margot believed the woman was entitled. Her own behavior was inexcusable and her reasons for not coming clean, calling Benji and Andy, or being upfront with the Bakers at the gala, sounded thin even to her.

"Of course," said Margot. "I can't imagine how it's been for you."

Annie leaned forward to top off her glass, taking her time, aware that she now had the floor.

"Eva's always been high strung," she said without a glance at her daughter. "She didn't talk till she was three. That was a source of concern. I always said it was exactly like Eva. She did what she wanted, when she wanted. But of course her brother talked enough for both of them. Conroy's at Stanford School of Medicine."

She said this like a proud hen, but she didn't look proud. She looked wrecked, with heavy bags under her eyes. An anger line creased her forehead and one muscled leg was thrown over the other, foot twitching.

"It was the same with the baby. Birdie. She would not be talked out of it. Would not be helped. Wouldn't tell us who the father was, so we could get him to help."

"I regret that," said Margot.

"We tried!" said Annie. "Ethan was beside himself. I think Eva thought her father would do the boy harm."

She looked at Margot, as if she expected some kind of rejoinder. What did she want to hear? *I understand*? And how bizarre, to talk as though Eva wasn't listening to every word.

"She's a good girl," Margot said, which came out sounding more earnest than she intended, as if she were trying to earn points with Eva. "I'm impressed by her, I mean. What she's done. Raising a child is hard enough with two parents. To raise a boy by yourself, I can't imagine."

"We do try to help," said Mrs. Baker, swirling her glass of red wine, gazing into it.

"I didn't mean—"

"She won't let us! She keeps him away from us, from me!" She sat up in her chair, animated. "Sometimes she and Ethan and Birdie go out for pizza. But not me. She doesn't want me anywhere near him. I think she wants to hurt me because she says I paid more attention to Conroy than I did to her." Lifting her wine glass and sitting back, she added, "She's not wrong. I did."

Margot shifted on the couch, glancing at Eva. "I'm sure it's hard, trying to balance two children."

"She was more difficult, that's all there is to it."

As Margot watched, appalled, the woman emptied her glass, then languidly lowered her arm, holding its rim with her fingertips. "What about you? How did you end up here?"

Margot gave a half laugh. "It's not the end of the earth."

"But you can see it from here!" She slapped her thigh in mock amusement at this tired phrase. Margot didn't react.

"You play cello. Did you never want a career?"

"I have a career."

"I mean, an exciting one. In Europe or New York. Somewhere big! With prestige."

Again, Annie came forward to refill her glass, unconcerned that she might have offended Margot.

"We all have a vision for our lives," Margot said carefully. "You shape it and it shapes you."

In response to this platitude, Annie Baker rolled her eyes with an exaggerated smirk.

"I suppose I did want more," Margot admitted.

"What happened?"

"I don't know, exactly. Life happened," she said with a mirthless laugh.

Annie Baker snorted in agreement. "And now you're a grandmother. Suddenly you're much further along on the journey than you thought."

"I wasn't going to have children," Margot continued. "I had an abortion when I was seventeen."

Annie Baker froze with her glass halfway to her mouth. Eva's eyes snapped open. She didn't move a muscle but looked wild with surprise. Margot felt a warm deflation. Confessing shut down the magnetic power of the thing. In one instant it became a decision among thousands, even millions of decisions she'd made in her life. How wasteful, to have spent the decades harboring that wrong turn. But Nigel wasn't even a turn, more a speed bump, was all.

"I've never told anyone," Margot said, breathless but smiling. "Feels good to say it. Validating."

She waited. If Annie Baker said anything patronizing, Margot would kick her out. She said nothing, only lifted her glass in a silent toast.

How ridiculous I've been, thought Margot. How poorly I've behaved! I'm injured and I act like a child. My little rebellion. My grandchild's been taken and I had a part in it.

"Are you all right?" asked Mrs. Baker.

Eva was watching her, too. Margot's hands were clenched and her jaw pulsed.

"No," she said. "I am not all right. I only realized it now. I am not all right with any of this."

Annie Baker leaned back in her chair. "Welcome to the club," she said with a sad, frail smile. "I'm sick of talking. How about you put on some music. Classical music. Something slow and sad and lovely."

Margot saw that she was serious and immediately liked her better. She crossed to the stereo and cued Tchaikovsky. In times of tumult, her habit was to return to the Russians. She played the fourth movement of Tchaikovsky's Sixth Symphony, so well-known in tragic movies or love scenes. The opening notes of sorrow constricted her chest. This music could embarrass some people. Students were uncomfortable with the emotion and drama. Tonight it brought tears to her eyes.

She looked over, thought she saw a matching shine in Annie Baker's gaze. The crescendo five minutes in was heartbreaking: the horns were more majestic than she remembered and the longing in the strings was difficult to bear. The intervals of stunned silence followed by more of that sweeping, foreboding beauty said so clearly that this was the music of a terrible farewell.

When it was over, Mrs. Baker was asleep with the wine glass poised on the armrest. Margot stood to remove the glass, set it on the table. She got a blanket from the chest in the corner and covered the woman, thinking she'd go up to bed. In the end she couldn't leave them. She didn't want to be alone. She got another blanket and lay down on the couch, her shoulder immobilized by a throw pillow, legs hanging off the arm and the blanket hanging from her feet like a curtain.

Thirty-one

Eva's phone vibrated before it rang. She opened her eyes as it started its chugging dance across the coffee table. She jolted awake and snatched it.

"We got him," said Evans. His voice was calm and steady as he reported where to meet them. Eva stopped listening as soon as he said the name of the hospital. She hung up, jumped off the couch, crying, *Margot!* as she ran to get dressed.

Without discussion, Eva rode in the Suburban. Her mother followed in her own car. Margot drove with both hands on the wheel and kept the injured shoulder slightly forward. She stared at the road with her eyebrows up, as if it might get away from her.

"He's okay," Eva said after miles of silence. "He's going to be all right."

When they pulled into the hospital, an ambulance was unloading. Margot pulled in behind it and Eva jumped out, sprinting through the automatic doors to the triage area, where the nurse directed her to his gurney. Birdie was being rehydrated intravenously. A nurse was soaking his left hand in a tub of warm water. His eyes were open but he didn't look fully awake. Eva took his face between her hands, trying not to weep when he said, "I was brave."

Evans reported that Birdie was left with a granola bar and a water bottle, but the bar had fallen out of reach. Birdie had pulled one arm free—the one with the frostbitten hand—and reached the water bottle, drank the whole thing, which helped. Video surveillance put Dutch in the truck stop in Bonner, east of town, at nine a.m. on Saturday. He bought Ritz crackers, a sweatshirt, water and a backpack. Afterwards, he vanished. Probably got a ride with a trucker, Evans said. Birdie had been in the car all day and half the night.

Eva distinctly remembered packing granola bars and water that morning; Dutch had cared nothing for Birdie's survival, didn't even return to the car. Some time past three a.m., the night clerk took out the trash. The car was parked near the dumpster, which was fenced and locked. The night was crystal clear and cold, well below freezing. There would have been stars by the millions. The drone of I-90. The shine of the river in the valley to the south. The clerk lit a cigarette but without a coat could only take two drags before he turned to toss it. Realizing the car was not his coworker's, he crouched to see inside, and popped straight up again. A little boy was buckled into a car seat. He used the light on his phone to be certain.

At three-fifty a.m., the 9-1-1 dispatcher took information from a hysterical clerk who kept muttering, "Oh god, he's not moving. He's not moving!" An ambulance and a sheriff's patrolman were dispatched. The woman talked the young man through opening the car door—it wasn't locked—unbuckling the boy and carrying him inside. Here the two night employees stared at one another, horrified. They wrapped him in blankets taken from the shelves. Within ten minutes they heard the sirens on the highway, and this felt like way too long. The boy was bluish in the face and did not wake up, but he was breathing.

Birdie was discharged by four o'clock in the afternoon on Sunday. His left hand was wrapped in dressing. The extent of the frostbite wouldn't be apparent for another several weeks. Eva's father joined them. They gathered in the waiting room and Eva's mother asked again if she wanted to come home. Eva said, "We're going with Margot."

Which meant they were riding with Satterfield. Margot called him after she was treated by the on-call orthopedist, who ordered her to put her arm back in the sling. The bone had cracked again. She would have six more months in hardware and rehab, and he couldn't guarantee she would bow again. She was told not to drive unless it was an emergency.

The maestro waltzed through the automatic doors in his wool trench. With a top hat, the man might have stepped out of *Great Expectations*. Her parents swooned like he was royalty. He pulled off his leather gloves, holding out his hand to them. To Eva's chagrin, her father introduced himself as a "long-time symphony donor."

"Of course," Satterfield said, then turned to Eva and Margot. "Ladies."

"Lambchops," Eva greeted him, enjoying her parents' shocked dismay at the irreverent nickname.

Satterfield silently ran a finger over his left sideburn, fighting a smile. Her mother muttered, "Eva!"

Satterfield left his vehicle at the hospital. They rode in Margot's Suburban. As soon as they were on the road, he said, "I hope all this doesn't kill your parents' generosity."

Margot turned to him and said, "You shit."

Eva held Birdie and smiled into the dark of the back seat.

The mood at Margot's was nothing like the previous night's tense wait. It reminded her of a sleepover at a new friend's. She noticed things she hadn't before: the narrow, elegant phone table in the foyer, the hanging globes over the kitchen bar, casting an orange glow, the curve of the kitchen faucet, marble knobs on the cabinets.

They had stopped for Mexican carryout. Satterfield set it out on the counter bar while Margot changed clothes. Eva held Birdie, studying the refrigerator magnets. Benji wearing a suit, holding his violin. A younger Margot and large, blond Mr. Fickett.

"What's he like?" Eva asked.

"Andy Fickett?" Satterfield asked, following her gaze. "You'll like him. Most people do."

She turned. The sideburns actually made his gray eyes stand out. He was handsome, even more so, she imagined, dressed in a tuxedo, waving a baton. His face was kind and something else, curious, maybe. Open, which was rare in older people.

"But not you?" Eva guessed.

"Not me what?"

"You don't like Andy."

The corner of his mouth twitched. One eyebrow rose.

"You said *most* people like him," she explained. "As in, *most*, but not you."

"Not you!" Birdie repeated, reaching out to squeeze Eva's lips. His first unsolicited words! Her face lit up; she smiled at him, kissed his hand.

"We are very different," Satterfield admitted.

Eva moved to stand directly across the counter from him. Satterfield barely looked at Birdie but his eyes wandered over her with interest.

"You're in love with Margot," she said quietly.

Satterfield gave a loud barking laugh, tossing his head. Birdie started, but Eva was smiling. He recognized the merriment and clapped his wrapped hand with his naked palm.

"That's why you don't like Andy," Eva continued, nonplussed.

"Funny," Satterfield said. His eyes were amused, but the way they turned down at the outer edge made him look permanently sad.

"I'm right," Eva said. "It's obvious."

"You're very confident. I can see why Benji liked you."

The name slowed her down, which was surely his intention.

"No," Eva said, coming around the island. "In high school, I was nothing like I am now."

She sat on the stool next to him. Birdie sat on her lap. Satterfield wasn't the least flustered by their proximity. He put an elbow on the counter and let his forearm rest between them. His fingers were long and elegant, like Margot's.

"What do you mean?" he asked.

"I fit in."

Satterfield waited.

"I was just like everybody else," she explained. "I conformed. If Birdie hadn't come along, I'd still be mainstream and stupid."

"You certainly don't seem mainstream and stupid."

He gazed down at her like a school principal. She wasn't fishing for a compliment, but Eva liked hearing him say this.

"I am not," he continued, "nor have I ever been, *obvious*."

His tone was formidable, but his eyes danced with amusement. Eva gave a small laugh, and when Satterfield smiled, she said, "I'm afraid you are."

He sighed and said, "Really, I don't see what a tiny drug dealer has that I haven't."

"Nothing!" Eva cried, exploding with laughter. "I assure you! *Nothing!*"

Satterfield laughed too, which Birdie watched with interest. Still smiling, Satterfield filled a plate with tacos, chips and guacamole and slid it towards her. Eva wasn't hungry, couldn't imagine chewing, but Birdie reached out for a chip.

"*Does* Margot know?" she asked. "Are you two..."

He looked at her. "Eva. We are both married."

"That didn't stop her this weekend," Eva said.

He froze, holding another plate. She had shocked him. His eyelashes were perfectly straight and long.

"What do you mean?"

"Nothing," Eva said. "I shouldn't have said that."

He put the plate down and swung his body towards her, hands on his lap. "I saw them together, at Bruno's," he said. "A week ago. Is that what are you referring to?"

Eva glanced at the stairs. The weight of knowing, of being the only one who knew, was suddenly unbearable. She didn't want to tattle on Margot so much as offload the information.

"Her new injuries—he did that. Friday night, they spent the night together and he left her locked in."

She spoke quickly, in one long breath. Instead of the relief she expected, she felt guilty. Birdie turned to her, squeezing her face between his hands. Eva kissed him, but looked at Satterfield. He couldn't hold her gaze. Even in profile Eva could see his hurt, which confused her. They weren't married! And people their age ignored their feelings! Her parents and their friends seemed not to possess any, in fact.

Birdie reached for another chip. The sign of appetite thrilled her. She pulled the plate closer, offering him a forkful of taco meat, consciously disengaging from the complexity she'd just unearthed.

Margot's feet appeared on the stairs. Eva looked at Satterfield, who also noticed. He came off his stool to greet her with a kiss on the cheek, being careful of her arm. Eva watched them closely, mystified by the idea that people could leave their desires on simmer for decades.

Later, after Satterfield's wife picked him up, Margot showed Eva the keys to her Honda. The car had been parked since the accident. It was too low to the ground for Margot, so Eva might as well use it. She showed Eva Benji's room, where she and Birdie would stay. Just as they had last night, they settled on the couches downstairs. Birdie was rubbing his eyes on Eva's shoulder. Margot pointed, saying Eva should put him to bed.

"Are you kidding?" Eva said. "I'm not letting him out of my sight!"

He fell asleep on her shoulder as they reviewed the details of the weekend, starting with the moment Eva saw her at the bowling alley. Eva laid Birdie beside her on the couch, his head resting on her thigh. "You were higher than a hot air balloon," she said, which made Margot laugh. They discussed the falling dresser, and Margot grew almost somber. "It could have killed you!" she said.

They marveled that the events were barely forty-eight hours ago. Margot asked what it was like to overhear her mother speaking like that.

"You mean when she said Conroy was her favorite?" Eva shrugged. "It was nothing I didn't know."

"Is it true, you try to keep her away from Birdie?"

Eva felt her lips tighten, recalling her mother's defensiveness. *We do try to help!*

"My mother has done her damage. I'm not going to leave him unprotected."

"What are you afraid of?"

"She'll make him think he's not good enough. He'll be dragged all over to wherever she wants to go, to be shown off when she wants him to be charming, and then expected to shut down when she's busy. She expects compliance. He's an accessory to be put on and taken off as the mood hits her."

Eva's face felt hot. Her voice had risen. Birdie stirred and she put a hand on his back.

"Wow," said Margot.

Eva looked over. "You can see why I wasn't in a hurry to have more parents. I know it was selfish. I just couldn't risk it."

Margot's pity lifted a little. Eva was relieved. She said abruptly, "So you had an abortion."

Margot reacted with the tiniest jolt. She nodded.

"Why didn't you tell me? You let me march into that crowd of picketers, cursing them, when all along you had—" Eva stopped, unsure how to phrase what she wanted to say, sensing she ought to not say it. Margot had gone ahead with what Eva couldn't do, which mildly disgusted her. And that disgust was wrong, she was sure. It was what the fuckers wanted you to feel.

"You might have at least let on that you were once in my shoes," Eva said. "You had to face being pregnant, too. You let me go on feeling all proud of myself for what I went through, when you went through it, too."

Margot was still for a time. "It was different for me," she said finally. "I was younger than you were."

"A year! One year younger!" Eva cried. "I don't see how that matters. And it wasn't my age that kept me from having an abortion." Her heart was pounding again. This time she didn't stop. "I didn't do it because I didn't want to live with that, being someone who did that. One of *those* women."

Margot's eyes fell. She pulled her injured arm into her body a little tighter, crossed her legs. Eva wondered at herself, baiting the woman into self-defense. She knew Margot wouldn't apologize, didn't want her to. What right did Eva have to shame her? It ought to work the other way around. Eva was supposed to be all liberated and open about abortion and women's rights. So why was she accusing Margot of being horrible?

She wanted what she always wanted from her mother, Eva saw with embarrassment. She wanted Margot to pronounce that Eva and Birdie were the best thing ever. She wanted assurance that she hadn't made a single mistake. The fact that Eva and Margot chose differently made this impossible. One of them had to be wrong. But that was stupid. They both got to choose what was right for them, which was sort of the point.

"Eva, I did feel for you," Margot said at last. "All along I felt for you, for your situation. You think I didn't see myself in you? I was sympathetic. And guilty, too. You took a risk I couldn't take."

"I could say the same thing."

"The boy I met, the father—he was nothing like Benji, I can tell you that. I hate even the hint of comparison. Maybe that was why I didn't say anything."

"What was he like?"

Margot rubbed her temple. "Irresponsible. Self-absorbed. Cruel."

Eva looked up. "Like Dutch."

With a look of miserable agreement, Margot said, "Yes. Like Dutch."

She got up to make them hot chocolate and Eva was glad the subject was closed. She came back with a mug stuffed with marshmallows for Eva. Poking the white pods, Eva watched them drift. Would every night from now on feel strange and uncertain like this, Eva wondered. Were routine, ordinary nights a thing of the past?

"I've always thought I would die young," Eva said to Margot. "I don't know why."

"Oh, that," said Margot, unalarmed, resituating herself on the couch. "All young people think that."

"You did?"

Margot nodded, sipping from her mug. "It passed," she said, smiling.

Thirty-two

When Margot woke, the world was white. Five degrees warmer and the snow would have been rain.

Her body ached. She edged to the side of the bed, hooked a leg over the mattress, and pushed up with her hands, trying not to move her head. The snow fell down straight as a curtain. Already the hillsides and trees were covered. She remembered that Eva and Birdie were here and her heart leapt: the giddy thrill of a snow day.

She caught sight of herself in the bathroom mirror and was shocked. The discoloration had deepened around her collarbone and on her thighs. Her breasts looked pistachio green and her torso was pink with inflammation. Last night while Eva was in the bathroom with Birdie, Satterfield told her she looked "rode hard." They sat across the table from each other and the comment sat with them. He appeared to regret it but didn't say anything, only leaned back in his chair. Any minute his wife would arrive to take him home. Margot saw he was waiting for something from her.

"Eva told you about Dutch," she said.

In reply he gave a protracted blink.

"You can't judge," she said. "You of all people."

"I'm not judging."

"And yet you look—" she thought but could not say, *hurt*. How absurd! For the first time in her memory, he couldn't meet her eye. His gaze flitted to the far corner of the room, up the stairs, to the tabletop. She leaned back, too. The irony. The double standard!

"It was a mistake," she said, hating the impulse to explain and the shame bubbling up her throat. If it was this bad with Satterfield, facing her husband would be worse. Nothing in her life would remain untouched by these events, she understood. She was demolished. She wished she'd driven herself and Eva, left Satterfield out of this. Her ears burned. The idea that Douglas would blame her was infuriating, yet without the energy for rage, she was on the brink of despair.

Sensing this, Satterfield leaned forward and covered her hand with his long fingers.

"I understand," he said.

"You better."

He held her gaze, smiling. "If you would allow me a word about infidelity."

"The expert."

"Yes," he said, rueful. "You'll want to confess. You'll think telling on yourself will exonerate you. You're wrong."

The burning sensation intensified, moving from her ears to her cheeks. She had indeed imagined telling Andy, thought a confession might act as a reset button, reboot the marriage.

"Confessing is for the betrayer, not the betrayed." He withdrew his hand, watching her. "The betrayed don't want to know."

He was a melodramatic man. He took himself too seriously and he loved theatrics. But what he said made sense. Seeing this sober, wise side of him was unnerving. She shifted in her chair, was almost relieved when they heard the bathroom door open down the hall.

In the quiet, snowy morning, Margot crossed the hall to look into Benji's bed. Eva's body was cocooned around Birdie's, the covers tangled in her legs. This vision, combined with the snow, allowed the events of the weekend to recede. They could move away from all that now.

Downstairs Margot cooked bacon, warmed frozen croissants and made a pot of coffee, all with one hand. Piling cookbooks against the half wall, she could pin the bowl of eggs with her body and whisk one-handed. She was enjoying herself, working around the challenge when she heard something upstairs. She thought Eva must be up, then was certain she heard the front door close. Someone called hello. Her first thought was Annie Baker, the bloodhound. But the voice was a man's.

Only one thing on earth could disrupt this morning's delicious sense of peace, and it was happening. She dropped the whisk, feeling plundered. That's all she and Eva were to get. Just those few hours last night. It was a strange thought. They had a lifetime, after all.

"Smells good!" Andy cried, appearing on the stairs. "Who told you we were coming?"

Rooted in place, Margot's expression went blank. Her stomach flip-flopped. Andy was down now, coming towards her. His big, familiar shoulders and happy pale eyes, pleased to see her. He rounded the island but stopped short of embracing her, remembering, bless him, that reunions must be taken slowly. They had learned this over the years.

"We took the early flight," he said. "Surprise."

We, he said. From upstairs came a shocked gasp. Benji's feet on the stairs, his stunned face, even more adult than it had been at spring break. His shoulders were wide, his waist fuller. He had snow in his hair.

"Eva Baker is upstairs," he said. "In my bed."

"Who's Eva Baker?"

Margot stepped around Andy. She felt the crushed sensation she'd had last night, as if some force squeezed her torso, including the fracture. She tried and failed to speak. Eva was coming down the stairs, carrying Birdie. She was wearing Benji's clothes and her face was swollen with sleep. Birdie held his gauze mitten aloft over his mother's shoulder.

"I'm Eva," she said, joining the three of them.

Andy smiled with caution. Benji looked miserable. Birdie studied them until he recognized Margot, and cried, "Bacon!"

Andy laughed. "Who's this?"

"Birdie Baker," said Eva.

"This is Andy, my husband," Margot told her. "I think you know Benji."

The two young people exchanged a look. Eva mumbled hello and Benji nodded, the sides of his neck reddening.

"Shall we sit down," Margot said. "I've got breakfast almost ready."

Margot turned to the stove, putting her back to them. When she looked again they sat facing her like owls on a branch. Behind them the backdrop of white was like a stage set, out every window, as far as she could see. The people at the counter were thrown into vivid relief. Margot could see the shadow of stubble on Andy's face, the blue of Eva's eyes, Benji's nervously rumpled hair. Birdie sat in Eva's lap slapping the counter with his bandage, chanting the word *bacon*. Each time he spoke, he looked over at Andy and Benji to gauge their reactions.

Margot set down the plate of bacon. Birdie grabbed a slice with his free hand. There wouldn't be enough. She loaded the pan with more. The meat sizzled, sending smoke into the room. Margot emptied the coffee pot and dumped the filter to make more. She turned and everyone spoke at once. Margot blurted that Benji and Eva were in the same high school class. Benji complained that he needed coffee and Andy said the flight had landed twenty minutes ahead of schedule. Birdie stopped chewing. Eva grinned.

Margot was the first to begin again, saying, "Eva and I met recently. She and Birdie have been keeping me company."

"Terrific," Andy said, turning. "Are you a musician?"

Eva laughed. "Oh no, I'm not a musician."

Andy gave a bright nod. Margot knew he was trying to place her, wondering if she was a new student, maybe a new member of the cello group. He bit off half a slice of bacon, asking, "So how did you two connect?"

The women looked at each other. Benji's gaze didn't leave the countertop as he said, "A book group."

Margot's face grew warm.

"No," Eva laughed. "Not a book group."

"Okay... what am I missing?" Andy asked, scanning their faces. "Everybody knows something I don't."

Benji looked at his mother.

"You know, I think we'll pack up," Eva said, sliding off her chair. Birdie reached for his plate. Eva grabbed his bacon and headed for the stairs, leaving the stunned Ficketts looking after her.

"Eva!" Margot called. "Just give us ten minutes."

"Ten minutes!" she cried, still moving. "You're going to need ten years."

Andy looked at Margot. "Did we come at a bad time?"

"No! I'm glad you're home. Just—I'll be right back."

Margot heard Benji call after her but didn't stop. Eva was putting on her coat in the foyer.

"Please don't go," Margot said.

She said nothing as she grabbed Margot's car keys from their hook. Margot followed her to the front door.

"I want this moment behind us," she said. "We need it behind us."

"This moment is never going to be behind us, Margot. You're dreaming."

Margot followed her outside. The wall of snow beyond the porch stunned them all. For a moment they stood gazing at it. Birdie twisted in Eva's arms, pointing at Margot with his bacon. She grabbed his hand and kissed his knuckles, which made him smile.

"Say you'll come back," Margot said.

For a moment they faced each other, each of them recognizing the introductions, explanations and justifications ahead. The snow sounded like pennies on carpet. The cars were already covered. The muddy brown of the driveway had vanished and along the fencerow the budding willows drooped. Spring never was.

Eva stepped out. Margot went back inside for her snow boots and jacket, grabbing the shovel by the front door. Across the driveway, Eva and Birdie were obscured by the storm. She heard the Honda's engine start. Eva was buckling Birdie into the back seat. Margot attempted to scrape the windshield but had no strength. The shovel dropped onto the car's hood. Eva elbowed in beside her, using the scraper from the back seat. Margot dragged the shovel to the back of the car and began knocking snow off the trunk. Their bare heads were soaked in minutes.

Andy appeared in boots and his Carhartt jacket, holding the other shovel. He began digging under the Honda where old snow had piled up. Margot's chest swelled, watching his gusto. The man lacked suspicion, refused to hesitate. Benji joined them with the scraper from the Suburban. Margot stood back as the Fickett men unearthed the car. Eva got in the driver's seat. Andy and Benji stood back with Margot as she backed out. She drove in a wide circle, slipping around the driveway. Without a backward glance, she vanished into the storm.

Margot turned to the men. Andy clapped his hands and said, "Here we are, then."

Thirty-three

The snow blinded Eva. It behaved like heavy, wet hair. She squinted to see through it, hunched over the steering wheel. The small car tires grabbed the ruts on the muddy road and they were pulled from side to side. "Whee!" Birdie called from the back as they sashayed all the way to the pavement. Eva couldn't remember which way to turn. She chose what felt like the downhill direction. A second intersection felt vaguely familiar and she again tried for downhill. For miles there were no houses or landmarks she recognized but the snow seemed to lighten. Soon she could see the creek and traveled downstream with it towards Deaton. Finally, a gas station. The underpass.

In town she wasn't sure where to go. The condo was piled high with packed boxes. Her bedroom was in disarray. Some of her clothing was to be sold and the rest was in garbage bags. A mountain of shoes sat in the closet, waiting to be sorted. Was it last week she signed the buy-sell agreement or last century? For the first time, Eva regretted it. What she wanted right now was somewhere familiar and easy and paid for.

She skirted the north edge of town, heading for Lucky Lane, hoping to find Sully. She'd been unable to reach him by phone. He must know about Birdie and the abduction. The story was on the local and regional news. Eva, Margot, and Satterfield saw the story of Birdie's rescue last night. The truck stop attendant who found him was interviewed, as was Agent Evans, who called it a happy ending to an ugly twist in the marijuana raids.

Turning into the trailer park, Eva looked in the rearview mirror to see if Birdie recognized the place. She didn't see him and her throat caught. She stopped the car and turned. He was stretched out asleep on the seat, still belted in, his wrapped hand under his head like a pillow.

Sully's truck wasn't there. In the snow the trailer was uglier than usual. The brown lattice skirt had holes in it. The tear in the screen on the kitchen window looked bigger than she remembered. Eva rolled through the center circle, barely slowing down. Not finding him mattered less than she'd have predicted. In fact, everything did. Eva was altered. She knew it as soon as she saw Benji Fickett, a moment she'd imagined dozens of times over the years. Yet when the scene was upon her, she felt a grizzled indifference. Benji was nervous and suspicious, would not speak or look directly at her. Eva felt no shaky embarrassment, no urge to explain. They had sex, made a baby, and he was father. Eva and his mother were friends. The *Boy-meets-father* moment withered in significance after the boy had been abducted, spent the night behind a truck stop and nearly froze to death.

With Sully the situation was more complex. He had changed after she got fired. Her suspicion was that he preferred them to be a secret. He didn't want to be with her in public. She had hoped the detached weirdness she felt coming off him would settle down with time, but since leaving him in the police station, the feeling had cemented itself. She was hurt that he hadn't called. At the same time, her need to find him, her repeated, frantic calls might be a way to cover up her listless feelings. She missed him, but couldn't imagine what she'd say to him. The months of intimacy had been erased. He felt like a bad idea, a food that made you sick but you ate it anyway.

In the weather, traffic moved slower than usual. Eva recalled that it was Monday, almost noon on a regular business day. She turned towards the river, deciding to go to McLeod Park, the future. If she was honest, what she wanted was the past. Bethany Meyers and tall, blunt Kariss, her Unique Boutique crew. If she could walk into any room right now, it would be that store as it used to be, the warehouse of rooms. She would lie down on the log platform bed next to the five-thousand-dollar wood stove they pulled out of Hamilton, Montana. The display was meant to feel like a cabin on the river in July: you could imagine the grass hissing in the wind, the comforting buzz of crickets. Another favorite was the modern living room, white tuck-and-roll leather sofa with metal frame and a glass coffee table. In the boutique, you could move from one persona to another. You never had to choose.

There wasn't a parking space in front of the Rhino. She had to park by the interiors store half a block down. She left the Honda running to keep it warm. Birdie was still asleep. People passed on the sidewalk wearing ski parkas, carrying shopping bags with handles and little to-go boxes from the bakery. Even heavy snow didn't stop people from shopping.

A couple coming out of the interiors store caught Eva's attention. The woman was wearing a pantsuit, carrying a blocky purse over one wrist and holding an umbrella. She was speaking to the man over her shoulder. They were middle-aged, both well dressed. Eva was sure the man was her husband, though he appeared to be an assistant. The sight made Eva's throat close. Marriage! The diminishment in it. Couples were so *mean* to each other.

In her lap, her hands began to shake, precursor to all-out bawling. No one would notice, but it would be loud. She'd wake Birdie. She gripped the steering wheel to stop her hands. This was all wrong. Mrs. Fickett was right. McLeod Park was not for her. Even Sully had known. Some days at the boutique, fifty bucks was the total day's take. Fifty! The rent here was twelve hundred, plus utilities. You'd have to sell an awful lot of used goods to make twelve hundred bucks. The sale of the condo would get her through a year, maybe two, but what about after? And they couldn't live here. It was too cold. Birdie sleeping there was out of the question. She'd have to look for a rental, would probably need a roommate.

Getting out of the sale would be difficult, if not impossible. But she could get out of this place. She'd never see her deposit, not after painting half a rhino on the wall. But undoing the lease wasn't out of the question.

The roads were horrid. Snow routes had high spines plowed down their center; one lane traffic backed up streets all over town. Turning left was like gunning a motorboat through its own wake. Eva made her way through the greasy, congested streets to the rental office parking lot. A lone car was parked outside. She carried Birdie inside and he woke in her arms, asking where they were. "Just a little errand," she told him, as they ducked inside.

The phone was ringing. The secretary was the only person there, a thick-set woman dressed in polyester. She turned to look at Eva and Birdie as she snatched the phone out of its cradle. Her voice was gruff; the caller was clearly a tenant with a complaint.

"Have you tightened the washer?" she demanded, then sighed. "I'll make a note," she said and hung up, turning to Eva. Big in the shoulders, she wore no makeup and her hair was so short she looked skinned. Eva guessed she'd have a low tolerance for bullshit. It would be best to forego any charm.

"I've made a terrible mistake," she said in her clearest, most adult voice.

The woman's eyebrows raised a fraction. She didn't dismiss them, which was a start. Eva spoke without rush or panic, telling her the entire story of how she had rented the space hoping to open a business with money from her boyfriend's business profits, which had looked promising. The secretary shifted her weight and crossed her arms, but continued to listen. Eva mentioned the FBI raids over the weekend: her boyfriend was ruined, and now she was too.

"I was involved in all that," she said gravely. "Maybe you saw us on the news."

As if cued, Birdie picked his head up off her shoulder and looked at the woman. Eva explained about the kidnapping, knowing she was horrible to use their nightmare for leverage. But the woman was leaning a full hip on her desk now.

"You have rotten luck, kid," she said when Eva finished.

Her name was Lois. She shook Eva's hand as if to say, let's do this. She dug a set of keys out of her desk drawer and unlocked the agent's office. Piles of papers and file folders sat atop every surface. They were stacked on the floor and shoved into the bookshelves in the space over the books. Eva's heart sank.

"As you can see," Lois said, "the odds are good your deposit check is still here."

Moving to the far corner, she said, "I'll take this side, you take the opposite. I've found leases this way, pet deposits, you wouldn't believe it. Work towards the middle."

Neither of them spoke for the better part of an hour. Birdie played with Eva's keys, pretending to unlock the file drawers. Twice he knocked over stacks. Both times Lois hurried over cooing, "That's okay, sweetheart," and righted the mess. Outside the snow blocked the light. The room was dim and still. Lois snapped on the overhead fluorescent, which hummed above them as they searched. What a bizarre picture they would make from afar, rifling through this mess as if the world turned on finding that bad check. In a way it did, thought Eva.

An hour and half in, Lois gasped, holding up an envelope. Eva crossed the room, staring at her own handwriting. Lois grinned as she ripped it in half. Eva squealed with joy. Hearing his mother, Birdie trotted over, clapping with his big mitt. In a fit of relief, Eva opened her arms and squeezed Lois. The woman coughed with shock, but was smiling, pleased.

Thirty-four

Wearing her thickest socks, her injured arm tucked inside a parka zipped up over her head, Margot stood on the cliff top in the snow. Visibility was six inches. The house had vanished behind her when she reached the top of the stone steps off the deck. Unable to see the creek bed below or the ridge across the valley, she couldn't judge how far she'd walked. She thought of the owlets, separated by now, hovering near the trunk of a separate lodgepoles, waiting out the storm. What did they make of the snow? Without a seasonal disappointment—awfully late in the year for this—there would be no worry that spring forgot to come. It was people, with their expectations and hopes, that made endless difficulty for themselves.

Consider music. Difficult passages existed in most every piece, and some were challenging throughout. Prokofiev's Sinfonia Concertante, for cello and orchestra, was a beast. Schumann's cello concerto was intense from start to finish, even if you rehearsed for months. The cellist might easily feel inadequate. Margot reassured her students that the problem didn't lie with them. They didn't struggle because they weren't good enough. The piece was simply *that hard*.

In the end, the preparation, rehearsal and prayers would come down to the performance itself, little more than an extended moment, maybe ninety minutes. You hoped for the best, but you were only as good as what came to you on that night, in that moment. Maybe you didn't remember to play the

D on the C string, thus avoiding the awkward down bow, or you failed to lift your elbow to prevent over twisting the wrist: the performance would suffer. Still, the moment was upon you and you played.

This morning, Margot's performance was flawed. She was a weak storyteller. Some details were overemphasized, others were left out. She began with the phone calls last March and ended with the raids last weekend. The harpoon in the story was the kidnapping. She put it off as long as possible. She skipped Dutch altogether, getting at last to the three simple words that would change everything: *He's your son.* The men looked at her like she spoke another language. They stood in the dining room. Andy dropped into a chair as if his feet were kicked out from under him. Benji's fine, long fingers covered his face and ran through his unruly mane of hair. His reaction grew to an all-out tantrum, head rocking back and forth, making a high-pitched whine like a four-year-old protesting bedtime. "It can't be!" he screeched, his voice breaking. "This is bullshit! Oh my *fucking* god!"

Margot was appalled. She expected shock, but she never dreamed he'd cry. He wouldn't stop messing with his hair. Finally she grabbed a rubber band from the counter and thrust it at him. The sight of him gathering his hair in his long, gentle fingers stilled Margot's blood. He was so *easy* on himself. Like his dad.

"What am I supposed to do?" he hissed at her, his dark eyes flashing with anger. "Move back here and pick him up after school? No. I am *not* doing it."

Margot felt she'd been slapped. "You don't have to marry her," she told him. "You don't even have to be friends. But you can't ignore the facts."

Benji looked at his father. Andy, hands on the table, looked up at Margot.

"Why didn't you *call*?" he asked, incredulous. "I understand you're bad on the phone but Jesus, I think a grandson merits a ring." Then he did an incredible thing. He stood, raised a hand and said, "Vow of silence. Starting right now."

The move was unprecedented. Andy couldn't stand the quiet, hated the loneliness.

"Dad!" cried Benji. "For god's sake—"

"I'm serious. Ten hours of silence."

"Ten *hours!*" Margot said. "How can we—"

But Andy held up his hand. Benji spun around and marched down the hall to the practice room. Margot went upstairs to get her coat.

Here on the cliff, with no ceiling or walls, Margot stood inside her parka and felt the frailty of all life. How tenuous the whole endeavor turned out to be! Your worldview, how you felt about someone you'd known forever—your own child, for god's sake—could transform in a moment. A performance you could not undo. Her beloved son—*her boy!*—was a spoiled brat. She had allowed this, accommodating his talent, pumping him full of himself. *Fussing* over him.

She heard the delicate sound of snowflakes hitting her parka. Rocks and grass were covered. The sage shrubs looked like white boulders from a fairy tale. Without the view, the world was reduced to a vaporous cloud. She felt like the central figure in a snow globe being shaken by a massive, unseen hand.

Yes I did, Margot thought. I spoiled them both. Andy was also full of his own importance. She never minded his absences, even loved the silence and space. But all artists need a protector. For a time, Margot had a grandmother. When she died, Margot did her best. Andy was a place to pour energy, she thought, someone to protect besides myself. My own music! Satterfield was right. She ought to have formed a quartet, toured more. Something happened when you became a mother. Everybody said so. Did all parents face such a moment? The small hand that once held yours in the parking lot vanished, the most profound abduction.

Their melodrama enraged her. Of course they would not jump for joy. Did she expect them to be happy about Birdie? But the infuriating gasp of tragedy, as if Birdie *happened* to them. Perhaps their maleness was the problem. As a man, paternity could sneak up on you. It was the ultimate gender chasm.

She turned towards the house, understanding that the vow would have to be broken. Silence wouldn't help at this juncture, if it ever had. She marched back the way she had come, not sure what exactly she intended to say.

Inside, she stood in her dripping gear at the glass door to the den. Andy sat in his wingback chair, wrapped in a blanket, nursing a cup of tea. She opened the door and he held up his hand to silence her.

"Fuck the vow, Andy," said Margot.

Stricken, he put down his mug. She unzipped her coat, left it in the foyer. She sat on the couch to remove her boots. He watched her struggle to do it one-handed, then stood to help, pulling on the heel of one, then the other. He tossed them through the door to the tile floor.

"A grandson," he said, hands on his hips.

She nodded. He moved back to his chair.

"I'm sorry I didn't call you," she said. "I wanted to handle it. I thought—I didn't believe her. Truly, I thought she was lying."

"Did you tell anyone?"

"Douglas," she almost whispered.

His lips pursed in an angry line. He gave a quick nod, then another. Then he closed his eyes, leaned his head against the chair. The lines on his face looked deeper. Without the humor Andy was a much older man.

"I keep thinking about Benji's first bath," he said, eyes still closed. "We were exhausted. He wouldn't sleep in those early days, remember? We'd put him down and he'd cry. You bathed him in the kitchen sink, held him in your big hands and shampooed him like you'd done it a thousand times."

He opened his eyes but kept his head back, half smiling. "When you were done, you wrapped him in a towel and you said to me, 'This changes it. This makes it okay.' I knew what you meant. You were talking about the bomb that went off in our life when he was born. The damage got repaired by those moments after that first bath, the way it felt to care for him, to figure it out."

Margot waited, thinking he was going to criticize their early selves, how scared they were, and ill prepared, way too serious.

He lifted his head. His voice was deep but soft. "Benji didn't get any of those moments," he said. "You dropped a bomb on him, Margot, on both of us. No bath, no shampoo, no cozy towel."

She looked away, admonished. "I know it's a lot to take all at once. I didn't know how to prepare you."

He was staring out the window behind the desk where the snow kept falling. Finally he looked at her with determined eyes, his jaw set.

"Margot, what *happened* here? To your arm? Last time we talked you were doing well, then I get here, you're back in the sling, like you never went to rehab."

"I'm fine. I'm going to be fine. I had a little setback."

"You fell again? Can I see?"

She looked at him steadily, and slowly shook her head. "I didn't fall."

She saw him understand that there was a story, a big one. His eyes moved from determined to worried. He was probably thinking of Satterfield. Though he'd never admit it, he was threatened by their friendship, especially because they had music in common. But Andy wasn't someone who had to know for sure, about anything. The habitual, distanced expression came over him. He slouched his shoulders and let his head fall back again. He propped a foot up on the edge of the coffee table between them. Margot hadn't considered this tendency in him as a posture, yet his body moved into the zenned-out Andy, the man of impartial serenity, right before her eyes. His dispassion was a form of protection, she understood. This hurt him, not knowing. Her distance hurt him as much as his absences hurt her.

"We can make the child support payments," he said at last, resting a palm on his raised knee. "We can afford it. That's what my patent money has always been for, a way to keep making music."

"It's not about the money!" Margot cried. "He has a son! Our son has a son! To *raise*. That's what you do with children!"

His placid eyes inflamed her, which made no sense. She ought to be glad the subject was changed, that the focus was off her. The avoidance felt like a lie, however; like the vow of silence, it was a dodge.

"He should move home," she said, hating how petulant she sounded, as if she wanted to punish him. Maybe she did. "Eva's given up everything! Why shouldn't he?"

Andy lowered his knee and leaned forward. The blanket fell from his shoulders as he clasped his hands. In his deep, calm voice, he said, "Margot, Benji would be a terrible father."

Her stomach dropped. Andy rarely said a word against their son. Margot was hard on him, Andy defended him. That was the way it went.

"It would be a disaster," he continued, his eyes glistening with emotion. "He's not ready."

"He'll want to quit to school," she said. "This will be the excuse he's been looking for."

"He might, Margot. We can ask him to finish the year. But not to come home."

Outside the weather surged. The snow turned to hail that pelted the glass with eerie taps. They sat staring at one another. The worst part of a secret was the way it made you a prisoner. Her betrayal would grow, festering with power and threat. Margot could see what she had done to them, this weekend and before, not involving him. Outwardly, Andy was a simple man, liked easy tunes and playing for a crowd. But he could take in the implications of news like what she'd told him today in a fraction of the time it took Margot. He could infer. She often felt transparent around him, as if she was an easy read. Worst of all was realizing that she had never shared all of herself with anyone. She was that type of person.

Thirty-five

Sully, Gerald and Marvin spent the weekend hunkered in Marvin's living room with the blinds pulled. After leaving Paige's house Saturday morning, Sully found he couldn't face the mess at his trailer. He drove aimlessly for a time, planning his future. The seedlings that Dutch left untouched could be harvested in eight weeks. Without permits of his own, Sully supposed he'd have to go back to selling on the black market. That would require digging up his contact, a scummy guy who dealt to college kids and the Deaton blue collars. Until then, Sully was going to have to clock in at a job.

He drove to Gerald's house, woke him. Half dressed, he listened to the story of Sully's night at the police station. They wondered together what had become of their college crew. Gerald lost his phone in the mayhem, and Sully threw his off the bridge, so they had no way of finding out. They ordered several pizzas and drove to Marvin's.

The bong helped dim the fears of Dutch crashing the party, coming after them for not preventing this. In fact the raids were his fault. According to Evans, arresting Dutch was the real prize behind the statewide shutdowns. The men discussed the mysterious trio that appeared at the bowling alley, also after Dutch. Gerald deduced that those three strangers were the first domino to fall in a chain reaction. Marvin argued no, the feds would have had to plan something like this for months. Sully agreed. He reported what he heard from Evans about Carlos La Salle and Tristan Santiago. Not brothers after all, they were released from custody under the stipulation that they never return to Montana. This did not seem legal, but nobody was in a position to protest.

Their own losses were discussed, particularly Sully's—he'd come the closest to going to jail. Evans knew about Caitlyn and Paige, all about Sully's life. His plea bargain stipulated that he would call Evans immediately upon any contact with Dutch.

Evans was dreaming, Sully told them. "I won't hear a thing, unless the guy's a complete dumbass." The other two gazed at him, inferring the unsaid: if Dutch reappeared, Sully would wring his neck.

Saturday evening a Helena grower was all over the Internet. Marvin's phone kept beeping with texts and emails about a man named Chase Winters. His outfit, Blue Sky Medical, was shut down permanently due to the discovery of firearms on the premises. There were four co-owners and all were arrested that morning. Winters had gray hair, was the father of a teenager, and looked like your neighbor, the kind of guy with a pop-up camper parked in front of his house. He insisted he was in compliance with state law, claimed to know nothing about the firearms. While his partners accepted plea bargains, he demanded a trial. He was an instant hero to the ruined growers across the state.

The three men watched the local news, wondering if Winters would be interviewed. They saw fellow business owner Harvey Mankiller, a cigarette jammed between the first two fingers of his left hand, his face swollen with indignation. "This is bogus!" he cried. "Over four hundred patients are without medicine because of this!"

Mankiller and his wife, Shirley, were under house arrest, all accounts frozen, over a million dollars in assets. Up in Smoke, their business, was one of Montana's largest—their warehouse served dispensaries in Deaton, Helena, and Bozeman.

"They've bankrupted us!" cried Shirley, her face streaked with mascara.

"I can't watch," said Marvin, picking up the remote.

But Sully said, "Wait."

Dutch's picture flashed on the screen, the old photo Evans had shown him.

"That's not Dutch," said Gerald, bong in hand. "They've got the wrong guy."

"It's an old picture, Gerry," scoffed Marvin.

"Quiet!" cried Sully, grabbing the remote.

Dutch was missing. There was a manhunt. Eva was on camera, weeping. A photograph of Birdie.

"Holy shit," muttered Marvin

Sully sat perfectly still. The news he was trying to avoid now hit him in the chest.

They described Eva's car, and Birdie, a three-year-old wearing a blue coat. Sully felt his body temperature spike. He put a hand on his throbbing heart. He tossed the remote and stalked back to Marvin's spare room, slamming the door. He paced, pulling his hands through his hair. Instinct told him to go to her while reality told him to stay put. He had a kid to think about, an ex-wife, child support to pay. He was robbed, his trailer was trashed, he couldn't even look after his daughter. The FBI had him by the short hairs. He threw himself on the soft twin bed, which nearly bounced him onto the floor. He hollered into the mattress, muffling himself with a pillow as best he could. They could hear him out in the front room, the walls were no thicker than in his trailer. He screamed anyway, his body tense, his legs rigid, a seizure of rage.

The following day, the New Leaf had become mythical. In twenty-four hours, the place went from a brick-and-mortar business to an emblem for what might have been. Marv and Gerald reminisced about the massive harvest, replaying pivotal moments of the past nine months: Gerald scoring the PVC pipe from a job site, Marvin buying his first suit. They sentimentalized the hope of legitimacy, the year they became "providers" instead of "dealers."

Sully couldn't stand it. He'd never been grandiose in his hopes, didn't want to join the fucking school board. He was finally a taxpayer, thought people might look him in the eye, that his lifelong sense of being locked out of the party might come to an end.

Marvin and Gerald brought up the New Leaf clientele, the "poor sick people" who had to go back to "Big Pharma," for their needs. Sully had gone in for this argument when they started the business, but now he heard it as false compassion. This kind of moaning about unfairness was little more than couch-surf complaining. He hated the inertia. Romanticizing events as recent as last week, falling back so easily on cliché, only proved their attachment to the status quo. They didn't want to get off the couch, had no interest in paying taxes or any sort of participation. Neither, for that matter, did Dutch. Dutch wasn't lazy, he was a pirate. He loved his status as an outsider, cultivated it. He hurt people.

The depth of Sully's contempt scared him. Eva had ruined him, her unfaltering belief that he knew what he was doing, that he wouldn't fail. Her faith had elevated him, making him unfit for his own kind.

Chase Winters, the Helena hero, was interviewed on the Sunday evening news. Sully, Gerald and Marvin were eating Thai food. Nobody had left the house. Marvin had it delivered. They all three stopped chewing.

"There but for the grace of God," muttered Marv.

"Shush," cried Gerald, turning up the volume.

"This is about the violation of constitutional rights," claimed Winters from the steps of the state legislature building. The crowd of pot advocates cheered. A group had pooled money to meet his bail. Marv and Gerald cheered. Sully did not cheer. The trial wouldn't take place for months. Winters didn't have a chance

Next came news of Birdie's rescue. A clerk was interviewed. Eva's parents shielded her from the cameras but Sully glimpsed Birdie in her arms. He couldn't swallow, had to spit the food into a napkin. He had been certain the boy was dead, he now understood. Margot Fickett was in the background. The two of them got into a vehicle. He could feel Marv and Gerald watching as he let out a sob of relief. He stood. He was going home.

That week, the sun came out. Everywhere he went Sully was confronted with flesh, the meaty, white limbs of drivers in tank tops and pedestrians in shorts. In Walmart, where he went to replace his shower curtain, shoppers wore flip-flops, a barrage of exposed, misshapen toes. At the lumber store, looking for scrap wood to repair his walls, the men in the chilly bays wore shirtsleeves and went hatless.

Sully could not make sense of what went on in his trailer. His bedroom closet was wrecked—he threw out one of the sliding doors—but his grow room looked untouched. His seedlings were fine, his lights and carbon filter intact. The curing jars, though empty, were neatly stacked on their shelves, lids replaced, barely out of place. He stood in the doorway thinking of Dutch's womanish beauty, his feline movements and nimble hands. Though the news story suggested it, Sully didn't believe for a second that Dutch took the kid on accident. He was immune to distraction, wasted no energy, noticed everything.

On Tuesday morning there was a knock on his door. He was awake but not up. His first thought was Evans, come to say they were taking him into custody after all. Fraudulence. Erroneous judgment. Stupidity.

He pulled on sweats and grabbed a T-shirt, hurried down the hall and swung open the door to find Margot Fickett. Behind her, a sunny day. In the center of the gravel circle, the grass was blindingly green. The willow had buds all over it.

"Oh," he said.

She looked as startled as he felt. She had a startled way about her, in fact, surprised and observant. He recalled her last Friday, glassy-eyed with a fixed smile, standing at Dutch's side. His last glimpse of her was her back squeezing through the crowd.

There was nothing glamorous about her this morning in her dark coat, her limp hair and tired eyes. She looked more like the woman he'd found asleep in her own backseat. Did he look as altered as she did now, he wondered. Sober and tired, he supposed so.

"I'm looking for Eva," she said.

"What's happened?"

Irritated confusion swept over her. She was in a hurry. He glanced over her shoulder at the black Suburban, whose engine idled. A man he didn't know was at the wheel, another figure in back.

"Who's that?"

"My husband," she said. "Can I come in?"

Sully opened the screen door. She stepped inside. He shut the big door behind her. For a moment they were awkwardly close to one another.

"You're wondering how I found you," she said.

He wasn't, but he said, "Yes."

"Your ex-wife."

There was an image, Margot Fickett and Paige Caruthers.

She stepped around him, into his kitchen. Moving stiffly, she lowered herself into one of the chairs. He was stunned by the physicality of her, here, in his trailer. Warily, he pulled a chair out and sat across from her.

"We looked everywhere. Her condo says 'Sold.' The rental space in Mc-Leod Park is vacant. I was sure she'd be here."

He shook his head, his mind buzzing. His gaze fell to her arm in a sling, inside the jacket. Following his gaze, she said, "I re-broke it."

"At the bowling alley?"

Her eyes darted. "After."

Dutch. Every bad thing would go back to Dutch. His throat was thick with guilt, calculating. Sully was the reason Margot Fickett met Dutch. Sully was how Eva met Dutch. He was a conduit of pain.

"I haven't seen her," he said.

"Did you hear about Birdie?"

He nodded, scratched the back of his head, unable to meet her eye. "I haven't seen Eva since Friday night, at the police station. She was released before I was."

"She left my house Sunday morning."

He watched her turn to the front room, notice the trash bags, the ruined medicine cabinet on the floor, the hammer on the coffee table.

"Do you know what went on here?" she asked, turning back to him.

He stopped the nervous jiggle in his left leg, waiting. Margot's long throat moved as she swallowed, gazing at him.

"Saturday, early, Eva came here. She walked in on Dutch."

Her voice was flat and civil. She had no intention of leaving without telling him, making him hear it. Sully's tongue felt thick in his mouth. The news report had said the kidnapping occurred when Dutch took her car. Sully had imagined it happening in a downtown parking lot, or at the New Leaf. In truth he had not allowed himself to wonder about the details, the timing of it all. He put together the evidence: the broken closet in his bedroom, the front door left open.

"He took Birdie from my place? From right here?"

Mrs. Fickett nodded. Sully's breath rushed out his lungs. He had to lean forward, elbows on his knees. He was wrong not to contact Eva. He ought to have gone over there, hunted her down.

"She's with her parents," he said, sitting up. "Has to be."

Margot asked for the address, but Sully didn't know the address. He'd only been there once. "It was on the river, the Bitterroot. Southwest of town."

"They're donors," Margot said, standing. "The symphony office will have the address."

Sully followed her to the front door where she turned, hand on the door-knob.

"They're all right, Sully. Birdie's okay. Eva will be okay."

"No thanks to me," he said.

She didn't reassure him but her bottomless brown eyes said, *Or me.*

Thirty-six

On her second morning at her parents' house, Eva opened her eyes to a view
as familiar as her own reflection. Her second-floor bedroom had south-facing
windows that stretched floor to ceiling. Because Eva had taken her canopy
bed with her when she moved, an air mattress on the floor was the best her
parents could offer. Her room was an office and storage closet. She might
have taken the guest room, once her brother's, but she gave that to Birdie,
opting for the comfort of this view. She could see the entire backyard, the
buck-and-rail fence marking the property line to the shared acreage along the
river. The cottonwoods were still leafless, their branches thin and hopeful.
On sunny spring mornings like this you could almost feel the willows greening up. The ice would be gone from the riverbanks now, except in the deepest
bends. If she followed her favorite trail to the swimming hole, there would
still be pockets of snow hiding in recesses and underbrush, receding but not
yet demolished by the sun's fingers.

Eva lay on her mattress gazing at the view, listening to the voices downstairs. She checked her phone. Only seven a.m. and Birdie was up. Yesterday
it was the same. Her father got up with him, a heroic attempt to make this
feel like a sleepover. Though neither of her parents ate gluten, they found an
old box of Bisquick and her dad made pancakes.

When they showed up here, her mother put on hot water to make
them tea. Eva hated tea. Her mother rummaged around for something

Birdie would eat, but they didn't have any dairy products, either. Their flustered excitement was difficult to take, though of course she didn't make a habit of dropping in on them. She couldn't expect them to be ready. Eva hoped to see a glimpse of the woman in the police station yesterday, the one who ate the donuts, and later drove out to Grant Creek with pizza, talking to Mrs. Fickett late into the night. That was a mother Eva could get behind, somebody who consumed donuts and drank wine like a normal person, who cried in the ER waiting room when she saw the Bird on his gurney.

Alas, that was not the woman who sat next to Eva on the couch, demanding, "What happened to Margot Fickett? Why aren't you staying there like you planned?"

"You can stay here!" her father interjected with a withering look at his wife. "We don't mind! As long as you need!"

Her mother couldn't help the suspicious aggression. Who could, in a house like this, with its angry, exposed beams and so much glass? The emotional mother was pinned down by the efficient, anxious perfectionist, wringing her hands because she had no groceries and there weren't clean sheets on the guest bed.

"Benji Fickett has come home," Eva told them.

Her mother gasped. In the chair opposite her father's body jolted with surprise.

"I don't think Margot expected him, or her husband—he came too. So I left."

"Does it mean—what does it mean?" asked her mother, aghast.

"That you'll be meeting him soon, I suppose," Eva said. "Both of them."

She felt the familiar exhaustion, an old, stubborn reluctance to explain herself to them. But this time, Eva ignored it. Determined to behave like a grown-up, she shocked them by not losing her patience. Thanking her mother for the herbal tea she wouldn't touch, she told them about the sale of the condo. Her father contained his disappointment to a grim frown, but of course he already knew her plans, had seen the For Sale sign in her yard. Her mother acted like Eva was refunding a Christmas present. She protested, wanted to contact a lawyer, try to undo the sale. Eva felt like an actress, ignoring her pumping anger. She didn't scowl or roll her eyes as she explained that papers were signed, a title company was involved, and the closing date was set. Her mother sighed in resignation.

Eva continued, keeping her voice calm and neutral. She thought of Margot and kept her back erect, did not jiggle a leg or gesture wildly or over-emphasize words. She told them about the space in McLeod Park, quietly enduring the gasps about high rent. Her father scolded her about writing a bad check; she let him finish, then described this morning's successful efforts to get it back. She told them she still had furniture in the space. She didn't have details worked out yet, but she'd get her property back.

Her efforts paid off. Nobody raised their voices or stormed out of the room. For a time, no one said a word. In the corner, Birdie stacked his wooden blocks, no easy task with his gauze mitten.

"You want to open a shop?" her dad asked finally.

"Yes," she answered. "Like the one Bethany had, Unique Boutique."

"You loved it there."

"I did, Dad." She smiled at him, relieved. He seemed to hear her, at least a little. Her mother sat with her legs crossed, quite still, which Eva took as a good sign.

The day unfolded slowly. They all three seemed struck by a bizarre shyness, a lack of ease. Her father almost walked in on her in the bathroom, wrenching the knob she'd locked. He apologized profusely when she came out, which somehow made the situation more embarrassing. Her mother was startled to find her in the laundry room, screamed like she'd seen a mouse. But it was Birdie who made the situation unendurable. He rifled through their things, messing with the TV remote, opening and closing the roll-top desk, endlessly picking up objects of interest in the great room, artifacts from other continents like an ivory chess set from India and grass dolls from Africa. Each time he picked something up, her mother hurried over to take it from him, redirecting him to the sad box of blocks. Her father finally fetched a cardboard box from the garage and went around the room loading up the valuables: two wooden gazelles from Indonesia, blown glass figurines from Italy, ceramic pineapples from Hawaii.

On Monday her parents ignored Eva's insistence that they go to work like any other day. Her mother said the studio wasn't yet open for business and her dad, not wanting to miss anything, took a sick day. He made pancakes again. They didn't listen, which wasn't news. Her mother had her write a grocery list for her trip to town and Eva included a copy of the newspaper and the Nickel Pincher, a free publication listing rentals in Deaton. This wasn't going to work, not beyond this week. They all knew it, even if no one would say so.

Tuesday midmorning, Eva stepped out of her shower and heard voices. In the Outlaw subdivision, full of huge ranchettes, people didn't drop by. Eva stood in her towel at the top of the stairs and recognized Margot's voice. A shot of joy. Rescue! She hurried to get dressed, not the least bothered that Birdie had taken every item out of her purse.

"Oh give that to mommy," she said, crouching to take a lighter from his hands. "Guess what? The giants have come!"

By the time Eva got downstairs the Ficketts had filed into the Bakers' great room, the courtroom, as Eva thought of this unfriendly place. The beams frowned and the symmetrical windows gazed from either side of the massive chimney. Margot was on the settee, back rigid, her broken wing resting in a sling. Eva's mother was in the kitchen making tea. Her father stood next to Andy by the hearth. Benji sat on the couch with his back to her.

"Cozy," said Eva as she entered, holding Birdie.

All eyes turned her way. Eva let Birdie down and he ran to Margot. Smiling, the tall woman came to her knees to embrace him with her good arm. Leaning back on her heels, she let Birdie perch on her thighs. "Who's that?" he asked, pointing at Benji.

Everyone inhaled, waiting. Now wasn't the time to spill the beans, Eva thought. She was about to speak, but Margot said, "That's my son, Benji. And over there is Andy, my husband."

Birdie considered a moment, then wrapped an arm around her neck, careful of his bandaged paw. "They want to be friends," he said.

Margot nodded. "Yes, friends."

Choking with emotion, Eva stepped deeper into the room, hands on her hips, facing them. The perfectly arranged room came at her, the stuffed fish on plaques hanging next to family photos and framed art, all that she despised in the Baker world. Her mother approached with tea on a tray for god's sake.

No sooner was the tray set on the coffee table then Birdie came over to mess with the ceramic sugar bowl, stirring with the delicate spoon. Her mother lifted the bowl out of his hands, announcing that the sugar would be on the mantle. Then she shouted, "That's hot!" warning him about the teapot. Birdie jumped, frightened. He trotted over to Eva, starting to cry. Eva picked him up and whirled around to bark at her mother, but before she could speak, her eyes rested on Benji Fickett. He had his mother's dark, gentle eyes, now clouded with fear. The room was bright. Sun poured in from the upper windows, yet he looked like any second a dragon would be released. His thick dark hair was pulled back. He was lovely. Not attractive to Eva, but lovely all the same. Long fingers gripped his knees. His wide mouth looked ready to smile or frown, depending on her. For the first time Eva wondered what it would have been like to have told him when she found out she was pregnant. If they had sat here together confessing to her parents, if she had not taken the advice of her coworker Kariss, navigating this whole experience on her own.

Eva did an extraordinary thing. Remaining silent, she sat down on the couch next to him. He let go of his knees, gave his legs a quick rub. Andy Fickett was watching her. What had Margot told them? What did they know of the past months? Of last weekend? Eva took a deep breath. She loosened her arms and let Birdie turn to stare at his father.

From the settee by the hearth, Margot said, "You were supposed to come back."

"Was I?"

"You were. I made you promise."

Eva pressed her lips together, rubbing Birdie's back.

"We got tired of waiting, so we came looking for you."

Eva shook the wet hair out of her eyes. "I got out of the lease in McLeod Park. You were right, it was too expensive."

"And your condo is sold?"

Eva nodded and felt her mother start to say something. Margot beat her to it.

"Live with us," she said. "In Benji's room."

The air in the room seemed to thin. Eva heard a high-pitched ringing in her ears. Her eyes darted to Andy, then her father. In her lap, Birdie lay his head on her chest. She turned to Benji, whose kind eyes were upon her. He nodded. The boy's self-possession, his open, comfortable way was impressive. Even Sully wasn't this composed.

"She's fine living here with us," said her father.

"Of course she is," said Andy, nodding. "We just wanted to offer, to leave it open."

He smiled at Eva. Incredible. Her mother was saying that really, she was fine staying in her old room, but when they met eyes, she allowed her voice to trail off. Eva would go with the Ficketts. The look she gave her mother said as much. Her parents would be hurt, but relieved.

She stood, speaking to Birdie, asking him if he was tired. She walked him to the area behind the sofa and stood rocking him, letting the attention slowly fall away from her. Her mother asked Benji about school. He said he was studying classical performance but that he was in a rock band, which he loved. He liked his professors, but "with these new developments," school was up in the air, he said.

"You mean fatherhood," Eva's mother clarified. She was never one to make things easy.

Benji nodded. "I can't get used to how that sounds," he said. "I didn't know, you see. Until Sunday."

Benji turned to look over his shoulder at her. Eva loved how he spoke, how intelligent he sounded. Her parents were startled by his frankness, which she also loved.

From his place by the hearth, Andy said, "We think it's best to talk about it, just air out whatever comes up."

In response, her mother grimaced, her attempt at a polite smile. Eva glanced at Margot, who looked sympathetic. Her nostrils flared with what could only be suppressed amusement. Still rocking her boy, Eva smiled back. It was a delicious shared moment. She had to look away to keep from laughing. Birdie's eyes had the faraway look of sleep, but she doubted he'd drop off with so much company.

"I suppose it would take a while," said her father at last. "To get used to being a parent, I mean."

"Yes," agreed Eva.

Benji turned, twisting his body to face her. "But you seem so good at it," he said. "You're a natural."

Eva flushed. There was no hiding how this pleased her.

"I'm very impressed," he added.

"Me too," said Andy.

The tension in the room began to leak away. Eva looked at her mother, expecting snideness. Instead, she was smiling. She almost looked proud. Margot lifted her mug of tea, smiling.

With Andy and Benji helping load her things, it took only one trip in and out of the house. Benji drove his mother's Honda, while Eva and Birdie rode out to the canyon with Margot and Andy. They took the perimeter highway, skirting town, and for miles no one spoke. Eva wondered if it was tension she was feeling between them. Did Andy know? Neither of them seemed angry or suspicious. She looked down to see that Birdie had fallen asleep, leaning against her.

"What about Benji?" Eva asked. "If I'm in his room."

Margot looked at Andy, and again Eva wondered what she'd confessed, if this marital deference was guilt. She was being so polite.

"Benji will go back to school," Margot said, turning her head but unable to twist further. "I thought I'd make him come home to help, but he can't, Eva. He can't live without music, and he—he's just not the kind of kid who could move home and get a job. Andy made me see it. I hope you understand."

"I never said I wanted that," Eva said from the backseat.

"Some people are good at a few things," Andy said. "Really good. But for all the rest of it, they need help." He met her eye in the mirror. "I'm like that."

She thought of her brother, Conroy. He was older, but even when they were little she was more capable, less dependent. He was their mother's favorite because he needed her more.

After a time, Margot spoke again. "Would you be all right if Benji spent time with Birdie?" she asked. "Not alone. You'd be there, too. At the park, the museum. Anything."

"Like a playdate?"

"Yes, I guess so."

"He wants that?"

"He does," said Andy. "And so do I, if you wouldn't mind."

"Sure," Eva said, trying to picture it. "What do I tell Birdie?"

"The truth," Andy said. "Benji's his dad."

When they got to the house, Eva moved Birdie into Benji's bed without waking him, then joined the Ficketts in the living room, where they wanted to have a family talk. When she met Benji's gaze, his eyes darted away, but as soon as she looked elsewhere, she could feel his intense, curious eyes. Eva didn't love the scrutiny. She fought the feeling that she and the Bird were something he'd tell his friends. His lack of shame was notable. She wondered how their conversation went, how they'd decided to come get her. When Margot told him had he said, *Oh, neat?* Doubtful.

Andy spoke with great earnestness, explaining that Benji would come home every weekend until summer, and then he'd come when he could. They had discussed it. The Ficketts were great discussers, Eva saw. They did not have shrill debates. They were slow and polite. The Ficketts stopped short of asking Eva's permission, wanting to know if she was "satisfied" with the arrangement. She stared at them, shocked.

"He can do what he wants," she said without looking at Benji. "He doesn't owe me."

"We want you to be comfortable with the situation," Andy said.

"Comfortable!" she cried. "I'd be more comfortable if you stopped asking me was I comfortable." Turning to Benji, she said, "Look, there isn't any rulebook on this. Even if there was, I'm pretty sure we wouldn't be in it. Just be natural. Spend time with him. Let him get to know you, the real you, not some nervous, Mr. Gotta-do-it-right."

The Ficketts blinked at her, and at one another. Margot didn't try to hide her smile, which began the minute Eva started speaking. Looking at his mother, Benji lost his alarm and half-laughed. She had been overly blunt, Eva supposed. Looking at them, she marveled. So careful. So fucking *happy*.

Andy helped Eva move the remaining furniture out of the McLeod Park space to a storage unit near the river. They took what remained in the condo as well, and spent days packing up the rest of her things.

Benji slept on the couch downstairs. Helping her do laundry, he commented on the tiny T-shirts and little jeans. Everything about him, the way he phrased his questions, his open fear, his lack of self-consciousness, amused Eva. He was the exact kind of person she suspected he was back in high school. Nice. Preoccupied, a little clumsy and shockingly comfortable with himself.

On a warm, dry day, Eva and Benji took their son to Cutbank Park, where there was a fenced playground for toddlers. Benji was the worst nervous dad there. "Won't he topple out of the swing?" he asked. "He'll be flung from the ride-on toy! Can he go down a slide?" He followed the boy everywhere, even hurried up the slide behind him. Birdie stopped him by holding out a small palm.

"You come down *after* me."

Looking down at Eva, he cried, "Can I? Am I allowed?"

"Yes!" she laughed. "No one minds! Go down the slide!"

"He'll fall back and crack his head!"

"If he falls off, he'll crack his head," she called from below. "But he won't fall."

"Are you sure?" Benji called, terror-struck. But it was too late. Birdie's little body was rocketing down the plastic chute. Benji let out a shriek and followed him down. At the bottom, he leaped over his laughing son.

He freaked out again as they were leaving. Outside the fenced playground, Birdie took off like a freed dog, running wildly through the grass. Benji ran after him, his long arms flailing, his face terrified, like a panicked, wing-flapping hen. Birdie loved a game of chase. He glanced over his shoulder, verifying the pursuit.

"Watch where you're going!" Eva heard Benji cry. She had to stop by the fence, doubled over with laughter.

When Benji went back to school, the house took on a different routine. Odd, no one having to get up for work. Birdie was often the first awake. Andy wandered the house in his robe, fiddle on his shoulder like a parrot. Margot took long walks in the fine weather. Eva was shocked by how much time the woman spent alone. As a couple they were careful with each other, no sarcasm or vitriol. Mostly the house was quiet in a charming, almost old-fashioned way. The idea of Benji away at school was also charming;

she imagined him crossing a campus somewhere, sitting in a classroom at a desk.

He returned full of questions, so many that Eva thought he must write them down. Sure enough, she caught him at the table one Sunday morning consulting a soft-sided notebook. It was written in pencil, a list with tiny gray bullet points. He asked about her parents.

"They're getting better," she told him. "They keep referencing the 'lost' condo. I think they're a little jealous, that I'm here and not there. But that just wasn't going to work."

Benji lowered his hands. After a pause, he asked, "Do they hate me?"

She saw that this mattered to him. He didn't want to be disliked. She explained that they had blamed him, because they needed her to be perfect. Go to college, get a degree, go out and be perfect.

"You were going to go to college?" he asked.

He was like a reporter, hungry for clues, tunneling down leads. Eva crossed her arms and sat back in her chair.

"It kind of killed them that I didn't go. Maybe that's what I wanted."

"To kill your parents?" Benji snorted. "I doubt that."

Eva watched him, thinking he was being snide. But he was serious. He meant that he doubted she wanted to kill her parents. Astonishing.

Another weekend just before semester's end, Eva and Benji took Birdie to see Andy's chicken coop. Andy had moved it to a far bend in the ditch below the cliff. Benji had his notebook, studied it a while, then asked her why she felt the need to be a hero.

"A hero?" Eva asked, confused. Like his mother, he had a blunt way of putting things. She liked it, but it could be disorienting. "How was I a hero?"

"When you got pregnant," he said. His cheeks flushed with embarrassment. "Why didn't you tell me? Why not answer my calls? You know, for a while that summer, I thought I was in love with you."

He was beet red now. Eva sighed. "I was worried about that. Shit. I didn't want to give you the wrong impression. I didn't know what I felt."

He glanced over, making sure Birdie was out of earshot.

"Pity, is what you felt," he said, practically spitting the word. "I finally decided that it was a pity fuck."

Eva stopped in her tracks. "It was not a pity fuck."

"Then what was it?" he asked, unable to look at her. "Why did you have sex with me?"

"It's kind of a stupid question, really," she said, sighing again. "I mean, why does anyone have sex?" She crossed her arms. He was looking at her. "Because I wanted to. I should also add that I didn't want to go to college a virgin, which won't make you like me any better."

He gave a little laugh.

"I was lame back then," she said. "People can change. I'm less lame now. I'm not a prodigy, like you, but I do learn."

Benji smiled. He had a good smile. She saw both his mom and dad in it.

"And also, lame people can do good things," Eva said. "Look at Birdie. He's not bad."

Birdie was running circles around one of the chickens, chanting something.

"No, not bad," he said, turning. "Really, Eva. He's great." Then, without consulting his notebook, he asked, "What about Sully?"

Eva began walking again. "What about him?"

"Do you still see him?"

"No." Eva hadn't seen Sully in a month. If she wanted to see him, she was obviously going to have to make the first move. She drove by the New Leaf once. It was depressingly quiet. She had driven by Lucky Lane, too, but did not turn in.

"So, he had a pot shop?" Benji asked, beside her.

Eva snorted. "Is that what Margot calls it? He had a grow warehouse and a dispensary. We were going to be rich."

"The night of the raid," Benji said. "My mother won't talk about it. I know something happened." He faced her. "I think she told my dad. They seem different. Distant. Kind of formal."

Eva didn't respond, though she wondered, too. She wanted Margot to be an honest person, to not lie. Yet how could they all live so harmoniously if she had confessed about Dutch? Margot seemed withdrawn, sometimes downright aloof. But without any knowledge of Margot before these last two months, Eva couldn't compare. Maybe she was like this at home, in private. Eva knew only that there was something sad about the woman's solitude. Maybe there was no point in confessing to actions that could not be undone, even if withholding made you sad.

Birdie made Margot happy. When they were together drawing on paper at the table, or playing outside off the deck, Margot was lit up and present, no longer a distant observer. She also lost the dazed, faraway attitude when she watched her son play his violin. Sometimes he and his dad played raucous duets. Eva and Birdie would clap, which made Margot laugh. Once, he played something he'd written, a melody so mournful that Birdie buried his head in Eva's neck. He played them snippets from his rock band, the Revelaires, haunting music he said was part of this summer's recording project. He was alive when he played, his eyes bubbling with excitement, his body animated with energy. How different this routine was from life in her boring, middle-class house! Evenings at the Bakers', everyone retreated to his corner with a device. Of course Benji was animated. Jesus, who wouldn't be, if you could do something like that, make that kind of sound? Why do anything else? Why sleep?

Benji took Eva and Birdie into the music room to show her what his father had invented, a small device meant to fix a bad sound, a wolf tone. It had to do with vibration and pitch. He explained it as flapping, unstable air, like when you were on the highway and someone in the car opened a window and the air stuttered so bad it made everyone scream until it was closed again. Andy's device could be permanently fixed with putty to the inside of an instrument, out of sight, and balanced the vibration, stopped the stutter.

Benji pulled a cello off the top shelf, maneuvering it like a whiffle bat, that carelessly. It reminded Eva of a girl she'd known in middle school who was shy and awkward at school, but in the corral with her horse, a creature big enough to crush her, her timidity vanished. Benji was like this in the music room, moving without hesitation, straddling the cello, his hands, his arms, his entire torso wrapped around the thing. He whipped back the bow and drew it across the string while moving his finger down the fingerboard. Near the bottom he hit the bad spot. An unmistakable howl. Birdie covered his ears. Benji lifted the bow, grinning. The boy trotted over to stand before him. With caution, he lifted a small finger to pluck one of the strings.

"Shall I do it again?" Benji asked him, laughing when the boy nodded. Again and again he demonstrated, thrilling Birdie. Eva covered her ears until finally Benji stood to pull down a smaller cello for Birdie to handle.

"You can manage the wolf with your bow," he told Eva over the screeching sound Birdie was making. "You can play around it. Sometimes a cellist can manage it by squeezing harder with her knees. A violinist doesn't have that option." He grinned. "I'm lucky. I don't have a howl."

"No wolf tone in you," she said, smiling. "What about your mom?"

"Probably, now that she hasn't played. She might get something close to a howl," he said. "A wolfy area."

Eva snorted. "That's priceless. I think my whole life is a wolfy area."

In late May, Eva finally drove to Sully's trailer. She and Birdie sat with the car running for a time, then she turned the key and got out. Holding Birdie's hand, they climbed the steps to his door. Someone shouted. They turned and saw Caity running across the gravel lot, coming from the ditch under the willows. Sully came behind her, hands in his pockets, watching their children hug. He looked skinny. She supposed she looked fat, eating all Andy's food.

"Your hair," he said.

She touched it, remembering. "Yes, it's dark. This is all me. Sort of."

He smiled.

"Is he okay?" Sully asked, gesturing towards Birdie.

Eva nodded. "You can see the frostbite on his fingers. But he's not going to lose them."

"I'm glad," Sully said, following the kids towards the ditch.

Caity's feet were wet. She was heading back in the water. Birdie followed but stopped when Eva called to him. "He can't get cold," she explained to Sully.

Sully nodded and directed the kids away from the water, over to a sand pile. They stood together, watching them play. This close to him, Eva missed him more than she had in weeks. His smell. The heavy, warm presence of him. Even parenting with him, discussing what the kids could do.

"How are you?" she asked.

He said he was working on a roofing crew. At home he was nursing his seedlings back to life, and he had sold a lot of the equipment from the shop.

"You won't try again?"

He shook his head. "It's pot in the master bedroom for me," he said.

She looked at him, smiling at this reference to their first date. He smiled too.

"Caity looks bigger."

"So does the Bird." He looked at her and took his hands out of his pockets, letting his arms hang. "I'm so glad he was okay, Eva."

She swallowed hard.

"If anything had happened to him, I'd..." he couldn't finish. His eyes flashed and shone; he had to look away. She couldn't guess what he almost said, and that was fine. She didn't want to say anything else about it.

"I'm getting to know Benji Fickett," Eva told him. "I'm staying with them for a while, saving money. I still want to open a shop."

They were both tense, wondering whether to wade in further, how to go about it. Two months ago they were waking in one another's arms, meeting secretly for lunch, knowing every hour of the other's day. Now they were comparing notes like divorced parents.

"Did you sell your condo?"

"I did. But I didn't rent at McLeod Park."

He didn't say anything. She knew him well enough to know that he hated trite responses like, *Great* or *Good for you*. She might have told him that Margot was helping her scout locations. They were looking at a neighborhood on the far side of campus, near the food co-op. She might have thrown herself at him. Things were different, obviously. She wanted to see him. That was all she knew, that she wanted to see him. Now she had.

"You should meet Andy Fickett," she said. "I think you two would get along. Would you?"

"Margot's husband?" Sully shrugged and nodded. "I'd like that."

Thirty-seven

Beethoven's Ninth was performed on Memorial Day, on one of those evenings when dusk lingered like smoke. Everything was new, the grass on the slope below the house, the leaves on the willows down by the creek, the fluttering coins of aspen leaves. Above the house the balsamroot nodded its cheerful yellow head and along the lane the lilacs let out their sickly sweet exhale.

Margot came into the kitchen from the music room. She wore a new dress, navy blue in a fabric that swung. Her injury was undetectable again—no more sling though she still hadn't held anything heavier than a toothbrush. Her student Pip followed her. He, too, was dressed in performance clothes, a coat, vest and cravat. He was talking, telling her about the 1824 premiere, about Beethoven's confusion. "He couldn't hear anymore, you know, and he lost his way. He was still conducting when the music stopped."

Margot stopped and turned to Pip.

"It would be awful, wouldn't it?"

He nodded, somber.

Benji came charging down the steps, so fast the house shook. Pip's face broke into a smile. Pip loved Benji, was maybe the happiest of anyone to have him home for two weeks. Both Pip and Margot gasped when they saw that Benji was holding Birdie in his arms. As soon as they hit the living room floor, Birdie waved his hands, giggling and crying, "Again!"

"Not again!" said Margot. "I can't watch," she said as they went up as fast as they came down.

Margot went out to the deck, over to the stone staircase that led to the rim. High above the house, Andy and Sully had set up the Adirondack chairs. This was their summer backyard. Moving their sitting area to the rim meant the snow was really gone, winter was a memory. Chairs on the edge of the world. Eva stood behind Sully. Her hair almost touched her shoulders and was dark, which made her look older. She wore maroon pants with a white blouse; in the long light the picture was like something out of another century.

Suddenly an inner trill began, a familiar yet uncommon sense of delight. Margot was prone to these moments when she was younger, after a performance in a distant city, or traveling with Benji for lessons. She had felt it occasionally with her cello group, and very rarely, on family trips with Andy and Benji. Safety was part of it, an absolute release of anxiety, a confidence that everything would be all right. No matter how tumultuous or harrowing previous events may have been, forces were angling, aiming you towards this precise moment. The tingling sensation of divinity dropped without warning. Grace, she used to call it.

Andy's involvement in these moments had diminished over the years. She was glad he was part of the picture now, conversing with Sully, both men with their legs crossed, engaged. They would be late, yet Margot hesitated, feeling the heightened awareness in her body, a sense of her physical self standing on the deck overlooking the hillside and creek, the people in the chairs in the last of the sun, the chill creeping out of the trees by the water. Risk was part of this feeling, she understood. Such enchantment would not be possible without threat.

"Departure time!" she called.

They met in the driveway. Margot loaded Birdie in the car seat in the Suburban. Pip and Benji sat on either side of him. Andy drove. Sully and Eva rode in his truck. The night deepened as they came out of the canyon into town. The rude difference between the two places was apparent: here were traffic lights, neon, people on the sidewalks. In town the lilacs were already fading and their overripe scent was cloying.

They crossed the river to park near campus, had to walk three blocks to the performance hall. Their large group moved in silence, diminished by town life. The trees and bushes were full, windows were thrown open. They saw families having dinner, or the bluish glow of televisions. Residue of the charmed trance skipped through Margot's blood. Stepping off the curb she saw lilac petals in the gutters like lavender glitter. As they neared campus, they passed other concertgoers, heard voices. How grand, to walk on the street in late May with your family, on your way to hear Beethoven!

Light spilled out of the performance hall. Walking in, Eva studied the crowd. "I feel underdressed," she said.

"Sully is the one who's underdressed," said Margot, smiling. He didn't look at her but she saw his eyes crinkle in amusement.

They took their programs and found their seats. Satterfield had reserved them a row at the top of the theater where the sound was best. Deep in the row, almost at the center, sat the Bakers, not speaking to one another.

"Oh my god, they came," Eva said to Margot, staring.

"They did."

"I guess I better sit by them."

"Yes," whispered Margot, waiting for her to go first. Taking Sully's hand, she started down the row. Pip sat between Margot and Andy, bouncing with excitement, and Benji sat on the aisle with his son in his lap, prepared to leave by the back door when the boy got antsy. Andy looked at Margot over the top of Pip's head. He reached an arm over the back of Pip's chair to touch the back of her neck. The lights went out. The curtain opened and the orchestra filed in. Excited applause filled the room for the first violin. The players stood as Satterfield made his entrance wearing tails and a bow-tie. And they were off.

Acknowledgments

Thank you to Maestro Matthew Savery and the Bozeman Symphony musicians for letting me lurk at several rehearsals. Special thanks to Principal Cellist Chandra Lind for her time and input. Thanks to cellist Kris Williams for sharing her story.

My brother Jim Stillwell was patient and willing to walk me through facts about grow light wattage and plant yield. Any mistakes in the details are my own. The courage and grace I witnessed in his final months are gifts I am still trying to comprehend.

I want to thank the random and beloved souls who have kept me on the literary path, a rich and endlessly varied route to take through life. Going way back, Dr. Hubert McAlexander was an energetic, passionate teacher who introduced me to the southern storytellers I was so astounded by. Melissa Tufts solidified my love of books. My first creative writing teacher, Coleman Barks, exemplified that life on The Path would not be ordinary. Kaylie Jones, who also walks The Path, offered a hand again and again. From the Wyoming years, I thank Richard and Perry Cook for the always open door and for providing writing space and time. Brenda Allen, Amy Andersen and Laurie Sain believed and encouraged. To the Laramie writers: thanks for all those Friday nights.

Early readers of this manuscript include my mentors and colleagues in the Warren Wilson College MFA program for Writers. The title was inspired by a lecture given by Kevin McIlvoy in January 2014. Other early readers include these generous souls: Amanda Peepe, Stefani Farris, Marilyn Guggenheim, Bridget Kevane and Cathy Copenhagen. Janie Osborne and Cindy Stillwell gave their time and enthusiasm. I am grateful to Kathy Stillwell and Roberta Tripp for their ongoing faith. Thanks to Tara Bishop, Laurie Kolwyck, Kris King and the artist Edd Enders, who allowed me to use his work on the cover.

To my immediate family, who lived with me and this book through the years it took to get it right, I send big love for this incredible life.

CHRISTY STILLWELL holds a BA in English from the University of Georgia, an MA in Literature from the University of Wyoming, and an MFA from the Warren Wilson College Program for Writers. She is the author of *Amnesia*, a chapbook of poetry from Finishing Line Press. Her work has appeared in journals such as *The Massachusetts Review, The Tishman Review,* and *Fourth Genre*. She lives in Montana.

TITLES FROM ELIXIR PRESS

Poetry

Circassian Girl by Michelle Mitchell-Foust
Imago Mundi by Michelle Mitchell-Foust
Distance From Birth by Tracy Philpot
Original White Animals by Tracy Philpot
Flow Blue by Sarah Kennedy
A Witch's Dictionary by Sarah Kennedy
The Gold Thread by Sarah Kennedy
Rapture by Sarah Kennedy
Monster Zero by Jay Snodgrass
Drag by Duriel E. Harris
Running the Voodoo Down by Jim McGarrah
Assignation at Vanishing Point by Jane
   Satterfield
Her Familiars by Jane Satterfield
The Jewish Fake Book by Sima Rabinowitz
Recital by Samn Stockwell
Murder Ballads by Jake Adam York
Floating Girl (Angel of War) by Robert
   Randolph
Puritan Spectacle by Robert Strong
X-testaments by Karen Zealand
Keeping the Tigers Behind Us by Glenn J.
   Freeman
Bonneville by Jenny Mueller
State Park by Jenny Mueller
Cities of Flesh and the Dead by Diann Blakely
Green Ink Wings by Sherre Myers
Orange Reminds You Of Listening by Kristin
   Abraham
*In What I Have Done & What I Have Failed
   To Do* by Joseph P. Wood
Bray by Paul Gibbons
The Halo Rule by Teresa Leo
Perpetual Care by Katie Cappello
*The Raindrop's Gospel: The Trials of St. Jerome
   and St. Paula* by Maurya Simon
Prelude to Air from Water by Sandy Florian
Let Me Open You A Swan by Deborah Bogen
Cargo by Kristin Kelly

Spit by Esther Lee
Rag & Bone by Kathryn Nuerenberger
Kingdom of Throat-stuck Luck by George
   Kalamaras
Mormon Boy by Seth Brady Tucker
Nostalgia for the Criminal Past by Kathleen
   Winter
Little Oblivion by Susan Allspaw
Quelled Communiqués by Chloe Joan Lopez
Stupor by David Ray Vance
Curio by John A. Nieves
The Rub by Ariana-Sophia Kartsonis
Visiting Indira Gandhi's Palmist by Kirun
   Kapur
Freaked by Liz Robbins
Looming by Jennifer Franklin
Flammable Matter by Jacob Victorine
Prayer Book of the Anxious by Josephine Yu
flicker by Lisa Bickmore
Sure Extinction by John Estes
Selected Proverbs by Michael Cryer
Rise and Fall of the Lesser Sun Gods by Bruce
   Bond
I will not kick my friends by Kathleen Winter
Barnburner by Erin Hoover
Live from the Mood Board by Candice Reffe

Fiction

How Things Break by Kerala Goodkin
Juju by Judy Moffat
Grass by Sean Aden Lovelace
Hymn of Ash by George Looney
Nine Ten Again by Phil Condon
Memory Sickness by Phong Nguyen
Troglodyte by Tracy DeBrincat
The Loss of All Lost Things by Amina Gautier
The Killer's Dog by Gary Fincke
Everyone Was There by Anthony Varallo
The Wolf Tone by Christy Stillwell